WALKING

APART

CATHERINE
FINCH

Chaffinch Books

This book is dedicated to all headteachers, teachers and their schools.

You are marvellous –
don't believe anyone who tries to tell you otherwise.

Chapter 1

It was dark when he slipped out of bed, collecting glasses, dressing gown and slippers from familiar places. He hesitated and listened to Helen's soft breathing before stepping onto the landing, closing the bedroom door gently. She needed to sleep. He had a vague feeling that her side of the bed had been empty in the early hours, although he hadn't stirred enough to check the time.

Downstairs, on the desk in the living room, he saw the closed laptop and neatly tidied files and papers as if a task had been completed. So, she had been up in the night working; it wasn't the first time. David frowned as he glanced over the spines of well-worn folders. They were neatly labelled with familiar titles, each illustrated with one of Helen's little stick-figures, some grimacing, others assuming comical poses, their hands and feet too large for the pencil-thin bodies. He let his face relax into a smile as he looked at the word *Inspection* next to the frantic figure crushed by a huge red balloon against a wall. The folders held the paperwork she despised about her job. The sketches showed a sense of humour that made it possible to keep going.

He filled the kettle, opened the door of the wood stove and spent five minutes coaxing the hot embers to life before stoking with larger kindling to set it roaring. He loved the fire. He loved it from the neat stacking of logs and the chopping of wood to cleaning the soot from the glass and reviving the flames each morning, finding great satisfaction in creating heat through his own efforts.

Years ago, they had opened up this part of the house to make a large kitchen dining room with a family sitting area. The lounge, which faced north, was cold and unappealing in winter, so they lived in here where the sun shone through the patio windows and the stove gave out a warm, soft heat, drawing everything towards it.

The kitchen was untidy, as they had neglected to clear up after last night's meal. It had been a relaxed Saturday evening when, for once, Helen had settled down to watch a film with him. A bottle of Rioja had slipped down easily with the generous platefuls of wine-steeped beef casserole that David had left to bubble all day in the slow cooker. The combination had left them both too sleepy to think about clearing up. He wondered, with some irritation, why his wife hadn't thought about loading the dishwasher when she had been up in the night – it would only have taken a few minutes. He cleared and stacked as the kettle boiled and then he started to make some coffee.

In his student days, when everyone used instant and buying Gold Blend was considered sophisticated, David had watched Michael Caine in the *Ipcress File* preparing coffee. Fascinated by the grinding of beans, the grains brewing in a cafetière, the black liquid in a white cup, he had searched for similar equipment – not an easy task in the late seventies. This coffee ritual started the day with a feeling of well-being, even before the caffeine had taken effect.

He heard a snap, then a thud as a sleek and very wet ginger cat dropped into the kitchen through the cat flap. Floss usually stayed out most of the night, returning in the early morning to warmth and comfort and breakfast. She headed for his bare ankles, but was shaken off after a wet rub around his feet.

'Get off,' he said. 'You can't stay out all night and come back in that state expecting a cuddle.'

He picked her up and carried her at arm's length to her basket to dry off, but what she really wanted was food, so the coffee-making came to a temporary halt.

Cat fed, they both sat by the stove, Floss washing and grooming and David cradling his cup, observing the attention she paid to every detail of her bedraggled coat as if he had never seen the performance before. They had found Floss as a young kitten, mewling and crying at the back door. Charlotte had brought her in. Big sister Elizabeth, suddenly the fount of all knowledge since she started sixth form, apparently knew where she had come from and was sure she would be drowned if she was taken back. Helen and David both insisted the kitten was not staying. More than ten years later she was still here. The girls – who had promised to look after her, pay for food, clear up any mess – had left home. She was his cat now; companion in the garden, observer with interest of all manner of DIY, biggest fan of his efforts of wood chopping to keep the house warm.

He added two small logs to the stove, adjusted the vent and crept upstairs. A feeble dawn was beginning to show as he opened the bedroom door, grey light seeping through the curtains. He reached for clothes without disturbing his sleeping wife, deciding to dress in the spare room, which felt cold. Then he crept downstairs and unhooked an old coat before stepping out into the chill, November morning. The rain was fine; a dampness in the air. In the east over the church steeple, a strip of pale clear blue caught David's eye, although the rest of the sky was a uniform cloud cover of Lancashire grey.

He made his way between houses to the village, passing the butcher's, the small supermarket and the hardware shop where he paused. For twenty-eight years it had been his shop. He had always considered it his and Helen's, although she was less interested after taking on her first school as headteacher.

He had been working through endless accountancy exams when his grandfather died. As the family recovered from their grief, it emerged that Grandad had a considerable amount of money in the bank together with a very saleable house, and David, as an only child of an only child, was to be the recipient of a good part of it. He and Helen, married for two years, started looking for a family home in one of the popular Ribble Valley villages, a prospect quite out of the question before the legacy.

David pulled his hood up and recalled a spring afternoon when they found themselves in the small village of Fellburn, considering an estate of fourteen new properties. The agent in the show home sent them to wander around the village, look at the range of shops, admire the pretty church and imagine their offspring walking to school with friends. It was during this wander, which was rather slow as Helen was due to give birth in less than a month, that they had passed the hardware shop.

The shop window was full of randomly stacked boxes. Everything looked neglected, but there were a few customers, all men, with lists in their hands, who left with paintbrushes and paint, paper bags of nails or, in one case, a splendid looking garden rake. Helen put a hand in the small of her back and sank onto the nearest bench.

'Sorry,' she said, 'got to sit down.'

'You can't sit there.'

'Why not?'

David pointed to a sign on the bench which said £55. 'Look, it's for sale. It isn't a park bench.'

'I don't care,' Helen responded. 'If someone wants to move me they can just try.'

David peered at the small adverts in the window. He read some of them aloud to his disinterested wife. One of them, slightly larger than the others, caught his eye.

This shop for sale.
Business premises with large flat.
Apply within.

It was a handwritten sign in black marker pen.

'Go in if you want to,' Helen said, and then with a quick laugh, 'but don't come out owning a shop.'

David smiled at her. 'Of course not, but if you don't mind being left here for a few minutes I will pop in and take a quick look.'

He saw Helen close her eyes and turn her face to the warm sunshine. He knew she would be lost in thought about the new house, and would already be planning a visit to Laura Ashley.

The bell clanged alarmingly as David entered the shop. He breathed in the familiar smell of wood shavings and compost. At an early age, he had developed a fascination for this kind of store. He loved browsing the nuts and bolts, investigating the latest equipment in the tool section leaving with grubby fingers and dust on his shoes. This place was more like a haphazard storeroom. Customers waited patiently at the counter. They turned as he entered, offering various grunts and nods as some sort of greeting. David nodded in return, then tried to head off down a small aisle, which was blocked with stock. His vain attempts to explore further were thwarted by an impenetrable wall of 20-litre bags of chippings. Glancing around, it didn't take him long to realise that nobody was browsing. An item was requested and the shopkeeper found it, put it in a brown paper bag or wrapped it in newspaper, and then money changed hands.

As his fellow non-browsers were being dealt with, David poked around in some boxes of different sized screws. He needed to buy something. He couldn't just walk out, but what could he ask for at the counter? Blades for the Stanley Knife perhaps? The door clanged shut and the brown-coated proprietor sought out his remaining customer.

'Can I help you?' he asked.

'Err, yes, I need some… actually...' David hesitated and took a breath. His next words came with some surprise. 'I wanted to ask about the shop being for sale.'

Helen had almost dozed off by the time he emerged. He blinked as his eyes adjusted to the sunlight and wondered how he was going to share the feeling of excitement and apprehension growing inside him. He had a sudden whim to buy this shop and manage it as a business, rather than buy one of the new houses. He had arranged with the owner and his wife to come back and look around the whole property, including the flat, when the shop closed in an hour's time. He could not imagine for one moment that Helen would even begin to consider any of this to be a good idea.

He placed a hand on her bare arm. She opened her eyes, looking the perfect image of a very young, expectant mother, which prompted David to say, 'I love you,' then, 'come on, let's go to the pub for a drink.'

Standing in the drizzle almost thirty years later, he recalled the battle he had fought, firstly with Helen, then with his parents about buying the hardware business. His future career in accountancy had stretched into the future with life-sapping greyness. It had taken a stubborn determination to stand his ground and to change the course of his career, but there had been no regrets, none. Once purchased, he never looked back, and the shop had flourished. Boxes were emptied and organised, shelves filled and, in later years, a spacious conservatory built where customers and friends came to share a pot of tea and discuss their various projects, from painting a door to building a house. Despite competition from the large DIY stores, a bit of imagination and a lot of hard work ensured that it continued to be a success. The flat provided a home for the family until, several years later, Helen got her wished-for house in the village.

David was pleased to see that the shop was still doing well under the new owners, but he missed it. Assuming responsibility for the domestic chores while Helen still worked was all very well and he was glad he could support her, but it didn't fill the void.

At this early hour, everything was closed. He thought he might wander down later in the day to chat with Mike, the current owner.

He continued through the village to the newsagent's where he found Reg and two Sunday paper boys busy loading bags and trolleys. As usual, it was Reg doing all the talking.

'David, you're up early,' he remarked. 'Look at

these two lads, in their prime and still half asleep. You sure you don't want a Sunday round mate?'

'Thanks Reg, but no thanks. Anyway, these guys need the cash more than I do, don't you lads?'

Both boys grinned politely and mumbled unintelligible responses. Reg grabbed a couple of chocolate bars and held them out.

'Right, now get on your way. We'll see if a bit of sugar can wake you up.'

The boys took the bars and left the shop with their trolleys.

'That was kind of you Reg.'

'They're good lads those two. Always here on time, and the Sundays aren't easy, especially on a morning like this.' Reg handed over a copy of *The Observer* and *The Times Educational Supplement* for Helen.

'Sorry about that one being late,' he said.

David shrugged. Helen had grumbled a little as she liked to go through the *TES* on Friday evenings. He had been secretly pleased when it hadn't arrived. They had talked about their trip to Australia in March to see their daughter, Charlotte. It had been far more interesting than listening to Helen's sighs and tuts as she read out the latest unrealistic announcement by yet another Education Secretary who thought he or she had a bright idea.

'You heard about the village school?' Reg asked.

David looked surprised. 'No, not heard anything.'

Reg looked secretive and lowered his voice as if the empty shop was listening.

'Inspectors were in last week. Didn't go too well.' Reg delivered this with eyebrows raised, and then, in a tone suggesting that he understood these things, followed up with, 'I thought Helen would have heard, her knowing the headmaster.'

'How do you know it didn't go well? I thought an inspection was confidential until the report's published.'

'Etta told me. She's been taken on as a part-time teaching assistant after all those years as a volunteer.' Reg seemed rather pleased to be the bearer of this piece of information, especially as it was obviously news to David.

'Don't repeat this to anyone else, Reg. You might get Etta into trouble, and you wouldn't want to do that just as she's started a new job.'

Reg spluttered a bit then started backtracking.

'Well, I only said something to you because I thought you and Helen would know. I wouldn't tell anyone else.' He paused. David guessed he was mentally counting who he had told. Then Reg threw back, 'Funny Mr York didn't tell your Helen the school were having an inspection.'

David also thought this odd, but he didn't tell Reg. He knew how closely Helen had worked with Simon York when he came to the school two years ago. Helen, as an experienced headteacher, had been Simon's mentor. She had seen him through a difficult start, which hadn't been helped by the previous head, George Walker. With his huge personality he had charmed parents, controlled the staff and managed almost everything himself. When Mr Walker left, the school's problems had come to light. Simon was a reserved, less self-assured character, but he was slowly gaining the trust of the community. He had a young family with two boys under the age of three. David knew all too well the long hours the teaching profession demanded of staff and he felt sorry for the guy who found himself being pulled in all directions.

He paid Reg and was back out into the grey morning. The Observer was already encased in plastic, but he slipped Helen's paper down the front of his coat to keep it dry. He mulled over the news, thinking how important village schools were to their communities. There was no anonymity for the staff, and certainly not for the headteacher. Everyone, governors, parents, children, even the vicar wanted a part of you. Helen had spoken up for Simon on several occasions during his first few years in the job and David remembered her fury, when, following a difficult governors' meeting, she had needed to defend his right to paternity leave, convinced some of the governors thought they owned him and his family.

David walked back the long way round, the cold air polishing his face. He needed to think. Unlike Reg, he didn't consider this news with relish, and dreaded imparting it to Helen, who would, predictably, add the village school and Simon to her already huge workload, as if it were her duty to rush in and rescue the situation. As a result, there would be more late nights, paperwork to read, frantic tappings on her laptop and endless phone calls, the gist of which he never seemed to understand.

One of Helen's sketches came to David's mind; the small, helpless figure crushed against a wall by an expanding red balloon.

That man, he thought, is me.

Chapter 2

Helen awoke from a bizarre dream, her sleep coloured in shades of red and purple. Her nights were full of dreams, vivid and wild, at times too frantic to drop her into the deep, refreshing sleep she needed. And waking up had become jolting and sudden, tipping into panic until she could focus on the day ahead and find a sense of calm. She glanced at the clock, stretched her limbs and considered the prospect of a free Sunday.

A faint aroma of coffee and toast was drifting from downstairs. David would be back from the newsagent's by now. Helen went through a short series of stretches before she got out of bed, but there were days when everything seemed to ache, whatever she did. The doctor blamed the menopause, as he probably did for all the ailments of women in their 50s. David offered little or no sympathy as long as she chose to carry on working. He had told her on more than one occasion that running a huge primary school and supporting other schools as an adviser, was too much.

'Tea?' David asked as she entered the family room.

'Yes please,' she replied, covering a yawn. She ran her fingers through her blonde hair, shaking it into place. 'Did you pick up my *Times Ed*?'

David indicated the paper. She reached for it and skimmed the front cover with a snort. A photograph of a frowning Mitchel Groves, the current Education Secretary, had been linked to the caption; Teachers to work longer hours.

Helen turned the smug face of Groves to the table with a satisfying slap and flung herself onto the old sofa in front of the stove. After thirty-five years in the profession, fifteen as a headteacher, she had seen it all before.

'It's pathetic,' she remarked. 'He's just another politician saying what he thinks the electorate want to hear.'

David put a china mug of pale-coloured tea in her hand. 'I thought it was a dreadful photograph,' he said. 'He seems to have the knack of always looking straight at you, like Mum's picture of the Spanish man in the hat.'

Helen couldn't help smiling. David noticed the smile and said, 'I never found that Spanish man the least bit funny. In fact as a child I was quite scared of him.'

'It isn't the picture,' Helen said pointedly, 'it's your mother.'

Helen knew that David loved his mother and father, but she always thought that her parents-in-law belonged to another age. When she and David had celebrated their silver wedding anniversary a few years ago, Marjorie had congratulated them on being together for so long.

'I was never sure you'd make it this far,' she'd said. 'After all it must be a strain on a marriage when the wife has a full-time job.' She squeezed David's arm and spoke close to his ear, but loudly enough for Helen to catch her words, 'Well done dear, I'm very proud of you.'

As she'd moved away with a sideways smile, Helen had turned to David and hissed furiously, 'What, proud of you, but not both of us? Proud of you for doing…'

'Shh,' David had put a finger to his lips. 'Don't spoil the party. Look, Auntie Beryl has just arrived.'

Taking Helen's hand, he led her across the room, whispering, 'Proud of me for putting up with you for twenty-five years.' At the time, his words had merited a sharp poke in the ribs.

'So,' Helen asked, 'did you have a good walk?'

'Bit wet and drizzly but I had the village to myself. Reg was full of his usual early morning nonsense.'

'I suppose newsagents have to like getting up early.'

David seemed to hesitate, then he took a breath.

'When I picked up the papers,' he said, 'Reg came out with an odd bit of gossip about the village school.'

Helen frowned and looked up.

'I haven't seen Simon recently, he didn't need me. But now I think about it, there were two missed calls from him at the end of last week. What did Reg say?'

'He said that Ofsted have been in.'

Helen rested the mug on her knee and looked at her husband in disbelief.

'How could they have an inspection and me not know about it?'

'You were in Birmingham until yesterday afternoon, how could you know? And anyway, there would have been nothing you could do.'

Helen bit the side of her finger and tried to recall her movements over the previous few days. David took the mug from her as it looked very near to tipping over, then he gently moved her finger away from her mouth.

'Don't,' he said.

'What exactly did Reg say?'

'He said that the inspectors were in last week and it

didn't go too well. When I pointed out that the information is confidential, he said he thought you would have known.'

'I'll have to ring him. I knew they were due an inspection this year, but there shouldn't have been any problems. And why didn't Debbie text me?'

David said nothing. He sat down and picked up the paper, shaking it out before turning the page. Floss opened one eye, disturbed by the sudden noises around her since Helen had come downstairs.

'Well, don't ring him yet, it's too early on a Sunday. I'll make you some breakfast.'

Helen got up and strode off to get the phone. 'Too early?' she called back to David. 'With his two little boys, he'll have been up since six at least.'

David sighed. Last weekend Helen had taken a phone call from a staff member who had spent the night in hospital miscarrying a first baby. The lady needed comfort. Time off had to be arranged for her and then a supply teacher for the class organised. There followed more phone calls from other staff members asking how the woman was. Sunday had been taken up with all of it. Helen was only trying to help people, but it had been another opportunity for an argument to erupt about her retiring.

'And who would do all this if I went?' she had said angrily.

'Someone would do it. There are others, younger and fitter than you who would do it very well.'

'So you think I'm too old for the job?'

'I didn't mean it to sound like that,' David said, 'what I meant to say is that I care about you, about us. We're not getting any younger and I want us to have some time together. I'm tempted to buy a motor home and bugger off without you.'

Helen had smiled a little at the prospect, but David wasn't smiling.

'I don't want to lose any pension for the sake of going early,' she said, 'you know that.'

'And the more you gain in pension, the more we lose in time,' he answered, turning away. 'When I agreed to sell the business, you agreed to think about giving your notice.'

'Oh come on David, that's not exactly fair,' she retorted. 'Neither of us knew it would sell so quickly.'

'That was a year and a half ago. You know you could have retired last year when you were fifty-five, and been grateful for the right to do so.'

Helen seemed sympathetic to David's logic but was struggling to understand her own feelings about letting go.

'Well, you can't have the years back,' he said eventually. 'We had so many plans. Now, all you can think about is work.'

That was last Sunday, and this one seemed to be following a familiar pattern. Helen came back, phone in hand. David put the newspaper down and looked at her over his reading glasses.

'So?' he said.

'So, gossiping Reg wasn't wrong. Ofsted were in last week and it wasn't good. Simon says he rang me, then sent me a text after the feedback on Friday evening, but I definitely didn't get it. I feel terrible for them. After all that stuff they went through last year, I thought they were doing fine.'

'It wasn't a long phone call.'

Helen breathed out heavily, then she said, 'Simon's coming round after lunch, when the boys have a sleep. I had to say yes, he sounded so downcast and weary. Sophie isn't very strong, you know. She's depressed again.'

'He's coming round today?' David stated the obvious with frustration.

'Yes, this afternoon.' He sensed she was trying to soften this when she added, 'He won't be here long, I promise.'

'And I thought after your nocturnal session we might actually get a Sunday together, have a walk or something.'

'David, he really sounded terrible. I've seen good headteachers resign over stupid comments by Ofsted inspectors who are so far removed from the classroom they don't know which end up a child is any more. And I feel very guilty that he couldn't get hold of me.'

'OK,' he said, 'but we're going out to eat tonight. I'll book a table at that Italian in Clitheroe.'

Helen put her arms around his neck and kissed him.

'Thanks,' she said, sounding relieved that there wasn't to be another battle. 'Really, David, thanks.'

David pulled her onto his knee encircling her slim frame, his fingers resting on her ribs.

'We don't do this enough,' he said.

'Do what, hugging?'

'Yes, just hugging, touching each other. I don't think you're real sometimes. You flit about like a bloody fairy, I can't pin you down.'

'It won't always be like this, I promise.' David kept hold of her, even when she wriggled to get up.

'No,' he said firmly. 'You're not going just yet.

Simon York can have you this afternoon, but I've got you now.'

Helen stopped struggling, so David pulled her closer. The sudden ringing of the phone made them jump.

'Don't answer it,' he said, but she was pushing away from him already. Of course she would answer.

'Hello. Lizzie? Hi, you're early, everything OK?' There was a pause and the sound of a voice, indistinct and muffled, at the other end.

'I see, yes I can chat now rather than later. No, you're not disturbing us.' Helen nodded to David and mouthed, 'All OK,' before settling down on the sofa for what would almost certainly be a long conversation with their elder daughter.

David put on an old fleece and went out to his shed. It was after ten o'clock, so he put the radio on and chopped up enough kindling to light the little wood burner. If Helen was going to be busy most of the day he would give himself some shed time. Before long Floss had joined him, seeking warmth and the chance for an uninterrupted snooze.

Everyone joked about men and their sheds, but David decided that it was, on the whole, women who claimed the house. They chose the furniture and the colour schemes, they changed the curtains and carpets when there was nothing wrong with the old ones, decorated rooms, and then re-decorated them in what seemed a very short space of time. So the shed was a present to himself on selling the business. He built the basic model, then insulated it, found an old bench and a couple of chairs, and painted the inside three different colours – much to Helen's astonishment.

'I like colours,' he had said, justifying the blue,

purple and green. 'The house is all neutral and I like that too,' he had added quickly, 'but this is my space and I wanted these colours. And there were three tins of paint left in the garage.'

He sat in an old wicker chair and reached for the photograph frame he had glued together yesterday. He removed the clamps, carefully testing each corner. It wasn't an expensive frame, but for almost thirty years it had held an enlarged photograph of a much younger David and Helen on their honeymoon in the Lake District. They were looking at the camera; he seriously, she with a half-smile. Whenever he looked at the image, he could almost smell the scent of roses which had bloomed incredibly in the gardens and he could feel the warmth of her skin where his hand had, rather furtively, been resting on her bottom. She's never understood, he mused, that I enjoy taking care of her, not just with the everyday stuff, but whenever she's upset or worried or just exhausted with it all and I love it when she needs me.

They had spent their honeymoon at a hotel near Windermere, where they played tennis, learnt to water ski, ate magnificently in the hotel restaurant and wallowed in unfamiliar luxury. They made good use of the king-sized bed, shared long baths and talked endlessly about each other. He already knew about her father who had left when she was thirteen. His departure had given Helen the determination to look after herself and her sister and not collapse helplessly as their mother had done. He had tried to press her for more.

'It was, literally, a light bulb moment,' Helen had said one evening over dinner as she recalled the weeks after her father walked out. 'I was appalled to discover that Mum couldn't do anything for herself, not even change a light bulb. After that, believe me, I learnt to do plenty of things, and I made sure Julia could do them too. Mum had no idea about paying bills, arranging insurance, getting a simple plumbing job done. She panicked about everything. So, I told her to leave it to me, and she did.'

'You did everything?' David asked.

'Mum cooked and shopped and looked after us, did all the stuff she did when Dad was around, but that was all she seemed capable of.'

'Was your father abusive? Violent?' David instinctively took her hands in his as if to shield her from the past.

'No, he wasn't violent, I never saw him raise a hand to Mum, although he didn't hold back with a smack on the legs where we were concerned. He needed to prove he was the boss. Julia and I are both strong characters, probably like him, so Mum couldn't cope with us. But do you know what the worst thing was? I always knew that deep down, he didn't like us. He never spent time with us, never showed us any affection. I can't remember sitting down as a family for a meal or watching television together and, believe it or not, we never went on holiday. Mum was devastated when he walked out. I was delighted. It was the best thing he ever did as a father. I've never seen him since and I've no wish to see him again.'

David pressed her hands together and covered them with his own.

'I'll always look after you,' he said.

Helen raised her eyebrows. 'I don't need looking after,' she replied.

It wasn't quite the response he wanted.

The next afternoon, following a very competitive tennis match, they walked back to their room. David was the victor, but Helen was smug having won more than her usual number of games and she made a point of letting him know how pleased she was with herself.

'You're too bloody confident,' he said teasingly. 'Good thing I can always beat you at tennis. At least on the court you know your place.'

Helen took his hand and raised her face for a kiss. 'You knew what you were getting into,' she said, 'so don't start complaining now because it's too late.'

'There's such a thing as over confidence,' he said as they climbed the stairs. 'It can put people off.'

Helen looked at him as he unlocked the bedroom door. 'I don't know what you mean,' she said.

David's thoughts returned to their conversation of the previous evening, when he had felt a desperate need to protect her, to do everything he could to make her happy. He took a deep breath and tried to find the right words to express himself.

'You're so independent,' he said, 'I don't feel I'm necessary to you sometimes.'

'You don't like me being independent?' Helen asked, dropping the racquets on the floor with a clatter and flinging herself on the bed. David sat next to her, wishing he'd never started this.

'I love you being independent,' he affirmed. He tried to think it through, to express his feelings without sounding ridiculous. He kicked off his tennis shoes and lay beside her.

'Remember last year when we climbed Helvellyn? Paul and Gail had cried off, so it was just us.'

'I remember,' Helen said, ruefully. 'Sunny when we

set off then that howling wind and rain all along Striding Edge. I was terrified.'

'Exactly! You were terrified and I wasn't. And you let me hold your hand all the way – you wouldn't let go at one point, and I got you along the edge and to the summit. Helen, you really needed me for a short time and I loved that feeling.' He turned on his side to face her. 'My first girlfriend Lucy was needy, clingy. Bloody hell, I would never want you to be like that. I love your confidence, the way you have a go at anything you want. But there's something inside me that wants to look after you, wants you to need me just a little bit.'

Helen lay very still, then turned her face towards him.

'But I do need you,' she said. 'Not just on Striding Edge, but with the ordinary things that happen every day. I need your company, because we do things together that I love. I need your sense of humour. I need you to mend my car because I haven't a clue where the engine is.' She smiled and touched his fingers. 'Just because I'm not feeble and demanding, it doesn't mean I can manage without you. And anyway, how about you being dependent on me?'

David put his hand on her bare leg and started moving it along her thigh, under the short tennis skirt.

'I definitely need you,' he said.

'But only for that?' she teased. 'You mean you only require my services for sex?'

David took his hand away. The conversation had changed tone now. He'd show her who needed who.

'I'm not reliant on you for sex. I could get it anywhere!'

'Really?' she said, jumping to the floor. Then, humming softly, she proceeded to take off every stitch of clothing as if he wasn't there.

David watched with an air of pretend indifference. She went through to the bathroom, closing the door behind her. He heard the shower running. It was too much. He waited, then undressed and went to join her.

The door was locked.

'Helen' he shouted. He shook the handle and shouted again.

'Can I help you?' she called.

'Open the bloody door!'

'Temper temper.'

Half amused, half annoyed, he shook the door, contemplating whether to give it some brute force and what the bill might be for repairs if he did. For a moment, he listened to the running water, then he heard a soft click.

David replaced the photograph behind the glass, smiling to himself. He looked at the young faces and thought that even now, years later, he was still trying to get the upper hand.

Chapter 3

Only when his wife and boys were asleep did Simon York finally get in the car to go over to Helen's. For a few seconds he sat there, hands gripping the cold steering wheel, concentrating on breathing calmly and watching the rain make watery patterns down the windscreen. Finally, he started the car and set off for Fellburn.

This journey was a familiar one, taking him away from Blackburn to the hills and farmland of the Ribble Valley. On most mornings it was a pleasure, lifting his spirits and reminding him of long rambles with his father along the rivers Ribble and Calder. Pendle Hill was magnificent in all seasons. It dominated the skyline, sometimes white with snow or summer green with pasture, often wearing a thin shroud of drizzle and mist, its broad summit hidden from view. The legends of witchcraft were well known locally, but Simon always felt that the hill guarded the real truth. The view was only spoilt by the cement factory, which continually puffed out a grey plume above Clitheroe, disgorging its own sorcery.

But there was nothing uplifting about this Sunday afternoon. Simon was as miserable as the weather and it made him realise that the drive had recently become less appealing. He contemplated his failure as a headteacher and hoped desperately that Helen's clear thinking could offer him a lifeline.

Simon remembered the first time he met Helen. She was presenting a course designed to encourage aspiring headteachers. After a tedious two hours looking at management of school budgets, during which he and another deputy head called Philip had exchanged bored glances, a tall, slim woman breezed in and demanded everyone's attention.

'Don't take notes,' she told them. You can pick up a copy of my summary on your way out. I'd rather you listened and asked questions.'

She entertained, threw in anecdotes about her own school, and talked with great enthusiasm about the job of a headteacher. At the end of her session, when they broke for lunch, Philip turned to Simon and whispered, 'What's her name, I didn't catch it?'

'Helen Richards. She's head of St Mark's, a large school near Accrington.'

Philip sighed. 'I think I'm in love. I could listen to her all day.'

Simon laughed, but Helen had made a great impression on him too. He admired her honesty about the job, and her energy. She spoke her mind about education and seemed quite unafraid of standing by her beliefs. He wondered if he would ever be like that.

During the lunch break, Philip seemed determined to meet her.

'Come with me,' he said. 'I've got to talk to her.'

'What about?' Simon asked. He also wanted to speak to Helen, but lacked Philip's confidence.

'Anything at all, come on, or I'll go on my own.'

They cleared their plates at the end of what, for them, had proved to be a disappointing buffet lunch. The caterer had seemed intent on covering everything in breadcrumbs, and dessert was a plateful of biscuits.

Coffee cups in hand, they crossed the room to where Helen was sitting. Simon felt like a fifteen-year-old trying to speak to a sixth former he fancied. Helen looked up and smiled as they approached.

'Hi, I'm Philip from Dale Street School,' Philip announced. 'We really enjoyed your session. May I ask you some questions?'

Visibly pleased that they were keen, Helen invited them to pull up chairs to join her. As Philip talked, Simon studied her in more detail. He could see the strength in her expressive blue eyes, and her way of smiling as she listened was encouraging. As she answered Philip's questions, amongst the common sense and straight talking, there was humour, almost mischief in her voice. Then she turned to Simon.

'So, what appeals to you about the job of headteacher?' she asked.

Simon hesitated long enough for Philip to joke, 'He just wants an office door with his name on it, don't you Simon?'

Helen looked again at Simon, waiting for his response.

He began hesitantly, amazed that she was giving him her full attention. 'I've watched my own headteacher at work and thought; I could do your job.'

Helen raised her eyebrows with amusement. Simon thought that maybe his answer had been too cocky, too presumptuous, but he was wrong.

'You're almost there if you're thinking like that,' she said.

'Almost there?' Simon asked.

'When you look at your boss and think; I could do your job, you're almost there. But when you look at your boss and think; I could do your job and, I could do it even better than you, you know you're ready for the next step.'

Neither Philip nor Simon spoke. Both young men were thinking through Helen's words.

'Don't take yourselves too seriously,' she said looking at their faces. 'You'll know when you want to start applying for headships.'

Simon took a deep breath, 'Actually,' he said, 'I've applied for the village school in Fellburn, perhaps you know it?'

'Ah, Fellburn,' Helen said. 'Come and have a chat when we finish this afternoon.'

'You jammy bugger,' Philip said as they walked away from Helen's table. 'You owe me a pint for taking the initiative. I think I fancy her even more now. Did you notice a wedding ring? I'm going to look out for all the courses she's doing and get booked.' He rambled on, much to Simon's amusement, as they settled down for the next session.

At the end of the day, Simon wondered, as he collected his notes, whether Helen would have forgotten about him.

'Look,' Philip said. 'She's coming over. I'll leave you to it mate.' He winked knowingly, and hurried away.

Helen perched on the table and Simon slid back into his seat. For the second time, he felt privileged to have her full attention.

During that conversation, almost three years ago, she had told him everything she knew about the village of Fellburn and its school, laying out the challenges and the potential pitfalls. She questioned him about his experience and he described how he had moved quickly through the stages of his career. He went away feeling energised and confident.

Looking back, it had all happened surprisingly easily. When he was a deputy head, he was popular with the children and the staff. The confidence he had in the classroom spilled out into other areas and Simon had felt ready to go further. As a man, it was almost expected of him to move into the top job – and to do it quickly. His first application at the age of thirty-three, barely a month after the course, was successful.

Simon arrived at Fellburn School with the optimism of his relative youth and high hopes that he could serve this village community and become a respected figure. The school had been graded as *outstanding* in a previous inspection and he thought he was taking on a smoothly sailing ship. George Walker, the retiring head, was a man of vigorous handshakes and charming smiles. Simon noticed how his voice boomed around the school as he made his presence felt. He had been at Fellburn for more than twenty-five years, taught some of the children of his previous pupils and was an important public figure in the village. But the smiles and joviality masked a management style where the boss controlled everything and the staff were way behind the times.

When he started his headship, Simon was invited to choose a mentor and he requested Helen. They worked well together. She never told him how to do the job, but helped him develop his own style. She was there when he needed advice, and she had fought his corner when necessary. Recently her visits to his school had declined as the two years of entitled support came to an end. He had tried to contact her when he received the call from Ofsted last Wednesday but had been told she was away, and his calls and texts to her mobile had remained unanswered. He thought it would all be fine. He never expected that the frosty-faced inspector would slap a *Requires Improvement* rating on the school.

As he drove, Simon thought about his young family, safely sleeping at home. Jim had been the easiest to settle. At two-and-a-half he still loved his naps and, with only three turns of the musical box, he was asleep. Sophie had fed Billy, who, in contrast to his older brother was fretful, and was wearing out his already fragile mother. Simon had rocked him to sleep, then made Sophie a drink and left her dozing under a blanket on the sofa, Billy in the Moses basket by her side. He loved his sons, fed them, changed them, played with them, but right now, the only thing he could feel was a great weariness that squeezed out all emotion until everything was flat. He didn't know how to help his wife. Emerging from post-natal blues following Jim's birth, Sophie had unexpectedly become pregnant with Billy, and now, with the demands of both boys, he was once again watching helplessly as she slipped back into anxiety and depression.

After twenty minutes, during which the rain continued to pour and spray leaked through the door seal on his car, Simon arrived in Fellburn. He turned up the hill to Helen's. As he pulled into the drive she was there, opening the front door. They had always greeted each other with a handshake and a smile, but as he entered the hall she gave him an unexpected and very reassuring hug.

'*Nil illegitimi carborundum*,' she whispered in his ear. 'Don't let the bastards grind you down. David has a tie with it on. Come in.'

David greeted Simon and gripped his hand.

'How are the boys?' he asked.

'Taking up all our days and nights, but they're fine. Jim's really coming on.'

'I'll brew some tea then I'll leave you two to talk,' he said. 'Sit down Simon.'

Simon sat in the old armchair by the stove and took great pleasure from the fact that someone was looking after him. The cat opened a sleepy eye, stood up in her basket with a stretch and jumped lightly onto his knee. He stroked her head, but she seemed to change her mind, and went to seek out the source of more interesting noises in the kitchen.

David cut two slabs of ginger cake and put them at Simon's elbow, then said he was off to Mike's. Simon stared at the cake. It was so long since someone had looked after him, even in the simple action of making a mug of tea, that he could easily have wept. Helen settled into a chair opposite and said, 'Right, tell me all about it.'

He took a breath and gathered his thoughts.

'They rang on Wednesday lunchtime, came Thursday morning and left Friday. Just one inspector; a rather large, grim-looking woman who could give a patronising smile if she wanted to.'

'What was her name?'

'Janine Brown. Late fifties, said she had been headteacher at three schools. I had a bad feeling the minute she shook my hand. I've been through Ofsted visits before, met some lovely inspectors, but she had it in for us before she came.'

'How were the staff?'

'Terrified. Julie pulled it off in reception, and Debbie, as expected, was brilliant, but none of the others rose to it. Sally threw a wobbler after her lesson observation. We struggled to calm her down. At the end of the first day, Mrs Brown asked for more evidence, so I was up most of Thursday night, rocking Billy with one hand, tapping the laptop with the other.'

'What about good behaviour?' asked Helen. 'All the clubs you run, the events with the parish? You do all that so well.'

'Yes, that was good, but you won't believe what she said when I took her to see the craft clubs. More than half of the children stay on Wednesday after school to do craft. She took one look at the knitting and I could see she thought it was all a bit superficial, so we showed her the blanket the children had made with squares to send to the orphanage. She beamed at them with her false smile, then, as we left the room said to me; "This is all very well, Mr York – but we are not the Brownies". I felt so humiliated.'

Helen's eyes were wide. 'That's a completely unacceptable and unprofessional thing to say. How dare she? What a miserable cow.'

Simon seemed to sink even further into the chair. 'There just aren't enough hours in the day,' he said. 'I'm there before anyone else in the morning and last to leave at night. I thought I was getting parents and the village on my side. A lot of the inspector's criticisms relate to things I haven't had time to change, but the local people won't see it like that, they'll think: new head takes over and two years later the school goes from *Outstanding* to *Requires Improvement*. Thank goodness that banner we had on the railings saying; "Welcome to our Outstanding School", blew away when we had the storms. Do you know a woman actually brought it back all ripped and muddy, she said it had landed in her garden? I just stuffed it in the bin.'

Helen took the chance to smile. 'Those banners are

expensive, boastful crap. When George put that one up I wanted David to go along after dark with a marker pen and write: *So bloody what?* over it.'

Simon finished his cake and took a mouthful of tea.

'What you need,' she said, 'is to stay calm and get through the next few weeks. The task in front of you is far too big to start unpicking all at once. They'll monitor the school for eighteen months and you'll have the Local Authority all over you like a rash, but nothing will happen during the Christmas period. And you won't always feel like this Simon, believe me.'

Simon bent his head. 'This time last week,' he said, 'we were, technically, still an outstanding school. How can a perfect stranger walk through the door and get to know us well enough in two days to say we're in the requires improvement bracket? It's a terrible way of judging schools.'

Helen agreed. 'We waste hours guessing what the inspectors want, then trying to make sure they get it.' she said.

Simon still looked completely miserable.

'I feel so ashamed,' he said. 'I'm worried that tomorrow I won't be able to find the strength to support the staff.'

'You will, because you have to,' Helen said firmly. 'Things will come out of this that you least expect and looking back, it will all seem quite different.' She reached over to touch his arm.

'Your priority now is your family, and those little boys. Now, have another piece of David's cake, you look like you haven't eaten for a week.'

Simon found himself feeling a little more positive, but he knew that however encouraging and helpful

Helen tried to be, in the end it would be down to him.

It was almost dark when David returned with a sack of wood ends for burning. He said, 'It was packed in there again, must be the weather. Mainly Dads and kids. The coffee shop's going great.'

'Is this the hardware shop?' Simon asked. 'Oliver and Matthew, Mike's boys, come to school. I like Mike.'

'Did you know Helen and I had it for over twenty years?'

'I did,' answered Simon. 'It's a hardware shop with a cafe?'

'It's called Nuts 'n' Bolts. When Helen and I ran the shop, we realised that customers often wanted to come in and chat about their projects, so we had the conservatory built and put in a coffee machine and a couple of benches. Sometimes we would put biscuits out for people to help themselves, then customers started bringing their own and one lady, whose husband came in regularly, sent cakes. I subscribed to some magazines about DIY and it became a sort of meeting place.'

'Yes,' Helen added with a laugh, 'for all the boring old farts in the village!'

'You including me in that?' David challenged.

'Of course,' she said.

David ignored her and carried on talking to Simon.

'Mike and his wife have extended the building to make it a proper cafe with a bit of a garden centre. It's going well, attracting walkers and visitors to the village, but it'll never be quite the same as in those early days.'

Simon grinned. 'What a novel idea,' he said, 'and it's the only cafe around here, apart from the pub.'

'Yes,' David said with a grimace. 'Best avoided on a wet Sunday afternoon when half the village kids are in with their dads playing with the Lego. Mike usually closes at three on Sundays, but there were still some customers when I left.'

'I need to get back,' Simon said reluctantly.

'Ring me next week,' Helen said, 'when you get the draft report. You can challenge stuff you know. By the way, how did your governors get on?'

'Now that,' Simon replied, 'might be one good thing to come out of this. They didn't fare too well. When George was there he did everything so they sat back and let him get on with it. Yet they're a very dedicated group, and the new members are keen to do a good job. I've introduced some training, but as you know, some of them have been reluctant to change. Now they'll have to.'

'That's good,' Helen insisted. 'But I think they'll be behind you. Janice is very shrewd – she's turning out to be a good Chair of Governors.'

'There's so much asked of them,' he said, 'to say they're only volunteers.'

'They're there to support you, and the school, and they should be doing that.'

Simon grimaced and shook his head. 'It's the parents.'

'Don't think about the parents, you can't do anything about that at the moment. You'll get through this, Simon, I promise. Take it a bit at a time.' She added, 'You're a good headteacher.'

'Am I really?'

'I know you are. I hope you're not doubting my judgement – it's a brave man who does that.'

Simon left Fellburn, only too aware that he would be driving back again the next morning. School life, including the knitting club, would go on as usual and some of his more vulnerable staff would need him to encourage and support them. He recalled a speech made by a head of Ofsted who claimed that, "Stressed and unhappy teachers mean the improvements you're making are obviously working." Simon had mulled over this statement many times. It was incredulous.

'You're so wrong,' he shouted, banging the steering wheel with an anger that startled him. It came from deep within, born out of frustration, exhaustion and his feelings about the unfairness of a system that put complete idiots in positions of power.

Thank goodness, he thought, at the heart of this crazy system there are still people like Helen.

Chapter 4

When Helen left early the next morning, she'd reminded David that she would probably be late home. He'd been surprised. She insisted it had been mentioned, but as he couldn't be bothered to argue, he let her go with barely a peck on the cheek.

They had eaten out the previous evening, but instead of it being the relaxed sharing of a few hours together, Helen had pushed the food around her plate and left half of it. She complained about the service and had been irritable with him, as if all her patience had been used up dealing with Simon. Once home, she had packed her bag and laptop ready for the next day, said she was exhausted and had taken herself off to bed. He had envisaged a quite different end to the day.

David watched her car pull away, then furiously chopped up more kindling, even though the box was almost full. He replenished the log basket, put the washing machine on and mentally ran through an evening meal that wouldn't spoil if kept waiting. By the time all that was achieved, he felt better.

He intended to visit his parents, but it was too early yet as they were never up and about until mid-morning, so he enjoyed a quiet hour browsing the internet and planning visits and sightseeing for the trip to Australia at the end of March. Helen, after much persuasion, had asked the governors for a few extra days leave, so they would have almost three weeks away. He was looking forward to spending time with

Charlotte and staying with friends, Chris and Jenny, who had emigrated ten years ago. The flights to Melbourne were booked and he was enjoying researching the city and the surrounding area.

The ten o'clock news was just starting as he got in the car and set off for the short drive. His parents had lived in the same house at the end of a neat cul de sac in the pretty village of Whalley since David was at primary school. They had both celebrated 80th birthdays, but they were still active, still mentally sharp and still stuck in a time warp somewhere in the middle of the 1960s.

During his teenage years, it had gradually dawned on David that most of his friends had very different, often far less orderly home lives than his own. Mums worked, dads cooked, Sunday lunch was sometimes bacon sandwiches and it was quite normal to have to move newspapers, toys or clothes when you wanted to sit on the sofa. In contrast, John and Marjorie had a somewhat timetabled existence where routine was very important. Marjorie always seemed to defer to her husband's wishes but in reality, she ruled the roost. After years of feeling frustrated with his parents' views and their way of life, he now accepted them with some amusement and much affection.

As his car crunched on the neat, gravel surface of their drive, he glanced up at the window and was unsurprised to see his father's head pop up above the newspaper. He let himself in, shouted a greeting and found his mother sorting out photographs which she had spread out across a table in the dining room. Immediately he spotted the same honeymoon photograph he had been looking at in his shed the day before. Marjorie looked up, smiled and offered her cheek for a kiss.

'How are you David? Still at a loose end?'

'I'm fine. I promised to help take that rubbish to the tip for you, so here I am.'

'Well it's coffee time in fifteen minutes.'

'I'll have tea, Mum,' he replied.

'Your Dad has a nip of brandy in his, you know,' she said. 'I'll put some in yours, keep out the cold.'

'I'll pass on the brandy thanks, too early for me.'

'Well, it's up to you.'

'I was looking at this one yesterday,' he said, holding up the honeymoon picture. The frame needed mending.'

'Do you know, I wondered where it had gone when we visited a few weeks ago. I thought Helen had moved it or something,' Marjorie said.

David smiled. 'You don't miss a thing, do you?'

'No, and don't think I wasn't aware of the atmosphere between you, either.'

'Really?'

'Really. But you probably don't want to talk about it, so I'll leave it at that.'

'I'll go and have a word with Dad,' David said, getting up. When he came back, Marjorie was still sorting and filing.

'Look at that one of you and Lucy.' His mother held up a snapshot of David with his first girlfriend. 'She was a lovely girl and very pretty. I'm sorry we never kept in touch. She married someone from Skipton I think. I still have that vase she bought me for my birthday.'

David sat down. 'There's no need to keep it, or the photo,' he said with a short laugh. 'Thought you would have thrown it away long ago.'

'Now, now, no need for that. Your first love is always special.'

'Mum, do you realise it was almost forty years ago? I was eighteen.'

David took the photograph and looked at himself with his first girlfriend. Lucy was a round-faced, blonde-haired girl, who had adored him. She came for lunch every other Sunday and at some time during the afternoon would feel cold and end up wearing one of his jumpers. She asked for walking boots for Christmas, to please him, but she only wore them once when they tried to tackle a small fell in the Lake District. The boots rubbed and gave her painful and quite spectacular blisters that lasted for weeks.

'That was the day you left for university,' Marjorie reminded him. 'We went to the station to see you off. We were so proud.'

David looked at himself at eighteen; tall, short-haired, clean and bright-faced. He was wearing stiff, new jeans. Lucy was glancing up at him, but he grinned towards the camera.

'You didn't look like that when you came home for Christmas,' Marjorie said with a wry smile. 'Let me see if I can find a later one.'

She sorted through the piles before pulling out a small photograph.

'There,' she said. 'That's when you first brought Helen to see us. Dad took that in the garden. I think it was the summer after your second year. Look how you've changed.'

David reached for the snapshot and gave a short laugh. His hair easily touched the neck of his shirt and a dark fringe shaded his eyes. He was glancing at the camera without smiling. A denim jacket rested casually over his shoulder and the jeans looked like they had never seen a washing machine, never mind an iron. Helen was wearing a tight black tee shirt and a long Indian print skirt that reached the flat leather sandals she had worn all that summer.

'Wasn't that after you came back from Cornwall?' Marjorie asked. 'You look so brown the pair of you.'

'Yes, I think it was. We stayed here for a few nights then we drove back to university in Helen's car.'

'I worried about you going on that holiday,' Marjorie said. 'And we didn't know Helen then. When you said you were going away with your girlfriend, just the two of you, I didn't know what to think.'

David passed the photograph back to his mother.

'Well,' he said, 'you needn't have worried. It all worked out very well in the end.'

'I'll go and put the kettle on,' she said.

David picked up the photograph again and looked at his younger self. There was nothing in the face of the youth looking back that gave any hint as to how he was feeling. Despite the moody, self-assured gaze, he had been desperately in love with this beautiful, lively girl, who seemed to have such a zest for life, such a strong desire to experience everything as fully and as deeply as she could.

They had started going out together during their second year of university. It had been casual at first, with David careful not to reveal how keen he was, sensing that Helen would perceive this as weakness on his part. When he suggested a holiday that summer, he was quite elated at her enthusiasm to spend the time exclusively with him.

Cornwall had been a revelation about how life

could be lived in all its richness. They had walked the coastal paths, sunbathed on remarkably quiet beaches, had swum in the sea and invented wonderful meals cooked on the primus stove they carried with them. The weather was hot and there was a rare exotic feeling about the sultry evenings. One afternoon they avoided the official site on their route and pitched the tent by a deserted beach. As the sun set, Helen suggested a swim and, much to his surprise and delight, stripped off her shorts, pants and top and headed, naked, to the sea. He could still remember the seductive glance she threw him as she turned and walked across the sand. David had reached for the camera and taken a few shots before joining her. Now, years later, he found himself grinning at the thought of his mother filing those particular photographs away with notes on the back. He would hunt them out when he got home.

The snapshot in his hand had been taken a few days after Cornwall, when he had first brought Helen to meet his parents. Marjorie insisted they stay a few nights, although he was so desperate to keep the feeling of exclusiveness he had with Helen, it was with some reluctance that he agreed. In contrast to Lucy, who had always been very gentle and unassuming, Helen seemed rather outspoken and full of confidence considering it was a first visit to her boyfriend's parents. She had teased David throughout the meal, and he could see his mother found it embarrassing. As they started to clear the table, Helen said to him, 'Come on you, this is our job, get yourself in that kitchen,' and she insisted that Marjorie, having made the meal, should sit down and leave them to wash up. He remembered his mother's horrified face when she caught the two of them flicking tea towels at each other, David with bubbles in his hair and Helen with a splash of water down her front.

'All done,' Helen had announced. 'Where's your Dad? I want to talk to him about when he was in Cyprus.'

'He's in the lounge.'

David remembered making a point of neatly folding the towels in front of his mother and hanging them on the rail.

'Great,' Helen said. 'Are you making coffee? You know I'm rubbish at it.'

She bounded out of the room and spent the next hour deep in conversation with John.

Marjorie gave David a steely look.

'Just be aware that I've made up a bed for Helen in the guest room,' she said firmly.

'Of course,' he said.

'What you get up to on holiday or at university is up to you, but this is my house and given that you're not married...'

'Mum, it's fine. Helen thinks the guest room is lovely.'

'Good, well I'll not mention it again.'

David related the conversation to Helen later that evening as they sat on the swing seat in the garden. He suggested he would sneak in to the guest room when the house was quiet.

'You will not,' Helen said with mock indignation. 'I wouldn't want to incur the wrath of your mother. And she does have a point,' she added primly, 'we're not married.'

'Helen…'

'And another thing, I think it's time I had a couple of nights off. You quite wore me out with all the demands you made of me in that tent.'

David grabbed her round the waist and pushed her down on the cushions. The seat swung wildly.

'I don't remember,' he said grinning fiercely, 'noticing any complaints from you.'

'I wouldn't have dared,' she said. 'I was completely at your mercy.'

David sighed as his mind wandered through the memory. How old would they have been, perhaps twenty? Marjorie noticed his amused expression when she came back with a tray of hot drinks and a plate of flapjacks.

'What's making you look so happy?' she asked.

'Memories,' David said replacing the photograph.

A voice drifted in from the lounge.

'Are we having coffee?'

David looked at his mother with some amusement. 'Still can't make his own?'

'He's becoming hard work,' she said raising her eyebrows. 'You don't know what I have to put up with.'

'It's on its way,' she called back. She took one of the coffees and a small plate of two flapjacks, neatly placed on a napkin, then she walked through to the lounge.

'Right,' Marjorie said returning to sit with David. 'Now, where were we?'

The next photographs to appear were of Elizabeth and Charlotte, from babyhood through to degree ceremonies. David knew how much his mother doted on the girls. She passed him a photo of a grumpy looking Helen holding Lizzie in the hospital.

'Lizzie was only a day-and-a-half-old there,' Marjorie said. 'Do you remember? Helen wouldn't let us visit that first day, said she was too tired.'

'I do,' he said, 'but it was me as well, we wanted Lizzie to ourselves.'

'Well, I remember Helen being quite miserable when Lizzie was born. Look at her there. When I had you, we tidied ourselves up a bit for visitors. I don't think she'd even combed her hair.'

David looked. Helen was trying to smile, but it was unconvincing. She wore a nightshirt with a stain on the front and her hair was tied in a messy ponytail. He recalled how hard Helen had found the first few months of motherhood. She had cried almost every day for a fortnight and kept saying, "I'm not in control of myself any more."

Helen's own mother had visited in a vague sort of way before disappearing, but it was Marjorie who came to help in the early days. For a while Helen allowed herself to be looked after, although she resisted much of Marjorie's advice about feeding and sleeping routines. When Helen began to feel better, David had tactfully asked his mother to call less often as he could see she was beginning to annoy Helen. It wasn't the first time he had needed to be there as a buffer between the two women.

Marjorie handed another photograph to David. This time she was holding Elizabeth in her arms.

'She was a beautiful baby,' she said fondly. 'Just like you. It brought back so many happy memories. To this day I can't understand why Helen had to rush back to work so soon.'

David shrugged. 'It was an agreement we made when I took on the business, you know that. If I bought the business, she would go back to work. At least we had one secure wage that way, and she wanted to go back. Helen would have hated being at home all day.'

'I remember trying to persuade her,' Marjorie said, 'but she wasn't having any of it. And look what a disaster that first childminder was. A good thing I was on hand to step in.'

David took another photograph, this time of the girls in matching lilac dresses and white socks. At six, Elizabeth looked serious and slightly uncomfortable. Charlotte, however, who loved dressing up, held the perfect pose, her head on one side, her hand daintily pulling out the folds of her skirt. Helen preferred her daughters in practical clothes, all-in-one suits and, when they were older, dungarees and boots. Marjorie bought them floral dresses, frilly pants, ribbons and bonnets, and she knitted cardigans with lace collars.

'I never had a little girl,' Marjorie said, 'so I loved buying pretty things for them.'

'Helen wasn't so keen, was she?' David remembered. 'She wanted them in practical clothes so they could play outside and get dirty.'

'Well, they didn't get dirty when they came here, did they? Do you remember?' said his mother, pointing at the photo. 'Charlotte tripped over the corner of the flower bed after that was taken and we ended up in casualty having her stitched up.'

'Heedless child,' David said. 'She hasn't changed.'

'David, that's not true. You and Helen always compared her so unfavourably to Elizabeth.'

'We didn't,' David said defensively. 'We don't. But she was so accident prone. She doesn't think.'

'Don't be too hard on her. She managed to get herself off to Australia for a year, didn't she?'

'With a lot of help, she did. She thought she could just book a flight and go.'

'That was her spirit of adventure. Charlotte's a lovely girl, so pretty and popular. Is she still with her new boyfriend?'

David nodded.

He sat with his mother and continued to browse. His father wandered in and the three of them enjoyed the rest of the morning lost in memories.

'Goodness,' said Marjorie looking at the clock. 'Lunch will be late today. Can you stay for soup and a sandwich dear?'

David refused. 'I've lots to do,' he said.

'Lots to do? You're retired, love, your time should be your own now. Are you still doing all the housework?'

'More or less.'

'And Helen's still involved in that extra work at other schools?'

'For now she is.'

'You look tired. You look as if you don't know where to put yourself.'

David didn't like the turn the conversation had taken with his mother. 'I'm fine Mum and I'm busy. I'm leading a few walks with the rambling group, I go down and help Mike at the shop, and I always liked cooking, you know that.'

'There's a bit more to looking after a home than cooking,' Marjorie said. 'I know how hard it is.'

David kissed his mother, said goodbye to both his parents, then loaded the car with the rubbish and left.

Over lunch, Marjorie shared her concerns with John.

'He doesn't look happy, and I can't put my finger on it.'

John, usually reluctant to comment on Marjorie's

opinions about most things, agreed with her judgement of David's mood.

'They used to share the household chores,' she continued. 'In fact, I quite admired the way they managed, especially when the girls were still at home, but now David seems to do everything. That's not good for a man, surely?'

'I know it seems odd to us,' John replied, 'but Helen's working full time. David's at home all day. Seems fair enough to me. And she's retiring soon, so it'll all settle down then.'

'Well I'm not so sure it will. She always wanted to be top dog in that marriage and now she's got her way. She'll have him running around after her while she swans off being Mrs Important Career Woman. He should have put his foot down a long time ago.'

John sighed. 'You're interfering, love. Whatever's gone on between David and Helen has worked for years. I'm sure David won't be put upon. But I agree, he does seem a bit deflated.'

'And he won't discuss it if I mention it, so there's no point trying.'

'Talk to Helen, then.'

Marjorie nearly choked on her last mouthful of soup. 'What? About who cleans the bathroom? Who does the washing and ironing? I don't think so.'

'No, about David being unhappy. She loves him, doesn't she? She might be too busy, too wrapped up in her job to have even noticed how he feels.'

Marjorie dropped her spoon in the empty bowl and looked at her husband intently.

'Do you know, John,' she said, 'I think that for once, you have hit the nail squarely on the head.'

Chapter 5

The school hall was in darkness on that first afternoon in December, except for one candle glowing softly on the Advent crown. Helen slipped in at the rear of the hall and listened to Simon as he led the act of worship for parents and children. He stood at the front looking very much the young, confident headteacher. As the teachers took their classes away, he smiled at children who were leaving quietly, raised his eyebrows at those spoiling the moment and then took the time to speak with as many parents as he could as they helped him, and some of his staff, stack chairs.

This is a great little school, with a good headteacher leading it, Helen thought. I can't bear to see him go through this – he doesn't deserve it. It may hit the local press in the next week or so and he'll need to be tough and stick to what he believes in. I only hope he can.

Simon spotted her and mimed, five minutes, before disappearing into his room with an anxious looking parent. Helen knew that five minutes would probably become fifteen, so she admired the displays of children's work before deciding to go and have a word with Debbie, the deputy head. Debbie was a good friend of Helen's. Unlike Helen, who had worked in several schools, two as headteacher, Debbie decided that teaching, not management was what she preferred, so, when she came to Fellburn as deputy head she had stayed. She was a familiar figure to everyone in the village, walking to school each day, organising Parish events, happy to mix her home life with her work.

Debbie was not in her room, but Helen could hear voices further down the corridor coming from the infant classroom where Sally was the teacher. As Helen entered she saw Debbie sitting on a low infant-sized table with her arm around Sally's shoulders.

The girl glanced up.

'Hi Helen,' she sniffed. 'Simon said you were coming in tonight to go through the report with him. I'm sorry, this comes over me sometimes. I've been fine all day really, with the children, you just have to get on with it, don't you?'

'Don't mind me,' Helen said. 'I'm here to help and I don't blame you for being upset. This Ofsted report, it's not your fault.'

Sally's eyes filled up again and her face crumpled.

'But it is, I feel I've let everyone down.'

Debbie gave her another hug.

Sally was in her mid-twenties, but she looked much younger. She was a dark-haired girl, whose wide eyes and gentle voice could effortlessly engage the infants in her class. Helen had observed her teach and knew that she was doing an excellent job.

'You haven't let anyone down,' Debbie insisted.

'But she said my lesson was inadequate in places, that I wasn't pushing the more able children, and I know that's one of the main criticisms.'

There was a pause, then Helen asked, 'And do you agree with her?'

'Yes. I completely froze, she made me feel so uncomfortable in my own classroom, standing there with her clipboard. The kids were fantastic, but there were so many things in my plan that I forgot to do. She stood there looking irritated the whole time, and she kept banging her head on the puppets.'

Helen looked up at the puppets; strings of clown bodies, each lovingly decorated by the children. Some of the painted faces showed wry expressions – eyes on a slant, noses off-centre and mouths in various grotesque shapes and grimaces. She couldn't help smiling. Pausing for breath, Sally continued.

'I thought that because you've all seen me teach, that I was a good teacher, not outstanding yet, but a good teacher. When I tried to tell her what I'm usually like, she said, "You're only as good as your last observation". For me, that means one thing – I'm inadequate!'

'No,' Debbie said vehemently. 'You've put that idea into your head yourself, Sally, and it's rubbish.'

Helen pulled up a little chair and sat down. This was a young, talented teacher, distraught over the insensitive words of a supposed professional who should have known better. She needed to get a grip and see the situation as it really was.

'Sally, I'm tired of all this Ofsted speak about outstanding, good and inadequate. They're only words. You're a super teacher. Your classroom is bright and lively, you have a lovely manner with the children, who all think the world of you. You have creative ideas.' Helen indicated the puppets and a glorious display of Christmas trees, each lit with a twinkling light. 'You're well-organised and the children make good progress with you, not just academically, but also in the way you help them grow up and get ready for the juniors. Now think about this, if Debbie, Simon and I are all telling you how good you are, and we know you, yet Madam inspector who doesn't know you is telling you something else, who are you going to believe?'

Helen waited until Sally had to admit, 'I suppose I believe you and Debbie and Simon, but she was Ofsted and…'

'Ofsted, it's only a name, a word!' Helen's voice showed her frustration. 'Look, forget them and their terminology. I'm weary of hearing teachers and schools described in their words. I think it limits the vocabulary we use to talk about our teaching. This is a wonderful little school, you are an inspirational teacher. Debbie here has heaps of experience and real integrity. Simon is an intelligent and caring headteacher. Now, have you heard me use any Ofsted words there? Outstanding, good, requires improvement?'

Sally shook her head, but she was listening intently and Helen knew that she had to choose her words carefully. There was much at stake here. She had seen good teachers give up after Ofsted inspections, and change career completely. Sally was young and Helen knew she would be a great loss to the school and to the profession if she decided it was all too much and left.

'You'll teach some great lessons, Sally. There'll be days when everything goes superbly. You'll also have some terrible lessons, when you'll come out of this classroom and think, huh, that didn't work, I won't try that again. No one can be brilliant all the time, and most days, you'll be like every other teacher in this land, and you will do your best. This job isn't a science, it's an art. You can't follow a procedure and out pops learning, you have to feel it, adapt it, love it and hate it, all in the same day. It isn't a tick-box sort of job, although they keep trying to make it one. It's much more complex than that.'

Helen paused for breath. 'Look at me. I want you

to stop thinking in Ofsted terms about your teaching. Yes, they'll come back and there'll be more observations and judgements and we'll play their little game, because we must. But eventually they'll go and you will carry on doing your best for these children.'

Debbie gave Sally another hug. 'We're in this together,' she said. 'It isn't just you. Simon said last week that the important thing now is to ensure that all the arrangements for Christmas go ahead as usual. He did a lovely advent worship and we have to do the usual festive things too.'

'I know you're both right,' Sally admitted, wiping her eyes and getting up from the table. 'And, Helen, your words are very wise, but it's hard to feel enthusiastic. My stomach churns and I'm going through everything automatically.'

'Well, grit your teeth and go through it then,' Debbie said briskly. 'We've all been there, haven't we Helen?'

Helen nodded. 'My staff think I'm really calm, but inside I'm frantic. David says I'm like a swan: it looks like I'm gliding effortlessly across the water, but no-one can see me paddling like fury underneath!'

Sally managed a weak smile. Sandra, the teaching assistant who worked with her, and who hadn't said a word all the way through, started gathering up the children's work and arranging chairs and tables.

'Come on, we need to get sorted out for tomorrow, Sal,' she said. 'When the kids arrive in the morning armed with their craft stuff for the card competition, we need to be ready. Do you think they care about some old bag of an inspector? They won't even remember she's been here.'

Sally gave her nose one last blow and seemed to be

making a determined effort to stop crying and start moving. As Debbie and Helen started to leave, she touched Helen's arm.

'Thanks for that. I know you're right and I will be fine.'

'You're young, Sally,' Helen said, thinking of herself as a young teacher. 'I found it harder to put things into perspective when I was your age. You do get better at it, believe me.'

Helen followed Debbie back into her classroom and closed the door.

'She'll get there,' Helen said. 'You'll all get there in the end.'

'I'm already there,' Debbie retorted. 'I'm retiring in the summer, I'm getting out. But you know what'll happen next, don't you? They'll send in advisers and the Intervention Team and start monitoring everything. We'll have observations each week, checks on planning, extra training after school – believe me, if some jumped up Literacy Consultant starts telling me what to do I'll show her the door smartish.'

Helen perched on the edge of a table. 'They're a really talented team, Debs,' she said, 'full of great ideas. And the kind of support you'll be offered, it's all free.'

Debbie didn't say anything for a few moments. She straightened a pile of books on her desk, then she sat down.

'I think,' she said carefully, 'that my real concern, Helen, isn't Sally, or Simon, or this school for that matter, it's teaching in general, because things can't carry on the way they are. Sally and her generation have years to go and I'm not sure that all this pressure will keep the best teachers in the job. The phrase you used about teaching being an art not a science or a tick-box exercise, is so true, but it's what some people expect it to be. I never heard that inspector use the word children, but she did use the terms more able, less able, special needs to describe them, as if the group they belonged to was what they were. They're all individuals.'

She picked an exercise book from the top of the pile. 'Like this kid, Laura, aged ten, her mother walked out last week, can you believe it? She struggles a bit with maths but writes a cracking story on a good day, and what's more, she's great at comforting the little ones when they fall over.'

Helen nodded in agreement, but found she had nothing more to add to a conversation she and Debbie had shared many times.

'Are you looking forward to finishing next summer?' she asked.

'Yes and no. I'll miss everyone, but there's a lot I won't miss. What about you? You're a year older than me. Have you any plans to finish?'

Helen hesitated.

'It's complicated,' she said. 'I mean, what are you going to do when you leave?'

Debbie gave a short laugh. 'Nothing and everything. I've no worries on that score.'

'I'm frightened I'll miss the challenge, the being in control of it all, the opportunity to change things or make new things happen. Some days I hate my job. On others, I'm so fired up by it I can't imagine school not being a part of my life.'

'What does David think?'

Helen paused. 'If I'm honest, he's desperate for me to give my notice.'

'Helen,' Debbie said with sudden urgency, 'then you've got to do it. Life is short, there's another world out there.'

'You sound just like David. He keeps threatening to buy a motor home and bugger off.'

'Well I wouldn't blame him one little bit,' Debbie said. She looked straight at Helen. 'It's not coming between you, is it?'

'A little, yes. I suppose it is.'

'You're looking tired. Are you still losing weight?'

Helen was becoming irritated by this subject. David referred to it all the time, Lizzie had mentioned it a few weeks ago, everyone seemed to think it was an issue, but it was nothing. She could see what the scales were telling her. She knew that every pair of trousers sat further and further down her hips and she was well aware that on some days she ate so little because the action of putting food into her mouth seemed unimportant. What she didn't know, couldn't seem to work out was why she was letting this happen, and why watching her weight drop off was making her feel quite energised. It had become yet another issue between her and David and the more he encouraged her to eat bigger portions, the more he argued with her about what she left on her plate, the more she would dig her heels in. Meals were becoming tense affairs. She thought guiltily about a previous evening when she had hidden a portion of chicken in a tissue as he had left the table to fetch something.

She tried to shape a vague answer for Debbie. 'Yes, but it's no big deal. I'm always stressed and tired at this time of year, you know what it's like.'

But Debbie seemed determined not to be fobbed off.

'I know exactly what it's like, Helen. The staff room is full of chocolates from parents, the kitchen sends mince pies through almost daily, there's always someone bringing in homemade cakes and we have Christmas parties where food and drink are a main feature. I can't keep the weight off. So, what's wrong with you?'

Helen sighed. 'I'm busy and I'm stressed, that's all. I'm sure I'll put some weight back on over the holiday.'

'Well make sure you do,' Debbie warned, 'or I'll be coming over to your place to help David force-feed you.'

Helen was relieved to hear a knock on the classroom door, which provided a welcome distraction. Simon put his head round.

'Sorry if I'm interrupting something, but Janice is here. I think we'd better get started. By the way, it's starting to snow. Tell the staff to get off home,' he said to Debbie.

'Right,' Helen said getting up, better get this over with. 'Are you joining us Debs. We're going through the report?'

'No, Simon asked me to come, but I've too much to do, and it'll make me cross.'

Simon and Helen left and made their way to his office, where Janice, the Chair of Governors was waiting. After a long day in her own school, Helen felt a wave of exhaustion wash over her. The emotional chat with Sally had left her drained and the prospect of going through the report with a fine tooth comb wasn't filling her with joy. She decided she'd try to let him and Janice do the talking as it was, after all, their school.

As the meeting progressed, it was interrupted by a number of phone calls, a parent at the door with an anxious child who had forgotten his homework and the verger asking about the school's rehearsal schedule for the carol service in church. Brian had let himself in and was wrapped up in bobble hat, scarf and coat, his shoulders white with flakes of snow.

'You're covered,' Janice exclaimed.

Brian seemed oblivious to the icy crystals which had sprinkled the threads on his knitted hat, and, Helen noticed, to the puddle he was making on the floor.

'I'll give you a ring in the morning,' Simon promised. 'I know how important it is to get the Christmas tree up in church.'

'Friday,' Brian said. 'You're welcome to come in any time but Friday. We need a whole day to do it properly.'

At the end of the evening, the report dissected in great detail, they e-mailed a response to Ofsted. Simon peered through the blinds of his office and said, 'Heck, it's really sticking.'

Fine flakes were falling steadily, covering cars, houses and the road to the school.

'Get out of here, Simon,' Helen said. 'Janice and I are on foot, you need to drive home tonight.'

Simon started to gather up papers and folders.

'Leave them,' Janice said. 'Just go. In fact, we should all be going.'

They stepped out into the snowy silence. Janice scuttled off to her cottage in the village, Simon put the alarm on and locked up while Helen started to brush some of the snow from his windscreen.

'You should be fine when you get to the main road,' she said.

'Thanks again,' he said. 'I'll ring you.'

'Drive carefully. And don't worry about anything.'

Then, rather unexpectedly, Simon kissed Helen on the cheek.

She watched as he got into his car and drove carefully out of the car park onto the road, following the dark tracks made by other vehicles.

Helen put her hood up, glad she had called at home earlier to leave the car, change shoes for boots and her coat for a ski jacket. Her breaths were splintered by the cold, but the snow was calming, beautiful. It fell thickly in flakes that were beginning to form a muffling blanket across the village. She thrust cold hands into her pockets, breathed in the freezing air, made footprints along the path. As she walked, she wondered what sort of mood David would be in when she arrived home. Part of her wanted to carry on walking, thinking only how to place her feet carefully without slipping. The action of putting one foot in front of the other, making regular shapes with her boots in the snow was quite enough to think about for the moment. Everything else could be pushed into a faraway place at the back of her mind, a knot to be unravelled when she had warmed up.

Suddenly, a dark figure was there on the pavement in front of her, shining a torch. She would have lost her balance if the person hadn't reached out and grabbed her arm.

'I wondered where you'd got to?'

She breathed out a gasp of relief and said, 'You frightened me.'

David took her hand. 'No gloves?'

'I left them in the car.'

He covered her hand with his, placed it in the pocket of his coat and started to lead her home.

Helen felt as if the whole scene was quite surreal and, without warning, a huge swell of emotion welled up from deep inside, overwhelming her as it spread.

Her eyes filled with tears. With one blink, they were streaming down her face, wetting the front of her coat with the melting snowflakes. As they reached the front door, David released her hand and turned away to unlock. She swiftly wiped her face with a sleeve. In the hallway she could smell cooking and felt her stomach slide uncomfortably, as if the growl of hunger was pawing a tight knot of anxiety.

David, who was taking off his shoes and pulling on slippers, looked up.

'Are you all right, love?'

Helen reached for a tissue. She knew she should thank him for coming out, be grateful he wasn't showing more frustration about another late evening, let him look after her. Instead she passed him the wet coat and said, 'Of course I am, don't fuss. It's so cold.'

She noticed him turn away, his shoulders slumped, and she wondered what was wrong with her, wondered where the passion for their marriage had gone and why she couldn't talk to him. It was as if part of her wasn't functioning and all her energy was directed towards her work, with nothing left over. David had done the difficult thing; given up the shop that he had loved, so what was holding her back?

Rubbing her hands together, Helen shivered, but it had little to do with the cold. It came from deep within, much deeper.

Chapter 6

Manchester, on a bright winter Saturday in December, was exactly how Lizzie liked it. She couldn't wait to get out of the apartment into the colour and noise of the city and feel the sharp cold air on her face and in her lungs.

Pete, who was still in bed, and reluctant to let her go, pretended to be cross that she was leaving him.

'I haven't seen you all week and now you're swanning off with your mother for a day's shopping, leaving me all alone.'

'Not all alone,' Lizzie said. 'I've left you a list, lots for you to do babe.'

'Don't go.' He took her hand and pulled her across the bed. Lizzie lay on top of him, boots, scarf, coat, and kissed him.

'I have to go now,' she said. 'I'm meeting Mum at Victoria and it will take me a good twenty minutes to walk. Come with me if you like, just for the walk.'

Pete considered.

'No, I've got my list, so better get started. Now get off you great lump, you're squashing me.'

'Charming.'

Lizzie was quite the opposite of a great lump. She was tall and slim, like her mother, but she had David's dark hair and blue eyes. She had inherited the intelligence and single-mindedness of both her parents and, from an early age, showed a determination to be independent. She was six when she announced to David that she could walk to school on her own, and didn't need him to accompany her the short distance from the flat above the shop to the village school. Helen, always very direct, said, 'You're too young, wait until you're in the juniors,' but David had approached his daughter's request differently.

'I'd be rather sad if I couldn't walk you to school any more,' he had said.

Lizzie remembered looking up from the string of beads she was threading in a particular sequence of colours. 'Why would you be sad?' she had asked.

'Because that's my favourite time of the day. Mummy has gone to work, Charlotte is at Brenda's and it's our special time together.'

Although she was only young, Lizzie had never forgotten how she felt at this point. She wanted, quite unexpectedly, because it wasn't something she did very often, to cry.

Still threading the beads, she said in a small voice, 'Well that's all right Daddy,' but the overwhelming feeling of having hurt him caused a tear to splash on her hand.

Lizzie remembered Mum coming back at this point and asking what was wrong. She had said nothing, put down the beads and climbed onto David's knee, burying her face in his shirt.

'She's fine,' David said, waving Helen away. 'We're both fine, aren't we, Elizabeth Jane?'

Lizzie had learnt at an early age that her mother would boss, reprimand, give orders and lay down the rules. Her father, on the other hand, discussed things, showed disappointment when they misbehaved, managed them much more subtly, and, as teenagers, probably more effectively.

Manchester seemed to have a life of its own that
morning. Snow was lying in icy lumps but the city had
shrugged off the grey skies and burst into winter with a
dazzle of sunshine that seemed to hide around corners
and flash unexpectedly. The wind blasted her as she
passed the Beetham Tower and tugged strands of hair
from where she had tucked them under her scarf. She
stole a glance upwards in the direction of Cloud 23, the
bar where she had first met Pete three years earlier.

She felt fantastic. It had been a good week at
school. The constant effort of trying to engage
teenagers in the world of numbers wore her out, but
there had been some highs in her classes over the last
few days, when she saw inspiration dawn and
understanding become clear.

Lizzie couldn't wait to see her mum. They loved
their shopping days. Usually Lottie would be with them
and sometimes even David, who was patient, but would
take himself off if a shop didn't interest him. He was,
however, very good at paying for lunch and carrying
heavy bags. Lizzie often thought that being the father
of girls suited him.

She crossed St Anne's Square and enjoyed a quick
look in the windows of the designer shops, shaking her
head in disbelief at the prices of handbags and shoes
and simple garments displayed on stick-thin
mannequins. As she passed the Printworks, she threw a
coin in the bucket of a woman muffled up in layers of
coats and scarves who leant against the wall outside
Victoria Station. Then she spotted Helen emerging with
the crowds. She shouted, 'Mum!' Helen waved and
headed towards her. They hugged each other. Looking

more closely at her mother, Lizzie thought she looked tired.

'Good journey, Mum?'

'Interesting. I sat with a quartet of old ladies so I had to listen to their gossip for most of the journey.'

'You eavesdropper,' teased Lizzie. 'I'm surprised you didn't join in.'

'Too young. I'm dying for a coffee. Where can we go?'

'M & S is on the way. It'll be packed, but we may be lucky enough to get a seat.'

Lizzie was right, the cafe was packed, but they noticed a couple gathering up coats and bags to leave.

'I'll get the coffee, you get in over there, Mum,' Lizzie said.

Helen jostled her way through the tables, avoiding prams and parcels and people's legs to sink into a chair almost before the couple had left. Suddenly, a red-faced man was at her elbow. He banged a fist on the table.

'We've been waiting for this table,' he insisted loudly.

'So have we,' Helen said, plonking her handbag on the table top as if to reinforce her claim.

'I think you'll find we've been here longer than you,' a voice piped up. Helen turned to see an equally red-faced woman standing behind the man.

'Well I'm here now, and I don't think you've even ordered yet, have you? My daughter is already in the queue getting our drinks.'

'You should find a seat first,' the man said.

'That's what I *am* doing. Don't tell me what I should and shouldn't do.' Helen's voice rang out loudly and crossly, as if she was talking to a child at school. 'I've got this table and if you wait patiently instead of standing there being so rude to me I am sure there will be another one free soon.'

Lizzie, waiting to order, had witnessed the scene. She was mortified. Everyone seemed to be turning around to look at her mother. She didn't know whether to stay in the queue or lose her place and go over to calm things down. What was Mum thinking of to get involved in a slanging match over a cafe table? Fortunately, the man and his wife decided to give up, and with several non-festive, indeed disparaging remarks, they shuffled off.

'And a merry Christmas to you too!' Helen called after them as they turned to leave.

When Lizzie came over with the tray of drinks and cakes, Helen had piled up the previous customers' crockery and was wiping the table with a napkin.

'Mum, what on earth was all that about?'

'Mr and Mrs Angry thought this table belonged to them. Don't worry about it.'

'But you shouted at them, everyone could hear you.'

'Well, they shouldn't have been so rude. Forget it, they've gone now.'

Lizzie unloaded the tray and stowed it by the side of her chair. She took a sip of coffee and glanced at her mother. Helen was checking her mobile.

'Are you all right Mum?'

'Don't you start,' Helen snapped, dropping the phone back into her bag. 'I've already got your dad on my back about workload and long hours. I am absolutely fine, busy, yes, but that's how I like it.'

Lizzie was hurt and a bit deflated. This was supposed to be a happy day out, a day she had been looking forward to. The scene with the man and his wife had unsettled her. It wasn't like her mum to behave like that. She sipped her coffee not sure what to say.

Helen seemed to sense her daughter's unease and said, 'Lizzie, I'm all right. I'm sorry I made a scene, I felt the guy was trying to bully me. Now, you said on the phone you'd had a great week. Why don't you tell me about it?'

Lizzie launched into everything that had happened that week. Mother and daughter worked in different spheres of education, but had much in common. They shared a love of watching children and young people learn, they relished a challenge, they both liked to be in control, especially when that control and respect was well-earned. When Lizzie was younger, they had frequently clashed and she had used her four years at university to put some distance between herself and her mother. Unlike her younger sister she had never come back home to live. Now, with an interest that fuelled many long phone conversations about their work, they had become great friends.

'So,' Lizzie asked, 'how're things with you? Last time we spoke you were worried about the village school.'

'To be quite honest, Lizzie, I'm furious,' Helen said. 'Furious with myself for being in Birmingham when Simon needed me, and furious, no what's worse, livid, with that Ofsted woman. I was there until nine on Tuesday evening going through the report with Simon and the Chair of Governors. The bloody thing's full of mistakes and discrepancies.'

'How is he?'

'Simon? Feels rubbish, dreading the outcome of the report becoming public knowledge and then the press getting hold of it, which they will of course. But he'll survive. He's a good headteacher.'

'Last time I spoke to Dad, he said you hadn't been home much before nine all week. You'll wear yourself out, Mum.'

'Oh he's exaggerating. I've had busy times before, and as far as Simon goes, I genuinely care about what happens to him and to the school.' Helen drained her coffee cup. 'Now come on, let's hit the shops.'

They left the cafe and set about the serious business of shopping. Christmas presents were high on the list, but they both loved browsing the innumerable racks of clothes. They separated in the larger stores, meeting up by the changing rooms with armfuls of garments which they tried on, swapped and, more often than not, returned to the bored-looking assistants. After a quick look around the Christmas market stalls, they lunched at a little restaurant near St Peter's Square.

'Wine?' Lizzie asked.

'I think we ought to.'

'Shall we text Dad? Let him know how we're getting on.'

'You text him,' Helen said shortly.

Lizzie glanced at her mother in surprise.

'Mum... have you two had words?'

She noticed her mother's face darken. Lizzie suddenly felt afraid. Helen didn't elaborate.

'I think,' Lizzie said cautiously, 'if you've had words, you'd better tell me.'

Helen didn't know where to start or how much to tell her daughter about the row that had erupted the previous evening. David had obviously been brooding for hours but, as far as she was concerned, it had come from nowhere and spun alarmingly out of control until they reached a point where they were both intending to hurt. They had always challenged each other, often in fun, occasionally in anger, but last night's harsh words, her own and his, still resounded in her head.

She had been late, which was not unusual. She had sent a text letting him know that a child protection issue needed sorting out. When she finally arrived home, it was after eight o'clock.

He was flicking through the channels as she walked into the sitting room. She dropped her bags on the floor and exchanged shoes for slippers, but he barely looked up. Friday night was when she usually managed to get away by five and she insisted her staff did the same. There were very few exceptions to this rule, but this was one, and it had been difficult and upsetting. She was absolutely worn out, beyond hunger, but in desperate need of a glass of wine.

She started an explanation, but David was obviously not in the mood to listen and, although Helen felt guilty for being so late and genuinely sorry that their Friday evening was spoilt, she also felt a huge sense of injustice at his stony silence. The last few hours had been hell. For God's sake, it wasn't her fault she had been detained for so long.

'You've obviously eaten?' she remarked, looking at the cleaned kitchen. A single plate had been placed in the middle of the table, as if to reprimand her, the meat and vegetables unappealing under a damp layer of cling film.

'It needs microwaving,' he said shortly.

Helen looked at the plate. Normally David would have got up, kissed her, taken her bags, microwaved the meal for her. This show of petulance irritated Helen.

She took the plate and put it in the fridge with a slam of the door much harder than she intended. David looked up.

'I think,' she said, 'I'll make some toast.'

David had switched the television off, thrown the remote on the chair and left the room. Helen heard his feet on the stairs. She waited, but he was obviously not coming back down. How dare he behave like this, she thought. I've been at work for more than twelve hours today while he's been here pleasing himself and now I'm expected to placate him for a situation that wasn't my doing in the first place. She felt tearful, cross, but above all, overwhelmingly tired. She could let him stew, like some sulking child, but that wasn't in her nature, so, anger rising, she followed him upstairs.

He was lying on the bed, hands behind his head. He looked straight at her, his mouth in a hard line, his chest rising and falling with each breath. She returned his gaze.

'Why are you behaving like this?' she said. 'I've had a dreadful day. I thought I'd be home hours ago, but I had to stay until the children concerned were safe. I don't want a row about something that was quite unavoidable.'

David got up. She pulled out the stool at the dressing table and sat down, her back to him. She started to wipe away make-up and take off her jewellery.

'You really think this is only about tonight?' he said incredulously. 'You really think I am so angry because of tonight?'

'Yes, unless I've done something else to get on your nerves, which isn't difficult at the moment.'

'Helen, tonight's issue isn't your fault, I'm quite

aware of that, but it only highlights the fact that you have still done nothing about giving your notice for next summer. How do you expect me to react? All these late nights, the work you bring home, the way you ignore me half the time and seem intent on this mission to transform the whole education system single-handedly...'

'A slight exaggeration,' she said, still not looking at him. 'But you seem to be getting a few things out of proportion, don't you?'

'Really? I'm getting things out of proportion? Helen, you run your own school, advise others, you're off presenting courses all over the place and now, as if all of that wasn't enough, you feel you have to interfere in the village school.'

'Interfere?' Helen swung around sharply. She was incensed. 'If interfering, David, is what you imagine I am doing at Fellburn, then there is absolutely no point carrying on this conversation. I refuse to argue with someone who, frankly, hasn't got a bloody clue.'

'You're the one without a bloody clue,' he shouted. 'You won't eat, can't sleep, don't take an interest in anything normal any more. I'm trying to plan this visit to Australia and you're showing so little enthusiasm I might as well go on my own.'

David crossed the room and put both hands on the dressing table with enough force to make a tall bottle of perfume fall heavily on its side. Helen wanted to stand up so that she was facing him, rather than looking up at him, but there wasn't room, so, with elaborate care she put the bottle straight and took off her earrings. She knew he was desperately trying to calm down but she was so tired, so insulted by his words, she couldn't find it in herself to care about his anger.

'I am asking you again,' he said slowly, 'to finish work in the summer as we agreed you would do two years ago. Helen, I can't answer for the consequences, for both of us if you don't do this.'

'What's that supposed to mean? Are you making some sort of threat?'

David didn't answer. Finally, Helen did stand up, pushing the low stool away so that it toppled to the floor with a thud.

'I will finish work when I choose,' she said quietly, furiously. 'I don't know what you mean by consequences, but I won't be forced into doing something that's not right for me.'

'And what about what's right for me?' The heat had gone. He sounded defeated, almost pleading. She knew that if she reached out to touch him it would all be all right. He would hug her, she would probably break down and cry with exhaustion. After, they would talk, apologise, she would get her glass of wine, they would both go to bed and hold each other before they slept as they had done almost every night of their twenty-nine-year-long-year marriage. But something inside Helen, something screwed up and tight, stopped her from reaching out to him, so she said, 'I'll think about it. Now I want to go to bed. I'm up early in the morning to get the train to Manchester.'

To her relief, he left the bedroom. She undressed, got into bed and within seconds her pillow was wet with tears.

Lizzie waited for her mother to speak.

'Mum?'

Helen snapped back into the present, mentally

shaking herself. She looked at her daughter and said cautiously, 'Yes, I suppose we did have words last night, just words, nothing to worry about.'

'Why?'

'The usual; the thing we always have words about at the moment.'

'Your job? Retiring?'

'Both.'

'You didn't have a big row?'

'No,' Helen replied.

Lizzie didn't believe her.

'The thing is,' Helen continued, 'I said I would think about giving my notice for the summer. I was tired last night and because of that, I wasn't exactly truthful with your dad.'

'What do you mean?'

'What I haven't told him is that I can't give my notice for this summer, in fact I don't think I can give it now for at least another year.'

Lizzie was puzzled. 'Why not?'

'Because yesterday Bridget came to me, quite out of the blue and presented me with her letter of resignation. She's quitting in July. I can't let the school start the year next September with a new deputy and a new head.'

Lizzie sensed the beginnings of an alarming rift developing between her parents, feeding a fear in her own mind of what might happen if the two of them couldn't sort it out. She sincerely wished Lottie wasn't so far away. Dad will explode when Mum tells him what she's just told me, she thought. And I think he'd be right. Lizzie recalled all the conversations she had shared with her father on this subject. She felt that Mum was seriously ignoring his wishes.

'You could still give your notice,' she said. 'It's not ideal for the school, but it's a situation that will have happened before. They would manage you know.'

'I don't want them to manage, I want to leave that school on a firm footing for the future so they can keep making progress. How do you think I'd feel if things started to fall apart after I'd left?'

'It won't fall apart, you're not indispensable, Mum. And anyway, whatever happens after you've gone is none of your business.'

Helen looked at her daughter. 'You've no idea, Lizzie,' she said, impatience in her voice. 'You look at things like Dad. Leading a school isn't like running a shop. You're not handing over a building and some stock, there are people at the heart of it – and children and their families.'

'I know that,' Lizzie said. 'But for Dad's sake, you need to think about it. You need to put him and yourself first, for once.'

Her mother picked up a serviette and started wiping the table, then she stacked the two plates, clattering the cutlery on top, pushing the whole lot to one side.

'It's out of the question, Lizzie,' she said, in a voice Lizzie recognised from her teenage years. 'It's not up for discussion.'

Chapter 7

David was up early on the Saturday morning of Helen's day out with Lizzie. He slipped carefully out of bed, and made a start clearing the driveway in the half-light before she was awake. Snow still covered most of the village as there had been fresh falls during the week. He could hear the shouts of excited children, shrill in the cold air, and as he straightened up to lean on the shovel and survey his efforts, he noticed a group in hiking gear. The thought of a long walk, a fast-paced, exhausting walk, where all he had to do was stride out, follow a familiar path and allow his thoughts to roll around in his head, was very tempting. If it hadn't been so dark when he had woken up earlier, he would have gone off on his own, because the prospect of facing Helen after the harsh words they had exchanged the night before was depressing his spirits.

As he shovelled snow from the drive, David wondered what to say to her before she left. There wouldn't be time for a long conversation, but something needed to be said that would at least point them back towards normality, even though reaching it would no doubt take some time. He replayed parts of their angry exchange and knew he shouldn't have accused her of interfering, it was unfair. It was meant to hurt, to belittle her work, to put her down and he was wrong to do that. But he had no remorse about any of the other things he had said, and at least she was now in no doubt about how strongly he felt.

And what had he really meant when he had thrown

in the word consequences? If they carried on as they were, David could only see them growing even further apart, so that in itself was a terrible consequence. But was there something else behind his words? Would either of them ever turn away from their marriage?

I am in no doubt, he thought, taking a breath of cold air, that I love her. We've been together for so long and shared so much. But I want the other Helen back; the funny, challenging, excitable Helen who was up for anything, who couldn't care less what people thought, who was sexy and mischievous and had such a great need to love and be loved. She's shutting me out. Her work-world is getting bigger and our world is contracting and becoming small and, for her, rather tedious.

In the past David had occasionally wondered if she had ever been tempted to have an affair, and this thought crossed his mind. She met other men in her advisory job, spent nights away and she was an attractive woman. How would he feel if he found out she had slept with someone else? Angry? Betrayed? But he would also feel a sense of injustice. Here he was, prepared to look after her, do all the house stuff, pander to her every need while she worked and he was at home, so to find out that she was taking some pleasure with another man would be soul destroying.

As he pushed aside the last pile of snow, David allowed himself a smile. He had married a strong woman, and, if he was honest, she had usually had the upper hand in their marriage. But it had worked, and almost thirty years later, here they were. I am so proud of her, he thought, but sometimes I wish I could break through all this toughness and get at the Helen who can be vulnerable and who needs me. It seems as if it's work she needs. Her job challenges her, excites her and I don't.

The front door opened and Helen appeared, car keys in hand. She looked at the drive and the heaps of shovelled snow on either side.

'You've worked hard,' she said, but her tone wasn't very encouraging. He remembered that they had both, quite deliberately, taken great care not to touch each other in bed last night. They always started the night close together, his knees tucked behind hers, his chest touching her back and his arm over the dip of her waist. Had she been waiting for his touch? He had been too angry to even think about reaching across the bed. And in the midst of their angry exchange, as he had stood over her by the dressing table, he could, quite simply, have lifted her from the stool and shaken her. David knew he would never hurt her, but he had been overcome with an overwhelming desire to do something that would put a stop to the harsh words they were throwing at each other.

'I'll take you to the station,' he said.

'You don't need to, there's plenty of parking, and besides, I don't know which train I'll be on coming back.'

She unlocked the Audi and threw her bag across to the passenger seat.

David watched her. The word sorry, was hanging in the air, along with I love you, but they evaporated in favour of, 'Enjoy your day, give my love to Lizzie.'

She glanced in his direction. 'I will. Don't bother to cook for tonight, we'll be eating out at lunchtime.' With that she got in the car and drove away.

Her last words about not making a meal did nothing to improve his mood. Not only was she implying that she didn't want to eat with him later, it was also another excuse for her not to eat at all. This was an issue that both concerned and annoyed David, and over which he had absolutely no control. Helen had always rejected food when she was worried, it was a familiar pattern. She stopped eating properly and lost weight but as soon as the crisis was over, she would usually pick up and start eating normally again.

This time it was different. David had noticed that over the last few months, she had been leaving food on her plate, complaining she was too full, and he had seen her throwing food away when she thought he wasn't looking. When they ate out, which they both usually enjoyed, she would order starter-sized portions then complain something was either too tough or too salty to eat and leave half of it. He knew from the feel of her body that she was losing weight. What he didn't know was how a slim, intelligent, fully grown woman, could do this to herself. For a while he had tried to cook the food he knew she liked, had teased her, encouraged her to eat. When none of that worked and he became more frustrated, he ended up arguing with her about it, and each meal became yet another battle, so for the moment, he had given up.

David cleared the rest of the drive. Floss made delicate footprints across the low wall around the garden, seemingly unperturbed by the change in the colour of her world. She came to sit on a dry patch of stone. He picked up a handful of powdery snow and tossed it lightly in her direction, watching as the crystals showered over her in a sparkling dust, which she shook off with some disdain.

'Not in a very playful mood today?' he said. 'Well, that makes two of us.'

He stood the shovel by the garage. A couple of walkers caught his eye. He raised a hand to Debbie and Ross who were striding out in wellies and thick coats. They looked ready to tackle an expedition to the North Pole.

'Hiya,' Debbie shouted. 'What a stunning day.'

'Lovely,' David replied. 'Where are you off to then?'

'Thought we'd do the Three Village Walk,' Ross said heartily. 'A drink in each pub.'

Debbie shook her head and rolled her eyes, 'Look what I have to put up with. He's impossible. How we're going to survive retirement next year, I don't know. Can he come and share your shed, David?'

David gave a short laugh. 'Anytime he wants, as long as he brings some beer. Better still, I'll help him build his own.'

'Are you and Helen off for a walk later?' Debbie asked.

'She's gone to Manchester shopping with Lizzie. I'm going to a meeting with the walking group at 10.30, but I might get out this afternoon.'

'Let us have your programme of walks for next year,' Ross said. 'We'd like to come again. They seem a lively lot.'

'Oh, they're that all right – a good example of how to grow old disgracefully.'

Debbie laughed. 'They sound like our sort of people,' she said. 'By the way, I noticed that Helen looked a bit weary when I saw her last Wednesday in school. Is she OK?'

'She says she's fine,' David replied.

'She might say she's fine, but what do you think?'

David shrugged his shoulders, but really didn't

know how to answer. Debbie was a good friend of Helen's. Perhaps he should tell her how concerned he was, but it was too complicated now, too personal.

'She was a great support when she came into school last week,' Debbie added. 'One of our young teachers was losing the plot and Helen knew exactly what to say to encourage her and make her feel better. She's very good at that sort of thing, David.'

David wondered how good she would be if he started to lose the plot, or was Helen's sympathetic side only reserved for people at work now? He couldn't remember the last time she had shown any concern for how he was feeling. At that point, he had a sudden desire to be by himself.

'Enjoy your walk,' he said cheerfully, bringing the conversation to an end. 'Must go, the cat needs her breakfast.'

He watched Debbie and Ross stride off hand in hand, their breaths caught by the cold air. Ross turned to say something and Debbie gave him a playful shove with her elbow. David wished he and Helen were setting off for a good walk in the easy, relaxed way they used to before she became so busy.

He spent an hour in the shed working on the little carved box he was making for Lizzie for Christmas, but gave up when his hands became too cold. Then, just before 10.30, he locked up and set off for the meeting.

When he arrived, the cafe was almost full, but it wasn't difficult to spot the walking group who had gathered around one large table. They had already spread out maps and papers between the coffee cups and cakes. Bob, the Chair, was trying to keep order and two of the women were sharing an iPad and making good use of the recently installed Wi-Fi to research car parking, cafes and pubs. Another couple were perusing the maps and consulting guidebooks and David couldn't help laughing at Dan who was making short, but rather messy work of an enormous chocolate muffin.

David enjoyed these meetings and he started to feel his mood lift a little. The committee were, indeed, a lively lot and he liked the planning as much as going off to do the walks.

'Sorry I'm late,' he apologised, then added with a grin, 'snowed in.'

'You only live around the corner!'

'Had to dig myself out. Now, what have I missed?'

'Dan, as usual, wants to tackle something really grand this year,' Bob said. 'Only for those who are up for it, and unfortunately that won't be me.'

'Great Gable?' David suggested, looking round for Mike or Rosemary, to order a drink. He pulled up a chair.

'We'd be up for that,' Dan's wife, Tina said. 'We need a good day, so we'd better plan that one for the summer.' She turned to her friend Karen. 'What about you? You haven't found any of the walks too hard have you?'

Karen had joined the walking group, introduced by Dan and Tina, in September. Recently divorced, she was trying to get her life back together. Tina had told David that Karen's husband walked out after twenty-five years, leaving her a small fortune, but nevertheless, she had found the divorce hard to cope with. On the last few walks, David had enjoyed Karen's company and he admired her determination to get over the breakdown of her marriage and start living her own life. It made him wonder how he would manage if he was suddenly single. It wasn't a pleasant idea.

'It sounds rather scary,' Karen replied. 'Is it a really high mountain?'

He shook his head. 'It is a big walk, but it's not dangerous or anything. Helen and I have climbed it lots of times, and we took the girls when they were fairly young.'

Karen was hesitating. 'I've only done a few walks with you all, perhaps I need to do a longer walk first and see how I get on.'

'Good thinking girl,' Tina said. 'You might surprise yourself. You've surprised me recently.'

David noticed that Tina's last comment had made Karen giggle.

'What have you been up to?' he asked.

Karen started to blush and pretended to glare at Tina.

'You said you wouldn't tell anyone about the naked swimming,' she said, nudging her friend.

David looked in mock horror and said, 'I'm shocked Karen, quite shocked.'

She gave him a shy smile before answering. 'Seriously, David, do you really think I would allow Tina to persuade me to go skinny dipping?'

'Well, let me know when you're doing it next time,' he said, 'I'll come along.'

'David, behave yourself,' Tina wagged a finger at him, 'or I'll tell Helen.' She turned back to address the group. 'Now, what about this big walk?'

Around a neighbouring table a group of young mums with an assortment of babies, toddlers, young children and all the paraphernalia that went with them, were involved in a lively discussion about fundraising for the village school. Both groups had spent liberally on coffees and cakes, and David could see how proud Mike was feeling as he surveyed his successful business.

'It's great to be your own boss,' David had told him at the time of the sale, 'but you need to know the drawbacks. Trade can be up and down, you can't afford to rest on your laurels and expect the customers to come in. It's long hours and short holidays and everyone expects weekend and bank holiday opening, now.'

Mike had seemed very confident. 'Never been frightened of hard work, have we?' he said to his wife. 'It's a grand shop you've built up, but we've loads of plans, haven't we love?'

'I'm taking on the cafe side of things,' she enthused, 'and we might develop the range of plants and gardening products.'

'Well, there's a great deal of opportunity there,' David agreed.

'Did your wife ever get involved?' Rosemary asked.

David had pulled a face at this suggestion.

'Helen always wanted her own career. She helped out a bit in the early days, more so when we lived upstairs in the flat, but since we bought the house, and especially since she became a headteacher, she left it to me.'

'We're in this together,' Rosemary had said proudly. 'It'll be both of us, and the boys when they're older.'

David had wished them well, slightly envious of their joint enthusiasm for the business.

Rosemary appeared to be working hard that Saturday morning. She brought David his usual espresso and asked if anyone needed a top up. Almost everyone did, so she went round the two groups, chatting, laughing, returning Bob's cheeky comments, then sitting down with the mums.

'I'm having five minutes,' she called to Mike.

As the morning went on, David realised how absorbed he had become in the meeting and how much better he felt. By lunchtime they had a good programme of walks planned, some more challenging than others, and several cups of coffee and two of Rosemary's home-made cakes had added to his feeling of well-being.

As the meeting broke up, Bob, who had been talking to Karen, came over.

'David, you couldn't help this lass out, could you? She says she needs to call a plumber just to bleed two radiators and mend a tap. It'll cost her a fortune.'

Karen was protesting that the cost didn't matter, but Bob was having none of it.

'David's handy and he can come anytime, can't you David?'

'I'll come over,' David said. 'You live at Copster Green, don't you?'

Karen hesitated and David thought she was going to protest again, then she said, 'Yes, it's the second cottage on the lane, the one with the blue door. Come over next week and I'll show you the radiators. It doesn't matter if you can't do it.'

'He'll do it in seconds,' Bob said, 'and then he can show you how to do it yourself.'

David turned to Karen. 'Have you got a radiator key?'

She shrugged her shoulders.

'It's like a little wing nut that fits on the valve.'

'I don't think so, I haven't seen one.'

'People usually put them in a kitchen drawer.'

'Honestly, I'm quite useless at this sort of thing,' she said. 'I'll have a search.'

'Don't worry, I can bring one. Which day's best for you?' he asked.

'Thursday, in the morning perhaps?'

'Fine,' David said. 'I'll see you then.'

'I knew you would help her out,' Bob said, as Karen made her way out of the cafe with Dan and Tina. 'Wish I was twenty years younger,' he added to David. 'I'd be getting to know her a bit better. She's a real sweetie. Can't believe any man worth his salt could up and leave her like that.'

'Did you know him?' David asked.

'Everyone sort of knew him. He was the 'Young' in Thomas and Young Engineering.'

David's eyes widened. 'Was he? I heard he sold his half of the business a few years ago. I hope she got her fair share.'

'Oh I think she did,' Bob replied, tapping the side of his nose. 'Those cottages where she lives go for a bob or two, and she doesn't seem to have a job. Tina and Dan live next door. They've really taken to her. I think she's getting over the divorce but I can't see her staying single for long, mind.'

David thought about Karen as he walked through the village and wondered how a long-term marriage could break down like that. Bob was right, Karen was an attractive lady and she had a good sense of fun, although compared to women like Helen and Debbie, she seemed rather shy, lacking some confidence. Some might call it feminine, but David struggled with what that meant these days.

Once home, he felt a bit deflated and started

mulling over what he wanted to say to Helen when she returned. His phone beeped. It was a short text from Lizzie saying they were having a good day. He noticed that it was his daughter and not Helen who had sent the message. Probably insignificant, but his wife could be making a point. He hoped she wasn't confiding in Lizzie. You shouldn't burden your children with problems in your marriage, it wasn't on, and the last thing he wanted was for either of his daughters to worry about their parents. Life was challenging enough.

It was dark when he heard Helen's car pull onto the drive. The door slammed. There were footsteps then a key in the lock, a dropping and rustling of bags and the sound of boots hitting the hall floor. David was watching television when she came into the living room. He was unsure how she would be feeling and how he would respond. Helen headed for the kitchen saying, 'I'm desperate for a cup of tea, the train was packed,' but she didn't look at him.

David switched off the TV, placed the remote carefully on the table and walked over.

'Leave that,' he said. 'I'll make the tea, you sit down.'

It was hard to read her mood. She looked up at him and said, 'I can make it myself.'

'Helen, I...'

She sighed and raised her hands in a weary gesture.

'I want to make you a drink, that's all.'

She dropped her hands. To David, she wasn't looking at him, but rather through him, to a space somewhere beyond, somewhere she seemed to want to be, rather than with him, in their kitchen. David wanted to take his wife in his arms and hold her. A few days ago it would have been the easiest, most natural thing in the world to do, but now, it was almost as if he didn't know how to do it. He wanted to say that they needed to sit down and talk. Instead he said, 'So, how's Lizzie?'

'She's good, really good. Enjoying the job, but looking forward to a break. And Pete seems fine as well. They can't come on Christmas Day this year as they're going to Pete's parents in Wales.'

'That's a shame. It'll be a quiet Christmas then.'

'Yes.'

The kettle boiled. David made two mugs of tea and they sat at either side of the sofa. Floss wandered over, as if looking for a knee, but, possibly sensing the tension, changed her mind, and flopped in her basket near the warmth of the stove. David asked a few more questions about shopping and Manchester. He told her about the meeting and how busy the cafe had been that morning. Helen listened, offering one word answers to his questions, as if she was deliberately rationing her words.

David took a deep breath and said, 'You may not want to, Helen, but we have to talk about last night.'

It took a while before the ensuing silence was broken, then she said, 'I really don't know what to say to you.'

'Well, in that case, I'll start, because I do know what I want to say to you.'

Helen looked up, met his eyes briefly, then glanced away.

'I'm sorry we got so angry with each other, and I'm sorry I wasn't more sympathetic about you being late. But for me, it was yet another evening waiting for you, another spoilt meal, another long day on my own. I said some things I shouldn't have said, but I did it because I was angry. In the end, I just want you to stop being the person you are now and go back to how you used to be.'

He paused to give her a chance to speak, but this time she didn't even look up at him. He ploughed on, regardless.

'You're so stressed, you don't look well, you have all the time in the world for your job but none for me, for us. To be honest, I didn't think retirement would be like this and if I had known, I wouldn't have sold the business, because at least when I was working, there was some balance between us. Since I stopped, you seem to work longer and longer hours and you're taking on even more. As I said last night, I want you to finish, or at the very least I'd like to know when you plan to finish. For me, it's as simple as that.'

He leant forward, elbows on his knees and waited. Helen put her mug of tea on the low table and then leant back, resting her head against the sofa. For a while she didn't speak and her expression gave nothing away. David could only assume that she was keeping something very important to herself.

'You said that if I didn't finish work, there would be consequences.' She turned her head to look at him. 'What did you mean exactly? I've been thinking about it all day.'

'I meant consequences for us, for our relationship, for our marriage.'

David found the silences unsettling. He would rather have her angry, as she had been the previous evening, because this lack of communication on her part served no purpose and was getting them nowhere. He was beginning to feel frustrated, so he tried another approach.

'I feel really fed up,' he said. 'I love you, Helen, but we aren't in a place where we seem to be able to love each other. I want to do things for you, you know I like looking after you, but it's so one-sided.' He wanted to mention the lack of any intimacy in the bedroom, but thought better of it.

'Well,' he said shortly, 'that's everything I want to say. Now it's your turn.'

She waited, then said, 'I need to tell you something, and you won't like it one little bit, but I have to tell you.'

So, this was it. Her change in behaviour, the distance between them, it all boiled down to one thing – she was having an affair. On reflection, it would have been so easy for her; the nights away; the late evenings at goodness knows where. It was probably a colleague or some smart-suited inspector, someone with a fast car and a huge wallet and nights away on expenses, someone who didn't need to spend his days chopping up wood and looking after the house and feeding the bloody cat. David sat up, ran his fingers through his hair, looked at her. With a pounding heart he opened his mouth, but the words seemed to stick in his throat. He took a deep breath and tried again.

'Whatever it is,' he said, 'you'd better get it over with and tell me.'

She was doing everything to avoid meeting his gaze, biting the skin down the side of her nail and considering it intently, leaning down to scratch her foot, shifting to pull her legs up underneath her body. He watched the fidgeting and waited. She glanced at him briefly, then looked away.

'Something happened last week, something that has now made it quite impossible for me to finish work next summer. Bridget came to see me and she handed her notice in. If I finish at the same time, the school will start in September with a new head and a new deputy. I can't let that happen, it could damage all I've tried to do at that school over the last few years, and you know how hard it's been to get everything back on track.'

David felt his body trembling, his pulse racing. He stood up and walked to the kitchen, placing his hands firmly on the unit dividing the two rooms. So, he had feared the worst and it hadn't happened. His assumptions about her having an affair now bordered on the ridiculous.

'Are you all right?' Helen asked.

David kept his head down, willing the thumping in his body to return to normal. She got up and came over to him.

'David, you're shaking,' she exclaimed, as he raised his head to look at her.

'I'm fine,' he whispered. 'Honestly, I'm fine.'

They stood for a moment. David could see she was confused by his reaction to the news, probably expecting him to be angry rather than in shock. She reached out, put her hands over his hands and said, 'I'm sorry, but you must see how it is.'

He came round to give her a hug, but they were both tense, both standing very still, both touching the other without any real feeling. Helen let go first and said, 'I need to sort out the shopping and I need a shower. Are you sure you're all right?'

David nodded. 'Yes, you go and do that. Do you want any supper?'

Helen thought for a moment. 'Perhaps some ginger cake and another drink,' she said, 'but you make something if you're hungry.' She left the room and he could hear her gathering up packages and bags before heading upstairs.

At that moment, what David really wanted to do was to go and sit on his own in his shed, but it would be freezing out there. Instead, he reached for the bread and opened a tin of beans – not a great meal for a Saturday night. As he waited for toast to pop up and beans to warm, he set about the mechanical task of emptying the dishwasher, his anger abating as he organised cutlery and put plates and dishes back in cupboards.

By the time Helen came downstairs in her dressing gown, he had eaten. She put the television on. The chance to talk had passed and David knew he was quite beyond any further discussion. His initial sense of relief had been replaced by frustration as her news about Bridget sank in. He wanted to probe further the reason she would have to stay on for a full year, but he hadn't the strength for another argument that evening.

They passed mundane, stilted comments about the day, about what Lizzie had been up to, about what they were watching on television. They discussed opening a bottle of wine, without coming to any sort of conclusion. By nine o'clock, Helen was almost asleep and decided to go to bed. David banked up the stove and followed her upstairs.

She was sitting on the bed looking at her phone.

'Lizzie,' she said, reaching over to plug the phone into the charger.

The neckline of her cotton nightshirt had slipped down over one shoulder and the desire to make love to his wife was suddenly overwhelming. David undressed, then he sat on the bed and took her hand. Helen seemed to understand his need and as they slid under the duvet, she reached for him and let him do what he wanted to do, but with limited response. When it was over, David felt wretched, almost as if she had allowed him to access her body to soften the blow of the news she had delivered earlier. It had been without passion, unemotional, and, worst of all, it couldn't be called making love because there was no tenderness, no affection.

As he lay in the darkness, he had the distinct feeling that there was still more to be faced, and that only by saying it, honestly, calmly, and listening to each other's thoughts and feelings would they begin to resolve this tension between them. But will we say it? he thought. Will we actually find the space and time to sit down with each other and say it?

As he drifted off to sleep, David wished he could feel more hopeful that they would.

Chapter 8

The year after Karen Young celebrated both her 50th birthday and her silver wedding anniversary, her husband came home one evening and dropped three bombshells that would change forever her view of the past and devastate whatever hopes she might have had for her future.

Nothing about Guy's departure that spring morning had prepared her for the coming storm. With a kiss on her cheek and a vague reference to what time he might be home, he had left the house. Mild weather enticed her into the garden later in the day, and she intended to ask him if he thought she should ring the gardener. Her husband returned in the evening, a little earlier than usual, sat next to her on the sofa and said, 'There's no easy way to do this, Karen, so I'm going to come straight out with it. There are three things I need to tell you.'

Karen had no time to say or do anything, because he didn't stop for breath. The words sounded rehearsed, as if he had spoken them aloud to himself to ensure that what he said would be crystal clear.

'Firstly, you need to get a solicitor, because I want a divorce. I will make things as easy as possible, but there will be a considerable amount of money involved, so you can't sort it out without a professional. Secondly, my share of the business has been sold, finalised today. I'm not going back to work, ever. Half of the proceeds belong to you. If it's any consolation, you won't need to work again, and, if you invest wisely, you'll never have any worries about money. Thirdly, I'm going to live in Florida with a couple of mates I met last time I was there on business.' At this point he did stop for breath, then finished with, 'I'm sorry.'

Karen felt as if all the fluid in her body was steadily draining towards her feet, leaving her with a strange light-headedness and a mouth so dry she could hardly speak. She heard herself say, 'There's a shepherd's pie in the oven,' then, realising the foolishness of the words added, 'but you won't be wanting any of that now, will you?'

'No. I'll go immediately,' he said. 'I think that will be the best for us both.' He went upstairs and came down less than half an hour later with two suitcases. Karen had stood at the bedroom door as he packed, crying, begging him not to leave. But leave he did, without touching her, no pat on the shoulder, no squeeze of the hand. He didn't even look at her.

She had wept for a month, every day the same, every morning an impossible battle with herself to get out of bed and perform the most basic of tasks. Their younger son, Alex, moved back home for a few months to be with her. He had looked after her gently and patiently, well beyond what might have been expected of a young man in his 20s.

'I should have known,' she said to Alex during one of their late-night conversations with a glass of whisky or wine. 'Why didn't I know? What did I think our marriage was about? He's ruined my past and my future. I did everything right, I tried to love him, but your Dad never showed much emotion. I thought all marriages were like that.'

'It wasn't you Mum,' Alex repeated patiently. 'It

was him.'

Karen frequently looked at her younger son and was glad he didn't resemble Guy in any way. He was a neat, fine-featured boy with dark hair that fell across his forehead. Night after night Alex listened as his mother voiced her anger, her complete incomprehension of what had happened and her fear of being alone.

After disbelief came fury, then a desperate analysis of every detail of their marriage. Finally, there was sadness, which brought a surprising feeling of peace, and Karen began to have moments where she glimpsed a life for herself again.

Almost a year after Guy had left, she sold the family home and bought a cottage. Karen started to plan, to make decisions, to organise and take charge of her future. She enrolled on a course of practical philosophy, offered her time to a local charity shop, joined an over 50s rambling group. It was on her first walk with this group that she met David.

Tina and Dan, her new neighbours, had persuaded her to join a walk in the summer starting from Fellburn. Karen was surprising herself. The philosophy sessions were encouraging her to understand her own feelings, to see life around her in all its colours, to appreciate living in the moment. She was doing things she had never done before, including going to Spain for a week with Tina and her friends, where they had swum naked in the villa pool at midnight, giggling like teenagers.

'I've wasted years and years trying to be normal,' she said, as they shared one of many jugs of sangria. 'It was like travelling through life in a car with tinted windows; I never saw what was going on outside.'

'I didn't know your husband,' Tina remarked, 'but he sounds like a boring bastard.'

Karen had thought about this. 'Definitely boring,' she said, 'but not quite a bastard. He left me the proceeds of half the business.'

The women insisted that she deserved it.

Karen loved her new friends. They joked about their husbands, put them down, laughed at their ineptitudes. They had careers, had brought up children but without the total self-sacrifice that Karen had accepted was her only role in life. Her sons had turned out to be fine young men. She knew this was mainly her doing, as Guy had taken little interest, always using the business as an excuse not to spend time with the boys. Karen wondered, now she was alone, whether she should have paid a little more attention to her own needs.

Once home from Spain, her confidence growing, she had bought a new car, had her hair coloured and visited both the theatre and the cinema on her own. When Tina suggested joining her and Dan for a ramble with the group, she reflected that she had never done much walking, except the odd stroll.

'You'll like the group,' Tina said. 'They're an enthusiastic lot, especially some of the old boys. There's a widower called Bob who runs the group. He's a scream. He has everyone in stitches.'

'I might get left behind,' Karen said, but Tina had scoffed at this idea.

'There'll be walkers a lot slower than you. And next Saturday will be a walk in the park. You won't even need boots.'

So, Karen had gone. She had enjoyed the walk, loved the scenery, laughed with Bob, who seemed to have a zest for life and a sense of humour that defied his years and, at the end, accepted a coffee from David

Richards, who had sat down and asked if she would be coming along next month.

David had led the walk on that particular day and taken charge of the party in a firm yet relaxed way. When Tina had disagreed about the route, he explained his choice patiently but stuck to the plan; when Bob's boot lace broke, he produced a spare; when a lady ran out of drinking water, he shared his own. Twice he had asked Karen if she was all right. She had enjoyed the attention and the feeling that someone cared about her. Karen considered him as they talked. He was tall and lean, dark hair turning to grey, quite at ease in casual walking gear.

'I've never been a walker,' she said to him. 'You're all so keen, I haven't even got the gear.'

'You only need boots, a waterproof and a rucksack.'

'I've got wellies.'

'No,' David said. 'You'll need some boots, that's if you want to do some longer stuff.' He gave Karen a list of the planned walks.

'I'm useless,' she said, looking at the list. 'I think I've led a very sheltered life. I don't even know where half of these places are.'

'You don't have to know. We often car share for the walks that are further away. Plenty of us enjoy leading, so no map reading skills needed.'

His encouragement and enthusiasm made her think what a kind man he was. She had already begun to realise how dull and emotionless her husband had been, and how that had rubbed off on her. It wasn't too late to change.

In the car, on the way home, Tina chatted away

about the walking group and Karen, in the back, half-listened. Then Tina said, 'And you met David, he's a lovely man.'

Karen was suddenly more interested. 'He bought me a coffee,' she replied, 'and gave me the list of walks for the next few months. Yes, he is lovely. He asked if I wanted to join the group again.'

'He's married,' Tina said, glancing over her shoulder. 'Sorry.'

Karen shook her head, made a face as if it didn't matter, and wondered why David wasn't wearing a wedding ring. Somewhere inside her there was a slight disappointment. But of course he would be married, as all the best men of his age seemed to be.

'His wife, Helen, sometimes walks with us,' said Tina, 'but she hasn't been recently. She's very pleasant. When they both come, they don't stick with each other like some couples do, they get round and talk to everyone.'

'Career woman,' Dan said.

Karen detected a faint note of disapproval.

'And a very successful one,' Tina countered, then to Karen, 'She's headteacher of a big primary school, but she always seems to be off at conferences and stuff. I think she visits other schools to advise.'

Karen was depressed to hear about yet another feisty, independent woman. For the umpteenth time, it made her wonder what she had done with her life. How had she let the years slip by without actually achieving anything herself? Looking back, it had been like a sort of sleepwalking.

'What does David do?' she asked.

'Retired now, just over a year I think. He used to own the shop where we have our meetings, but the cafe was much smaller then.' Tina launched into a long description of David and Helen, although she did admit that it was David who was the regular walker, often leading groups, especially when they visited the Lake District.

'There are some mid-week days out,' Tina said to Karen. 'You could go on those if you wanted.'

As they neared home, Tina asked her in, but Karen declined, saying she was tired. She took her bag from the car, kissed them both, as everyone seemed to do as a greeting or a goodbye these days, and walked up the garden path to her cottage door.

She paused, glanced around, and took stock of the profusion of early autumn colours. It was as if nature was holding on to the rich bloom of summer before a storm stripped the trees or a surprise early frost withered the leaves of late flowering shrubs. The garden was wearing a rich, yet slightly faded look, typical of good weather in September, but there was a brittle, last gasp feeling about it all. Before long, everything would finally give in to winter.

It was this front garden, the path down the middle, the quaint symmetry of the cottage with a door perfectly positioned between two windows, that had sold the place to Karen. It reminded her of the *Play School* house. Inside, the previous owners had modernised beautifully and very comfortably, yet with great respect for the age and character of the building. Karen loved it, and felt, almost childishly, that it loved her back.

Once inside, she took her shoes off, emptied her bag, then filled the kettle as she thought about the day. She had enjoyed the walk, but if she was honest, it had been another occasion when she found herself thinking about men. Being married to Guy might have been a rather flat, eventless existence, but she missed, quite dreadfully, being one half of a pair. She realised that although she envied women who seemed to have it all, she had been comfortable as a dedicated wife and mother, and this life she had now, although exciting at times, was missing something vital. For a moment, she gave in to tears, then took hold of herself and stopped.

Tomorrow, she thought decisively, I will go into town and get kitted out for this walking business. Then she wondered where on earth one went for outdoor gear. Tina would know. Karen stepped into the back garden and peeped over the fence. Tina was banging boots on the stones to dislodge mud and grit. She noticed Karen.

'So, you want that drink after all?'

Karen hesitated, thought about the tea she was intending to make, then said, 'How about wine? I've got some white in the fridge, almost a full bottle. I'll never drink it all on my own.'

It was blissful sitting on Tina's patio in the late afternoon sun. Dan had gone to visit his mother, so the two women settled into the loungers. Karen was glad she was not alone. She sometimes worried that her neighbours would tire of her, would think her too needy.

'I need to buy some walking boots, and a waterproof coat,' she said, gathering up a small handful of peanuts and popping them in her mouth one at a time. 'The sort of stuff you and Dan have. I've never bought anything like that before.'

'You do want to come again,' Tina said, 'great.' She proceeded to go through the multitude of shops selling outdoor clothes and equipment; there seemed to be so much choice.

Tina sat up, crossed her legs, and faced Karen.

'Today,' she said with a grin, 'did you...?'

'Did I what?'

'Did you, how shall I put it, fancy David?'

Karen gave a snort of indignant laughter.

'Whatever makes you say that?' she giggled.

'I could tell by the way you were looking at him. I'd say you were flirting, my girl.'

Karen started to protest but her friend interrupted.

'Hey, we all fancy David. You must have noticed those gorgeous blue eyes, and he's such a gentleman, pays attention to everyone.'

'But,' Karen said wistfully, 'he's married, as all the nice ones are. Bloody hell Tina, I could fancy Dan if he wasn't married to you.'

'Have him, take him,' she joked. 'You'd soon be passing him back over the fence, what with his dirty socks and beer breath.'

Tina stretched her back and lifted her arms in what Karen assumed was a yoga stretch. She envied Tina's slim, toned body, which was a couple of years older than hers, but remained taut and strong. She made Karen feel plump and rather saggy. She shifted position and wondered if a few regular walks would improve her figure.

'If,' said Tina, 'you've started fancying men again, and don't think that's only something we do when we're young, you'll need to start looking... seriously!'

'Looking? God, I wouldn't know where to start.'

'There's loads of places. And there are single men in the walking group, but possibly not for you.'

'It's a shame Bob's old enough to be my dad,' Karen said, remembering how much he had made her laugh. 'It's a shame David's married.' She took another sip of wine.

'You could try internet dating?'

'Absolutely not. I've heard that's just full of weirdos who want to get you into bed.'

'Not true,' Tina said. 'Who told you that?'

'I think it was Guy, believe it or not.'

'Humph, sounds like the sort of small-minded comment your ex would say.'

Tina relaxed her stretch and lay back. 'I have two friends who found partners and married them, and that was through internet dating. They were both divorced and couldn't face going out to try and meet someone. Both attracted some horrors, but eventually, each of them found their perfect man.'

'I'm not sure…'

'Of course you're not sure. It would be something completely new. But it's taking the initiative, and Sue, one of my friends, said how exciting it was and how in control she felt. She also said that there are a lot more men out there searching for women than the other way around, so, the man supermarket shelves are well-stocked. All you've got to do is get your shopping trolley and load it up with… suitable products!'

Karen laughed. 'Well I'll be choosing my shop wisely,' she said. 'Waitrose or Booths rather than one of the cut price ones.'

The women chuckled. Karen said she had an image in her mind of various shapes and sizes of men sitting hopefully on supermarket shelves. Tina described the miserable ones waiting in the cooler with the out-of-date foodstuffs. By the time Dan returned, they were helpless with laughter and he was surprised that only a single empty wine bottle sat on the table between them.

Karen refused when Tina suggested opening another.

'No,' she said, wiping her eyes with a tissue. 'You're both at work tomorrow, it's all right for me.' Somewhat unsteadily, she got to her feet.

'Hope your shopping's successful,' Tina said.

'Ah, yes, that's why I came round in the first place. I'll come tomorrow and give you a fashion show.'

Dan's eyes widened. 'Can't wait,' he said.

'He gets turned on by hiking gear,' Tina joked.

'I love a woman with a rucksack,' Dan said suggestively, 'especially if she's carrying my sandwiches.'

Tina thumped him and he made exaggeratedly hurt noises. Karen mused over the fact that she had never fooled around with Guy like that.

She pushed her way through the gap in the fence after hugging both of them, grateful for their company, knowing that the mellow, wine-soaked feeling would soon begin to wear off. She needed to do something to stop herself getting upset, so she rang Alex for a chat.

'Come over next weekend, bring Suzy,' she said at the end of the call and he promised he would. Then she rang her mother in Scotland, who claimed she was fine, but then proceeded to tell Karen in great detail about all her aches and pains. By the end of the conversation, she was tired and needed something to eat. Tina had told her she had a great figure but Karen was constantly aware of her tendency to put on weight, so she made a salad sandwich, leaving out the mayonnaise, and ate it sitting on the sofa in front of the television.

She thought about the internet dating suggestion. There was no harm in giving it a try. Tina was right, at her age she couldn't go and sit in a bar and wait for Mr Right to turn up, she would have to take the matter into her own hands and do something positive. Perhaps she could ask Tina for the phone number of one of these friends so she could talk about it first. She thought about her shopping the following day and looked forward to spending as much or as little as she wanted, a luxury she was enjoying, although she still felt that it was Guy's money rather than her own. She reflected on the lovely walk, the open spaces, rivers and hills she had never known were on her doorstep.

Once the cottage doors were locked, she climbed the stairs, showered and settled into bed. Then she allowed herself to think about David.

Chapter 9

As Simon walked through his school a few weeks before Christmas, he reflected on recent events and realised that, as usual, Helen had been right. A month ago, he and his staff were picking themselves up off the floor as the inspector left the village in her silver Mercedes. Now, unbelievably, they were gradually getting back to some normality.

The school was decked out in sparkle and colour, almost as if the Christmas decorations and the displays each class contributed to the hall had to be extra special this year. Everyone wanted to prove that this was a splendid school which would carry on being splendid in spite of some judgements made by a complete outsider. And there was some praise, which Simon had read and re-read and quoted to his staff.

The inspection report had gone out on the website, and, as Helen had predicted, the response from parents had been minimal. One mother had come in, demanding an appointment. She berated Simon about standards and poor behaviour and said she would be taking her children away after Christmas, which he sincerely hoped she meant. He was on the verge of offering to contact alternative schools to ask about spare places, but out of professionalism, he'd held his tongue. That mother's relationship with the school, despite many efforts to build bridges, had always been difficult.

Sometime after, a father had plonked himself in

the office and used some rather colourful language to describe the uselessness of inspections and the government, which Simon had agreed with in a very blokey and quite unexpected conversation.

Finally, Mike and Rosemary had arrived with a pot plant to tell him that they still thought Fellburn a great school, far better than the one their boys had come from. After that, the staff settled down, the children carried on as if nothing had happened and Simon felt his stress levels reducing.

The snow had caused some disruption, but although the cold weather had continued, no more had fallen and he was grateful that he could get to school each day. When the weather was very bad, he found that the decision about closing rested firmly with him, and it was a great responsibility. People would moan whatever you did, but if he decided to close, it caused great inconvenience to working parents. If he opened and there was an accident on the narrow lane to Fellburn, he would feel it was his fault. The police advised, the council promised to grit, but didn't, and no one would actually tell him what to do. With everyone's safety in mind, he had spent a few early mornings walking the last part of the lane in the dawn light to assess conditions.

Soon, school would close for the Christmas break, when he could once again devote himself to being a husband and a father. Sophie was still vulnerable, slowly gaining more confidence in herself and her ability to look after the boys, but Simon could tell she was as exhausted as he was. He knew that what they really needed was some time together.

He continued his walk back to the office, hearing children's laughter and chatter as he crossed the hall.

Three small boys were carrying a huge cardboard model of a crane. When they saw him, they did their best to speed up. The expression, more haste, less speed, crossed Simon's mind. The boys were forced to stop when their enthusiasm to reach him caused the mechanism at the top to fall off.

'What have we here?' Simon exclaimed.

'It's a crane.'

'We made it.'

'It really works!'

'It did work,' one of the trio said, folding his arms and shaking his head. 'Now look what a mess we've made.'

Simon couldn't help smiling at them.

'Bring it to my office,' he said. 'We'll patch it up, no one will ever know.' He looked around. 'Quick, before anyone notices.'

The boys collected the broken pieces, and with Simon's help, got the model to his room and placed it gently on the floor. Gill, the office manager, came through with the diary and said, 'Wow, you've made a crane.'

'It needs mending,' Simon said to her. 'Don't tell anyone.'

'Not a word,' she replied, kneeling down to look at the damage. She passed Simon the desk-diary and pointed to a date. 'Think you've double-booked yourself there.'

Simon took the diary and checked with the calendar on his tablet. As he flicked the pages and moved things around, Gill got to work with sticky tape and glue with as much enthusiasm as the boys. In no time, the model was fixed and the three designers solemnly demonstrated its stability. Simon sent them back to class with stickers and a promise to show the rest of the school the contraption as part of his next assembly.

He settled down at the computer to clear e-mails, answer some, delete others, note what he would need to ask Helen the next time he saw her. Later, he enjoyed a lively lunch hour with a group of infants, then joined the School Council to discuss events leading up to the end of term. He ate his own sandwiches with three of the dinner ladies, who never failed to amuse him with stories of the school in days gone by. Carol had attended as a girl, seen her own children and then grandchildren sitting in the same classrooms where she had learnt her letters.

'They say education's gone downhill,' she often said. 'But it's far better than when I came here. And I can't do the maths they do in the top class, now, no way.'

Simon was grateful for his lunchtime staff and the teaching assistants who supported the children in the classroom. He considered them the unsung heroes, working away in the background, and he wondered what he could buy them for Christmas as a gesture of thanks. A box of chocolates hardly seemed adequate.

The children joined their classes for the afternoon and he returned to his office. After barely ten minutes, Debbie came in clutching a copy of the local newspaper. She looked at him, and he knew exactly what she was about to say. His mood plummeted.

'So,' he said. 'It's hit the paper?'

'Nothing more than we expected,' she said. 'It's fairly short, and almost entirely made up of chunks from the report and your quote, of course.'

'How did you get that copy of the paper?'

'Etta brought it in after lunch.'

Simon sighed. 'Etta, I might have known. I suppose living above a newsagent's she was bound to see it.'

'She thought she was helping. She said that Reg is refusing to display the headline board outside the shop.'

'It's on a hoarding? What does it say? Surely it can't be as important as all that?'

'I don't know,' Debbie said. 'Take a look. It's only a short piece and on the fourth page.'

She handed the paper to Simon. He read the article, then passed it back.

'You're right,' he said. 'It's just repeating what the report says. Oh well, we knew it was coming. Perhaps I'll give Helen a ring.'

Debbie seemed slightly irritated. 'You don't need to ring Helen,' she said shortly. 'What can she do?'

Debbie's reaction surprised him. She had overstepped the mark but nevertheless he decided to defend his comment.

'I thought she should know, that's all.'

'Haven't you noticed, Simon, that Helen isn't great at the moment?'

He recalled the last time he had seen Helen. He hadn't noticed anything different about her.

'She seemed fine when I saw her,' he said.

'Well, she isn't fine, believe me. She's very tired and she's taken on far too much work over and above running her own school. I'm worried about her.'

'To be quite honest, Debbie, I hadn't noticed she wasn't well.'

Debbie shrugged and shook her head. 'You wouldn't, you're a man,' she said. 'Look, can I tell you something else while we have five minutes?'

Simon closed the door. The two of them sat at each side of a low table and Simon wondered what Debbie was going to say. He was desperately sorry she was leaving in the summer. It had taken them two years to realise and appreciate each other's strengths. At first, he knew she had felt him too young and inexperienced to be her boss. He found her resistant to change and he had also sensed some resentment on her part when Helen had started visiting as his mentor. But all that had passed. He appreciated Debbie's experience, and her talent as a classroom teacher, and now she supported him wholeheartedly.

'This support you're getting from Helen,' she said. 'I thought it was finished.'

Simon frowned. 'The official support for me as a new head has finished, that was only for the first two years.'

'But she came last week for the evening meeting with you and Janice, and she was in before school earlier this week.'

'She always said I could ring her anytime. I couldn't get hold of her when Ofsted called and I felt guilty that she didn't know we were being inspected. I suppose she's visiting in her own time, now, and I'm grateful she's there to keep an eye on things.'

Debbie looked directly at Simon. 'You can manage this school without Helen,' she said. 'You can get out of the Requires Improvement category with the staff you have and, more importantly, you can do it using your own skills and common sense. I know Helen means well, but it really isn't her problem.'

Simon ran a hand through his hair, scratching the base of his skull. He wasn't sure how to respond. Was Debbie criticising him, his leadership? In the end he said, 'I'm not sure what you're getting at?'

Debbie sighed. 'OK,' she said, 'here it is. I'm Helen's friend and I'm concerned about her because she seems rundown and overworked. She's doing too much and, as usual, when she sees a need to get involved, she wades in. You're quite capable of moving this school forward on your own. Don't forget, I'm not leaving until next summer, and by then you'll have another deputy in place. I'm not saying don't keep Helen informed, I'm saying be aware that she could do without any more hassle. I've known her and David for many years and just as I think you need more time with your family, Helen needs more time with David. I wouldn't say this to anyone else, Simon, and please don't repeat it, but things aren't great between them.'

Simon pondered this. He should have noticed that Helen wasn't herself.

'That's not good,' he said. 'I hope they can sort it out. I called at their house a few weeks ago and I thought they both looked fine.'

'They will be,' Debbie said. 'But remember what this job can do to a person. Don't, under any circumstances, neglect your little family.'

'I won't,' he said. 'But going back to what you mentioned about me leading the school – let me get this straight, and I want you to be honest – you're really saying that I should stand on my own two feet?'

'Exactly, but only because I know you are more than capable of doing it.'

'Thanks for the vote of confidence, I appreciate it,' Simon said.

'Right, I'm due in Class Two to cover for Sally. I promised them some more Horrid Henry.'

Debbie got up and left.

Simon tried to remember how Helen had looked the last time he saw her. He couldn't recall her looking tired. And I do still need her, he thought. I look forward to her visits. She has such energy, she makes me feel... he wasn't sure how she made him feel. Was it attraction? Surely not, she was much older than him, and theirs was a professional relationship. Yet since the inspection she had treated him more as a good friend, and the last time she had sat in his room he had felt himself looking at her in a different way and feeling strangely invigorated. There was something going on that he couldn't get his head round.

Debbie was right, though. It was time for him to be his own person, manage his role without continually referring to Helen when making decisions.

'And the first one I'll make is to throw this rubbish in the bin,' he said aloud, rolling up the local newspaper into a tight missile shape and jettisoning it neatly into the waste paper basket. He felt much better after that, then he changed his mind and retrieved it, smoothing the pages out carefully; after all, it wasn't his newspaper.

Later, when most of the staff had already left for home, Simon zipped up his laptop case and reached for his coat. It was another cold, still evening. A few flurries of snow had whisked around earlier, but the roads were fairly clear and his drive home was remarkably easy. He passed two gritters spreading salt across the carriageway and he hoped that they were heading for the more remote, minor roads, specifically those in and around Fellburn.

Pulling into his drive, he felt a desperation to be out of the car and inside his house where he could take his wife and two sons in his arms and hold them. He noticed coloured lights in the window. Sophie had said she would decorate the house with Jim that afternoon when Billy took his nap. The fact that she had done it made Simon's heart sing. He crossed the path carefully, his feet crunching on the icy surface, then he opened the front door and shouted a greeting. An enthusiastic three-year old bounded into the hallway.

'Daddy, guess what we've done?'

Simon scooped him up and held him.'

'Something nice I hope?'

'Very nice.'

Jim wriggled to be put down. 'Wait,' he said pushing the door to the lounge and peeping in. 'Right, you can come in.'

Simon peeped round the door. Sophie was kneeling on the floor holding Billy, with Jim by her side, the little boy unable to contain his excitement. The Christmas tree had, quite obviously, been decorated with the help of a very small child. Only the coloured lights had been hung neatly, illuminating the darkness in the rest of the room.

He expressed enormous surprise, great wonder that Jim had done so much of the decorating on his own, disbelief that it had only taken them the afternoon to complete everything.

An hour of cuddling Billy and reading to Jim followed, until both were put to bed, red-faced and sleepy.

Sophie headed for the kitchen to lay the table for supper. Simon reached out as she passed, wrapping his arms around her in the sheer joy of seeing some sparkle in his wife's face.

She returned his hug. 'How was today, then?'

Simon opened his mouth to describe his day, then

changed his mind. 'It was fine,' he said, 'but let's not talk about school. I'd rather you told me about what you've been up to. It's so great to come home to all this.'

'I was a little anxious when I woke up this morning,' Sophie said, 'and at first I wasn't sure I was up to much, but we had a good morning and Billy seemed more settled. This afternoon, I managed to get the buggy in the car and decided to go to the garden centre to buy a tree. Mum and Dad came round later and Dad helped me get the tree upright. Some of Jim's decorations need rearranging, but we had such fun.'

'Don't you dare rearrange them,' Simon teased. 'I think they look perfect as they are!'

Sophie laughed. 'Let's eat,' she said, 'I'm starving.'

After supper, Simon insisted that she left the clearing up to him, banishing her to the lounge. He hummed his way through the washing up, finding pleasure in the simple task. His thoughts returned to the newspaper report about his school, but he felt strangely unmoved. He had been dreading seeing what he considered to be his failure, made public. Now that it had happened, it didn't seem as bad as his imagination had led him to believe.

Perhaps, he thought as he attacked the burnt sides of the casserole dish with a pan scrub, perhaps I am learning to have some confidence in myself.

Kitchen cleared, crockery draining, Simon carried two glasses of wine through to the lounge, where Sophie was tidying up the Christmas tree. She was wearing his old jumper over leggings, and for the first time in ages, Simon looked at his wife and allowed himself a desperate hope that she was feeling better. Her fine, blonde hair had grown recently, framing her slight features and her face seemed to have a brighter look. Sophie smiled at him. 'Sorry,' she said, 'I had to rearrange some of the decorations.'

She finished straightening the angel, then came to sit next to him on the sofa, resting her head on his shoulder, wrapping her arm under his shirt to lie beneath his ribs.

'Thanks for putting up with me,' she said. 'I know I've been awful. I know I need to be more supportive.'

Simon felt a rush of love, protectiveness, determined to see himself and his wife through this difficult time.

'We'll be fine,' he said. 'We have everything going for us and I don't care how long it takes for you to get your confidence back. I know it'll be all right in the end.'

'But what about you? All the stuff at school?'

'I'll sort it out. It won't be easy, but both Debbie and Helen believe in me – that means a lot.'

They sat without talking, then Sophie said, 'I saw Helen's husband, David, today, at the garden centre. At least, I think it was him. He wasn't with Helen though.'

'Well, he wouldn't be, Helen would be working.'

'Yes, I thought that. We were waiting at the entrance for the hail shower to stop, and he rushed in with some dark-haired woman, about his age, quite attractive I suppose. I noticed her because she was in walking clothes, but she had a huge sparkly handbag. It looked rather odd.'

Simon thought about the conversation he had shared with Debbie earlier that day, and remembered she had hinted that things were not good between Helen and David. It was ridiculous to put two and two together and make anything out of it.

'Probably just a friend,' he said.

Sophie sat up. 'When I realised who it was, and it was David Richards I'm sure, I thought that. Then, as they went past me, he said something and she looked up at him and laughed and touched his arm in a very familiar, almost affectionate way. It was as if they were sharing something, not exactly intimate, but very close all the same. If I hadn't known it was him, I'd have thought they were married or something.'

'Did you see them again?'

'No, we left as soon as the hail shower eased off. It was fleeting, but the sparkly handbag and her hand on his arm stood out in my mind.'

Sophie lay back against Simon's arm again, then she tensed as a faint cry started upstairs.

'Billy,' she said. 'I'll feed him then he might go right through.'

She got up, kissing Simon before she left the room.

He switched off the Christmas tree lights, locked up, moved the last few items of crockery from the drainer and put them away, then followed her upstairs. He wondered if things between Helen and David were worse than even Debbie knew. Surely not. It was only a few weeks since he had visited them the weekend after the inspection. He had thought at the time that they seemed so relaxed in each other's company and he remembered imagining himself and Sophie with grown up children, pleasing themselves on a Sunday afternoon. The woman Sophie had seen was certainly a friend, that's all.

But Sophie had described a certain look and a touch. She noticed many things that usually escaped Simon's attention, such as whether people wore wedding rings or who might have lost or put on weight.

Where people were concerned, his wife showed an astuteness which often surprised him.

He hoped that on this occasion, she was wrong.

Chapter 10

If Simon had decided to phone Helen earlier that afternoon, Jen, her business manager, would have said she was unavailable. Helen had walked out of a long lunchtime meeting and entered the office just in time to grab the edge of the desk and crumple to the floor against one of the filing cabinets.

She remembered hearing Jen's voice somewhere in the distance telling her to put her head between her knees but, although she could hear the voice and could feel a pain in her back, she seemed incapable of doing anything. When she opened her eyes, it was to see Jen kneeling beside her and, apart from the pain, things started to clear.

'Are you all right?' Jen asked, holding Helen's hand, her face full of concern.

'I think so, I don't know what happened.'

'You fainted. Have you ever passed out before?'

'Never.'

'How do you feel now?'

Helen put a hand behind her back to see what was causing the pain. A drawer handle was digging into her spine. She eased herself forward, wincing.

'Ouch, that's better.'

'You still look very pale. Have you had lunch, Helen?'

'No, the meeting went on far longer than we thought so I haven't had time. I'm not hungry, but I do need a drink.'

'I think you need to go home and rest. People don't faint for nothing. And you need to eat something. Maybe your blood sugar is low.'

Jen helped Helen up and into a chair, then made her a cup of tea. Helen was grateful there were no other office staff working that afternoon. She experienced a strange sense of unease at what her body had inflicted on her, as if it had acted without her permission and done something independent of her will. It was most unnerving.

'I'll drive you home,' Jen said firmly. 'You've no appointments this afternoon.'

'I was planning to meet Bridget after school.'

'She'll understand. You can do that another day.'

'Things get so tight at this time of year, it's hard to rearrange.'

Helen felt a knot of fear in her stomach at the prospect of her schedule being jeopardised by her own inability to keep up with it. Some of the staff had been ill recently, with flu and colds. Perhaps she was going down with something.

'You're right,' she said. 'Yes, I should go home. There are some reports to do before the end of the week, I can work at home, get them out of the way.'

'Leave the reports, you need to rest. Will David be in?'

Helen tried to think. She couldn't remember him saying anything about going out, but then she hadn't really spoken to him that morning. In the back of her mind, she was sure he had said that something was happening later in the day.

'He should be in.'

'Shall I ring him?'

'What, now?' Helen sat upright. 'No, of course not.

I feel fine, Jen, really I do. I think you're probably right, I need to eat my lunch and then take it easy for the rest of the day.'

She took a gulp of tea. 'I hope I'm not getting flu or something.'

'I'll go and tell Bridget I'm driving you home.' Jen set off for the door, but Helen was determined to take control of the situation. She didn't want Bridget knowing she had fainted, and she especially didn't want David to know. He seemed to seize upon the least sign that she wasn't coping with everything. It was becoming an issue that rumbled on; he taking the opportunity to comment if she seemed tired or short-tempered; she continually feeling the need to prove that she was coping effortlessly; neither of them being honest. If Helen had taken the time to really think it through, she would have realised that this wasn't a battle to be fought, it was a challenge for both of them to face together.

'No,' she said sharply. 'I'm quite fit to drive. I'll eat a sandwich, get all the paperwork together, then I'll go. The traffic isn't too bad at this time of day, I'll be home in half an hour.'

'Helen, I can't let you drive. What if you fainted again?'

'I won't faint again,' Helen said. 'And there's no need to tell Bridget, or anyone else about this.'

'You're hopeless, you know that? Sometimes I don't think you take advice from anyone. Well, I'm telling you, you shouldn't drive.'

'Thanks for your concern, I appreciate it, but I'm absolutely fine now, honestly.'

Jen turned away and started to open the post with the paper knife, stabbing at the letters and ripping open the envelopes.

'You're the boss,' she said after a minute. 'She looked up from the messy pile of discarded envelopes and junk mail. 'But I want a text when you get in, otherwise I will ring David.'

'I promise,' Helen said. 'I'll get my things.'

As Helen drove home, it started to snow again – wet, sleety flakes in Accrington, finer, icier flakes as she neared Fellburn. This winter was showing some real bite, which was unusual before the Christmas holidays. By the time she pulled onto the drive, it had stopped, but a light covering had dusted the trees and fields and covered the lumps of snow that remained from the last fall. Thankfully, David's car wasn't there, although she had rehearsed what she would say to explain her early arrival, using paperwork and the need to have some peace and quiet away from school as an excuse. She sent Jen a cheerful text before getting out of the car.

As she pressed send, she was aware of a face at the window and a gloved hand tapping the glass. Helen turned to see a figure wrapped up in thick scarf and woollen hat, her cheeks bright with cold. It was Rosemary.

'Hang on,' Helen mouthed. She reached over for her things, then opened the car door, forcing a smile. Much as she liked Rosemary, this wasn't a good time for a chat.

'I'm going to collect the boys from school and I saw your car. Can I ask you something, Helen? I won't keep you for long.'

'Of course, but come in for a minute, Rosemary.'

'I've got my wellies on. Really, it's very quick.'

Helen unlocked the front door, dropped her school stuff on the floor and invited Rosemary, boots and all, to step into the hall.

'Right,' Helen said, 'how can I help?'

Rosemary pulled the scarf away from her face and took off her gloves.

'You know Mike and I are helping to run the parents' group at school, now? Well, we had a meeting last night and someone had an idea. I said I'd see what you thought about it before we mentioned it to Mr York.'

'Go on.'

'Schools put banners up, don't they? Sometimes it's a quote from Ofsted, like the one on the way to Blackburn that says; Welcome to our Outstanding School.'

Helen rolled her eyes. 'Don't like them myself,' she said. 'Banners are all very well to draw attention to an event, maybe, but I don't put up free adverts for supermarkets at my school just because we're collecting tokens, and I would never boast about an Ofsted rating. Anyway, how many schools leave them up when they look tatty and blow about in the wind because no one can be bothered to move them?'

'I agree,' Rosemary said. 'But we feel that both the staff and Mr York need a boost. We want to put up our own banner saying how good we think the school is.'

She groped in her handbag and pulled out a piece of paper with prints of various banner designs, handing it to Helen. The designs were simple, yet colourful. They welcomed visitors, quoting the perceived attributes of Fellburn School.

'I need to know,' Rosemary said, her cheeks beginning to glow in the warmth, 'I need to know if we're allowed to put up a banner like this, or can you only do it if Ofsted say you're a good or outstanding school?'

Helen thought briefly, then answered, 'I'm quite sure that schools can put up whatever banner they like, as long as it isn't giving false information or is offensive in any way. I think it's a great idea, Rosemary, but don't use the word good, Ofsted use that word to rate schools. I'd use wonderful or caring or welcoming, whichever word you think best describes the school. Then make it clear that it's something the parents want to say. Run it past Mr York, but I'm sure he'll be fine with it.'

Rosemary stuffed the paper back in her handbag.

'Great, we'll get on with it then. Rachael has a friend whose company make banners so it won't cost much. We feel so annoyed about this Ofsted thing, we want to do something to try to put things straight.'

'Good for you. Simon will be delighted.'

'We're worried about him,' Rosemary said. 'He looks so tired and sad since the inspection.' She put her gloves on and pulled her scarf around her face. 'I mean, he's a lovely man. Some of the girls on the committee quite fancy him you know!'

Helen laughed. 'He's a good-looking guy,' she said, 'but he's very happily married and the proud father of two little boys.'

'Oh, it's only in fun,' Rosemary added, seriously.

'I'm joking,' Helen said. 'If I was twenty years younger I could fancy him myself!'

Realisation dawned and Rosemary's face broke into a smile.

'Thanks, Helen.'

'Thanks for calling. Is everything all right at the shop?'

'Great. Busy, but that's how it should be.'

Helen opened the door and Rosemary stepped out into the cold giving a wave as she strode out across the road towards the school.

Helen shut out the freezing air, removed her coat and went into the family room. It was warm and there was a smell of meat braising. In the kitchen area, pans of prepared vegetables stood in water. She paused for a moment, then remembered something David had said earlier that morning about his parents coming to eat with them. The thought depressed her and she felt weary. She would have to behave pleasantly and make cheerful conversation so that Marjorie wouldn't say, as she so often did, that Helen was looking tired.

She pushed her laptop and school bag under the desk. A plastic box with two cheese sandwiches fell out of the open bag followed by a green apple that rolled across the floor. Helen looked at her lunch dispiritedly. The apple had travelled between home and school for three days now, and was looking bruised and pitted. She wondered why she had bothered to think she would ever eat it. It went in the bin with a sharp thud and was closely followed by the sandwiches. In order to hide the evidence, should David decide to play the detective, she tore off two squares of kitchen roll and placed them over her uneaten lunch, then she deliberately left her empty sandwich box in the sink.

She went upstairs to change, choosing jeans and a thigh-length jumper, which hid the looseness of the trousers.

I'll have a few minutes lying down, she thought, then I'll get the reports done.

The bed was so welcoming and comfortable that for once she could close her eyes and clear her mind.

When David came home an hour later, she was dozing. Floss had sneaked silently into the bedroom and curled up on the other side of the bed, ready to leap off when she detected any movement.

Helen opened her eyes to see David picking up the cat and throwing the creature out of the room. It was dark, the only light seeping in from the landing. He reached out to switch on the reading lamp as she turned over, then he sat on the bed, looking huge in his thick fleece, bringing a scent of the outdoors into the bedroom. Irritation surfaced because he had interrupted her slumber, yet perversely, she was annoyed with herself for being asleep when he returned.

'I'm glad you managed to get home early,' he said.

Helen sat up and rubbed her eyes. 'I thought I'd better not be too late with your parents coming over. I must have dropped off for a moment.'

'It's after five o'clock. They'll be here soon.'

'Has the snow stopped?'

'Yes.'

Helen noticed that David was looking at her intently. Instinctively she knew that he had sensed something wasn't quite right, so she got up from the bed and rummaged in the wardrobe for her slippers, asking about his day. She headed off any questioning as they went downstairs.

'You've been walking?' she asked, watching him put more logs on the stove.

'Yes, by the Lancaster Canal. We walked it a few years ago if you remember. Then we had a coffee at the garden centre.'

'A good crowd?'

'The usual mid-week walkers. Stunning weather until after lunch when the clouds came over and we had a few flakes of snow, then hail.'

Helen set out the cutlery and placemats on the small table in the living room, as David checked the casserole.

'Wine glasses?' she asked.

'I think so. Dad will want a glass of red.'

Helen set the glasses down carefully, thinking about when she had fainted earlier. She remembered that she had eaten very little all day and resolved to try to make the best of David's cooking.

Marjorie and John arrived in a flurry of cold air, exclaiming loudly about the weather and the lack of grit on the frosty roads.

'I said I'd pick you up,' David reminded his mother, but she was adamant they weren't so old that they needed a taxi service.

No, Helen thought looking at her mother-in-law, that's because John always drives. She took their coats, thinking that John was looking frailer and less confident than he used to be. He had broken his wrist due to a fall a year ago and the accident had left him rather cautious and slower in his movements. Marjorie, on the other hand, seemed to be in the same robust state of health she had always enjoyed.

'I can't wait to talk to Charlotte,' Marjorie said as David took coats and ushered his parents into the warmth. Helen looked at David.

'Have you organised a Skype call?'

'I told you this morning, didn't I? If we call at eight, it's early morning for her. She said she'd be up.'

Helen doubted that her daughter would be out of bed at that hour and said as much.

'Yes she will,' David contradicted her. 'She sent a text this morning to say she would.'

'Well, we'll see,' Helen said. 'Now, are we having drinks?'

David poured his mother a small sherry and opened a bottle of red for his father and himself. Helen refused a drink. She was feeling light-headed again and was unsure how alcohol would affect her, so she sat next to Marjorie and asked the usual polite questions about friends and family, leaving David to get on with whatever needed doing in the kitchen.

'Oh, I forgot to tell you, we've brought the local paper,' Marjorie added, when she had finished updating Helen with their news. 'There's an article about the village school. Well, it's a report really.'

Helen felt a wave of nausea wash over her. 'Fellburn village?' she said.

'Yes,' Marjorie replied, reaching over to where John had put the paper. She flipped the pages over, folded it back neatly and presented it to Helen.

'Look, it doesn't make very good reading, Helen. The inspectors found a lot of things that need improving.'

Helen took the newspaper and read the short report. The headline was simple: Village School told to Improve. Some journalist, probably a junior on the team had cut and pasted chunks of the inspection report, deliberately pulling out all the negative and none of the positive comments. Simon's quotation was earnest and sounded sincere in a desire to take all the advice given and to remedy any shortcomings. She handed the paper back to Marjorie.

'Rubbish,' she said. 'It's a great little school.' She got up. 'I must ring Simon.'

'Now?' David said from the kitchen. 'You have to ring him now?'

Helen had already left the room. David picked up a tea towel to wipe his hands and followed her into the hall where she stood fidgeting, the phone to her ear.

'Surely he won't still be at school, Helen. Can't it wait? Leave it until tomorrow.' Helen waved him away irritably, but he stood over her as she waited for someone to pick up the phone. When there was no answer, he took the phone out of her hand and replaced it in the cradle.

'David,' she exclaimed. 'I was going to try him at home.'

'No, you're not ringing him now, especially not at home. It'll wait Helen, we've got guests. Just for once, leave your work at work.'

Helen made a grab for the phone again.

'Don't!'

David's voice made her jump. She hesitated, suddenly lacking any energy for another row, especially not with John and Marjorie in the next room. She glared at him, expecting some sort of apology, but he had already left the hall.

Helen took a deep breath, smoothed her hair with hands that, to her surprise, were trembling, and followed her husband back into the sitting room. She said little as Marjorie shook her head and said what a shame it was about the school. David called everyone to the table and the meal passed with pleasant conversation about Lizzie and Charlotte, the visit to Australia and arrangements for Christmas. Helen accepted a glass of wine and, finally, felt hungry enough to eat most of her meal.

She cleared the table, insisting that David leave her so he could set up the Skype call with Charlotte. She moved crockery and pans with a weariness that only a long, long sleep could cure. It was as if she needed to hibernate; sleep away this freezing winter and wake to blue skies, spring sunshine and the first daffodils. As she held this thought, her eyes almost closed and a glass dish, slippery with soapy water left her hand and shattered on the quarry-tiled floor.

David had an armful of extension leads and the laptop, so it was John who came to help.

Helen was close to tears, but she managed to hold them back as she found the dustpan and brush.

'I'll do it,' John insisted.

'Bloody stupid thing to do.'

'Well, I agree with you there, Helen. I always thought you were a clumsy oaf!'

Helen smiled at his teasing, picking up the larger shards with careful fingers, as John swept.

'You won't be walking around in your bare feet, will you?' John said. 'Auntie Bea dropped a milk bottle once and my cousin Walter got a piece in his foot two weeks later.'

'It was William, not Walter,' Marjorie called from the lounge.

John winked at Helen and mouthed, 'Walter,' then called to his wife, 'William, yes of course dear, how remiss of me.'

Helen giggled softly and took the dustpan and brush from John.

'Thanks,' she said. 'You're a knight in shining armour.'

Quite unexpectedly, her father-in-law gave her a hug. He knows I'm on the edge, she thought.

Suddenly, she heard Charlotte's voice, followed by Marjorie, who exclaimed with delight at the wonders of modern technology.

They talked for the best part of an hour. Charlotte looked sleepy at first, then someone passed her a coffee and waved to them all, and by the end of the call she was giving them a guided tour of the apartment with rapid sweeps around the rooms that made Helen feel dizzy.

'Slowly,' David told her, then, 'put it down, Lottie, you're making us feel sick.'

Marjorie insisted on hearing every small detail about her granddaughter's life in Melbourne. In the end, Helen could see that David was desperate to talk, so she suggested Charlotte say goodbye to her grandparents and the laptop was moved to face the small sofa, where she and David sat down together.

As Charlotte chatted and Helen listened, she thought how energised her daughter seemed to be. Despite the poor screen colours, her skin was obviously tanned and her blonde hair streaked by the sun. She giggled, recounted events with great enthusiasm and made Helen envious of her youth and vitality.

If I stood next to her, Helen thought to herself, I'd look like a shadow, sort of washed out and faded. And that's exactly how I feel. Even my thoughts seem wispy and unreal sometimes.

Suddenly she realised that Lottie wasn't talking to David, she was asking her a question. Helen focussed on the screen and sat up.

'Sorry, I didn't catch that?'

'I said, what do you want to do, Mum, when you come over in March?'

Helen hesitated. It had been David who had done most of the research about Australia. She hadn't shown much interest.

'I'm not sure, really,' she said. 'I'd like to spend time

with you, sit on the beach, read some good books.'

'Well, Dad and I will leave you to the beach and we'll go and paint Melbourne red, white and blue!'

'Sounds great to me,' Helen replied. 'I'll be on hand with the bail money when you get each other into trouble.'

Charlotte laughed and began a tale of friends who had been picked up by the police after a night out. Helen and David listened until their daughter glanced at the time and said she had to get ready for work. The call ended with reluctant goodbyes and promises to keep in touch.

Without warning, David leapt up suddenly to move the laptop, dragging wires across Helen, forcing her to move out of the way. She was about to protest, when she perceived a glimpse of sadness in his face. Marjorie dabbed her eyes, John picked up Floss, settling the cat on his knee and Helen turned to stare at the flames in the stove.

'How can you bear her being so far away?' Marjorie asked, but neither Helen nor David replied.

Later that evening after David had gone to bed, Helen stayed up to write at least two of the reports. She thought about the closeness between Charlotte and her father. It had showed through very strongly tonight; it was almost tangible. Even though they were both thousands of miles apart and their voices were not always synchronised with the image, the bond was tight, making her feel excluded at times.

She closed the laptop and the folder of notes, poured a glass of water and paused for a moment to drink it.

He's only upstairs, she thought. Yet if I'm honest, I

feel that it's me, not Lottie who's more than 10 000 miles away. The way things are, David and I couldn't even use Skype to reach each other.

Too tired to consider these thoughts any further, she rinsed the glass, switched off the lights and went to bed.

Chapter 11

Karen always dressed carefully, but this morning she had taken a long time to try on, and subsequently change her mind about various items of clothing. When she was married to Guy, she had regularly used make-up, kept her hair short and neatly cut and, even in jeans, had always gone for a smarter look. But her attitude had changed. She'd let her hair grow out into a softer style, and found that she liked the casual clothes that Tina and some of the other women wore. It felt liberating to choose flat shoes rather than heels, which did little more, if she was honest, than hurt her feet and slow her down. This morning she decided on a pair of casual jeans, and a neatly fitting jumper that brushed softly against her skin.

She ran a duster over the surfaces in the small lounge at the front of the cottage, glancing up every so often to check if David's car had arrived. It would be the third time he had called over the last few months to do *man jobs* as they both referred to them. As she waited, she re-lived the afternoon walk by the canal the previous week, and wondered if he had given it more than a second thought.

She had accepted a lift from him to the garden centre where the group walk was to begin. It was cold, but they were a good-humoured party and the blue sky and thin December sunshine invigorated them all as they wrapped themselves up in thick coats, scarves and hats.

Karen noticed that David left his coat in favour of a green fleece jacket. On the previous walk, he had wrapped the fleece around her shoulders when she had shivered during the picnic stop. It still held the warmth from his body, with a faint scent of wood smoke and oil.

'Will you be warm enough without your coat?' she asked.

'I don't feel the cold, and we'll keep moving today,' he said. 'It's too chilly to stay outside for long.'

Karen enjoyed David's company, but Bob got him involved in a long conversation about politics, which didn't interest her in the least, so on this occasion she spent most of the time with Irene and Jane, two lively ladies in their seventies. She had met them on previous walks, but only shared a few passing words. They were proud to tell her how old they were and how important it was to keep fit. Both women were full of energy and moved with long, comfortable strides. They asked Karen about her husband and children, which Karen found she could describe honestly, now, without feeling any shame at being a divorcee.

'I divorced my husband twenty years ago,' Jane said. 'He was a waste of time. Unfortunately, it took me nearly twenty-five years to finally get round to doing it. When Irene's husband died, she came to stay and, would you believe it, she never went home. We were always good friends and now we live together.'

'We're not lesbians,' Irene exclaimed looking at Karen.

'I didn't think you were,' Karen said hurriedly, a little perturbed at the comment.

Jane laughed at Karen's serious, slightly shocked expression. 'Irene's always saying that. I think she likes to surprise people. You can shock quite easily at our age if you use some bad language. She said, "Oh, bugger it", last week. You should have seen the face of the lad in Tesco who overheard!'

'It wouldn't have mattered if you were lesbians,' Karen said. 'I'm very open-minded, more so since my divorce. People should live in a way that makes them happy.'

'And *are you* happy?' Irene asked.

'I'm happy now, this minute, walking in the sunshine and the cold, talking to you. I might feel a bit down sometimes, but I'm learning to appreciate the days when I feel good and accept that there are days when I don't.'

'Good for you,' Jane said. 'I like your attitude. I expect you've had a difficult few years, haven't you?'

'It was such a shock when my husband left me,' Karen admitted, 'but it's made me see things quite differently and I'm beginning to like my freedom. I can please myself, do what I want to do. I don't have to put anyone else's needs first.'

The walk was, for the most part, flat, and kept mainly to the canal towpath which was icy in places and muddy where the sun had managed to find a way through the trees. Karen was enjoying the secure feeling of wearing well-fitted, expensive hiking boots with two pairs of thick socks to cushion her toes and keep them warm.

By three o'clock the sky had darkened and the first flakes of snow began to fall, tossed about by a gusty wind. Before long, a brief, swirling blizzard was spattering their cheeks, settling on woollen hats and scarves. Just as quickly it passed over, but the early sunshine never returned and when they got back to the cars, it seemed dark, even though it was still mid-afternoon. Despite thick, sheepskin mittens, Karen's fingers were frozen. She sat under the hatchback of David's car fumbling uselessly with the laces on her boots. Everyone else seemed to have sorted themselves out and were heading inside for a hot drink.

'I'm sorry,' she called out. 'I can't undo these laces.'

David came around to help her, laughing when he saw the great knots she had tied.

'I didn't want them to come undone on the walk,' she explained.

She watched as he proceeded to unpick a series of granny knots. For a moment, something inside took hold, encouraging her to reach out and put a hand on his shoulder. He looked up and smiled, then carried on with the task. She regained her senses, sliding her hands under her thighs out of harm's way, wondering what on earth she was thinking.

David finished undoing the laces. He removed the boots and passed her shoes. Karen pulled them on and started shoving the boots into a plastic bag.

'Not like that,' David said. He took them from her and tucked the laces inside, slapping the boots together to remove some of the mud. As he put them in the bag he said, 'When you get home, lay them on a piece of newspaper on their sides to dry out. In a few days the mud will have hardened and most of it will come off with another good thump against a wall. Then you need a stiff brush to remove the rest.'

It was a small kindness, but Karen felt a rush of gratitude. She wanted to hug him, touch him again, but standing in the biting wind in the garden centre car park, she didn't dare. Instead she said, 'I've never got them so muddy. I think I've got a little brush at home.'

'Leave them until I come round next week,' David said. 'When I've put up those shelves, I'll do them.'

'Would you? That's so kind. I'd really appreciate it, David.'

She reached for her handbag, an expensive and, for the occasion, quite inappropriate leather design with sparkles on each side.

'Unless I'm mistaken, it's my turn to buy you a coffee,' she said.

David was grinning at something. Following his line of sight, she immediately realised why.

'You don't think this bag goes with the walking clothes? I know it looks ridiculous, but I didn't have time to change bags this morning, you were early, remember?'

Still smiling at her need to explain, he locked the car. 'Hey, I'm no expert on women's accessories,' he said. 'Looks great to me. Come on, there's a piece of carrot cake with my name on it in the cafe.'

At that moment, a shower of sleet swept across the car park. David took her arm. She held the handbag over her head and with the wind catching their laughter, they made a dash for the entrance of the garden centre.

When David dropped her off later that day, she invited him in, but he declined.

'My parents are coming over,' he said. 'But I'll see you next week, we said Tuesday, I think?'

Karen confirmed this, waved him off, then, following his instructions to the letter, she dutifully placed her boots on a piece of newspaper to dry out. After that, each time Karen stepped past them to use the back door, she thought about David undoing the laces, taking them off her frozen feet and then giving her a rather serious lesson in mud removal.

I'm going to keep this in perspective, she'd said to herself. I like his company and I'm grateful for his help with the radiators and stuff. But he looks after everyone when we walk, not just me and he's happily married. When I think about him it gives me a good feeling and I like it, but that's all it is; all it will ever be.

Now, less than a week later, she found herself watching from the lounge, a brief flicker of excitement warming her insides as his car drew up. She watched him pull out his overalls and pick up the now familiar blue tool box before slamming the boot shut. He opened the gate, pushing it back to click, then walked down the path towards the house. She waited for the second knock, then stuffed the duster in a drawer. Taking a quick look at her hair in the mirror, she opened the door, standing aside to let him in.

'Good morning,' she said.

'Radiators still hot?' he asked as he sidled past her into the narrow hall.

'Warm as toast.'

'And the tap?'

'Not a drip. You're a marvel.' She closed the door.

David snorted. 'No, not a marvel.' he said. 'A man with a toolbox and half a brain. Right, what about these shelves then?'

Karen spent the next few hours holding screws and screwdrivers, passing rawlplugs and the hammer and using the spirit level and tape measure to level brackets and planks of wood. The time flew. They chatted as they worked, enjoyed Radio 2, battled out the Popmaster quiz with Ken Bruce and by lunchtime had two sets of shelves, one in the spare bedroom and another in the kitchen, firmly on the wall.

'Lunch?' Karen said. 'That is if you aren't rushing off somewhere?'

'Lovely.'

'It's only soup. I've already made it.'

David whistled softly to himself as he cleared up the tools and washed his hands at the sink in the kitchen. He peeled off his overalls revealing jeans and a checked shirt, the sleeves neatly turned over. Karen watched him and thought how solid his presence felt. He seemed to fill the room, to give it life and energy.

They shared the soup and bread, then she insisted he stay for a cup of tea and a slice of home-made lemon cake.

'Guy never did anything like putting shelves up or mending stuff,' she said as they sat opposite each other in the conservatory. 'I wanted to have a go, but there was only so much I could do on my own. I once put an IKEA table together and a bloody leg fell off when we had visitors. I thought it was quite funny, but Guy didn't, and he never let me buy any flat-pack furniture again.'

David gave a short laugh. 'Never let you? If I tried to tell Helen not to do something, she'd go and do it anyway to prove me wrong and make a point.'

Karen smiled at him and shrugged her shoulders. 'It wasn't like that with Guy,' she said. 'I went along with everything, mainly because I thought he was always right, which,' she added, 'in retrospect, he wasn't.'

'He built up a good business, didn't he?' David said. 'I'm not defending him, but he must have got some things right.'

'Oh yes, no doubt about that, but do you know, I would give up all the money and the financial security it brought us to have been married to a man who had feelings, showed some passion, not only about me, but about anything other than his business. I mean, surely it's possible to have someone who can be your best friend as well as your husband?'

She could see that David was struggling to comment, but she decided to press on with a question.

'You've been married for a long time, haven't you? Are you and Helen best friends?'

If she was expecting a quick, confident reply she didn't get it, and was surprised when he hesitated again.

'I'm sorry,' she said. 'You don't have to answer.'

David shook his head. 'No,' he said, 'it's a fair question, and I would have to say, yes, for most of the thirty-five years we've known each other, we've been best friends, with few exceptions. But... well, at the moment, we're in the middle of one of those exceptions.' He looked straight at her, smiling a little, but she sensed that something had been left unsaid.

Now it was Karen's turn to fumble with her words, to struggle to find the right response. In the end, she said, 'Would it help to talk about it?'

David put down the mug he had been cradling and ran a hand through his hair.

'It's nothing, really, and I'm sure we'll sort it out, but things have changed since I sold the shop 18 months ago, and to be honest, being retired hasn't worked out as I thought it would.'

Karen listened as David described the impasse that existed between himself and Helen. She watched his hands as he spoke, noticed the short, clean nails, the broad fingers and the innate strength in his wrists and forearms. She made herself take in every word, otherwise she knew that her thoughts would imagine his hands touching her and although those thoughts were lovely, they had to remain inside her head. And it was important to listen – he was sharing some very personal and emotional details.

'Can I ask a stupid question?' she said when he had finished.

'Fire away.'

'Have you told her how you feel? Does she know?'

'She knows. And that's something I'm finding hard to understand. You see if it was the other way around, I'm sure I would look at us and at our relationship, and I would do what she wanted me to do, because that would make me happy too.'

'She's obviously a strong character.'

'We're both strong characters and,' he added quickly, 'that's always been a good thing – I mean, it's worked. She had her career, I had the business, and between the two we had each other and the girls. Even when both of us were busy with work, we always found time to be a family, to do things together. The girls have both left home now, probably for good, and since I gave up work, I feel as if things aren't balancing themselves out.'

'I've never met, Helen,' Karen said, 'but those who know her, such as Tina and Dan, say such nice things. But she does sound very,' she searched for a word, 'very driven.'

She noticed a slight pause, then David said, 'You're right. Helen is an amazing woman and I love her very much. She drives herself to ensure that the children at her school get the very best. But she's taken on too much and the most frustrating thing is that I can't do anything about it. I want to take hold of everything that feels wrong and sort it out to help her, help us, get through this. But she won't let me anywhere near.'

Karen wanted to tell David that she thought he was the amazing one. She wanted to say that Helen was very fortunate to have been married to him for so many years and to have this sensitive, caring man as her husband. Karen knew that in Helen's place, she would follow him to the ends of the earth if that was what he wanted. For a moment she experienced a stab of anger, which was ridiculous as she had never met Helen.

'Have you spoken about this to anyone else?' Karen asked.

'Not really. A few of our friends have guessed that something is wrong and Helen doesn't look well, which is prompting people to ask about her.'

'But I don't know Helen and I've only known you for a short time, so I'm wondering why you're talking about it to me.'

David, who had been playing with a splinter in his thumb, biting it with his teeth, sat up.

'Well, you asked me, and really, I suppose I was ready to talk to someone. In a way, it's easier to talk to you because you don't know us very well. I feel I can trust you to keep this to yourself.'

'That,' she said, 'goes without saying.'

Karen went to a drawer and pulled out her sewing basket.

'Let me get that splinter for you. Alex was always getting them when he was a child. I'm an expert at pulling them out.'

'It won't hurt, will it?' David asked, putting on a rather unconvincing show of pretend fear.

'Not if you keep very still.'

She knelt next to him on the sofa and took his thumb in her hand, squeezing the fleshy part. The end of the splinter stuck out and Karen realised that this would be an easy task.

'Look away,' she commanded. 'I'll warn you if I have to start going deeper.'

David took a deep breath and turned away.

Karen could feel her knees touching his thigh, the hairs on the back of his hand, rough to the smoothness of her palm. She wanted the moment to expand, to fill the room until she had absorbed every small detail so it would always be clear in her mind.

Slowly, with a few gentle touches of the needle, she eased the tiny fragment of wood free and held it out for David to see. He breathed a huge pretend sigh of relief.

'Thanks nurse Karen,' he teased, patting her knee with his other hand. 'You're much more patient than Helen.' For a brief second, their eyes met, then they both got up, she to return the needle to the sewing box, he saying it was time he was on his way.

'You've forgotten a promise,' she chided.

David looked puzzled. 'You'll need to remind me.'

'My walking boots. You said you'd clean them.'

'You're right, I did,' he said. 'I saw them by the back door earlier. Thanks for reminding me.'

He took the boots outside and Karen watched him remove chunks of mud from the soles using a tool from his penknife. Then he banged them together to dislodge any remaining earth, and, using the little brush she had found, buffed the heels and toes to bring up the colour and remove any remaining dust and dirt.

'There you go,' he said, handing the boots back. She inspected them closely, then she said, 'Hmm, not bad, but I do think a few more opportunities to practice would improve your technique.'

David grinned and shook his finger at her. 'Your

turn next, and I'll supervise!'

'I'm a slow learner,' she retorted, putting the boots away. 'I think I'll need another demonstration before I have a go myself.'

David laughed and shook his head. 'Women,' he said. 'You always get your own way in the end.'

Karen had run out of quick replies so she smiled, but it did make her wonder if this comment reflected David's experience with his wife; did Helen always get her own way?

He collected his tools, threw his coat over his arm and made for the front door.

'Thanks,' she said simply, as he stepped outside and turned to face her. 'I'm so grateful, David. And if you ever need to talk about anything, don't forget, I'm a good listener.'

'I'll remember that,' he said, meeting her gaze. He kissed her lightly on the cheek and was off down the path. He stowed his bag of tools in the boot, then turned, reminding her about the next walk, saying goodbye with all those meaningless, *take care*, *speak soon*, *catch you late*r little phrases which, for Karen, seemed to dilute the moment.

She closed the door and went back through the house into the conservatory. The weak December sun was brightening the room. She lay down on the sofa, hands behind her head, her eyes closed to the light and re-lived every tiny detail of the morning they'd just shared.

Chapter 12

Two weekends before Christmas, Pete drove Lizzie's car from the city of Manchester to the hills of Lancashire. They frequently disagreed over who should drive, but on this occasion, Lizzie was still feeling half-asleep and wanted to sit in the passenger seat and look at the scenery for the hour-long journey. Pete was obviously pleased, but after ten minutes of sighs and sharp intakes of breath from Lizzie, he pulled over.

'What's the matter? Is there a problem?' she exclaimed, as he stopped the engine.

'Either I drive and you relax, or you drive. It's all the same to me, but I don't want to go all the way to your parents with you watching my every move.'

'You go too fast, I feel nervous.'

'You drive then.'

Lizzie looked out of the window. She hadn't been looking forward to this day of visiting. She was tired and more than ready to break up for the holidays, which were a week away, but seemed quite unattainable with the mountain of work she had to complete before the end of term. She would have preferred a Sunday morning in bed with the papers; Pete making coffee and warming croissants, the radio on in the background. Then, after lunch, they could have taken a brisk walk to join the crowds at the Christmas market, where the great northern city of Manchester briefly, and very successfully, transformed itself into something more European and rather exotic.

'I would prefer you to drive, Pete.'

'Well keep quiet then, woman,' he said good naturedly. 'You have to trust me.'

'I'll try, but it would help if you slowed down a little bit, please.'

Pete started the car and pulled away, smiling to himself, but he did slow down and Lizzie started to relax.

'Anyway, what's the matter with you?' he asked as they left the city and headed north. 'You usually love visiting your family.'

'I wanted a day at home, our usual Sunday. I needed a lie-in.'

'You'll get two weeks of lie-ins soon enough. Think of me, I only get a few days.'

Lizzie sighed, 'I know. I suppose, it's not only that. Things seem very tense between Mum and Dad. I told you how Mum behaved when we went shopping a few weeks ago. I had a long phone call with Dad last Wednesday and he seemed so flat. Every time I asked about Mum he made sarcastic comments, such as, "I don't know I never see her", or "don't ask me, I'm just the house-husband". It isn't like Dad.'

'Have they had a row? Your parents don't normally row, do they?'

'Not really. I never remember them shouting at each other or getting heated. They argued occasionally, still do, but I've never seen them get really angry.'

'I've told you before about my parents,' Pete said. 'They were always shouting at each other, but it never lasted long. Sometimes Mum would throw things – she had a dreadful temper.'

'Did she throw things at your Dad or at you?'

'Never at us kids, but boy could she rant when she

was on her high horse. She threw things at my Dad when she really lost it; terrible shot, usually missed him.'

'It didn't frighten you? I would have hated to see my Mum and Dad fight,' Lizzie said.

'We were used to it, and they always made up. It'd be a big row, everything out in the open, then she'd be asking him what he wanted for dinner.'

Lizzie thought about this. 'I still can't believe your parents were like that, they always seem very affectionate.'

'Oh, they are. They've calmed down a lot now and, looking back, I think most of the rows were about us kids and things have probably improved since we all left home.

'Fifth,' Lizzie said.

Pete looked at her.

'The car, it's got five gears.'

Pete changed gear with exaggerated care.

'Thank you so much for reminding me,' he said reaching over to squeeze her thigh. Lizzie slapped his hand. 'Keep your eyes on the road,' but Pete kept his hand where it was although he did as he was told.

'I think my parents never got into a really big row,' Lizzie said, 'because usually, Dad gave in and Mum got her own way. The one thing they didn't agree about, though, was Lottie. Dad always defended her even when Mum was telling her off.'

'Telling her off about what?'

'You know, she's untidy and disorganised, she's always losing things, and she's quite incapable of thinking ahead. But Lottie had Dad wrapped around her little finger. Mum and I could see it, but he couldn't, still can't.'

'I really like your Dad, but I'll bet he was a

pushover with three women in the house. Hey, do you remember last year, when we arrived on Christmas Day?' Pete said with a grin. 'We turned up a bit early and caught your Mum and Dad *at it* on the sofa.'

'They were not "at it" as you so nicely put it,' Lizzie said indignantly. 'They were fooling around.'

'Good job we arrived when we did, or they would have been.'

'Pete, stop that. The one thing you can't do is think about your parents having sex.'

'Oh, right, so your parents only did it twice then?'

Lizzie slapped him playfully on the arm, 'That's enough!'

Pete grinned at her. 'You're such a prude.'

'I am not. Only where my parents are concerned. Now shut up and concentrate on your driving!'

Lizzie was beginning to feel better. As they were spending Christmas with Pete's family this year, this visit was to deliver presents and to see everyone. Today they planned to call on her grandparents first, then go for Sunday lunch to the village pub with David and Helen. She hoped the mood between her parents would have improved.

They dropped down from Rossendale and the sight of a snow-capped Pendle Hill against blue sky lifted her spirits. By the time they arrived at her grandparent's, she was genuinely pleased to see them and feeling less tense.

Marjorie, wearing the Christmas apron that Lizzie had bought her last year, was at the door as they got out of the car and hugged them warmly.

'Come in both of you. How are you? Has the traffic been bad this morning? Sundays are almost as busy as the rest of the week now.'

Lizzie did her best to keep up with the barrage of questions as Marjorie took their coats. The house exuded its familiar mix of smells – furniture polish, baking and Marjorie's rather old-fashioned perfume. Lizzie breathed in and seemed to absorb a feeling of peace, of being cared for and fussed over and loved.

They sat in the lounge and enjoyed a pleasant hour drinking coffee and eating home-made cakes. Pete, always sociable, charmed Marjorie and engaged John in a conversation about the local football team.

'We would have come out for lunch with you,' Marjorie said, 'your dad asked us, but we're going next door this evening. It's a sort of pre-Christmas drinks and nibbles.'

'You could still have come, Grandma,' Lizzie said.

'No, two outings in one day is a bit much for us now,' she said, lowering her voice. 'Grandad likes to have a sleep in the afternoon, otherwise he's dozing off in the chair by seven o'clock.'

'I rest my eyes a bit.' John winked at Lizzie. 'She thinks I'm asleep, but I've heard her carrying on with the window cleaner.'

'John,' Marjorie said. 'What *will* Pete think?'

'I'd think, well done you,' Pete said to Marjorie. 'Nothing wrong with a bit of carrying on, is there?'

Marjorie laughed. Then she said to Lizzie with a knowing look, 'I think your Dad's carrying on.'

Lizzie, eyes wide, looked at her grandma. 'What do you mean?'

'I'm only joking,' Marjorie added in the face of Lizzie's concerned look. 'He keeps visiting a woman who's joined his walking group. He goes round to her house to mend stuff for her. Your mother knows of course.'

'He hasn't mentioned it.'

'He won't have, it's nothing, but I've been teasing him a bit. Right, anyone for more parkin?'

Lizzie and Pete arrived in Fellburn as the church clock struck noon. Families, lively groups of children and worshippers young and old were leaving the church after morning service. Lizzie was reminded of the vibrancy of her childhood village and she felt a sudden need to be part of it once again, rather than being a very small, anonymous fragment of a huge city. Pete pulled into the familiar cul-de-sac and parked the car neatly by the pavement. David opened the door as they walked down the drive and Lizzie had to hold back from throwing herself into his arms, the need to feel the familiarity of her dad almost getting the better of her. She desperately wanted to prove to herself that everything was well.

They carried in a pile of Christmas cards and gifts. Pete shook David's hand, Lizzie allowed herself to be hugged, but kept a firm grip on her emotions, then Helen was there to embrace them both. The house, Lizzie thought, looked much the same, with Mum's laptop and folders open across the table, and Floss dozing in her basket. There were no Christmas decorations yet, but she knew that her mum had never liked bringing the Christmas tree in too early. Dad beckoned them to sit down and put another log in the stove.

'We've an hour,' he said. 'I've booked for one o'clock. I thought the Hare and Hounds would be best as we can walk.'

'Great,' Pete said. 'Do they still do giant Yorkshire puds?'

'I hope so,' David replied, 'because I'm looking forward to one.' Then, turning to his daughter, he asked, 'How were Grandma and Grandad?'

Lizzie picked Floss up and settled the cat on her knee, then said, 'Fine, in fact really good. Grandma had lots to say, as usual, but Grandad was on good form too.'

Helen sat next to Lizzie and asked her about school and for the next few minutes, Pete and David were shut out of this conversation. Eventually, David raised his eyebrows at Pete and interrupted.

'How about if we meet you at the pub?' he suggested.

'I suppose so,' Helen said, glancing at him.

David left with Pete as Lizzie continued to describe to her mum an observation of one of her lessons by the head of maths. The session had gone very well, despite a group of fourteen-year-olds who could be difficult to motivate.

'Good for you,' Helen said when her daughter had finished. 'It's great to get good feedback, especially when it's from someone you respect.'

'It is good, Mum, but the next lesson I had with this class was awful. What if she'd been observing then?'

'But she didn't, did she? Hopefully she'd know you well enough to understand. We've all had dreadful lessons.'

Lizzie looked at her mum with an expression of disbelief.

'Even you?'

'Especially me! I had a pretty horrendous hour in the reception class last week when I was covering. I don't know how anyone copes with a class of under-fives every day of the week. They wore me out, I can tell you.'

'You still look worn out,' Lizzie said, taking the chance to use Helen's own words to ask how things were with her mother.

'I'm all right. Like you, I can't wait for the holidays to start.'

'Is Dad still mad about you saying you can't finish next year?'

'He was. He's resigned to it now, I think. He hasn't mentioned it for a while.'

Lizzie wondered where to take this conversation next. She wanted to hear some reassuring words, some details that would confirm that things were fine with her parents. So far, the sight of her mother looking thin-faced and tired, and her father seeming too bright and breezy, was not putting her mind at ease.

'Is Dad busy?'

'You'll have to ask him. He seems to be very involved with the walkers. There's a walk every week and he leads quite a lot of them.'

'You don't go any more?' Lizzie asked.

Helen shrugged. 'He used to ask me, but I don't have time, and some of the walks are midweek.'

Lizzie took a deep breath and said jokingly, 'Grandma says he's got another woman.'

Helen laughed. 'That's just like your grandma to make something out of nothing. The "other woman", as Grandma calls her, is Karen, she's recently joined the group. Dad's been to do some DIY or something at her place. She's divorced and for some reason doesn't seem to have found the *Yellow Pages*.'

The clock in the hall struck the half hour prompting Floss to leap off Lizzie's knee, startling them both.

'Stupid animal,' Helen said. 'You wouldn't believe she's nearly twelve, would you?'

Floss stretched and arched her back before settling, as only a cat could, in front of the stove.

'Do you remember when Lottie first brought her in?' Helen said.

Lizzie replied that she did, realising that her mother had neatly changed the subject and there was little chance of changing it back.

After a short walk, they met up with David and Pete, who were already on a second pint and deep in conversation with a group of guys who were propping up the bar. David bought his wife and daughter a drink and indicated the table he had reserved. Pete mouthed, 'Would you drive home?' to Lizzie, pointing to David as if to confirm that it was her father's fault he would be over the limit. Lizzie shrugged, but a subsequent nod of the head confirmed her agreement. She sat down with Helen.

Lunch passed fairly amicably, but, as David and Pete tucked into giant Yorkshire puddings, Lizzie noticed that her mum was furtively passing much of her food over to Dad, who didn't seem to notice his plate was being replenished. The conversation never stalled, but nevertheless, Lizzie became miserably aware that the atmosphere between her parents was tense. Her mother and father chatted away, both to herself and Pete, but spoke very little to each other. There was no interaction between them at all, apart from a short exchange about how they would settle the bill.

'There's no touching, no shared smiles, no teasing each other,' she thought. 'It's nothing but stony faces and blank looks, as if they're putting on a show for our benefit.'

Back at the house, in spite of Pete's protest that they had plenty of time, Lizzie declined coffee. She kept smiling throughout the afternoon, but the longer she spent in the company of her parents, the more anxious she felt and the more she desperately wanted to get away and distance herself from the cause of her anxiety. Dad, she noticed, was slightly drunk and seemed to be full of good cheer. He hugged Lizzie enthusiastically as they were leaving and slapped Pete on the back as he shook his hand and wished him Merry Christmas. Her mother was quite sober and rather quiet.

'I'll ring you on Christmas Day,' Helen said. 'Hope the end of term goes well.'

'It will,' Lizzie said. 'Look after yourself, Mum, and remember, Christmas is a holiday. Leave the work at school and spend some time with Dad.'

Helen gave her a final hug, but to Lizzie's consternation, didn't seem to think that her comment merited a reply.

'Are you all right babe?' Pete asked as they drove away.

'No, I'm not all right,' she said. 'I'm worried. There's something wrong, Pete.'

'Things were a bit tense,' he said, thoughtfully. 'I usually feel so relaxed with your parents, but they did seem, well, sort of different – different in the way they acted with each other I suppose.'

'You know we were saying before that your parents are still affectionate, well that's how Mum and Dad used to be. Usually, he's hugging or touching her, sometimes as if he can't keep his hands off her. Last Christmas, when we walked in on them on the sofa, well, that behaviour used to be quite normal. But today,

I could almost see the distance between them. There was no affection, no humour.' The churning in her stomach seemed to intensify. Lizzie could feel tears welling up.

'And I don't know what to do,' she said, panic in her voice. 'I mean, how do you talk to your parents about their relationship. Bloody hell... they're your parents?'

Pete hesitated. 'You're right,' he said, 'it's a difficult subject. But think about this – if you and I were having issues, you'd talk to your mum, wouldn't you?'

Lizzie wiped her eyes with her sleeve, but she couldn't stop the flow. Fear had set in and was engulfing her, making it hard to think straight.

'I might do, yes.'

'Well, your mum or your dad might want to talk to you.'

'But they won't, will they? And what if Grandma's right and Dad is playing away? I know she said it in fun, but it might be true. I couldn't bear the thought of either of my parents being with someone else.'

'Look, you need to pull over and calm down,' Pete said. 'I wish I hadn't had that second drink now, then I could have driven home.' Lizzie indicated, pulled in and switched the engine off. She rummaged blindly for tissues in her handbag. Pete put an arm around her shoulders.

'Now,' he said firmly, 'all of this is speculation.'

'I know that, but could you bear to see your parents splitting up?' Lizzie threw at him between sobs.

She could see that Pete was thinking about this, then he said; 'I might have to one day, and so might you. Who knows what the future holds and why it happens? But it hasn't happened yet, has it?'

Lizzie said nothing.

'Has it?'

'No.'

'Well, let's worry about it if, and when, it has.'

They sat in silence for a few moments, then Pete said, 'Tell me, who knows your parents best of all? Who's a good friend?'

'Debbie and Ross,' I suppose, Lizzie replied. 'They live a few doors away. Mum and Auntie Debbie are close, have been for years.'

'Speak to Debbie, then. Say how worried you are.'

'I could do that. But I'm scared that if I start digging deeper, it won't make me feel better, it'll make me feel worse. I could uncover what I really don't want to know.' Lizzie started to cry again. 'Grandma said she was joking, but what if Dad really has got another woman? And on top of all this, Mum looks so ill.'

Lizzie could feel her world of twenty-seven years fragmenting in front of her, life as it had always been scattering into pieces that she was quite helpless to pick up and put back together.

'I'm sorry,' she said to Pete, sobbing uncontrollably. 'But I can't get this into perspective. If Lottie was here instead of on the other side of the world, I'd talk to her, she's usually more optimistic than me.'

Lizzie dried her eyes again, determined to stop the crying and get a grip, although the sobs continued long after the tears had stopped. Eventually she felt composed enough to drive and concentrate on the rest of the journey. As she parked the car in their allotted space near the apartment, she started to hiccup uncontrollably, which had them both laughing.

'I love you,' Pete said. 'And I'm here for you,

whatever happens. You don't have to be brave on your own.'

'Thanks,' she said. 'That's just what I need to hear.'

Lizzie pushed her cold hand underneath his coat as they walked away from the car. She was glad of the warmth from his body and the rock-solid feel of him at a time when the foundations of her life seemed to be shifting uneasily beneath her feet.

Chapter 13

The temperatures dropped suddenly, more snow fell and the wintry weather was forecast to stay well into the New Year. David went out each morning to de-ice Helen's car, the cold taking his breath, the clear skies promising another vibrant but bitter day.

Some schools had closed early for the Christmas break, but Helen managed to keep hers open and struggled into work every day. She brushed aside David's offers to drive her to Accrington himself when the roads were particularly bad. On the last day of term, she set off but returned minutes later, on foot, furious with another driver who had skidded and blocked the road from the village.

'Ring the school,' she barked at him. 'Tell Jen I'm on my way. I'm going to get a spade.'

'You ring school, I'll get a spade. For goodness sake Helen, calm down. You can be late for once.'

He ignored the look she shot him and went off to get a snow shovel.

David walked back to where the road was blocked and thoroughly enjoyed the next half hour throwing grit under wheels, driving one car out of the deeper snow for a nervous driver, laughing with the other guys, most of whom he knew. Helen stood aside, mobile phone to her ear. She let him kiss her on the cheek before she drove off, but seemed irritated by the fact that her husband had more or less turned the problem into a social occasion. David was tempted to tell her to lighten up. A word of thanks would have been polite.

Helen arrived home that evening complaining of a sore throat. By morning she had coughed herself hoarse and when she made it downstairs, all she could do was collapse on the sofa flushed and aching.

'It's flu, they've all had it,' she croaked.

David wasn't overly sympathetic.

'I'm not surprised you're ill,' he said. 'I could see this coming. You've put in too many hours recently, you still won't eat properly and you've no reserves to fight it off.'

'Thanks for the support,' she replied.

'I'll drive to the chemist,' he said. 'What do you think will help?'

Helen reeled off a few medicines then declared that she'd go back to bed.

'I suppose there's no point trying to make you something to eat?'

Helen thought about this. 'Yoghurt would slip down, or perhaps some soup later.'

David shook his head and reached for the car keys.

The roads were clear, but temperatures had dropped well below freezing again overnight. The snow, dusted with frost, sparkled on the fields and hedges making the drive to Clitheroe quite magical, and the sharpness of blue sky and early sunshine lifted David's spirits a little. He tried to feel some sympathy for Helen. The last thing she would want was to be ill in the holidays. It wasn't fair to blame her. Hopefully she would be feeling better by Christmas Day.

David had always been grateful that Helen never made a big fuss about Christmas and treated the day as one where a traditional dinner with family and friends, followed by a few silly party games was enough to keep everyone entertained and relaxed. He remembered the perfectly planned Christmases that his mother had engineered when he was a boy, when the wrong sort of crackers bought by his father or overdone parsnips could spoil her day.

As he drove, his thoughts drifted back to when the girls were younger, small enough for him to carry both of them downstairs at once. One of them, usually Lizzie, would reach down to open the door revealing the piles of presents he and Helen had wrapped up together. Lottie had retained an innocent approach to life, keeping up the pretence of believing in Father Christmas until her early teens.

Last year had been the first Christmas morning when neither of their daughters had been at home. Lizzie was in Manchester with Pete, but she had promised they would come over early to help with food preparation. Charlotte was skiing in France. David recalled waking up to a quiet house, missing the usual excitement of stockings and family presents. The weather had been bright in a fragile winter fashion with mist on the hills in the morning and cool yellow sunshine later in the day, fading away by mid-afternoon. It had been mild in comparison with this year's big freeze. He and Helen had exchanged gifts, enjoyed a glass of Bucks Fizz in bed and then planned the day.

He remembered getting up first, keen to make a start on preparations in the kitchen, checking Helen's list, humming along to the radio. They were expecting a houseful for dinner. He peeled and chopped, organised steamers and roasting tins, and filled his lungs with the smell of the roasting bird which had been in the oven since the early hours. Floss sat neatly in a perfect square of sunlight on the kitchen floor.

'No turkey yet,' David said to her. 'You'll have to wait.'

Floss yawned showing her sharp white teeth then meowed at David hopefully.

'Oh all right then,' he said, 'we can both try it, make sure it's tender.'

He took the turkey from the oven and lifted the foil, then, with a sharp knife, he took a slice from the leg, tearing it into two morsels, one to eat himself and holding the other to cool for the expectant cat.

'There,' he said giving the meat to Floss, 'but don't tell the boss.'

He was sliding the roasting tin back in the oven as Helen appeared wearing jeans and a pale blue jumper. Her feet were bare.

'I can't find my slippers.'

David looked at his wife, wishing for a moment, that he hadn't been in such a hurry to leave their bed.

'You look very sexy without them,' he said, then added, 'and I like you in jeans.'

'What, these old things?'

'Any old things. During the week you look harsh and spiky in your high heels and suits.'

'And how do I look in jeans?' she challenged.

David considered. He disliked her work clothes. She might look fantastic in them, but the power-dressing brought a subtle change to her personality, gave her a sharpness. She was less his wife and more a public figure moving in echelons from which he was excluded. Wiping his hands, he came over to give her a hug and said, 'Actually, you look great in anything.'

'That,' Helen said, 'is a most unsatisfactory answer. You're playing safe.'

'And that,' he replied, 'is what men usually do to please their wives.'

As she turned, he flicked the tea towel, catching her neatly on the behind.

'Ow!' she exclaimed, whipping round with a look of mock fury. She shook a finger at him. 'David Richards, behave yourself.'

David dropped the cloth, but before she could escape, he'd grabbed her around the waist. Ignoring the protests, he bundled her out of the kitchen onto the sofa, pinning her down with his weight. A loose arm that was punching his back was soon captured and Helen couldn't move.

'Right,' David said, 'Miss very important headteacher. You're not at school now, so don't point your finger at me and use that bossy voice.'

'Well don't flick at me with the tea towel.'

'You used to love it,' he said, nuzzling his face into her neck. 'What time did Lizzie say she was arriving to help?'

'Any time now.'

'Well count yourself lucky, because if she hadn't been so keen to get here early I'd have been taking you back upstairs.'

Helen's retort was interrupted by a loud click followed by a call. The front door slammed shut. They froze. Lizzie and Pete burst in, arms full of presents. Lizzie looked at her parents in disbelief.

'Dad, what are you doing?'

David sat up feeling a tad foolish.

'Just reminding your mother who's boss,' he said in a matter of fact, this is quite normal behaviour, sort of way. 'And now, with that out of the way, I'll get back in the kitchen.'

One year on, David wondered when they had last been relaxed enough to play around like that. He parked the car in the one remaining space on the car park near the chemist. I'm scared of getting hold of her, he thought. Either she freezes or she pulls away or just stands there patiently until I let her go so she can escape to do something more important.

He spent what he considered to be a small fortune on cold and flu remedies. The over-enthusiastic assistant had slapped an inordinate number of packets and boxes on the counter and talked at great length about nasal sprays and cough syrups, and what you could and couldn't take at the same time. Unable to choose, he ended up buying most of what was on offer and, as he searched for his credit card, noticed the woman rubbing her hands together. Probably with glee rather than the cold, he thought.

He tapped in his pin, grasped the bulging bag and wished her a Merry Christmas. As he left the chemist's he noticed Simon and his family crossing the road. Sophie was struggling with the buggy which was weighed down with packages stowed underneath and two large bags swinging from the handles. Simon carried his older son. David remembered what a nightmare shopping could be with little ones.

'You've been busy,' he said, indicating the bags.

'Hello David,' Simon said, putting Jim down and shaking David's hand. The little boy swung round Simon's legs.

'Glad the holidays have arrived?' David asked.

'Yes, but no chance of a break with these two. Has Helen finished?'

'I think school has just about finished her,' David

said. 'I've left her in bed with flu.'

'Oh no, not at the start of the holidays, poor Helen.'

'And poor you,' Sophie said. 'Hopefully she'll be feeling better by Christmas Day. You'll have to take charge and look after her every need.'

'Well that's nothing new,' David joked. 'I'll let you get on. Someone,' he said, indicating Jim, 'seems to have had enough of shopping.'

They parted with Christmas greetings and an invitation to come over for a drink sometime. As he drove home, David recalled what Helen had said about Sophie being unwell after Billy was born. He thought she was looking great, as was Simon, considering how depressed he had been the last time he had seen him. The resilience of youth, he thought. I wish I was still in my 30s.

When he got home, he checked on Helen, who was asleep. On his way downstairs, David noticed that her school stuff, including her laptop and a huge bag of folders had been dumped in the hall. There was another bag of Christmas gifts and cards. On top of them sat her school diary. He picked it up and flipped through the pages. Every day was covered in Helen's neat pointed handwriting with various colours of highlighter illuminating the details. He turned to Christmas week, expecting to see it looking blank. He was wrong. There were three meetings scheduled, one for tomorrow, which she certainly wouldn't be attending, and two between Christmas and New Year. She was due back at school on the 5th of January, but she had noted events on the 3rd and 4th. So much for my idea of going away for a few nights, he thought irritably. There's no point suggesting it now.

He pushed the diary into the bag with the folders and carried the whole lot upstairs to the spare bedroom, keen to get it out of sight.

That done, he unfolded the Lake District map on the kitchen table and opened the iPad. If the weather was good, a small group of them were planning to climb Loughrigg Fell near Grasmere in February and he wanted to check out the best route and suitable places to park. Bob had been keen on the idea, and David had tried to persuade Karen to join them. He enjoyed her company on the walks, and found himself feeling disappointed if she wasn't part of the group.

After an hour of research, David e-mailed Bob some details about his preferred route, then he grabbed the bag from the chemist's and went upstairs to check on Helen.

She sat up rather painfully and attempted a faint smile as David put his head round the door.

'Do you feel any better?' he asked.

She shook her head. 'I'd love a hot drink,' she said.

David spread the medicines on the bed. 'Right, cup of tea coming up, or I could make you one of these lemon things.'

'I'll give one a try, but they always seem to set my teeth on edge.'

David made the drink and came back with two plain biscuits and a tangerine. His wife took the mug and wrapped her hands around it, but waved the food away. She had propped herself up against the pillows. David glanced at her, thinking how ill she looked.

'Where does it hurt?' he asked, sitting carefully on his side of the bed.

'My throat,' she said. 'It hurts when I swallow and I seem to ache everywhere.'

'Do you want me to cancel Christmas Day?'

Helen shook her head but looked completely miserable. 'Let's see how I feel tomorrow,' she said.

Two days later, on Christmas Eve, David rang his parents and said he would come over to them for Christmas dinner on his own as Helen was still not feeling much better.

'Don't want you and Dad getting flu,' he said to his mother on the phone. He also told Debbie and Ross he didn't think they would both make it for drinks in the evening, although he might call round later. Helen protested weakly, but David was adamant she needed to rest. The few times she had ventured out of bed, he had needed to be there with a steadying arm. When she asked for her laptop, he refused to get it.

'No,' he said. 'You've got your phone if you need to contact anyone, but you're not doing any work until you feel a lot better.'

'I'll get it myself when you're out,' she threatened.

'No you won't, you don't know where it is.'

'That's not fair, you've got me at a disadvantage.'

'That,' he said, 'is exactly where I want you to be.'

In the end, David quite enjoyed Christmas Day. It had begun with calls to the girls. Charlotte had enjoyed an Australian Christmas on the beach. She looked tanned and fluffy-haired and slightly drunk as it was after midnight over there. Lizzie and Pete were having a raucous time with Pete's extended family in Wales and they had to shout over the noise. Helen cried after both calls, apologising to David, saying that the flu had made her emotional.

He had lunch with his parents followed by a quiet evening with Helen watching her favourite film, Shirley

Valentine. It wouldn't have been his choice, but he found himself smiling at the humour and wondering what might happen if he buggered off to Greece and didn't bother to come home.

By Boxing Day, Helen had improved enough to demand access to her school bag and laptop, and to argue when David wouldn't get them. He had put everything away in the top of the cupboard in the spare room and piled other boxes in front in case she went looking. He decided to bargain with her.

'Right,' he said. 'You eat whatever I make for dinner this evening and I'll get your laptop.'

Helen complained. 'Can't I have it now?'

'After dinner.'

He could see that she was half-annoyed, half-amused, but the ploy worked and, later that evening, he watched her clear her plate with smug satisfaction.

'You're making me feel about ten-years-old,' she grumbled as he brought down the laptop and bag of folders.

'Well, start behaving yourself and I'll treat you like an old woman of fifty-six again.'

Helen pulled a face at him, prompting David to reach out as if to take the laptop away. She grabbed it with both hands, defending it with a cushion. He felt glad that they were almost back to their normal selves, sparring, but in the familiar, relaxed way.

She cancelled the meetings between Christmas and New Year and the days passed easily, watching films, reading and keeping warm. Simon, Sophie and the boys came round for a few hours one afternoon, and Simon told Helen about the banner the parents' group had put up. Otherwise there was very little school talk. David hunted out a box of Duplo bricks and thoroughly enjoyed a serious building session with Jim. Billy sat contentedly on Helen's knee playing with a set of keys.

On New Year's Eve, Debbie and Ross arrived for an early drink on their way to a party. After they left, Helen fell asleep in the armchair so David half carried her up to bed before settling down in front of the television to see the New Year in on his own.

David was contemplating a walk the next day, when the phone rang. It was Dan ringing from Karen's house to say that she had returned from a few nights away to find that her boiler wasn't working.

'I'm sure you once said it was like yours,' Dan said. 'But I can't see the pilot light.'

'Look in the oval-shaped window,' David told him.

Dan was rather vague. 'I still can't see it. 'We can call a plumber if you're busy, but we need to do something. The poor girl's freezing and they're forecasting minus seven again tonight.'

'I'll come over,' David said.

As David came off the phone, Helen looked up from her book.

'I need to go over to Karen's. Her boiler's on the blink.'

'Not odd-job Karen again?' she joked. 'Does she really want you to come over on New Year's Day?'

'That was Dan, not Karen.' David replied, rather annoyed by his wife's sarcasm. 'Anyway, why don't you come with me? You haven't been out for days. Even if you stay in the car, at least it's a change of scenery.'

She settled into the chair and looked aghast at the idea of moving anywhere.

'I'll get your coat,' David said.

Still protesting mildly, she allowed him to zip her into a ski jacket and find her boots and gloves.

'The brown furry boots,' she said. 'They'll go over these slipper socks. We're not going in for a drink or anything, are we? I look such a mess and I don't feel like making polite conversation.'

'You look lovely. Now stop worrying and get in the car.'

Helen did as she was told, complaining that he was behaving like a complete bully and seemed to be rather enjoying himself at the same time.

At Karen's, Tina and Dan were lighting her little log-burner in the lounge. Karen had plugged in some electric heaters but Dan was right about the freezing temperature in the house. David could do nothing with the boiler, so a plumber was called, who, surprisingly, said he would be there within the hour.

'Come and have a drink at ours,' Tina suggested. 'I'll do mulled wine to warm us all up.'

'Helen's in the car and I doubt she'd want to stay,' David said. 'She's still not over the flu and only came out for the drive.'

'Oh, but she must,' Dan insisted. 'We haven't seen her in ages. I'll go and persuade her.'

Dan brought a protesting Helen back to his and Tina's house, took her coat and sat her on the sofa, fussing with cushions and a footstool to ensure she was comfortable. Soon, Tina was handing round drinks of steaming ruby-coloured wine.

'This is Karen,' David said to his wife as Karen sank into the cream-coloured leather sofa on the opposite side to Helen.

The two women shook hands.

'Ooh, you *are* cold,' Helen exclaimed.

Karen rubbed her hands together. 'I'll soon warm up,' she said. 'I'm very grateful David could come over.'

'I'm sorry he couldn't do anything to help.'

'At least he tried, and he managed to get hold of a plumber.'

She passed Helen a plate of Christmas cake and mince tarts that Dan had put on the coffee table, but Helen refused.

David couldn't help thinking what a contrast they made. Karen looked glowing. She sat neatly, her dark hair glossy and sleek, the red jumper she was wearing giving her a bright warmth. Helen, who had tucked her legs up beneath her, was wearing an old grey sweatshirt over jeans and seemed to have been swallowed up by the cushions. Her bony wrists stuck out of roughly rolled-up sleeves and her face and hair lacked any colour.

David insisted they would only stay for a quick drink, but Tina's mulled wine seemed to revive Helen and she was happy to sit and chat until the plumber came and Karen's boiler was fixed. As they were leaving, Karen said to Helen, 'David's been great for helping me with jobs in the house. You're very fortunate he's so practical.'

Helen smiled. 'I couldn't have married a useless man,' she said, 'and I'm happy to lend him out sometimes. It's been nice to meet you Karen, to be able to put a face to the name.'

They were quiet on the way home, then Helen said, 'I like Karen, but you do know she fancies you, don't you?'

'That's understandable, most women do.'

'Seriously, David.'

'Karen's lovely, but she's not my type.'

'She's attractive,' Helen remarked, 'and she seems a nice person.'

'She's extremely nice and very patient. Do you know when we put those shelves up the other week, she held the tools, passed nails, did exactly what I told her. There was no moaning, no grumbling, no telling me how to do it.' He grinned at Helen. 'And, she makes the most divine lemon drizzle cake.'

'I'll bet she's also very good at telling you how wonderful you are,' Helen said, a playful note in her voice.

David turned to her. 'It might keep you on your toes if she does fancy me,' he said.

Helen laughed. 'There's only one person that keeps me on my toes,' she retorted, 'and that's me. So, if you fancy a bit on the side with Karen, off you go, if she'll have you. And anyway, she'll soon send you back when she realises what you're really like.'

David shrugged but said nothing. So what if Karen did fancy him a bit? It wasn't important. At that moment, he felt great. Helen was getting better and he had enjoyed pandering to her every need, bossing her a bit, taking charge of Christmas. Perhaps this is a good time to bring up her finishing work again, he wondered, glancing sideways. She had her eyes closed and her face looked white. Suddenly she sat up.

'I'm sorry,' she said, 'you'll have to stop. I'm going to be sick.'

David pulled in and got out. She lurched out of the car and bent over as he grabbed her around the waist. Helen vomited a violent red stream onto the frosted ground and, for a moment, he almost panicked as he thought it was blood. Then he remembered the mulled wine. He could feel the force of each retch, watching as the wine splattered across the snow. Someone will look at this tomorrow, he thought, and think there's been a murder.

When she said she'd finished, he helped her back into the car, the cold air making her shiver.

'Too much, too soon, love,' he said.

'And I thought I was feeling a bit better.'

'Dreadful waste of red wine.'

At home she headed straight upstairs, refusing food, accepting tea. David sat on the bed and they talked for a while, then, seeing she was exhausted, he rearranged the pillows to let her sleep. As he got off the bed, his phone beeped. It was a text from Karen, thanking him for coming over, saying how lovely it was to meet Helen. It ended with, *Looking forward to seeing you on the next walk.*

'Who was that?' Helen asked.

For some reason, he wasn't sure why, David said, 'Oh, nothing, another offer from Vodaphone.' Then he kissed his wife, turned off the reading lamp and went downstairs, humming to himself.

Chapter 14

Karen had always liked January. Other people moaned about the cold weather and the dark nights and the long months until spring, but she saw it as a clean break from the Christmas clutter; a white canvas on which to make strokes of colour in the blankness of the new year. This January came in with teeth bared, then lost its bite and slipped away into February almost unnoticed. The extreme temperatures loosened their hold and the blue and white sparkle of frost and snow degenerated into drab, grey rain that, on most days, fell in a steady drizzle.

She was glad she had met Helen on New Year's Day, but it had left her feeling unsettled. When David said his wife was in the car, her stomach had flipped uncomfortably and, for a moment, she was acutely aware of the clothes she was wearing, the amount of make-up she had put on that morning and her hands had instinctively run through her hair. The afternoon at Dan and Tina's had seemed very strange. Helen looked pale and washed out in her old clothes. This had rather disappointed Karen. In her mind, she had an image of Helen in a smart suit, looking well-groomed and confident, contributing intelligently and wittily to any social situation. What she didn't expect to see was this thin, angular woman who had sat quietly, smiling at Dan's jokes, answering Tina's questions, but never initiating conversation.

What Karen found most striking, although she

shouldn't have been surprised, was the way David looked after his wife. She observed how many times he touched her affectionately; resting a hand on her knee, kissing her on the mouth as he tied her scarf, putting his arm across her shoulders as they walked to the car. The rift he had described a few weeks ago wasn't evident at all. Helen's fragility had obviously brought out David's instinct to take over, and her acceptance of this appeared to have brought them closer together.

Karen's determination to get out and look for a new partner had stalled during the last few months. She had registered with an online dating site, but a few meetings with unsuitable men had put her off. If she analysed her own feelings, she would have understood that in truth, the loving, considerate, practical guy she was looking for, whose interests included walking, going out for meals and sharing cosy nights in, was someone exactly like David.

There were no more odd jobs in the cottage and anyway, she couldn't keep calling on him to do things, yet he was never far from her thoughts.

At the beginning of February, the walking group met for an afternoon drink at the cafe in Fellburn. She and David exchanged a few words. When she asked if Helen was well, he had said curtly, 'Well enough to go rushing back to school at the first opportunity,' but he didn't elaborate. He seemed subdued and contributed little to the meeting. As she was leaving, he touched her arm.

'I didn't mean to snap at you earlier,' he said.

'You didn't,' she insisted. 'But you don't seem to be yourself.'

'Sorry.'

'Come round for a coffee,' she said. He seemed to hesitate, then, his hand still on her arm, replied, 'I'd love to, but I might not be very good company.'

'Helen?' she asked.

'Sort of.'

'Come this afternoon.'

David opened his mouth to answer, but didn't seem to make a decision. He looked at her.

'Whatever it is,' she said, 'we can talk about it. Are your daughters both all right?'

David nodded. 'Yes, they're fine.'

'Just come,' she said, 'anytime this afternoon. I'll be in.'

He arrived soon after lunch and was leaning on the door frame holding a pot of hyacinths when she let him in.

'I saw you admiring these at Mike's earlier,' he said, 'so it's a thank you for noticing I needed a chat.'

Karen took the pot, exclaiming at the beauty of the early bulbs, protesting that he really had no need to bring gifts.

'I wanted to,' he said, following her in. He took his coat off and hung it over the newel post in the familiar way that Karen loved.

'Coffee?' she asked. 'I'll make a cafetière. I picked up that brand you recommended when I was in Booths last week.'

They sat in the conservatory, the rain pattering gently on the roof. There was no need for small talk. David, without waiting to be asked, launched straight in and told Karen that after a quiet Christmas, when things between him and Helen had seemed to improve, they were now as bad as they had ever been.

'Is she really over the flu?' Karen asked. 'It can

stick around for a while.'

'I don't think she is. She still has a nasty cough. I wanted her to take another week off. I even spoke to her deputy, who agreed with me, but Helen was having none of it. She's booked up with conferences and presenting courses and supporting other schools, and she's so irritable. To be honest, I preferred it when she was ill.'

'You were lovely with her at Tina's. She looked awful.'

'I like looking after her.'

'She's lucky,' Karen said. 'Most men would let their wives get on with it. I had a hysterectomy a few years ago. Guy felt uncomfortable because I'm hardly ever ill. He tried to ignore it, so it was the boys who looked after me when I came home.'

'I didn't know,' David said.

Karen thought for a moment. 'Is Helen at that time of life? It can really affect your mood.'

'I'm sure she is, but she would never admit that it was affecting her. She'd see it as a sign of weakness.'

Karen listened as David continued. She tried to make helpful comments, but found herself consumed by an overwhelming desire to touch him, to comfort him, to let him touch her. In the end, she got up from her chair and sat close beside him on the sofa, taking his hand in hers, trying to keep all her movements friendly and supportive. This can stay a friendship, she thought, or he can take it further, but he's got to make the first move.

David squeezed her hand looking down at the neatly painted fingernails.

'Nice colour,' he said. 'Helen rarely paints her nails.' He kept her hand in his for a while, then gently placed it on her knee before he stood up to leave. Karen tried to smile, but inside, she felt dismal. She had offered up an opportunity and he hadn't taken it. It appeared that he only thought of her as a friend, someone to lend an ear as he talked about his self-centred, miserable wife.

'You're walking on Sunday?' David asked.

'Yes. It's us two, Tina and Dan and Bob, isn't it?'

'I'm trying to persuade Helen to come. Loughrigg is one of her favourite walks.'

'Oh, yes,' Karen said with slight over enthusiasm, 'persuade her to come with us.'

'I'll do my best,' he said.

David kissed her on the cheek, which he always did now, took his coat and let himself out. Karen stood in the hallway feeling desolate and slightly used.

On Saturday evening, she was on the verge of sending him a text to say that she would give the next day's walk a miss. The weather was set to be fine but windy and she wasn't sure that battling her way over a craggy summit in a gale was how she really wanted to spend her day. As she picked up her mobile, a text came through from David. Apparently, Bob had cried off as his knee was playing up and Helen wasn't coming, so the remaining four of them could travel in one car. He would pick her up at nine o'clock. She realised the decision had been made for her.

They parked at Pelter Bridge near Rydal. Karen had the usual dilemma about how many jumpers to put on, which gloves she needed, whether to take waterproof trousers.

'Do you want to put your stuff in my rucksack?' David asked. 'Save you carrying it.'

'That,' said Karen gratefully, 'would be wonderful,

thanks.'

They set off along the lane, then turned up a track that led by Rydal Caves, passing a few other walkers who were also enjoying an early start and the brightness of the day. David took them into one of the caves, a yawning, man-made cavern, which had been fashioned for the extraction of slate. It was good to shelter from the wind for a moment. At the back, Karen noticed candle stubs positioned on stones jutting out from the walls.

'Imagine being here at night with candles,' Tina said looking round. 'Very atmospheric.'

'Could be rather spooky,' Karen said.

David adjusted the waist belt on his pack then ran his hand over a smooth piece of grey slate. 'I've read somewhere that students from the college in Ambleside used to come here to sing carols,' he said. 'Although I thought the place closed a few years ago.'

'What an amazing thing to do,' Karen exclaimed. 'Imagine the echo.'

At the mention of an echo, David and Dan started calling, listening to their words reverberate around the cave.

'That's quite enough of that you two,' Tina said. 'Come on Karen, they'll be singing next.'

The walk took them across Loughrigg terrace, where the sun came out long enough to turn Grasmere into a sheet of rippling blue water and illuminate the snow which lingered on the surrounding higher peaks. Once again Karen wondered how she could have spent most of her life so near to the Lake District yet have been quite ignorant of places like this.

It was a hard pull up to the summit and too blustery to stay by the cairn for too long. Karen stood between David and Dan as Tina took a photograph.

'Right,' Dan said looking at his map, 'we'll head off down the steeper route and see you two back at the car.'

Karen didn't know they were splitting up, but it seemed all arranged. Tina and Dan set off like two mountain goats, both full of an energy that defied their years.

'Come on,' David said to her. 'It'll be more sheltered further down.'

Karen followed him. The wind was fretful, surprising, blowing in sudden gusts, unbalancing them, tugging at their coats, their hair, loose straps on rucksacks and flattening clothes against their bodies. David found a sheltered corner where they paused for a moment, resting against a rock, its dark surface warm in the winter sunshine. They were both laughing and breathless. He reached for the map and traced the route with his finger. Karen watched.

'Do you know something, David?' she said, suddenly.

He looked up. 'No, tell me.'

'I'm happy when I'm with you. You're thoughtful, clever, and when you find these little tracks and paths you know exactly which way to go and I…' she hesitated, feeling the weight of the words – they could change everything in a moment. 'I just feel… safe.'

For a moment, she thought she was going to say loved, but she didn't.

He looked at her as if he knew. Reach out for me, she thought. I need you to reach out, once, take my hand and hold it, because it's what I desperately want you to do.

But he didn't reach for her hand. Instead, he smiled at her, looked away, re-folded the map into its natural creases and put it back in his rucksack.

As they left their shelter, the wind took a deep rasping breath and blasted them. Karen lost her balance and stumbled. He grabbed her arm to steady her, then, he took her hand.

She regained her footing, but she didn't let go and neither did David. No words passed between them as they negotiated the rest of the rocky path. Through her glove, Karen could feel the warmth of his hand and a deep rush of pleasure and fear opened up inside her. Once through the gate, David turned, gently pinning her against the wall, his body against hers, his hands pushing back her dark hair which the wind had tangled. He looked at her for a few seconds, then he kissed her, passionately, forcefully.

As he pulled away, the falling sensation in her stomach fuelled a desperation for him to kiss her again. She pulled off her gloves and stuffed them in her pockets. David paused, looked into her face, then he took her hand and led her down the lane to the car.

Chapter 15

They stopped for a late lunch in Ambleside with Dan insisting on fish and chips.

'You'll love this cafe,' he said to David. 'No frills, just top-class grub.'

Dan was right, the food was delicious. It was served with white bread and butter and mugs of tea. David was liberal with the ketchup, ripping the corners from three sachets, rolling up the plastic to release the red sauce. They laughed at Karen, whose greasy fingers refused to grip the tiny packet. David took it from her, briefly touching her hand. He made the tear then passed it back, glancing up to meet her eyes, before looking away.

The cafe windows ran with condensation. A fug of steaming food, hot drinks and bodies padded with anoraks meant that it was more than a relief to step outside and breathe the cold air. Dan put an arm around Tina's shoulders as they walked to the car park making David feel awkward. He put his hands in his pockets, and was grateful as Karen filled the moment with chatter about the day.

David drove, Dan bent his ear all the way down the M6 with stories about work, and the two women talked for a while in the back, before falling asleep. David grunted at Dan from time to time, but wished the guy would shut up and doze off as he desperately needed some space with his own thoughts.

At the cottages, everyone heaved their backpacks

and boots from the car and there were cheery goodbyes and reminders about the next walk. Karen was quiet as Tina and Dan headed off towards their front door. She looked at David.

'Come in?' she asked.

He shook his head, making a small gesture towards her neighbours' cottage.

'Better not.' he said. 'Look, I'm sorry about...'

'No, no, don't say sorry David, anything but that,' Karen said, a break in her voice, 'because I'm not sorry, not at all.'

'I didn't mean it like that,' he said putting a hand on her arm, struggling to express himself. It was as if his words were teetering along a wire, threatening to tumble if one came out wrong. He let his arm drop.

'You've been so good to me, Karen, and I think you're a lovely person.' David hesitated, ran a hand through his hair, the language inadequate for what he needed to say. 'I really don't know what I've started.'

She took a short breath. 'Ring me,' she said. 'Go away and think, David, then ring me.'

'I'll do that, I promise, before the end of tomorrow, I'll ring you.'

As he drove away, he glanced in the mirror, saw her pick up her things and turn down the garden path. He was overcome with a sudden urge to go back. The last thing he wanted to do was to go home, see Helen, give her a perfunctory kiss on the cheek – indeed that was the only sort of kissing they had done for ages – and think about what to do next.

I need to find a quiet pub and have a drink on my own, he thought. In the end, he stopped in a lay-by, and, as the noise of the engine ceased, he put his head on the steering wheel and allowed his emotions free rein in the space and the silence of the car.

'It was only a kiss,' he said aloud. 'I held her hand and kissed her, that's all.'

David leant back in his seat and knew that wasn't all. Guilt. It consumed him, made him feel dreadful, immoral, angry with himself. But beyond the guilt, there was also excitement in a brief moment, something taken instinctively. If he had let go of her hand after the wind caught her, that would have been the end of it. But he hadn't let go, hadn't wanted to let go, and the desire to kiss her had been overwhelming.

This can't go any further, he decided. I go home, review the fact that I'm married to Helen and tell her how much I love her. Things might not be great just now, but that's no excuse for me to be doing this. I'll tell Karen it was a mistake. David considered the word *mistake,* and realised how feeble, how weak it was. And anyway, he thought, it wasn't a mistake, I wanted to do it and right now, I don't want to go home to my wife, I want to turn back and do it again. And if Helen hadn't been so busy with work, she might have come on the walk, and none of this would have happened.

Immediately, David realised that he was being unfair and stopped himself. None of this was Helen's fault.

He switched the engine on, pulled out into the road and headed for home.

He tried to put Karen out of his mind and to think about Helen; all their years together, their lovely girls. He planned a conversation where he would tell her how much he loved her, how he missed the closeness they used to have, how he wanted her back and wouldn't make any more demands for her to retire from work as long as they could regain some balance in their relationship.

'I'll try and explain how I feel,' he decided. 'Perhaps I need to compromise a little.'

By the time David was almost home, he was quite clear-headed. Helen was his wife, and they loved each other and a difficult time did not mean that one of them should give up on the other and find solace in someone else. He would ring Karen the next day and explain, although he wasn't sure what he would say.

He turned into the drive and noticed Simon's red car parked in front of the house. He recalled Helen saying that Simon was coming over for a few hours to work on some document or other. Surely he wasn't still here? He took all the walking stuff out of the boot, carried it down the path and went in.

'Hello,' he called, dropping his rucksack on the hall floor. He undid the cords and pulled out the thermos and sandwich box.

Helen answered. David walked into the living room to find Simon sitting on the sofa with a laptop on his knee and Helen kneeling on the floor surrounded by folders and papers. He closed the door and looked at them.

'Are you still at it?' he said, annoyed that Simon was there.

'I'm sorry,' Simon explained. 'Jim tripped over this morning and caught his head on the edge of the table, so I spent four hours in casualty with him. Helen said to come over anyway, but it's later than we had planned.'

'Is Jim all right?' David asked.

'He will be. It was a straightforward gash. They've filled it with skin glue. We've been told to keep an eye on him, but he seems to be fine. I told Sophie to call me if there's any change.'

David picked a way between them to the kitchen area and started rinsing out the flask and sandwich box in sink.

'Have you eaten?' he called. 'I've had fish and chips.'

Helen looked up. 'Simon says he'll treat us to a takeaway later,' she said.

'Have you much to do?'

'We've only just started,' Helen replied. She picked up another sheet of paper and read aloud, prompting Simon to start tapping on his laptop.

David said nothing else. He felt excluded. Helen didn't ask how his day had been, and she gave him no more than a brief look as he crossed the room. In the hall, he sorted out his walking gear, deciding to go upstairs for a shower. The last thing he wanted was a take-away – some lifeless food in silver trays – and as much as he liked the guy, he didn't want to share this evening with Simon. He had pictured himself with Helen, glasses of wine relaxing them both, a chance to tell her everything he had planned to say, hopefully followed by a conclusion to the evening that would banish all thoughts of Karen.

He stayed in the shower for ages, gradually turning the heat up until it was almost too hot to bear. Then he lay on the bed in a towel, knowing how much it annoyed Helen, although she was obviously so engrossed in whatever they were doing downstairs she probably wouldn't notice the wet patches on the duvet cover. He reached for his phone, looked at it, put it back. He reached for it again started a message, then gave up, tossing it on the pile of clothes. A wave of tiredness washed over him, then a desperate need to close his eyes, to sleep for a long time and to wake up knowing that he was in control again and all the parts of his life that seemed to have fragmented were back in the right places. He shrugged the towel off onto the floor, slipped under the quilt and went to sleep.

When he woke up, hours later, he was aware that Helen was sliding into bed beside him.

'What time is it?' he asked.

'Midnight.'

'When did Simon leave?'

'Ages ago. I came up earlier to see if you wanted any supper, but you were fast asleep. I moved your wet towel,' she added.

Helen yawned, turned away from him and pulled her knees up, ready for sleep. David put his arm around her, but it felt different, less familiar, less comfortable. He heard her breathing change as she drifted off and realised that he was wide awake. Falling asleep earlier had not been a good idea.

As soon as he was sure that she was asleep, he rolled over and got out of bed. Then he went downstairs and put the kettle on. The room smelt unpleasant; greasy and stale. Helen had wrapped all the takeaway debris in a plastic bag and put it next to the bin. Unwashed plates sat in the sink. He turned on the tap and ran water to soak them. It never ceased to annoy him that Helen couldn't be bothered to do such a simple thing. And she had the nerve to mention his wet towel on the bedroom floor in that self-righteous voice of hers. At one time, he would have laughed off her bossiness, told her she wasn't at school with teachers and children who jumped at her every word, but that kind of humour seemed to have gone out of their exchanges recently.

He sat for a while with a hot drink and a packet of Digestive biscuits, managing to eat at least five, knowing that he ought to make a sandwich, but couldn't be bothered when it was far easier to eat straight from the packet.

Whatever I do next, he thought, someone gets hurt, and really, it has to be Karen. If I keep seeing her and if things develop, who knows where it will go? And the further Karen and I take things, the harder it will be to stop. I'll go and see her, talk to her, explain that as much as I love being with her what happened today can't happen again.

The voice in his head made it sound so easy, but what David wasn't acknowledging was that beneath all this calm straightforward reasoning, he was also feeling a huge sense of disappointment and a strong desire to kiss Karen again and more – in fact to do all the things he wasn't doing with his wife.

Karen appreciates me, he thought. She's so thankful for the things I do, she listens, gives me her time, she doesn't push me away when I look after her. Helen doesn't do any of that. She makes me feel like a spare part, separate from her very important work.

He sat for a while, wondering if this was really about punishing Helen. Unable to reach a conclusion, he rinsed out his mug and put the biscuits away, then washed the plates, took the rubbish into the rear porch and climbed the stairs back to bed.

The next morning, he was so tired he could easily have turned over when Helen's alarm went off. While she showered, he got up and padded downstairs in dressing gown and slippers. He rattled the stove with the poker, added logs, opened the vents and had it roaring by the time she came down.

'Shall I make you some toast?' he asked.

'No thanks. I'll have a quick cup of tea.'

David watched his wife gather up papers, pack her bag, close her laptop. He crossed the room, took the things out of her hands and encircled her in a hug, pushing his hand under the stiffness of her tailored jacket. He could smell the slightly acidic perfume she always wore for work.

'Hey,' she said, 'that's nice, but I'm on the last minute this morning.'

She gave him a squeeze, then pulled away.

'Are you late home tonight?' David asked.

Helen reached for her diary. 'I think I am,' she said. 'Yes, it's a governors meeting, I'd almost forgotten. Sorry, it'll be after nine o'clock. We usually get pizzas in, so don't worry about a meal.'

'What about tomorrow, Tuesday?'

'Tuesday.' Helen consulted the diary again. 'Shouldn't be too late then, but the rest of the week is busy.' She looked at him. 'Why?'

David said, 'I want to have some time with you, talk about Australia, perhaps. To be honest, Helen, I didn't want to come home last night and see Simon here.'

Helen carried all her bags to the door, then crossed to the kitchen to make her tea.

'It couldn't be helped,' she said, tossing a tea bag into the mug. 'Simon didn't want to spend most of the day in casualty you know.'

Once again, she made him feel as if he was being unreasonable.

'I know that. Don't be so patronising,' he said, irritation in his voice. 'I'm only saying how I felt when I walked in and saw him. Am I wrong to want to spend some time with you?'

Helen sighed. 'Not now,' she said. 'I really need to get off.'

'You haven't even had a drink.'

'I'll get one at school.'

He watched her slip into heels, check her hair in the mirror, then reach for a coat from the hall cupboard.

'Could you give me a hand?' she asked, slinging the strap from the laptop case over her shoulder.

David picked up the bags and followed her out to the car. She unlocked the boot and he stowed everything neatly, closing it with a thump. Helen kissed him on the cheek, saying she would see him later. She got in the car, started the engine and drove off.

A wet and bedraggled Floss walked across the lawn. She meowed at him and rubbed around his bare legs. David picked her up and took her inside, dumping her in her basket. This morning she would have to wait for breakfast. He reached for his mobile phone and sent a text to Karen saying he would come round to see her at whatever time she wanted. Her swift reply said, *Come anytime. I'm up now and in until eleven.*

David showered, dressed, fed the cat and left the house by eight o'clock. As he approached Karen's, he made the decision to leave the car further down the lane where it would soon be enveloped by the early-morning traffic and less visible. He walked the short distance to the cottage, the hood of his jacket pulled up against a persistent drizzle.

Karen was there at the front door before he had time to knock. He stepped into the hallway, his face wet with rain. As she closed the door and looked up at him,

David found all the previous evening's reasoning evaporating into thin air. The thoughts he had about moral duty and doing the right thing disappeared as emotion surfaced like a great air bubble, clean and clear, emerging from the depths of a muddy pond. He slid his hands around her neck and pushed his fingers into her hair before he kissed her. Then he held her close, feeling the softness of her body against his. She leaned into him, ignoring the damp coat, her arms around his back.

She moved away first, reaching up to touch his face. Taking him by the hand, she led him into the lounge where her little stove was struggling to get going.

'I've been trying for half an hour,' she said. 'The flames won't catch.'

David looked at the logs and the charred newspaper and couldn't help smiling.

'I thought Dan had shown you how to do it,' he said. 'You need some of the kindling we chopped up for you. You can't light a huge log from newspaper.'

David was relieved to be doing something practical. He took off his coat and, for the second time that morning, he revived a dying fire. When he had finished, he sat next to Karen and took her hand. She reached over to stroke his arm.

'Now what?' she said with a sigh.

David looked at her and said, 'I honestly don't know.'

Karen linked her fingers with his. 'Well,' she said, 'how about if I start?'

David said nothing. He wasn't sure he was up to this. He needed to sit close to her, hold her hand, stare at the flames in the stove, keep it all very simple.

'It's easy really,' she said. 'I've loved every minute we've spent together, almost since that day we first met in September. I love the way you look after me, tease me sometimes, make me laugh, and although I know you're married, I want to spend time with you. When we held hands yesterday and you kissed me, you made me feel something I haven't felt for a long time, perhaps never before, and I haven't stopped thinking about it.'

David squeezed her hand as if it was the only response he could give, as if there were no words he could offer that would come anywhere near to an expression of how he was feeling. Her body close to his was awakening desires and emotions that he had only ever had for his wife. As he listened he put a hand on her thigh and left it there. When she had finished, silence hung between them.

'You need to tell me how you feel,' Karen prompted. 'I need to know.'

He sighed, aware that she was right, but also how hard it would be to tell her the truth.

'Say it,' Karen prompted gently.

He looked at her. The first words would be the hardest, but they had formed in his mind as she was speaking. 'I'll never leave Helen,' he said.

Karen paused, then she said, 'I know that, so now you've said it and we understand it, try and tell me how you feel about me.'

David put his head back and looked at the cottage beams, then he put his arm around her and she rested her head on his shoulder. She said nothing, as if waiting for him to speak.

'I love being with you too,' he began hesitantly. 'I haven't only come here to mend stuff and put shelves up, I've also come to spend time with you. I enjoy making life easier for you, looking after you, and I don't mind that you can't light the stove, bleed a radiator or clean your boots, because I've so enjoyed doing those things for you. But, I have to admit, I'm scared of my own feelings, Karen, and I don't know where a relationship between us will lead.'

Once David started to talk, he found that he couldn't stop. He talked about Helen, his frustration at the emotional distance between them, his fear at one time that she might have been having an affair. He tried to explain his anxiety about the future if he and Karen continued to see each other, and if they did, how they could do it secretly, because a friendship was fine, but as soon as anyone guessed it was something more, the repercussions didn't bear thinking about.

'Yesterday,' he said, 'there was no plan, no thought, it was something instinctive that made me kiss you.'

Karen paused, then said, 'I would very much like you to do it again.'

And he did. Once, then a second time, then longer, more passionately, pulling her to him, feeling her body relax. It should have felt wrong, but it didn't. It felt as if he had been kissing this woman for years. He pushed her gently onto the cushions of the sofa, his hand finding the gap between her blouse and the top of her jeans where the skin was soft and warm. For a moment, he thought about how he had done this with Helen earlier and how rigid she had seemed to his touch.

Karen pulled away first, suggesting they move to the kitchen and make some breakfast.

David leant against the unit, watching her and he couldn't stop thinking how different she was to Helen. When she glanced up and smiled, there was a gentleness, a vulnerability that touched him.

'So,' she said as they sat opposite each other with a second cup of coffee, 'you do want to carry on seeing me?'

'Of course I do,' David replied placing a hand over hers, 'but I'm not sure how. I can't keep coming here, unless I can do it less obviously.'

'Let's take one day at a time,' she said. 'Don't think too hard about this, David, we'll just enjoy being together whenever we can. I understand how difficult it is for you and I promise I'll never push you into doing anything you don't feel happy about. I'm here for you, because I want to be, but you have your family to consider. I'm on my own. You need to take the lead, tell me when you're free to meet.'

'I can't believe you're so accepting, so patient,' he said. 'I don't deserve this, really I don't.'

Karen took his cup and set it down next to hers.

'You mustn't think you don't deserve me,' she said, looking into his face, 'because you do.'

David couldn't believe this was true, but he was feeling happier with himself, more confident that sharing this time with Karen wasn't so wrong, wouldn't compromise his married life. I need this, he thought. I seem to have to fight Helen tooth and nail, but there's no fight here. This woman has said she's here for me. When did Helen ever say that?

Karen said, 'Sorry, but you'd better go. It's my stint at the charity shop this morning.'

David gripped her hand. 'I might not let you go,' he teased.

'That sort of talk,' said Karen, 'is lovely, but it won't get all those second-hand clothes sorted out and put on hangers, will it?'

David released her and stood up to leave, promising to text her later.

'There's one more thing,' she said, as he pulled his coat on. 'It's something I've been thinking about.'

'What's that?'

'I know you're struggling with Helen and I know I've listened to you and tried to help. But if we continue to see each other, however bad you're feeling about things, I don't want to talk about her any more. We can talk about your girls, my boys, but not Guy and definitely not Helen.'

'I understand that,' he said. 'I won't even mention Helen. In truth, this is nothing to do with her.'

He left, glancing around guiltily. But he had nothing to fear, the lane was deserted. He headed back to the car with a sense of circumstances being different, now. The last time he had come to this house it was open and innocent, but in future he would have to be more careful.

The clouds were clearing to show patches of blue. David was aware of a change in the air which now seemed colder, drier, freshened by a sharp wind. He didn't think, he didn't look ahead with anxiety or anticipation. He allowed himself to take deep breaths, to enjoy the chill, to look up at the sky and feel light-headed, energised, alive.

Chapter 16

In the time it took to reach across the bed, and realise that David wasn't there, Helen was in the grip of a panic that clawed at her insides and took her breath. She lay still, one hand resting on her stomach, the other feeling the rise and fall of her chest. She put her mind to breathing, concentrating on the outward breaths. Little by little, she took control and the panic eased.

Every morning began like this, and the episodes weren't improving. In fact they were becoming harder to control. She had hoped that during this week, which was February half-term, the attacks would ease, but they had got worse, as if a break from the familiar morning routine had taken away some sense of purpose, and her thoughts had nothing to anchor them. She convinced herself that the problem was age related, another change in hormonal patterns affecting her mood, or her body still recovering from the bout of flu. The extra work she had taken on over the last year, on top of running her school, was most likely taking its toll, but stress was part of the job, always had been. She had never failed to manage everything it threw at her.

She looked at the clock: 7.45. Well at least she'd slept a little later, and there was a good day ahead. Lizzie was coming over and they were going out for lunch with Debbie. She checked her phone and her iPad for messages, then reached for her dressing gown and went downstairs.

David was reading the remnants of the Sunday newspaper, which would usually last him until the middle of the week. He looked up, then back to the paper, adjusting his reading glasses, reaching out to stroke Floss who was asleep on the sofa beside him. He was working at the hardware shop for ten days, covering while Mike and Rosemary took a well-earned holiday, so he was busy again.

He seems more content, she thought, but I don't feel that it's with me, with us. Perhaps being back at work is giving him a focus, a sense of purpose.

'Good morning,' he said. 'I was wondering if you were awake.'

'Get that cat off the settee,' Helen said, mildly irritated.

David scratched Floss's head. 'I can't read the paper when she's on my knee, she sort of slipped off. And anyway, how old is the furniture in here? We've had it since we bought the house.'

Helen, no longer concerned about either the cat or the settee, crossed to the kitchen area to put the kettle on. She was beginning to feel a little better; her breathing was steadier although her stomach still churned.

'Have you remembered that Lizzie's coming over today?' she said.

David looked up from the paper. 'Of course,' he replied. 'That's why I'm not going to the shop until lunchtime.'

'Is someone else covering?'

'Mike's dad.'

Helen brewed tea and came to sit beside him, putting her feet up on the footstool. Floss stretched and eyed her suspiciously.

'It's a shame you're at the shop all week,' she said, 'when I'm on half-term holiday.'

David looked at her over his glasses. 'Would you have wanted to do something?' he asked. 'Go away for a few nights perhaps? You always seem so busy now, even in the holidays.'

'Yes, I think I would,' Helen said. 'But I know it can't be helped. I hope Mike and Rosemary are having a good time in Tenerife. They deserve a break.'

She leant back in the chair, feeling calm enough to think about the rest of the day with some pleasure. David shook out the newspaper and folded it, running his fingers down the spine to sharpen the crease. Helen looked at him, noting the black trousers and white shirt. Before he left, he would probably put on a tie. In all the years he had run the shop, he never failed to look smart, even though it was the kind of business where customers came in wearing all manner of paint-splattered jeans and grubby overalls.

'I think,' Helen said, 'that you are rather enjoying being back at work.'

'You're right, I am,' he replied, laying the newspaper on the floor and transferring a sleepy Floss onto his knee. The cat started a deep rolling purr as he scratched her head and ears. 'It was different when I ran it, but I have to admit they've done really well to develop the business in the last eighteen months. The cafe is going great and Rose has a good sense of her market. There's quite a lot of passing trade at lunchtime now; drivers, workers who want a bit of lunch. Some are regular customers.'

'A bit like a transport caff,' Helen said with a short laugh.

'No, nothing like a transport cafe,' he replied.

'I didn't mean it like that,' she said. 'I'm really pleased they're making a go of things, it isn't easy with all the enormous DIY stores opening. I wonder if we could have done more when we had the business?'

'What do you mean, *we*?' David said. 'You were only interested in the shop in the early years. As soon as you got your first headship, you left it all to me.'

Helen didn't respond to this, although she knew it was true.

'Do you regret selling the shop when we did?' she asked.

David glanced at her briefly.

'No,' he said, 'not at all. I was ready to finish, you know that. My only regret – also something you know – is that you haven't finished working, but I don't want to labour that particular point any more.'

She studied the tea left at the bottom of her mug, then reached for his hand. He turned to look at her with some surprise.

'It will happen,' she said, 'I promise it will.'

David shifted in the chair before replying, nudging Floss gently to the floor. 'That isn't good enough,' he said, 'but I've realised that it will have to do for now.'

Letting go of Helen's hand, he took her mug to the kitchen, where he put it in the dishwasher, closing the door with a click.

'I took some cake out of the freezer, the other half of the fruit loaf I made last week. I thought you might like to have it with your coffee. Did you say Debbie was coming round?'

'Yes,' Helen said. 'We're going to the pub in Waddington for lunch. Lizzie said she would drive.'

'Sounds nice. I'll have coffee with you, then I'll have to go. I'll be in the shed, if you want me,' David said, reaching for his coat by the back door. 'I'm looking forward to seeing Lizzie.'

The door closed. She heard him putting shoes on in the porch. Helen watched through the window as he strode across the garden to the shed. She tidied the room a little, straightening cushions and moving clutter from the table. When everything looked tidy, she went back upstairs and got into bed to indulge herself in a blissful, uninterrupted hour of reading.

At half-past ten, dressed in her favourite jeans and sweater, she opened the front door to an enthusiastic Lizzie, who was full of news. When Lizzie eventually stopped to draw breath, she looked around and said, 'Where's Dad?'

'In his shed,' Helen replied. 'Go and get him. Drag him away from whatever he's doing in there, I need him to make some decent coffee.'

Lizzie went to find her dad and Helen unwrapped the slab of cake, cutting careful slices, making sure that there were some smaller ones amongst the arrangement on the plate. She watched her husband and daughter make their way across the garden, Lizzie turning to take David's arm, he laughing at something she had said. They looked animated and happy. Helen felt quite separate from them.

Is she like me? Helen thought, or is she like David? She seems more emotional than I am, or is she just less likely to hide her feelings? She reached for some plates and selected four china mugs from the cupboard.

'Debbie's on her way,' David said as he came in. 'We could see her from the garden.'

'I'll let her in,' Lizzie said, setting off through the hall. Helen heard the front door, then voices, but the conversation was hard to catch, and after a minute or two, she wondered what they were talking about. She left David making the coffee, reminding him that their elder daughter liked hot milk, and opened the hall door. Lizzie and Debbie were talking seriously, but smiled when Helen appeared.

'What's the secret?' she asked.

Debbie kissed her on the cheek. 'If I told you, it wouldn't be a secret, would it?' she said, jokingly.

Debbie shouted a greeting to David, who came across the room and gave her a hug. 'Ross OK?' he asked.

'Fine, as usual.'

'Tell him we're climbing Great Gable in May,' David said. 'It's a weekend walk so you could both come.'

'It's my knees,' she began in mock protest.

'Debbie, nearly everyone in the group has something wrong with their knees,' David said. 'We take our time.'

'I'll think about it.'

'You'll come,' he replied. 'Now sit down and I'll bring the coffee.'

'How's Simon?' Helen asked as Debbie settled into a chair.

'Great. Have you noticed the three banners on the school railings?'

'I noticed them as I drove in,' Lizzie said. 'I saw the words, wonderful and super. What's that all about?'

'The parents' group started it,' Debbie explained. 'After the inspection, they wanted to express their support for the school. Didn't Rosemary come and see you?' she asked Helen.

Helen nodded. 'I don't usually like banners,' she said, 'but I thought this was a good idea. I think it's the

'Super School' one that Rosemary and the other parents put up. I'm not sure about the other two.'

'One was Sunday School,' Debbie added. 'and the other is a complete mystery.'

'Sounds interesting, do tell,' Lizzie said.

But Debbie couldn't tell them anything, except that it had appeared overnight.

'Simon is so touched by all the support. I would never have thought that we would all feel like this just a couple of months after that awful woman inspector was in school, but we're buzzing. There's a great atmosphere. Simon was here a few weeks ago wasn't he,' Debbie said to Helen, 'writing the action plan with you?'

'Yes, we had quite a long session,' Helen said, 'but it all came together very well. I presume you've read it?'

'We changed a few things,' Debbie said casually. 'But overall it's got that particular bit of paperwork out of the way.'

'What did you change?' Helen was irritated at Debbie's rather flippant tone.

'I can't remember now,' Debbie said. 'Nothing major.' She gave a short laugh when she saw Helen's serious expression. 'Come on, Helen, give the guy some space to make a decision on his own.' She turned to Lizzie and asked how things were in Manchester and as Lizzie launched into her news, Helen found herself feeling rather annoyed at Debbie's barbed comment. But the conversation had moved on. It wouldn't have been appropriate to challenge it in the circumstances, so she bit her tongue.

David brought the tray of coffee and cake to the table.

'I can't believe we haven't seen each other since

before Christmas,' Debbie said to Helen. 'You and David must come over for a meal soon. We missed you over the holidays.'

'Are you completely better, Mum?' Lizzie asked.

Helen looked surprised. 'Yes, it was only a bit of flu.'

'Only a bit of flu,' David said. 'Enough to put you in bed for three days and have you throwing up on the way home from Tina's.'

Helen brushed away his comment, describing the whole thing as a humorous incident, certainly not something to be taken seriously.

'Not one of your mother's better moments,' David remarked.

There was a pause, then Lizzie asked, 'Are you still doing stuff for this Karen, Dad?'

'Not really,' he replied as he took the cafetière from the tray and started arranging place mats and mugs. 'But part of her rear porch ceiling has come down and Dan and I said we might tackle it for her.'

'Is Karen the one whose husband went off to America leaving her with a small fortune?' Debbie asked.

'Depends what you call a fortune,' David replied. 'She joined the walking group last year, that's how I met her.'

'I think I know her,' Debbie said. 'Her son had swimming lessons at the same time as Matt. What does she look like?'

'Oh, darkish hair, medium height,' he shrugged. 'Helen's met her, haven't you Helen?'

Debbie turned to Helen questioningly.

'Karen's a very attractive lady,' Helen said, grinning in David's direction. 'Now, there's a line from a song, what is it? All the right stuff...' she thought about the words again, then remembered. 'That's it. All the right stuff in all the right places. That's Karen,' she said, her eyebrows raised meaningfully, her mouth forming a rather suggestive smile.

David plunged the cafetière a little too abruptly, forcing coffee up through the spout to splash on the table.

'So, a bit different to you, then,' he said glancing up at his wife. The comment was delivered with a tight smile.

Helen came back at him sharply. 'All my *right stuff* is up here,' she said, pointing to her head, 'exactly where I'd prefer it to be.'

Lizzie jumped up. 'I'll get a cloth,' she said. 'Honestly, Dad, you don't know your own strength.'

She came back with a dishcloth and a roll of kitchen paper that she tore into sheets to soak up the coffee. Helen watched, wondering why her eldest daughter's hands were shaking as she dabbed at the pools of brown liquid. Debbie asked David how things were going at the shop and the next few moments were taken up passing cups and plates and slices of cake.

At a quarter to twelve, David stood up.

'Right,' he said, 'time I wasn't here.'

'I'll walk down with you,' Lizzie said. 'Is that all right Mum?'

Helen glanced up at the clock. 'Yes, we've plenty of time, I haven't booked, I didn't think we'd need to midweek.'

Lizzie got her coat. David kissed both Debbie and Helen on the cheek, and they left, Lizzie looping her arm through her father's.

Helen started stacking things onto the tray and

carried them over to the kitchen. David's remark came back to her and she thought, I don't care, then, almost immediately, actually I do care. The words hurt. It was as if he was defending Karen. She considered her own comment, which she had meant in fun. It had been said rather flippantly, but it was a compliment, not meant to be a criticism. Perhaps it was the way she had said it. In any case, he didn't have to be so touchy, especially in front of Lizzie and Debbie.

Debbie got up and leant against the unit which separated the living room from the kitchen. For a moment she watched Helen as she cleared up.

'What's up with you and David?' she asked gently.

Helen stopped what she was doing and wondered how to answer this question. Debbie had been a friend for more than twenty years. Their children had played together when they were small and David and Ross still enjoyed an occasional drink in the village pub. But how do you try and explain, even to a close friend, what's going wrong in your marriage when you don't even know yourself?

'It's nothing,' she said. 'Just a bad patch, everyone has them, don't they? We're both busy and it's hard to talk sometimes, but really, Debs, it's nothing.'

'Are you any nearer knowing when you'll retire?'

'To be honest,' Helen said, 'I'm not. David seems to have accepted that it won't be this year because of my deputy finishing, and I need to know her replacement has settled in before I give my notice.'

'That,' Debbie said pointedly, 'is an excuse.'

Helen finished in the kitchen and came to sit in the lounge. She was still irritated by Debbie's earlier criticism that she wasn't allowing Simon space to make his own decisions, and now her friend was delving into her marriage. Before she could respond, Debbie spoke again.

'I'm sorry if you think I'm interfering, and tell me to shut up, if you like,' she said, 'but I'm really concerned about you both.'

'You don't seriously think David's having a fling with this Karen person?' Helen said quickly, keen to move Debbie's attention away from herself.

'Obviously I don't, but,' she hesitated, 'how would you feel if he was?'

'Stupid question, because he isn't,' Helen said with certainty in her voice. 'And if he was, I am absolutely sure that I'd know about it.'

'How would you know?'

'I'd just know,' Helen said with exasperation.

'I'm sure you're right, but if you can, give Lizzie some reassurance, will you?'

'Lizzie?' Helen gasped. 'Why would I need to do that?'

'She's worried about you and David. She's sensed that things aren't right. I think David's mother said something before Christmas about Karen that unnerved her.'

'Bloody Marjorie,' Helen said. 'She has made some stupid comments about him going over to Karen's, hinting that there's more to it. She thinks she's being funny.'

'It isn't only that, Helen. Lizzie can feel an atmosphere between the two of you.'

'How do you know?' Helen asked sharply.

'I've spoken to her. She's told me.'

'I feel,' Helen said, controlling the anger rearing up inside her, 'that certain people are making more out of this than is necessary, and it *is* getting close to interference. My work, our marriage, David doing DIY for that woman and everyone seems to think there's an issue. And,' she added, looking at Debbie with the hint of a smile, 'if you mention one word about me losing weight, I think I'll have to hit you.'

Debbie laughed. 'That,' she said, 'was going to be my next question.'

'Don't even think about it, I'm a woman of my word.'

'I wouldn't dare,' Debbie replied, her hands raised, as if fending Helen off.

Helen sat back in the chair, stretched her legs and kicked off her slippers. Debbie was raising issues that she preferred to keep in the back of her mind, to ponder later when she was alone, possibly to talk about with David.

'David and I, we just need some time together,' she continued, 'but we might not get it until we go out to see Lottie at the end of March.'

'That's weeks off,' Debbie said. 'Have a weekend away, a meal out, a date night – that's what the kids call it now, and it's a good idea. Talk things through. Are you really so busy after the half-term holiday?'

'Doesn't bear thinking about,' Helen replied.

'School or advisory stuff?'

'Both.'

'I don't know how you do it.'

'If I'm honest, I love it. I love supporting other schools, mentoring new headteachers, presenting courses. I love running my own school, being the boss. I don't need to tell you how hard it can be sometimes, well, most of the time. It wears me out, but I have to admit I'm a little scared about giving it all up to retire.'

'You could leave school, stop having all the

responsibility of being a headteacher and still do the advisory stuff if you wanted to,' Debbie said. 'That could work, couldn't it?'

Helen pulled her knees up and wrapped her arms around her legs, lacing her fingers together, lining her feet up exactly.

'I had thought about that,' she said. 'In fact, it was almost a feasible plan. Then Bridget gave her notice and I had to shelve it.'

'Did you tell David about this plan?'

Helen considered this. 'I never got around to it, then it was too late.'

'Helen,' Debbie said. 'Why not?'

Helen opened her mouth to speak but ended up shrugging her shoulders.

Debbie sat up. 'You need to concentrate on David a bit more,' she said. 'Put more effort into that aspect of your life and a bit less into work.'

'He understands,' Helen insisted. 'He knows it isn't forever.'

They heard the front door open, then slam. Lizzie called out that she was back. The conversation was over, although it left Helen with a strong sense of loose ends, things she would need to secure in her own mind when she had space to think.

As the three women were leaving for lunch, she picked up a text from David saying he wouldn't be home until nine-ish as he was off to the warehouse after the shop closed with Mike's dad.

'Who was that?' Lizzie asked as she unlocked the car and slid into the driver's seat.

'Dad saying he won't be back until late. It's funny, usually it's the other way around. He's getting his own back.'

'Good for David,' said Debbie. 'So, you'll have his slippers by the fire and a meal on the table when he walks in, will you?'

Helen pushed the seat back and climbed into the car behind Lizzie.

'And do you think,' she said, 'knowing me as well as you do, that there is the slightest possibility of that ever happening?'

'Try it,' Debbie retorted, slamming the passenger door and reaching for the seatbelt. 'See what happens, you might be surprised.'

'I think Dad would be the one who was surprised,' Lizzie said. 'He'd think Mum was ill or something.'

Helen laughed. 'I could do devoted little wife if I wanted to,' she protested, a note of pretend hurt in her voice. 'You two have got me all wrong.'

Both Debbie and Lizzie contested this loudly. Helen smiled to herself, pleased to be with two people who knew her so well.

Lizzie set off and, as she and Debbie chatted in the front, Helen thought about the terse comments she'd exchanged earlier with David.

It's not good enough, she thought. We must find some time to talk, to be together, when work isn't at the front of my mind. I know I love him, but I can't seem to feel it. I can't find any space in my head that isn't full of an endless list of things to do. An image of her diary, chock-a-block with interminable appointments came to mind.

She caught Lizzie's glance in the rear-view mirror and smiled back brightly.

If she's noticed something's wrong, she thought, then David and I have to do something about it, and if people are talking about him visiting that bloody Karen, well, he should stop going. For goodness sake, the woman's got enough money to employ a proper handyman when she needs some jobs doing.

In her mind, Helen closed that particular issue. She would talk to David later and the problem would be solved. The rest of the day was about enjoying precious time with her best friend and her daughter.

Chapter 17

It was early March, cold, sometimes bright. Karen felt a sharpness in the emerging spring, a pale sun shining a little stronger each day yet still competing with a bitter wind. She could sense a difference in both the season and her mood.

David was constantly in her thoughts. Sometimes she would empty her head of everything, allowing the space to fill up with each fine detail of their last meeting and self-indulgent imagining of the next. She would lie for hours on the bed or the sofa, thinking, or sit in front of the television, seeing and hearing the programmes but with her thoughts elsewhere.

The previous Saturday, when Tina had called for a chat, Karen made coffee and found biscuits and listened as her friend talked, but she was relieved when Tina got up and reached for her coat.

'You're a bit quiet,' Tina said.

Karen brushed this off, saying she wasn't sleeping well.

'I wondered if you'd feed the cat for a few days?'

Karen was suddenly aware of Tina's words.

'You're going away?' she asked.

'Yes. We're off to York, Thursday to Sunday.'

Tina explained about their short break, the hotel deal they had managed to find, the sightseeing and walks she was looking forward to. Karen listened politely, but after Tina had left, she could remember very little about what she had said.

Early that morning, she watched and waved as Tina and Dan drove off, her mind awash with the possibilities, then she went into the kitchen to prepare a picnic. She buttered bread, lay ham in thick slices and cut sandwiches into triangles – because that was the way David always cut them. She noticed the rough grain of the bread, the smoky smell of cured meat and when she licked the smear of mustard from her fingers it was sharp and hot across her tongue.

She had arranged to meet David at eleven o'clock at a car park on the edge of a small village. He was good at finding quiet walks on less popular paths. Karen left the arrangements completely to him; keeping their relationship a secret needed to be his responsibility. This pattern of meeting some distance from home, sometimes for a walk, occasionally for lunch in a pub, had become the only way to remain discreet. Since the day he had first kissed her on the descent of Loughrigg Fell, apart from the group walks, they had met exactly half a dozen times.

As she wrapped the sandwiches and placed them in a picnic box, she wondered about what she was doing and where it could lead. She would always be waiting for him to be free to see her, never able to plan too far ahead, never spontaneous. This was what an affair with a married man meant. Yet he still wanted to continue, taking great care to plan things, taking account of what she preferred to do whilst ensuring they wouldn't be seen together. And that, she considered regretfully, must always come first.

She left the house, her hiking boots in a plastic bag, the sandwiches and a thermos of coffee in her rucksack.

She knew that when she got there, he would pretend to check how well she had cleaned her boots and he would take her gear and put it in his own rucksack. The anticipation of both of these simple things made her heart sing.

It was cold, but the blue sky was promising. Karen enjoyed the drive to Sawley and, as usual, found that David was there before her, sitting under the tailgate, studying the map. The car park was empty, the pub across the road not yet open. Karen parked in the opposite corner to David, turned the engine off and got out of her car. For a moment she paused, then, with a wild sense of freedom which fuelled her anticipation of the day ahead, she walked across, her feet almost bouncing and stood in front of him. He wrapped his arms around her and kissed her.

'Lovely,' she said, breathing deeply. 'I've missed you this week.'

She shivered as he pushed his cold hands under her coat and jumper where they reached the bare skin of her back.

'Sorry,' he said. 'I should have warmed them first.'

'Warm them on me,' Karen said, raising her face to his. 'I'll need another kiss if you want to leave them there.'

David looked serious as he kissed her again, and, not for the first time, she wondered what he was thinking. Was he making comparisons? Karen had said she didn't want to talk about Helen, but it certainly didn't stop her thinking about his wife. Did he still kiss Helen with such passion, touch her skin under her clothes? Perhaps they had made love the previous night, and now here he was being unfaithful, detaching himself from his marriage?

I don't need to know, Karen thought, don't want to know. This is today and he's with me, not her, and I'm going to enjoy it.

David released her and said, 'Go and get your things and we'll set off.'

Karen brought everything from the car and he transferred it to his rucksack as she put on her boots.

'Well done,' he said teasingly, noting the neat laces and the clean suede.

They climbed over the stile into a field. David took her hand, as he usually did. Sometimes they talked, sometimes they walked in easy silence, sometimes he stopped to kiss her or to put his arms around her. They halted briefly for sandwiches and coffee, but by this time the sun had faded and there were a few drops of sleety rain in the air. The last hour of the walk was a quick dash back to the cars, and they both ended up wet, muddy and cold. David helped her out of her waterproofs and unlaced her boots, which bore only a slight resemblance to the clean pair he had admired that morning.

'Leave them when you get home,' he said. 'I'll do them for you.'

'Come and do them now,' she said, looking at her watch. 'Surely Helen won't be home for a couple of hours and Tina and Dan are away until Sunday.'

David seemed to be thinking something through.

'Helen's away until tomorrow,' he said.

'Away overnight?' Karen held her breath, but she wanted to be sure.

'Yes.'

'Well, why don't you come back to my place and I'll cook us both a meal.' It was said casually, as if he could take her up on the offer or leave it.

She saw that he was hesitating. For a moment she was unsure of what he would say.

'I've a few things I need to do,' he said, 'but, yes, I would really like that.'

Karen wanted to say that the words "really like" sounded as if she was offering to open a box of chocolates rather than presenting the chance of a whole evening to themselves. Instead, she kissed him on the cheek and said, 'I'll see you later then,' the easy tone of her voice masking a tangle of knots forming in her stomach.

She drove home in a state of nervous excitement, which at times, bordered on fear. Then she made herself calm down. What was she afraid of; that he would try to take things further? Or was it that in reality, this lovely, thoughtful – yet married guy – would find that the next natural step, actually sleeping with a woman other than his wife, would be a step too far. Surely not. He was a man, he had desires and several times he had pushed his hand under her blouse or rested it on her thigh. Last week he unzipped the back pocket of her trousers as they walked and slid his hand inside to rest on her bottom. When she had raised her eyebrows at him in mock surprise he had said suggestively, 'Now I know why they make these pockets so deep.'

I'm trying to read him based on these little things, she thought, but do I really have any idea how he feels or what he wants?

As she showered, she tried to work out what she wanted, and that was just as difficult. But it needed to be clear, out in the open with no ambiguities. 'I want him forever,' she thought, 'but I know I can't have him. He'll go back to playing happy families because he's a good man and he won't be able to keep up this duplicity for too long. Sometimes I can feel his guilt, I can see that he's ashamed of himself. I need to tell him I know, and that it's normal to feel like that.

In the bedroom she stood in front of the full-length mirror towelling her hair. Then she dropped the wet towel on the floor, unfastened the tie belt and shrugged off her robe letting it fall around her feet. She wished she was slimmer, taller, less rounded. She turned sideways, pleased at the shape of her breasts, not so pleased, however, at the curve of her stomach. She rested a hand on her midriff, pinched the flesh, thought about the slim frame of his wife. A shiver had her reaching for something to cover herself. Nakedness made her feel vulnerable.

She chose underwear and clothes with the utmost care, taking from the wardrobe slim black jeans and a blue satin shirt with pearl buttons down the front. She spent a long time blow-drying her hair, putting it up, then taking it all down, shaking it out to rest on her shoulders. Her hands shook as she applied light make up and selected a favourite perfume. Finally, she put on a pair of embroidered Chinese slippers that David had once said made her feet look pretty.

Tidying the lounge, clearing the kitchen and putting a lasagne together helped to steady her nerves. She was sliding the dish in the oven when she heard a knock.

He stood there, clean-shaven, hair slightly damp, looking extremely handsome. He kissed her, breathed deeply and commented on the rich smell of cooking. Yet she noticed something unsure in his movements, some tension. Karen gave him a bottle of wine to open, then they sat on the sofa and he took her hand.

'I'll stay to eat,' he said, 'but I mustn't be too late back. Helen sometimes rings.'

Her heart sank. So, he had already decided that things had gone far enough, that trying to behave like a couple with her, eating together, sharing a whole evening – and possibly a night – was too much. We will never get beyond being good friends with affection for each other and a bit of very safe touching, which really goes nowhere, she thought. But I need this. I need to know about all of this and even if it seems selfish, he is what I need tonight.

She took a deep breath and said, 'Why have you come back, David?'

He looked puzzled. 'Because you asked me to come. Because I want to spend the evening with you.'

'And is that all?'

She could tell that he knew exactly what her words implied.

'It's a rare chance for us to do this,' he said. 'And no, I suppose that isn't all. If I'm honest, I thought that eating together might not be the only thing we would do this evening.'

Karen felt a tightness in her stomach; a grip of something pleasurable, yet sharpened with uncertainty. So, he had thought beyond a cosy evening in. She took a deep breath.

'If you can never leave your wife,' she said, 'and I totally accept that, where are we going? There's no future for either of us. Yes, we're enjoying each other's company. I love our time together, I love feeling your hands on me, and sometimes I've desperately wanted more, but we'll never have anything better than a secretive, once-a-week kind of relationship, will we?'

'You need to find a single guy,' David said, shifting

uncomfortably. 'You don't want me. You need to find someone who can provide some sort of a future for you.' He released her hand. She could sense his discomfort and knew that within a minute he could be gone.

'I *do* want you,' she said.

He paused, first looking at her, then turning away to consider her words.

'But wanting each other doesn't make it right, does it?' he said. 'I came back this evening thinking that we could take things further. But I've realised that not only would it mean I was, without question, unfaithful to my wife, I would also be treating you despicably, because this is an affair and an affair isn't what will eventually make you happy.' He shook his head. 'I'm torn, you must see that.'

'I do see, but I don't think you understand how I feel,' Karen said. She moved across the sofa to sit on his knee, where he encircled her with his arm. She wondered when he and Helen had last sat together like this. Did he sometimes pull Helen onto his knee to comfort her, or to touch her as a man might do with the wife he desires?

'I could never, ever, take you away from Helen,' she said. 'I wouldn't expect to. I wouldn't want to. I'm not a marriage breaker, and I know how you feel about your family. But if my philosophy classes and twenty-five years with Guy taught me anything, it's to seize the day, to live in the present. You're right, I need a man, I'm not good on my own, and one day I hope I will find someone, but,' she put her hand on his cheek and pulled his face round so that she could see his expression, 'it won't be you.'

'Then why?'

'Because I need to start somewhere. I'm so scared. I was only ever married to Guy, only ever had sex with Guy, I hardly kissed anyone else but Guy and, looking back, everything with him was diluted, weak, lacking any passion. I know absolutely nothing about falling in love, and I have to find out about myself and what I want.'

'But with me?'

'Yes. You are lovely and, unfortunately, I've fallen for you. But it's a sort of practice falling in love, I'm not sure that sounds very nice, but I can't express it any other way. You're unhappy at the moment with Helen, I know that, but you will get over it. With Helen, you have a long history, a shared life together and a future. You and I, we need each other now.'

She was aware of his hand on her hip, his breath on her neck, the warmth of him beneath her. She breathed in his familiar scent and thought that this was the right time, the only time.

'So,' she said. 'I suppose that what I'm saying is that if you want to stay the night, then it will be all right. Think of it as a separate thing, nothing to do with the future, no implications; you and I doing something we want to do now.'

She watched him close his eyes, rest his head back, breathe deeply.

How can I bear it if he says no, she thought? I want him to make love to me so much. I want him sleeping next to me in my bed, and if he leaves in the morning and I never see him again, I'll get over it.

She felt him stir beneath her, then he pushed her off his knee, almost roughly. For a second she thought he was angry at what she had said, but he grasped her hand, then, as if he didn't want to give himself any time to think, led her upstairs to the bedroom and sat her on the bed.

He reached over to switch on the bedside lamp and looked at her. 'You're quite sure about this?'

'Quite sure,' Karen said. 'But if I'm honest, I'm frightened. I don't know what to do. I'm scared that I'll be a disappointment to you.'

'It's a first for me, too,' he said sitting beside her.

'Of course,' she murmured. 'It's a first for both of us.'

As she lay back and tried to relax, he stroked her dark hair, laying out the strands on the pillow.

'Don't think about doing anything,' he said. 'All you need to do is try to tell me what feels right to you. If it's disappointing, and it won't be, it'll be my fault, not yours.'

Suddenly she was petrified. 'I've forgotten what feels right. I don't know if I ever really knew.' She could hear the alarm in her voice.

'Don't worry.' he said. 'Let's find out.'

Karen gave him a nervous smile.

'So, do you want me to get undressed?'

'Absolutely not,' David said. 'That's quite definitely my job.'

In the end there was no disappointment, no doubt. He was unhurried, gentle, seemed to know instinctively what she needed. There was one fleeting moment when she imagined him making love with Helen, and wondered if he was thinking the same, but the thought evaporated as briefly as it had appeared. When it was over he lay very still, his face almost touching hers, and whispered she was beautiful. Karen nearly said, thank you, but it would have been completely the wrong thing to say, so she said nothing. Instead she eased her body against his, ensuring that as much of her as possible was touching him.

After a few minutes, she remembered the food in the oven.

'Oh God, the dinner, it'll be burnt,' she exclaimed, sitting up, pulling the quilt to cover herself.

David smiled at her. 'I can't think of a better reason for letting it burn.'

Karen hesitated. She wanted to get her dressing gown from behind the bedroom door, but was aware of his eyes on her. She slid out of bed quickly, reached the hook and wrapped it around herself.

'I'll go and see what I can salvage.'

Ten minutes later, they were sitting at the kitchen table. The lasagne was edible, but Karen couldn't remember food tasting so good. David scraped the charred edges from the dish, insisting that it was the best part. Karen watched him, feeling different, still amazed at what had happened between them, realising that finally, she knew what the phrase, making love, really meant.

I had sex with Guy, she thought, sex, for years and years, I don't remember passion or tenderness. I certainly don't remember feeling like this.

'So,' she said later as they sat together on the sofa. 'How do you feel now?'

'Fantastic… and dreadful at the same time, if that's possible,' he said. 'What about you?'

'Just fantastic.' She took his hand, turned it over and kissed his palm.

'Stay,' she said, 'sleep with me in my bed.'

David was quiet. He seemed to be struggling with his thoughts. Karen held her breath. Then he pulled her to him, kissed her hair and said, 'I think I will.'

In the middle of the night, Karen lay awake listening to the heavy breathing of the man asleep beside her. She ran her hands over her body, touching where he had touched, recalling every detail. When they had come back to bed, they made love a second time, differently. There was less gentleness, less hesitation, more passion. Karen's negative thoughts about her body, her fear of being a disappointment, had evaporated and she felt completely intoxicated by their desire for each other. She wondered how Helen could bear to spend even one night away from him.

But it's also this, she thought, reaching out and touching him gently as he slept. It's his presence, next to me, all night. It's the way he pulled me to him as we drifted off to sleep, as if I'm being kept safe. I was lying when I said it was a practice falling in love, how could I have said that?

Karen knew exactly why she had said it. She had said it because it was the only way she could get him to stay. If he had thought for one second that taking her to bed would make it harder to break up when the time came, he wouldn't have done it. She had to persuade him that, for her, this was something she needed and he would be doing her a favour if he stayed.

I'm a fraud, she thought. All that rubbish about seizing the day, enjoying the present, not wanting to break up his marriage. If we carry on, if we have more nights like this, I will be desperate to hold on to him, and in time we won't be able to keep this a secret. Then his world will come tumbling down and I will be responsible.

The image of an old-fashioned pair of scales came into Karen's head, with herself on one side and David's family on the other. He was pivotal and could tip the balance either way. Deep down, she knew which side he would choose in the end, the pull of his family and his long marriage to Helen being just too strong. She put the thoughts out of her mind, concentrated on listening to his breathing, moving closer to feel his warmth.

'This moment,' she whispered to herself, 'has to be enough.'

Chapter 18

David awoke to pale light through crimson curtains and the feel of silky bed linen against his cheek. He was used to plain cotton in blues and greens, cool to touch, smooth. The room was warm, uncomfortably warm. At home they slept with the window open.

He glanced across to see that Karen had gone. In the middle of the night he realised he was sleeping on the wrong side, but perhaps the wrong side was the right side in this unfamiliar bed.

He sat up and wished he could leave quietly. There would have been something simple and uncomplicated about waking early, letting her sleep on as he tiptoed away to sort out his thoughts alone. There was no doubt about his feelings last night, but now he was less sure.

He threw the quilt off and straightened the bed, wondering whether to have a shower, on reflection deciding to make it the first thing he did when he got home. Dressing quickly, he checked his mobile for a message from Helen. There was a missed call from an unknown number but nothing else.

As he arrived downstairs, Karen was carrying a tray into the conservatory.

'I thought I heard you moving about,' she said. 'I've made coffee.'

She put the tray down and turned to him, reaching up to touch his face with both hands. He kissed her, but it was a little awkward.

'Thank you, David,' she said.

'No, I should be saying that to you,' he replied, which sounded rather feeble; an automatic response.

They commented on the weather, what she was doing for the rest of the day, when Tina and Dan would be back from York. They didn't speak about what had happened between them.

'I'll ring you,' he said. He kissed her as she stood by the open door, then he left, relieved to be outside, back in his own space again.

As he drove away, David found the word, unfaithful, rolling around in his head. And at what point did faithful become unfaithful? Was it sex? Was he still a loyal husband right up to the actual act, or was it that very first touch when the wind almost blew them off the fell and he grabbed her hand? He couldn't remember making a decision not to let go, nor could he remember deliberately choosing to kiss her by the gate. Last night, the things she said had been the catalyst. Minutes earlier he could have walked away, then they had reached, indeed crossed, the point of no return and desire was the only thing left.

He was surprised how easily he had blocked everything from his mind and enjoyed the closeness of a night with this woman, the touch of her hands, the softness of her body, the passion. Inevitably, when he had woken in her bed there was guilt, fear about what would happen next and an unexpected and perverse need to see his wife.

The phone was ringing as he walked through the door. His first thought was Helen, but the display read *International*. He looked at his watch and wondered if it was Lottie ringing from Australia. At the other end of the line he heard Chris in Melbourne, his voice serious. David knew immediately that there was something wrong.

'David, it's Chris. Thank goodness I've got hold of you. I'm afraid Charlotte's had an accident.'

Fear flooded through him and his hand holding the phone started to shake.

'What sort of an accident? Is she hurt?'

'She's been hit by a car. It's serious, but we've been assured that she has every chance of making a full recovery.'

'Tell me what you know,' he said.

He heard Chris take a deep breath, and for a split second, he tried to imagine the vast distance between them and the speed at which the voice was travelling across the miles.

'She was with Harry. They were crossing a road to get to work this afternoon. As far as I can gather, they crossed at the lights and a car hit them both.'

'Harry's hurt as well?' David asked.

'Yes, but with him it's just cuts and bruises. Charlotte came off worst. Harry remembers her going over the bonnet of the car and landing on the other side.'

'No,' David gasped. 'Tell me how bad it is.'

Chris seemed to be shuffling a piece of paper at the other end of the phone. 'She's broken her left leg below the knee, also some ribs, her collarbone and her right wrist. She took quite a blow to the head, which caused concussion, but they don't seem concerned about that.'

'What are they concerned about then?'

'Her leg, it's a bad break. She's probably being operated on as we speak.'

David's breath was coming in short gasps, his heart pounding in his ears, the thumps filling his head. Chris gave him the phone number of the hospital, then Jenny came on the line promising that they would do everything they could.

'Let it sink in,' she said. 'Talk to Helen, then ring us again later. Try not to worry, we've been assured she will recover. She's being very brave. You'd be proud of her.'

Cordless telephones allow for pacing about, up and down, stop, back again, so that when the call ended, David needed a chair. Floss jumped lightly onto his knee. He felt frozen, helpless. Yes, he must contact Helen, then Lizzie, then Australia again, but that was all giving information, passing on the news, it wouldn't help Lottie.

The instinct to protect his family had always been strong, and it was Lottie who had demanded and accepted her father's protection, who allowed David to take control and bail her out when needed, stand between her and Lizzie, take her side in a dispute with Helen. He was proud of the independence and single-mindedness of his elder daughter, but – and he had never untangled these thoughts for himself – he loved being needed by his younger daughter. As little girls, while Lizzie protested; "I can do it myself," Lottie said; "Daddy, please help me," and every time, sometimes in the face of Helen's protestations, he did.

Suddenly his mind cleared. It was simple; they had to be there, nothing else would do. They were booked to fly in three weeks. Their passports were in order, although he would need to check the visa requirements. He would ring the airline and bring the flights forward. At once David had a goal, a reason for taking action

223

and a confidence that he could make it happen to be with Charlotte.

He rang the hospital, but there was no more news as Lottie wasn't back from surgery. He left a message on Helen's phone, knowing she would be in the middle of her presentation at a conference in the Midlands. Well, too bad, she'd have to leave and come home. He left a message for Lizzie asking her to get in touch urgently when she could, then he contacted the airline, relieved to find that he could change the flights to the following day from Manchester. He booked a taxi to the airport and before Australia went to bed, rang the hospital again. Lottie was back in her room recovering from the operation.

He spoke to a nurse called Maddie. The gentle, Australian accent was full of reassurance and, as David said, 'Please tell her we love her and we'll be with her soon, 'he heard his own voice crack.

'You'll be able to speak with her yourself, tomorrow,' Maddie said. 'She should be up for a phone call, although it could be your night-time.'

'Thanks,' he said, wiping his eyes, 'thanks, but we'll be on a plane by then.'

'You're coming out here?'

'Yes. We're on a flight to Melbourne tomorrow.'

'That's great,' Maddie said. 'Shall I tell her?'

'Please, as soon as you can. Thanks so much Maddie. I know you will anyway, but please look after her, I love her very much.'

'We'll do everything we can Mr Richards. Don't worry. Charlotte is young and she'll get through this. I've seen them walk out of this hospital good as new.'

'Thanks,' was all David could manage as he realised that he could only control the fringes of this situation.

It was a brief respite to leave the arrangements and stand under a hot shower, to shave and smell the familiar soap, to clean every part of him. He rubbed himself down roughly, put on clean clothes and felt slightly better. Strong coffee was the next task, then he clambered into the loft to get the suitcases and spent a productive few hours organising paperwork and making lists of people to contact. Lizzie rang and David filled her in, briefly, knowing she would have to get back to class. She was obviously shocked and upset, but in her inimitable, matter of fact way, showed no surprise that her parents would have to drop everything and go.

'I'll come over later Dad,' she said.

David protested, but Lizzie said, 'Dad, I want to come, I need to see you both.'

He made a sandwich at lunch time, wondering why Helen had not returned his call. His message would have left her in no doubt as to the urgency of things. David got on the phone once again, called Helen's school and spoke to Jen in the office. She told him she would ring the hotel where the conference was taking place. Then he spoke with Bridget, the deputy, and explained about the travel plans. She was full of concern for Charlotte and accepted without question that Helen would be travelling to Australia earlier than planned.

'She'll worry that we can't manage without her,' she said, but we can. 'You need to be with Charlotte. Helen can keep in touch from Australia if she wants, but to be honest David, we'll be fine.'

David rang off, grateful for the concern and support. Now he needed his wife to call back.

It was after three o'clock when she finally rang. David outlined the news. A poor line and noise in the background meant he couldn't hear Helen's voice clearly. He was telling her to get home soon but drive safely when they were cut off.

By six o'clock, she still hadn't arrived and there were no messages. David was worried. He rang her school, but there was no answer.

Bloody hell Helen, he thought, this is the one time I need you to be here. Surely the traffic can't be that bad?

He tidied up, cleaned the kitchen, started to lay out clothes and collect documents together. At six-thirty he heard the car. The door opened, and Helen appeared, laden down with bags, some landing on the floor with a thump.

'Thank goodness,' David exclaimed. 'Where've you been? It's hours since you rang.'

Helen reached down to fling off each of her shoes and answered crossly, 'The traffic was dreadful and I needed to call in at school,' and then, in response to David's look of complete incomprehension, 'I'd left my phone on my desk yesterday. That's why I didn't get your messages.' She dropped a bag on the table then shed her jacket over the back of a chair, striding to the fire to warm her hands.

'Is there any more news?' she asked.

'No. We can ring at ten o'clock tonight. Are you all right?'

'Yes. I could have told you something like this would happen. She's such a scatterbrain. Thank goodness we signed for the extra insurance.'

David considered these comments rather harsh, but decided not to comment.

'I wish she wasn't ten thousand miles away,' he continued. 'I desperately want to be with her.'

'We're fortunate that Chris and Jenny are there.'

'They'll do whatever they can to help, but she's not their daughter, is she?'

David found Helen's lack of emotion bewildering. He started to tell her about the flights, but she interrupted him and said, 'David, I saw Jen and Bridget at school. They said you'd told them about Charlotte's accident and about changing your flight or something. Are you flying out to Australia on your own?'

'No,' he said. 'I've changed both flights, brought them forward. *We* fly out tomorrow.'

Helen looked at David intently, as if processing this information was an impossible task. She moved away from the stove and reached for her diary. With this in her hand she crossed the room again, flicking pages irritably. Suddenly, with a gesture of complete frustration she said, 'I can't go to Australia tomorrow.'

The previous twenty-four hours had been an emotional roller-coaster, the likes of which he had never known. Ultimately, inevitably, it all became too much. It took less than a second for David to explode with anger.

'What do you mean, you *can't?*'

Helen replied in a tired, flat way as if stating something very patiently to a small child.

'You know why I can't.'

'Know? I'll tell you what I know. I know one, essential, all important fact, Helen, and that is our daughter, our precious, lovely girl is lying in hospital in Melbourne and the only place that I want to be right now is by her side.'

David had expected his wife to come through the door anxious about Lottie, grateful that he had managed all the arrangements, even a bit tearful, needing comfort and reassurance, able to give him some comfort and reassurance. God knows he needed it. What he hadn't expected was this emotionless, cold detachment.

She put the diary down and yanked another folder from her bag. Documents spilled across the table, then she checked something, consulted the diary once more and crossed the room turning to face David. He tried again.

'She needs us, both of us,' he said doing his best to suppress his anger.

'She doesn't need us,' Helen snapped. 'She needs the nurses, the doctors, the care she'll get in the hospital. For goodness sake, we're going in a few weeks, that's when she'll really need us. You said we can phone her. You said the nurse will speak with us at any time. There's no need to start overreacting.'

That last word, delivered so pointedly, tipped David over the edge. He took three strides across the room, grasped her by the arms and pushed her against the wall. The diary went flying, papers tucked within its pages scattering to the floor.

'David, let go. You're hurting me.'

'I am not hurting you, I am holding you so that you will stay still long enough to listen to what I have to say. And when I have said it, Helen, I will let go.'

'For goodness sake,' she protested angrily, 'you don't need to hold me down to make me listen, let go.'

She pushed against him, but he held tight, waiting for her look at him. When she did, he relaxed his hold ever so slightly.

'Now,' he said, trembling inside, but determined to speak clearly. 'Listen, Helen, because what happens next is very important. Whatever you decide to do is up to you, but I am going to be on that plane to Australia tomorrow. I am going to be on it because my daughter, who means the world to me, needs me to be with her. I want you to come, because she also needs you, in fact we will need each other. So, you have a choice. I can't force you to do anything, but if you choose your job above Charlotte, I don't think I will ever forgive you.'

He felt her body tense, and David knew he had to let go. He didn't want to move. He was terrified that once he released her, things would never be the same again. If they could both stay here, charged with emotion, angry at each other, but touching, connected, close, there was a chance. He took her hands in his, grasping them together. She was so cold, so thin, so hard – like a piece of steel.

'I'm going to finish packing,' he said removing his hands. 'It's up to you.' He went upstairs and sat on the bed, furious with himself, furious with Helen.

After a few moments, he lifted his head. There were no sounds from downstairs, nothing. David listened. Still nothing. He stood up. Helen never did anything quietly. She slammed doors and moved with impatient feet. You always knew when she was in the house. Oh God, he thought, what if I've really hurt her? No, surely not. I just held her still.

David bolted downstairs into the living room. For one dreadful moment, he thought she had gone, then he saw her. She was in the same place but had slumped to the floor and was sitting with her hands around her knees, her head resting against the wall, tears staining her face.

'Helen.' David knelt in front of her. 'I'm sorry, I'm so sorry.'

She shook her head and reached out towards him

breathing in a gulp of air that triggered racking sobs.

'Talk to me, Helen, don't cry, please.'

But all she could do for the next few moments was weep uncontrollably. David stayed on the floor with her hands in his. As she began to calm down, he tried again.

'Helen, speak to me. What is it? I didn't mean to hurt you.'

She shook her head and he watched as she struggled to find some control. 'It isn't that,' she said. 'I'm sitting here and,' she took another sharp breath, 'I keep trying to think it all through and I can't.'

David was confused. 'You can't…. what?' he asked.

'I can't make a decision. I don't know what to do.'

He wasn't sure how to handle this. Should he order her to come to Australia? Should he help her think it through for herself, help her check her diary? Perhaps he had overreacted in booking the flights for the next day. She needed more time to make arrangements before she dropped everything. I haven't managed this at all well, he thought, so I need to handle it very carefully now.

He reached for tissues and placed them in her hand. Her face looked older, grey and weary, yet her position on the floor, her hair ruffled and damp, and the way she was wiping her eyes reminded him of a much younger Helen. He kissed her forehead.

'How can I help?' he asked. Her response, when it came, took him completely by surprise.

'I think,' she said, 'you need to tell me what to do.'

The front door banged and Lizzie called out as she pushed open the door.

'What's happened? Why are you on the floor?'

David got up and hugged his daughter. 'It's OK, nothing worse with Charlotte, it's Mum, she's,' he hesitated, 'she's finding the whole thing rather a shock.'

'Dad, I'm scared,' Lizzie said.

'I think Mum's scared, that's why she's so upset. But you and I, we have to take charge. There's stuff to do and I need you to help me.'

Lizzie took a deep breath. 'Right,' she said, 'what do you want me to do?'

The first job David gave her was to go over to see Debbie, tell her what had happened and ask whether she could feed Floss while they were away.

'Don't let Debbie come round,' David said. 'She'll want to, but I don't want anyone to see Mum like this.'

In the minutes Lizzie was away, he tried to get Helen moving. When she had asked him to tell her what to do, he had felt an enormous sense of relief. He was back in control, but he was worried. It was as if Helen was experiencing some sort of breakdown. He helped her up and sat her on the sofa.

'Have you eaten today?' he asked.

'A little at lunchtime.'

'How little?'

'Hardly anything. The other presenter was ill, so I did the day on my own. I didn't have time.'

'And no breakfast as usual?'

She shook her head.

'Right, I'll make you a cup of tea and some toast.'

'Tea,' she said, 'but I can't eat anything.'

David sat next to her and placed his hand on hers. 'You have to eat.'

Helen took a deep breath and closed her eyes, but he felt she was calming down.

When Lizzie got back, she brewed a pot of tea and made a plate of toast for all of them. David went through everything the doctor and then the nurse had said, his calls with Chris and Jenny, all the people he had contacted. Lizzie thought of a few more and she took their phone numbers. Helen said very little. She finished the drink, but only swallowed a few morsels of food. David ignored this. There was enough to face without another battle.

'Why don't you go and start laying some clothes out on the bed,' David said to her. 'Lizzie will come and help you.'

Helen went upstairs with her daughter. Minutes later, Lizzie was back down again. She turned to David.

'Dad, what's up with Mum? She's the organiser, the tough guy in the crisis. I've never seen her so…' she hesitated as if trying to find the words to accurately describe her mother, 'so lifeless. She's getting clothes out, but it's as if she's not really there.'

David didn't know how much to tell his daughter about the row and his anger and how Helen had seemed to collapse, but he needed to share it with someone, as he still wasn't sure whether to call a doctor.

When he didn't answer, Lizzie's tone became more urgent. 'Dad, something's happened, hasn't it? Tell me.'

David took a breath and thought about his words.

'Mum came home late. I was frantic with worry about Lottie, but also about where the hell she'd got to. I told her I'd changed the flights for tomorrow and she said she couldn't go, there was stuff in her diary that she couldn't cancel, and that I'd overreacted.'

'Bloody hell, Dad, she said that?' Lizzie gasped.

'I really lost it at that point. I don't think I've ever been so angry in my life, so I…,' he paused, 'I told her I would be flying to Melbourne tomorrow and that she could make a choice, but if she didn't get on that plane with me, I'd never forgive her. Then I disappeared upstairs and tried to work out what to do next. I didn't know how she would react, but what I did know was that I'd go without her, whatever she decided.'

Lizzie put a hand on his arm, her face aghast at what he was telling her. 'Dad, you poor thing, I can't believe she said she couldn't go because of work. So, what made her change her mind?'

'I came downstairs as it had all gone quiet and she was in a heap on the floor crying, not talking to me. When she did say something, it was that she couldn't make a decision and she wanted me to make it for her; to tell her what to do. Then you walked in.'

'She wanted you to tell her? Mum's never let anyone tell her what to do in her life.' Lizzie's voice was full of confusion.

'I'm not sure whether I ought to call a doctor.'

Lizzie thought about this, then said, 'I think you need to get her on that plane tomorrow. What's she been like recently?'

'Dreadful, totally consumed with work, never sits still, up in the middle of the night.'

'Not eating?'

'Hardly anything, and lying about what she has or hasn't eaten, and if I try to encourage her she gets all stubborn and eats even less.'

'Dad, you've had all this to cope with?'

Lizzie put her arms around her father. 'Why,' she whispered, 'didn't you tell me?'

He didn't answer. There was so much he couldn't tell his daughter; so much he probably couldn't tell anyone.

'Lizzie, I need to do something.' David tried to sound rather vague. 'I need to go out, it won't take long. There are maps and stuff that the walking group need and I have to give them to someone. Can you stay here, help Mum to pack?'

'I can do that,' Lizzie said, 'but are these maps so important? I could drop them off for you.'

'No,' David said, reaching for the car keys, deliberately not meeting his daughter's eye. I need to explain things. I won't be longer than half an hour.'

I don't know who I am any more, he thought as he drove away from the village. I desperately want to be with my injured daughter, I have to be a rock for my wife, who has collapsed so spectacularly, yet here I am driving in the opposite direction to see the woman I slept with last night. And what do I say to her? Thanks for the support, but my family need me now, I can't see you any more.

David pulled off the main road and drove up the lane to the cottage. It was pointless trying to hide the vehicle, there were more important things to worry about. He had no words ready, nothing. He got out of the car, walked down the path and knocked on the door. When Karen answered it, her face lit up, but he shook his head and said, 'I don't have long, something's happened.'

They stood in the hall as he told her about Lottie's accident and Helen's response. It was only a few hours ago that he had left this house, his mind tossing feelings and emotions around like bits of paper in the breeze. He had wondered what lay in the future. Now, the future was forcing his hand.

'You shouldn't have driven over,' Karen said when he had finished. 'You should have phoned me.'

At that moment, David knew exactly why he was there, why he hadn't picked up the phone to speak to her, why he had left Lizzie to cope with Helen. He looked at Karen, unable to find the words. To his shame he felt the unfamiliar sensation of tears welling up, spilling over as he blinked.

Karen reached up and touched his face. 'Come in for a minute,' she said, taking him by the hand and leading him into the lounge. David sat down, but he couldn't speak, the lump in his throat blocking the words. Karen sat close by, a hand on his arm.

'You have to go back home,' she said.

She waited as he regained some composure.

'You're right.' His voice sounded rough, unfamiliar inside his head. 'I don't know how long we'll be in Australia, but it could be for a while. I'm so sorry, but…'

As the words failed him and his emotions took over again, Karen reached for his hands.

'Sorry?' she said. 'Sorry about what? Last night?'

'I didn't mean that.'

'I'm not sorry about a single minute of the time I've spent with you. You've made everything in my life better, clearer, and what we've shared over the last few months and especially last night, it's part of us both now.'

David could see how desperately she was struggling to keep herself together. There were tears in her eyes, her mouth trembling. He reached over and put his arms around her, reluctant to let go, acutely aware of the time passing. There was a strong compulsion to keep hold, but also to release her and leave to return to his family who needed him.

Karen untangled herself and pushed him away gently. 'Go home,' she said. 'I'm sure Lottie will be fine. Shut our affair away in your head and keep it there for now.'

By the front door he grasped her shoulders.

'Find a good man,' he whispered. 'You deserve nothing less than that.'

As he stepped out along the path, David was blinded by an orange glow. Shy for most of the day, the sun was finding an opening in the ragged clouds. He turned to say goodbye, but the door was already closed.

Chapter 19

As he sat in the car outside Karen's cottage, David could have put his head on the steering wheel and wept. He wondered how much more anguish he could take. The need to be strong for Lottie and for Helen was the only thing keeping him together; this was not the time to indulge his own emotional release. He felt desperate leaving Karen, knowing that their brief affair was almost certainly over, angry with himself for letting it happen, yet unable to feel genuine regret that it had.

He started the car and tried to concentrate on what he needed to do before tomorrow. There was essential paperwork to check, suitcases to finish packing, the house to tidy up, although that would be the least important task. As he anchored his thoughts to planning the next few hours, he gradually found himself feeling more composed. It was as if he was standing still in the eye of the storm, seeing and hearing the events racing around him, but remaining detached. Whatever happened, if Lottie was all right, he had no doubt in his mind that he would cope with the rest.

Lizzie was on the phone when he walked in. She mouthed, 'Grandma'. David took the phone and spoke to his mother, going over their arrangements, reassuring her that he would ring every day. Marjorie wanted to speak with Helen, but David managed to put her off.

'She's in bed, we've an early start tomorrow. Yes, she's fine,' he lied. 'Don't worry, I'll contact you every day, but it won't be possible while we're flying.'

Moments later, after putting the phone down, he looked at his daughter.

'Where's your mum?'

'She's in bed. I don't know if I've done the right thing, but I gave her a sleeping tablet from a box I found in the bathroom cabinet. She's all packed, I think, but I've done most of it for her.'

'Is she any calmer?'

Lizzie paused. 'She says she feels panicky all the time. She kept asking where you were and when you'd be back. I tried to get her to look at clothes and think about what she wanted to take, but she didn't seem able to concentrate. What's more, she keeps crying.'

'I think,' David said, taking his coat off, 'that she's having some sort of breakdown. She's been on the edge for a while now and this news about Lottie might well have tipped her over.'

'Not Mum?' Lizzie said incredulously. 'Sit down, Dad, I need to try to understand this.'

David sat heavily in the armchair, exhaustion flooding through his body. He closed his eyes. He didn't want to start untangling everything, and anyway, he wasn't sure he understood it himself.

'Dad,' Lizzie said carefully, 'do you mind if I ask you something?'

David opened his eyes and turned towards her. He saw the faint frown lines, the blue eyes, which everyone said were his, but always reminded him of Helen, and the long dark hair tucked behind her ears. He wished she didn't have to go through all this with him.

'Ask whatever you want,' he said, 'as long as my reply doesn't need a lengthy explanation, I'm so tired.'

'Are you and Mum all right?' Lizzie said. 'You're not splitting up or anything?'

As expected, she had not minced her words and David knew that in spite of what had happened during the last twenty-four hours, he had to convince Lizzie that there was nothing to worry about. He sat up in the chair and met her gaze, knowing he would have to sound absolutely certain if he wanted her to believe him.

'We're not splitting up. Mum's stressed and there are things we need to sort out, but you mustn't worry about us, Lizzie. We'll get through this together.'

'I've been worried, really worried,' Lizzie said. 'You two seem so distant with each other, and when Grandma made a comment about you going to see that Karen woman, my imagination started running riot.'

'Well, you'd better stop it running riot because your mum and I are fine,' David said, passing his hanky to Lizzie, who had started to cry.

'I'm so glad,' she said. 'I couldn't bear it if you weren't. But I wish you'd told me how hard she's been to live with recently.'

'And what would you have done?'

Lizzie wiped her eyes and blew her nose as she seemed to think about this.

'Something,' she said. 'I could have done something.'

David looked at his watch.

'I think we can ring the hospital again,' he said. 'It's morning over there.'

The news from Australia was encouraging but rather non-committal.

'It's the best we can hope for, Dad,' Lizzie said having followed the conversation word for word. 'You'll get more details about it all when you arrive. Just be glad she's alive and at the other side of the operation. Just think, this time tomorrow, you'll be almost there.'

'You're right,' he said. 'We've got to get through the next twenty-four hours. Anyway, you'd better get off home now.'

'I'm going to stay tonight,' Lizzie said. 'I've rung Gina, head of maths, and she'll cover my lessons until lunchtime. I've also let Pete know I won't be home tonight, so it's all arranged.'

David started to protest, but Lizzie was adamant.

'When you've left I can clear up here, empty the fridge, stuff like that. You could be away for weeks.'

'Thanks,' David said, grateful to relinquish some responsibility. Lizzie seemed to be on a roll now, taking charge in the same way Helen would usually do in a crisis.

'Right.' she said. 'Go and get the cases from upstairs, they're ready on the landing. Check the passports and tickets and stuff, then you'd better get to bed. The taxi's booked for five, isn't it?'

'Quarter to,' he replied.

David went upstairs and looked in on Helen, who was fast asleep. He wondered how she would cope with the flight. Perhaps the long hours sitting next to each other on a plane would give them chance to talk things through. He and Lizzie made a final check, then they both went to bed. David slipped gently under the quilt. He listened to the sound of Helen's breathing and said a silent prayer for his younger daughter. His mind inevitably took him back to the previous night, but he let his exhausted body overcome thought and tip him into a restless sleep.

It was a relief to finally hear the alarm. David was out

of bed immediately, reaching for clothes. Helen didn't stir and he struggled to rouse her, but eventually she sat up.

'You need to get dressed,' he said. 'Everything else is ready to go.'

He tapped on Lizzie's door and she appeared, her hair in a rough ponytail.

Helen had managed to get up, but she was white-faced, holding her stomach. David passed her the clothes that Lizzie had helped her lay out and she dressed mechanically. He hugged her.

'Don't worry,' he said. 'This is the worst bit. We'll feel better when we're at the airport and we can get some breakfast.'

'Have we got the passports? she asked. 'I usually do all that.'

'All sorted. Don't worry,' he said again.

Within half an hour they were at the door waiting for the taxi. When it drew up, David took the luggage out and shook hands with the driver. He went back inside where Lizzie and Helen were holding onto each other. He put his arms around them both for a moment, then he took Helen by the arm and led her to the waiting car. He could feel her body shaking, either with nerves or the early morning cold, he wasn't sure.

Lizzie stood there wrapped in his walking coat.

'Look after yourselves,' she called out. 'Give my love to Lottie, and ring or text me every day.'

David came back up the drive and hugged her. 'Thanks,' he said. 'I don't know what I'd have done without you.'

It was with a sense of relief that he sank into the taxi seat, breathing in the minty odour of air freshener and cleaning fluid. From now on, the priority would be getting himself and Helen from one place to another, the rest was someone else's responsibility.

Manchester Airport was wide awake when they arrived, and so began the wearisome process of joining queues, sitting, waiting. David's stomach growled with hunger, the three slices of toast he had eaten the previous evening was a poor excuse for a meal. He ordered a full breakfast in a spotlessly clean but faceless cafe. Helen, sipping tea, looked at it incredulously and managed a faint smile at his hearty appetite. She was quiet. Usually she would have been browsing the shops, trying perfumes, commenting on the other travellers. This morning her eyes seemed blank. When he had finished eating, they found seats not far from the gate. She leant her head on his shoulder and seemed to sleep.

He gazed at a huge photograph of Sicily on the wall; blue-grey mountains and green fields and he pictured himself walking alone across one of ridges, the sun on his shoulders, breathing in the clear air. The laughter of the check-in staff interrupted his thoughts. A delay was announced and the waiting passengers sighed and shuffled in their seats. David watched a woman stand and stretch as if warming up for a long-distance jog. Suddenly, Helen straightened up and looked around, her hands shaking. She gripped his arm.

'I'm scared I'll be ill on the flight,' she said. 'We've never done long haul before. I'm scared I'll not be able to get on the plane.' He felt her cold hand in his, and he remembered previous incidents where she had been travel sick.

'Do you have any travel pills in your hand bag?' he asked. 'You always used to carry them.'

She rummaged in her bag and produced a tattered

strip of tablets in foil. They were at least a year out of date.

'I'll go and buy you some,' he said. 'You can't take those.'

"No, don't leave me. What if they start boarding?' She clung onto him again, her fingers gripping tightly. 'For goodness sake, this is pathetic,' she said. 'I can't believe I'm behaving like this.'

David put his arm around her shoulders. It was like holding a wooden doll. He could try to reassure her, tell her to relax, but she was way beyond such a simple remedy. Instead he said, 'Come with me, then. We'll both go.'

After the brief stop in Munich to pick up German passengers, David was relieved that Helen succumbed to sleep for most of the first flight. In the chemist's he had picked up a herbal remedy to calm her nerves as well as travel-sickness pills. Thankfully, the combination seemed to be working.

He wished he could have slept. He watched a couple of films, toyed with the trays of food and tried to settle in every possible position to snatch some sleep. Even when he found some comfort in the cramped seat, his mind wouldn't rest. He worried about Lottie. He wondered if she would walk out of the hospital as good as new, as the nurse had promised. What would the future hold for his daughter if there was permanent damage? This was a girl who loved swimming and skiing and running down the garden or on the beach full of her natural exuberance for life.

He wrestled with guilt and regret when he thought about Karen. One minute he had been in her bed enjoying a closeness and a passion that had felt like a

natural part of their relationship, then he was on her
doorstep knowing that it was almost certainly over. And
what if there had been no call from Australia, if Lottie
hadn't rolled over the car bonnet, what would he have
done then?

He watched Helen, sometimes touching her arm or
taking her hand. If she opened her eyes and met his
gaze, he smiled at her with as much reassurance as he
could muster. He wanted to tell her how distant she had
been recently and how it didn't matter any more as long
as both she and Lottie got better. As often as he could,
he told her he loved her, that things would be fine, that
they would get through this together. Sometimes she
cried quietly and reached out for his hand. All he could
do was take it and hold it, yet inside there was the
immense weight of his betrayal.

I'll have to live with this, he thought. I'm ashamed
of myself, mainly because I knew what the
consequences could be, but I still carried on.

It was early morning when they arrived in Singapore for
a three-hour stop over before the onward flight to
Melbourne. Helen seemed more awake and a little
brighter. After changing terminals, they found
somewhere to sit and he went in search of drinks.
When he got back, she was hunched up in the seat, her
head down.

'Helen,' he said. She raised her head, brushing tears
away with impatience.

David placed both cups on the seat beside him and
put his arm around her shoulders. He was running out
of things to say to comfort her, so he pulled her close.
He passed the hot drink and she appeared to feel better
after a few sips.

'One minute you look fine,' he said, 'then you lose it. What sets you off? Is it thinking about Lottie?'

Helen wiped her face on her sleeve. 'I'm not sure,' she said. 'It comes over me like a flood, and when it does, I've no control. A lovely Australian couple asked if I was OK. I felt so embarrassed.'

David sat forward, his elbows on his knees. His back ached after fourteen hours on the plane, and he was struggling to ease it. He said, 'Try to explain it to me. I want to help you, but I don't know how.'

Helen seemed to be thinking, and David waited before prompting her again. 'Please, Helen, try to explain what you're going through. I feel dreadful too. I ache. My stomach isn't sure what to make of the airline food and I'm worried about what we face when we get to Melbourne. I know we'll get through it somehow, and you have to believe it too.'

'It isn't that simple,' she said. 'It isn't only worrying about Lottie or about the stuff I've left undone at school.'

'Tell me what it is then.'

'I'm not sure you'll understand, I'm not sure I understand.'

'Try me,' David said. 'Try telling me how you feel and it might help us both.'

Helen took a short inward breath, then she exhaled slowly, as if using some trick to compose herself. She leant back in the seat.

'It's the panic,' she said. 'Sometimes I seem to be gaining control of myself, then I have an attack of panicky feelings, which start here,' she put a hand on her stomach, 'then spread out and I can't do anything to stop them.'

'Is it obvious when it starts?' he asked. 'Will I

know?'

'No, not really. I want to run away from it, like you would if it was real panic, like a man with a gun suddenly appearing. I want to run, but there's no point because I would only be taking it with me, so I hold it inside.'

'And you felt like this last night, when I told you about Lottie?'

'I've had these attacks for a few months now,' she said, 'possibly longer.'

David sat up and looked at his wife. 'A few months?' he exclaimed. 'Why didn't you tell me?'

'Because,' she said, her lip trembling, 'because I thought they would go away, like a sore throat or a cold. I thought I could get on with everything, keep busy, and they would stop. At first, they were only when I woke up in the morning, then I started having them during the day, and recently they've got worse.'

'Why didn't you tell me?' he asked again.

Helen let out a frustrated sigh. 'I didn't tell you, I haven't told anyone, because I thought I could sort it out myself. And you would have told me I was working too hard, doing too much, needed to retire, and that wouldn't have helped at all.'

'I would have been right,' David said, trying to sound gentle, exasperated that she had got herself into this state, although it wasn't the right time to say so, not yet.

They sat for a few moments watching a family establish themselves on a row of seats. The children were young, one barely walking. Both parents looked tired, but their off-spring sat patiently as Mum handed out biscuits and fruit. David watched the oldest child, a serious-looking boy, take one of the younger ones on his knee.

'Can you imagine doing this journey with little ones?' he said.

Helen shook her head. 'It feels like I'm dreaming, as if none of this is real. I feel as if I'm another person in another life.'

'Are you panicking now?' David asked.

'No,' she said. 'There's a knot inside me, but that's normal. I'm scared of the panic though, because I can't stop it once it starts. Do you remember I had this once before, when Mum died? It was soon after Lottie was born?'

'I remember you going to the doctor and refusing pills, but I don't remember it being quite like this. I still feel hurt, and a bit cross with you for not telling me.'

'You know I hate being ill,' she said. 'It makes me feel like I'm not in charge of myself.'

'But when you broke your wrist all those years ago and had that virus in your throat the year Lizzie went to university, now the flu this Christmas, you weren't like this. And because I knew you were ill, I could do something,' David said. 'How is admitting that you have panic attacks any different?'

'I suppose,' she said, hesitation in her voice, 'all those other things I couldn't help, so it wasn't a weakness. This isn't happening because someone has died, or because I've caught a virus. This is coming from inside of me, so it's my fault, it's a sign I'm not coping, and I couldn't bear anyone to think that.'

'Not even me?'

She didn't answer.

If he hadn't been so tired, so concerned about her state of mind, David could have lost his temper. To think she had brought herself to this through her own stubbornness, had carried on knowing it was hurting them, unable to give in and admit she was ill. And she'd told no one; not him, not even Debbie, her best friend. She'd put her own pride, her bloody mindedness, her need to do it all single-handedly or else lose face, before everything else that mattered.

And I haven't even started on why she's not eating properly, he thought. He put his arm round her again and wondered what to say next. I will tell her, he thought. When she's stronger, she needs to know exactly what I think.

'What can I do to help you?' he asked. 'I'm glad you've told me, I'm not sure I understand completely, but it's a start.'

'I don't know what you can do. I have to do this myself.'

'No, you don't,' he said impatiently. 'There must be something that will help, something I can do.'

'Just be with me, next to me, but then I suppose you've no choice for the moment, have you?'

The second flight passed much as the first. At one point, the pilot announced that they were flying over Western Australia, but when David looked at his watch it would be another five hours before they touched down, reminding him of the vastness of this country. Below them the red-brown earth and empty nothingness seemed to stretch relentlessly. He stopped quizzing Helen about the panic attacks, but insisted she told him when she was having one, even if there was nothing he could do. He suggested films for her to watch and found a selection of television programmes he thought she might like, hopefully to take her mind away from the continuing anxiety. When the food trays came he intervened as she tried to wave them away.

'There's usually fruit and yoghurt,' he said. 'At least try something. You have to eat, Helen, the steward on the last flight was concerned about you.'

She was surprisingly compliant and seemed ready to do what he suggested. It was as if everything she was going through had sucked the fight from her. He recalled her words from the previous night; "tell me what to do". If that was working for the moment, perhaps he needed to keep on doing it.

Watching her as she slept made him wonder where the years had gone. She was showing her age, regardless of the bright hair tone, which was a little too blonde for his liking. He preferred her natural pale-brown colour, although, like him, she was almost certainly partly grey. The weight loss had started to affect the shape of her face, which had lost its normal healthy look. He thought about their earlier conversation and wondered if he would need to find a doctor for her in Melbourne. The landing was bumpy. David took Helen's hand during the final approach and said, 'We're here at last. Any panics?'

'A few.'

'You didn't tell me,' he scolded.

'You were asleep.'

'No excuse. You tell me, Helen, every time, all right?'

She looked at him. 'I'm frightened,' she said, 'about what happens next.'

'So am I, but we'll cope. We need to see Lottie, then we'll take it from there.'

Helen rested her head on his shoulder as the plane started to taxi towards the terminal building. David turned to her and whispered, 'I love you.'

Helen kissed his cheek, 'I don't know why,' she said softly.

'No, neither do I come to think of it,' he replied. 'As soon as you're feeling better, and Lottie's on the mend, I'll expect you to remind me.'

Helen kissed him again. 'There,' she said. 'First reminder.'

'Well, at least it's a start, if only a small one.'

As they came through customs, they noticed a tall figure, waving madly. It was Chris, easy to spot amongst the crowds, with Jenny beside him. Jenny hugged them both and offered kind words and reassurance, although Helen seemed to have frozen. He knew she was in the throes of anxiety, so he put his hand in hers and did all the talking.

'Can we go straight to the hospital?' he asked.

Chris said that they could, and had assumed that was what they would want to do.

'It isn't too far from here,' he said. 'We saw Charlotte only this morning. She's a bit wired up to bits of medical equipment, but she can't wait to see you. The news about her progress is still very positive.'

'Thanks,' David said, 'for all you've done and for having us to stay earlier than planned.'

'Stay as long as you want,' Jenny said.

He was grateful for these friends. He had known Jenny ever since he could remember. When she married Chris, they'd been part of a larger group of friends, all with young families. Their boys had played with Lizzie and Lottie and the rest of the children for years until different secondary schools had loosened the childhood friendships established by their parents. Then, about ten years ago, Chris and Jenny had surprised them all by announcing their intention to emigrate and start a business in Melbourne. Helen and Jenny had never been very close, but David missed the couple, especially Chris, who was a keen hiker, DIY enthusiast and Friday night drinking pal at the pub in the village.

At the car, Jenny opened one of the rear doors to get in the back with Helen, but David shook his head.

'We'll both get in the back,' he said. 'Helen's exhausted, she may need a shoulder to fall asleep on.'

Helen had hardly said a word. Once in the car he pulled her to him and mouthed, 'OK?' She squeezed his hand, but he sensed she was struggling.

Chris went through all the practical information he had about Lottie, her boyfriend Harry and the accident. He paused, letting Jenny step in with more details.

'You'll like Harry,' she said. 'Poor guy feels terrible that she took the brunt of it.'

David listened, quizzing Chris about everything the doctors had said. As he built up a picture of the injuries, he began to feel calmer. None seemed so serious that they wouldn't heal with time. The journey passed quickly, swift carriageways emerging into city congestion then neatly laid-out suburbs. Chris negotiated the route with the ease of a driver in familiar surroundings. David had been momentarily distracted by the Melbourne skyline which was impressive, but as they approached the hospital, his stomach lurched.

He was glad that Chris and Jenny knew the way to Lottie's ward, as the whole place seemed to be a warren of corridors and stairs with a bewildering system of lifts. Helen's hand in his was hot and sticky, in spite of the cool air, but she kept her head up and responded to Jenny's chatter with smiles and nods and the occasional few words.

His daughter was in a small room of four beds.

Pushed back with a clip, her hair lay in limp strands, but apart from a bruise on her forehead, she looked tanned and surprisingly well. Her wrist lay over the covers in a plaster cast and it was the sight of the small, trapped fingers, curving out uselessly, that moved David.

She opened her eyes, saw them and her face broke into a huge smile, which soon became tears as both he and Helen hugged her carefully.

David wasn't sure what to say. How are you feeling? seemed inadequate. 'We've missed you,' was all he managed.

'I've missed you, too,' Lottie said. 'I'm so glad you're here. Chris and Jenny have been great, but I wanted you.' She dabbed uselessly at the tears and sniffed. David passed the box of tissues from the bedside cabinet, realising that he had spent most of the last two days passing tissues and hankies to the women in his life. Someday he would give in to his own emotions and have a good bawl, but that would have to wait.

He sat on the edge of the bed and took her hand. 'Well, here we are,' he said. ' You're going to get better and we're here to do whatever we can, so don't worry about a thing.'

'I feel so stupid,' she sobbed. 'I never realised a little accident could do so much damage.'

David shrugged. 'That'll teach you to look both ways.'

'I thought I had. That car came from nowhere.'

Helen sat in the bedside chair, listening. David glanced at her and it suddenly hit him how tired she looked and how strange he felt after the long flight.

He said to Lottie, 'We'll stay for a while, if you want, but we both need a good night's sleep. I don't think either of us realised how tiring that flight is.'

'Mum, you don't look too good,' Lottie said.

Helen pulled the chair round and managed a convincing smile. 'I'm exhausted,' she said.

'But you look…' Lottie hesitated, 'different, somehow.'

'She's fine.' David said. 'She just needs some sleep and some real food.' He turned to Helen. 'What happened to Chris and Jenny?'

'I think they must have waited in the corridor,' Helen replied.

'Pop out and see if you can spot them,' David said. 'Tell them we won't be much longer.'

As Helen left the ward, David took Lottie's hand and said quickly, 'Mum isn't very well, it's nothing serious, but she's been working far too hard and she's got herself very stressed. The shock of all this and the long flight haven't helped.'

'Her face looks different, sort of older and thinner.'

'She's lost a bit of weight recently, but I'm sure she'll pick up now she's away from work. Don't worry about Mum, she'll be fine, but don't be surprised if she doesn't seem herself. I wanted to warn you.'

'You're sure it's nothing worse, you're not hiding something Dad? I'm not so injured I can't take it, I want to know.'

'Honestly, love, she looks thin because she hasn't been eating properly. She's been so busy, you know what she's like. I'm sure that being away from it all will be good for her.'

'Lizzie's OK?'

'Lizzie's great and she sends her love. You'll be able to speak to her soon.'

Lottie's face started to crumple again and she

whispered, 'I'm so glad you're here.'

Much as he would have liked to stay at the hospital, David knew he and Helen needed to get some sleep and Chris and Jenny would want to get home. Perhaps they could consider hiring a car, even renting their own place for a month if necessary. They had flown out three weeks early, so there would be roughly six weeks before their return flights and Helen's school would re-open after the Easter break. But we'll stay as long as we need to, he thought, or even take Lottie home with us and I could look after her.

Helen returned, so he took the chance to talk through his daughter's progress with one of the nurses. David listened carefully, then realised he wasn't taking in much of the information as he found himself submerged by a huge swell of exhaustion. He gripped the edge of the desk.

'Are you OK?' the nurse asked.

'Jet lag,' he said. 'We've never done this long flight before.'

'You need to get home. I'll tell Lottie it's time she had some rest, give you the chance to leave.'

David almost protested, but the girl, who didn't look much older than Lottie, took complete charge, told her to say goodbye to the visitors and started to re-arrange pillows and check drips and tubes and monitors. Lottie said goodbye and David was grateful to see someone else taking care of things. He squeezed his daughter's good hand, kissed her cheek, said they would see her tomorrow.

He took Helen's arm as they left the ward to walk back to the car.

'How are you doing, love? OK?'

She nodded.

'Some tough times ahead,' he said, 'but we're all going to be fine.'

Helen was quiet, then she said, 'You're probably right, but I don't feel it yet, I can't even imagine feeling it.'

'You will,' he insisted. 'Then things must change, Helen. And I'm not just talking about Lottie, I'm talking about us.'

'I don't know how to change,' she whispered.

'Well I do,' he said, 'so you don't need to worry.'

They stepped outside the hospital into the warm, autumnal evening.

'29 degrees tomorrow,' Jenny announced. 'Now, I know Lottie's your priority, but you both look like you need a holiday. Stay with us as long as you like, you'll see we've plenty of room, enough for Lottie as well if she can't go back to her apartment when she's discharged.'

'You've done so much already,' David said, 'but thanks, both of you. We'll have to take things one day at a time.'

As they drove out of the city and headed down towards Brighton, where Chris and Jenny lived, David took in some of his surroundings and a sense of relief began to spread. They had managed the journey, seen their daughter and found reassurance from the hospital staff that she would recover. Just as importantly, he felt that his wife had spoken to him with some honesty. For the foreseeable future, his responsibilities were clear. What wasn't clear, and maybe never would be, were his feelings for Karen. Helen had said she kept the panic inside, told no one, coped alone. I have to do the same, he thought. I must keep this inside, but what if I can't? What if I end up having to tell Helen or worse than that, she finds out?

David's sigh was loud enough for his wife to glance at him. 'It's nothing,' he said. 'Another conversation for another day.'

Chapter 20

Looking back, Helen could remember little about the journey, from the wait at Manchester through to their arrival in Melbourne. At Changi Airport, Singapore, they had ventured out onto the orchid roof garden and retreated due to the intense humidity, but when David reminded her of this later, she had only a vague memory of it happening. What she did remember, however, in every painful detail, were the events of the evening before the flight; every word she and David had said to each other, the anger she saw in his face when he held her against the wall, the collapse of her own will to do anything. All of it was crystal clear.

As the weeks passed, she was accepting a gradual change in herself. At first, in between visits to the hospital, she needed to sleep, and if David wasn't nearby when she awoke, panic flooded through her and gripped and twisted deep inside until he returned. Whenever they left the house she held on to him. Eating, especially in front of their friends, was a trial. She found herself crying at unexpected moments, embarrassed and helpless. He was unfailingly patient, reassuring, but she wondered how he felt about this complete and utter dependence on her part that was so alien to them both.

'I'm sorry,' she repeated. 'I don't want to be like this.'

And David would say, 'there's nothing to be sorry for. Don't worry, we'll get through it.'

Towards the end of the third week, the need to sleep lessened, the panic attacks eased, and Helen realised she was regaining a little confidence. As her thoughts began to clear, she realised how dreadfully she had behaved on the evening before they left. What sort of a mother puts her work before a seriously injured child, however old that child might be? In her darker moments, Helen was appalled at herself; there was even a sense of fear at her own capacity to be so unfeeling, and she knew how badly she had treated David. He was the only thing that stood between herself and a complete breakdown.

When Lottie was discharged from hospital, she came to stay with her parents at Chris and Jenny's, recovering slowly, lapping up the attention but frustrated by her injuries. Helen enjoyed spending time with her daughter and the two of them tried to make light of the problems of washing and dressing and moving around. Every evening, David and Helen would carry her up to bed, usually after a few glasses of wine, so it was with good humour.

They met her boyfriend, Harry, when she was still in hospital and both liked the guy. He was working in Australia for a year before taking up a job as an accountant at the end of August back in the UK. Harry was an easy companion, besotted with their daughter and devastated that he hadn't managed to do something to avoid the accident.

The house in Brighton was delightful with cool, marble-floored rooms and a covered outdoor area leading to patios and a small pool. It was set a few blocks from the beach; the long promenade stretching towards the city in one direction and south along the

Mornington Peninsula in the other. As Jenny had said, there was plenty of room and even ministering to Lottie's every need didn't stop Helen feeling like she was on holiday.

She had started to think about her school and she wondered how Bridget and Jen were managing. She had been in contact by e-mail. Their replies were cheerful and positive but seemed deliberately vague. If she asked whether something had been done, the reply was always, yes it had, don't worry.

One morning, when Chris and Jenny were out, Helen sat in her bikini on the edge of the pool, her feet in the water. The sun warmed her pale winter skin and she knew she should find a shirt, but the combination of cold and heat was quite intoxicating, taking her to a place where her senses took over and all her thoughts settled. There was a scent of something strange and exotic in Australia, which she couldn't quite describe, and the light had a sharpness, sometimes a glare in the strong sun. She listened to the birdsong. It was more like random calling than song, different from the chatter of English sparrows and starlings and blackbirds. In that moment, alone in the garden, feeling the heat and letting all the sounds replace any conscious thought, Helen felt at peace for the first time in months.

David came across the lawn, picked up her towel and threw it around her shoulders.

'You'll burn,' he said.

It was a sudden intrusion; the peace had been disturbed. She shrugged off the towel.

'I think,' she said, swishing her feet about, 'that you can stop being so bossy.'

'Really?' he said, sitting down next to her, lowering his feet into the water. 'You're ready for that, are you?'

'I'm feeling more normal, more like me again.'

'Well, that's good,' he said, 'in one respect.'

She turned towards him, frowning slightly. 'What do you mean?'

'I mean it's good that you're feeling better, but I think we need to talk about what normal is, because I don't think you and I have had normal for a while.'

Helen didn't reply. She knew exactly what he meant, but was unsure how to respond. For over a year she had sometimes looked at her husband and wondered if she still loved him in quite the same way. When the business had sold, he seemed to lose some of his purpose, some definition as a person, and as she had carried on with her work outside their domestic world, he seemed to diminish into it. She tried to appreciate the cooking and cleaning and other household stuff that he did so easily, but it seemed trivial; her duties as a headteacher, Simon's school and the rest of her work becoming larger, more important in her mind. When she had been sharp with him, irritable or insensitive, he had retreated into his shed or gone off walking. Helen could recall occasions where he had tried to get through to her and she had dismissed him impatiently.

'Tell me,' she said, getting up and reaching for a cotton shirt as she crossed the patio to sit on one of the sun loungers, 'tell me what hasn't been normal.'

David stared into the water, then down at the ripples around his ankles. She waited.

'For the last few weeks,' he began, 'in fact since we came here, you've needed me almost every waking moment and I've been there for you. You won't drive or go out on your own. I've only this week felt that you could manage if I leave you in the house without me. Can you imagine how this feels when, for the last year, you've sometimes behaved as though my presence was quite unnecessary?'

Helen wished he would turn to look at her. She wanted to see his expression, gauge his mood, but he carried on looking at the water.

'I can't imagine,' she said.

'And you needing me like this,' he said, 'is fine. If I'm honest, I love it, Helen, really love it, because it's so much better than you not needing me at all, you pushing me away to go and do something more important, usually your work. When we both worked, there was a balance, and there could still have been a balance between us, but you just carried on tipping it your way.'

Helen felt the need to defend herself. Everything he said was true, but there were reasons why she had been so stressed.

'I don't think you've ever realised what my job's like,' she said. 'I have to put in hours and hours to keep my head above water, and now there are the other schools I support, the travelling about, the conferences. There's so much responsibility, so many things that need to be done thoroughly – I can't always delegate. It would have helped if you could have understood that a bit more.'

He got up suddenly and came over to where she was sitting. Helen could sense his annoyance as he dragged a sun lounger next to hers and sat down heavily. Her words of a moment ago about her job sounded petulant and defensive. I've said the wrong thing, she thought, of course he knows what my job's like.

'Let me ask you something,' he said looking straight at her, 'and I think you're well enough to hear this. Did you ever stop to think how I felt when the business sold? I admit, we were both surprised at how quickly Mike and Rosemary came along and wanted to buy it, and the sale made us financially secure for the rest of our lives. I felt so proud knowing that all those years spent building it up had paid off and I could relieve you of the stress because you wouldn't need to work any more. And then, when the initial euphoria of handing it over and banking the money had worn off, I missed it so much. You like being in charge, don't you? Well so did I, and not having that was like an essential piece of me was missing.'

Despite the heat, Helen shivered. His words were starting to bite and it hurt.

'You never told me any of this.'

'No, I never said anything because I knew I had to accept it, I couldn't go back, and anyway, I thought you'd be retiring soon and we'd be able to do all the things we planned to do. Then nothing changed. You wouldn't even discuss finishing work and I was left feeling more and more distant from you, and not having a clue how I was going to break through that barrier you put up.'

'You should have told me how you were feeling,' she said, hearing a note of desperation in her voice.

David snorted. 'That's rich coming from you.'

He flung himself back on the lounger. Helen could hear his breathing as she tried to sort out her own thoughts. She was starting to see things from a different angle and it felt uncomfortable. She glanced at him, this man she had lived with for almost thirty years, the father of her children. In a long relationship you shared so much, made it through the great, and the not-so-great, times together. But you changed, you didn't love in the same way in your 50s as you did in your 20s and 30s. I'm sure I love him, she thought, but like a lot of things just at the moment, I can't feel it. She admitted to herself how devotedly he had cared for her during the last few weeks and she swallowed to check the familiar bubble of tears that were welling up.

'I'm sorry,' she said.

He turned.

'You shut me out. It was as if I wasn't important to you any more.'

Helen sat up and took his arm.

'Don't let me get like that again,' she said softly.

David pushed her away.

'How?' he said, the anger in his voice unnerving Helen. 'How do I do that? You're a formidable force when you want to be.'

She put her hands to her face. 'But I can't stop myself.'

'Yes you can, you have to. Much as I would like to do it for you, Helen, I can't. I had to get blazing angry just to get you to listen to me, but let's face it, I can't make you do anything, you have to do it yourself.' He paused, then said more gently, 'Try to think about my feelings, sometimes. I do that for you all the time – when you let me.'

Helen pulled her knees up, wrapped her arms around them and put her head down. He was right in every respect, but she didn't know how to admit it and she had no idea where they went from here. She heard him get up and move to sit by her, felt his body next to hers, his arm across her shoulders.

'All I seem to do is cry on you,' she said, wiping her

eyes on his tee shirt.

'It's all right, I can take it,' he said lightly.

They sat in silence for a few moments. She said, 'now, sitting here with you, I can only say I love you, and I'm sorry.'

David took her hands. 'I love you too,' he said, 'and don't you ever forget it.'

'Is there anything else?' she asked. 'Is there anything else you need to tell me?'

She saw him hesitate, run a hand through his hair and she wondered what was in his mind.

'When was the last time we made love?' he asked. 'I don't mean the last time we had sex, I mean the last time you were actually there with me?'

Helen gave a shrug. 'I know, I know,' she responded, 'but I never seem to feel in the mood. It's probably my hormones, and when we get into bed at night I'm tired out. We're both older now, so…'

'Older? I might be older, but I still want to do it.'

'I'll try, I promise.'

'Let's try now.'

Helen smiled at him, slightly alarmed, a little bit pleased. 'Now?'

'Yes, Lottie's still asleep, everyone else is out.'

He took her hand and led her inside, across the coolness of the kitchen, through the hall and up the stairs. Helen could feel the beginnings of something familiar inside her and she knew that it wasn't another panic attack.

The bathroom door slammed and they heard Lottie shuffling about.

At the top of the stairs David stopped.

'Drat,' he exclaimed.

She felt his hand grip hers. 'You're not getting away

with this,' he said.

She grinned. 'What makes you think I want to?'

Helen began to realise that they were in Australia for a holiday, not just to look after their daughter. They wheeled Lottie down to the beach and lifted her onto the sand. She insisted on going in the sea, so, with much laughter and encouragement from onlookers, they carried her to the edge, where she paddled her good leg and even managed to splash David when he wasn't looking.

'Unfair,' he protested. 'I can't splash you.'

At this point, Helen, who was supporting Lottie, reached down and scooped a handful of water in his direction.

In the evening, David cooked for everyone on the barbecue. Harry called after work and wine was consumed in liberal quantities. Helen took the chance to thank their hosts for their hospitality.

'You must let us pay you or something,' she said.

'Absolutely not,' Chris responded. 'And anyway, when we come back to Lancashire next year, where do you think we're staying?'

Harry insisted on clearing up with David and cleaning the barbecue. Helen watched him kiss her daughter before he left. She was pleased with Harry. He seemed more sensible than some of Lottie's previous boyfriends.

As she loaded the dishwasher, Jenny waved Helen and David away.

'Get Lottie up to bed,' she said, 'this will only take me a moment.'

'I can do it myself,' Lottie said. 'Watch me.'

She sat on the bottom step letting the crutches

clatter to the floor, then she shuffled up the stairs backwards using her good leg and arm to push herself up. They applauded as she made the top step.

'Great,' David said, 'your mum and I can go and have another drink, leave you to get yourself to bed.'

Lottie pretended to whimper. 'I need my crutches, they're still at the bottom,' she wailed. 'Don't abandon me.'

David collected the crutches and took the stairs two at a time. Helen watched him pull Lottie up and place them under her elbows so that she could hobble into the bathroom.

'Mum,' she called, 'I need you now please.'

Helen smiled to herself. Lizzie would have worked out a way to manage all these things on her own by now, but Lottie had never felt the need to be independent if someone was there to help. As she climbed the stairs, Helen wondered briefly which of her daughters had got it right.

It had become routine for Helen to get Lottie into bed, then leave her talking with David for a few minutes. As she kissed her daughter and made for the door, he got up and followed her.

'Be back in a minute,' she heard him say to Lottie.

Helen was aware of him following her then taking her arm as she pushed open the door to their room.

'Don't undo a button,' he whispered, 'not one.'

Helen laughed softly.

'There aren't any buttons,' she said, her hands touching the shoulder ties on her dress.

'You know what I mean.'

'I think I can remember.'

He kissed her on the mouth and darted back to Lottie's bedroom.

Helen switched on the bedside lamp, then she slid open the terrace doors to let the cooler air into the room. She shook off her flip-flops and stepped outside, enjoying the smooth surface of the tiles under her feet. Gentle sounds; cars, occasional voices, a dog barking in the distance seemed to expand the night and she noticed the softness of lamplight between the trees. It was all enveloped in the exotic, earthy scent of this place that she was beginning to associate with a feeling of calm. It settled on her as she breathed. The sky was full of stars, strange constellations that seemed almost familiar, yet different in their brightness and their shape from those in a Lancashire sky. That's Australia, she thought. We recognise everything about it, but essentially, it's different.

She heard a noise and turned as David pushed the curtain aside. She started to ask if Lottie was all right, but he kissed her before she could speak, then took her by the hand and led her back into the bedroom.

He undressed her, ran his hands carefully over every part of her as if he needed to confirm something that he had never forgotten. She reached out to switch off the lamp, but he raised a finger and shook his head.

'No,' he said. 'You always do that. I want to look at you.'

They made love in their familiar, easy way and Helen was surprised at how readily she was able to respond. She was even more surprised at his passion. She felt as if he was trying to prove something to her, or was it to himself? Afterwards, as they lay on the bed, enjoying the gentle breeze from the open door, he put an arm across her body and said, 'That's better,' before falling asleep.

Helen lay awake for a while, listening to his

breathing. She remembered his words from earlier in the day, turned them over in her mind, realised that whatever had happened in the past year, this was a chance for change. She rolled onto her side and he pulled her close as he did most nights, even on those occasions when they had seemed to be distant and unhappy.

In the morning, he reached out for her, but she placed a hand on his wrist as she was already trying to steady herself through an attack of panic.

'Again?' she said.

'Yes.'

'In the morning?'

'Yes. Are you rushing off to work or something?'

'We hardly ever do it in the morning.'

'We could start,' he said. 'And anyway, it's night-time back home. My body clock hasn't adjusted yet.'

Helen turned to face him. 'I'm having a panic,' she said.

'So? It might make it go away.'

'You're not taking no for an answer, are you?'

'No. Now stop talking and trying to put me off. Relax. Let's try an experiment, see if it makes you feel better.'

Helen gave in. Later, as they dressed, she realised that there were a lot of things that unexpectedly made her feel better; spending time with Lottie and David, swimming length after length in the pool until she was exhausted, sitting in the garden emptying her mind so that her senses could take over.

I always believed that work and more work and keeping going cured everything, she thought. I was frightened of stopping in case I couldn't start again but

I was wrong, because you have to stop in order to change the way you do things. I needed this break, but I couldn't see it and no one could have told me.

Helen remembered fainting in the school office, the increase in the anxiety attacks, moments when she felt angry for no reason and then there was her worsening relationship with food. It had been so obvious that something was wrong.

After David had gone downstairs, she slipped out of her sun dress and looked critically at the mirror. Throughout her life, friends had envied her slim figure and long legs. She considered the reflection and tried to be honest. She placed a hand on her flat stomach, which was good and yet not so good. She had never minded having small breasts, but the area above was bony with arms that looked painfully thin, the skin hanging in fine creases that she hadn't noticed before. When she moved her hands to skim over her hips she felt the bones sticking out like two handles. But the worst part was her face. Jenny said she seemed to have lost weight from her cheeks and Helen had to admit that it added considerable years.

She recalled the conversation a few days ago. At times, Jenny irritated her. She had strong opinions and let you know about them. Yet there was an honesty in what she said, even if you didn't want to hear it.

'If you were a teenager,' Jenny had told her, 'one of your girls, for example, you would have been taken to see a specialist about this eating thing long before now.'

Helen hadn't known what to say. The thought of visiting a doctor, admitting she wasn't eating and then being told to eat more, seemed pointless. She tried to explain to Jenny how she felt, but it didn't make much sense, although Jenny listened and sympathised and asked what might help.

'Can we cook some things you like?' she asked.

Helen hesitated and thought about this. 'Yes,' she said, 'but I think it's mainly about letting me control it. If I can control the portion size, I'm more likely to eat it all. If I'm presented with a plate full of food I'm put off even before I've started, so I end up eating hardly anything.'

'Leave some,' Jenny said. 'No one's forcing you to eat it all, you're not a child.'

'I know,' Helen said, 'but it's something to do with having to clear your plate, like we were always expected to do as children. And David watches me like a hawk. Sometimes I push it all in a corner to make it look as if I'm only leaving a little bit.'

'David's doing his best,' Jenny said. 'He's worried about you.'

Helen sighed, 'I know,' she said, 'but when he tries to make me eat more it becomes a sort of power thing and it makes me worse.'

Jenny shook her head and looked at Helen in exasperation. 'David's worried. Come on, you're an intelligent woman, a headteacher. Either start eating more or you'll end up at the doctors. If you can't eat for yourself, do it to please David? Don't let it continue to be an issue, that's all in your mind. Do what he's telling you to do and be grateful he cares enough to keep trying.'

At the time, Helen had felt rather told off, but she accepted Jenny's words and now, looking at herself in the mirror, she knew that everyone else was right and she was wrong. Whatever this eating issue was all about, it was another thing that had to change.

She put her dress back on, thought briefly about England where they would still be wrapped up against the March winds and couldn't help feeling smug. Then, thoughts of school came into her head; end of term assessments, Simon, the conference she was missing. I need to ring them now I'm feeling better, she decided.

She ignored the unsettled feeling that returned to her stomach as she thought about her job and went downstairs to try and tackle some breakfast.

Chapter 21

'Cup of tea?' Jenny shouted. 'Or do you guys want a beer?'

David wiped his forehead and looked at Chris, who was holding the top of the fence post.

'Beer,' Chris said. 'It's scorching out here.'

David nodded and called, 'Beer please.' He steadied the base of the post as Chris hammered it into place, then the two of them slid the fence panel between the posts and stood back to check the level.

'Thanks mate,' Chris said, 'that's straight enough. Another job to tick off Jenny's list.'

'I've told her to give me that list,' David said. 'It's the least I can do in return for taking over your home.'

Chris waved David's comment away, then said, 'No worries. It's great to see Lottie improving, and Helen, for that matter.'

They sat in the shade, their first beers slipping down easily. Chris went to get two more cans from the fridge and David chuckled to himself as he heard Jenny remonstrating with him about his alcohol consumption. He accepted the can gratefully and the two men sat without talking, sipping this second one more slowly. After a few minutes, David heard heavy breathing and he knew Chris was starting to doze.

David reclined the lounger and lay back, trying to remember the last time he had felt so relaxed. Their time in Australia was coming to an end and some honest conversations and gentle hours doing slow, ordinary things together, such as walking on the beach or strolling to the local shops were drawing them closer. And Helen was still letting him take charge of everything. She was starting to tease him about being bossy, about his organisation of each day, yet she seemed calmer, more content. He never mentioned her school or Simon's school, or any of the other things she did as part of her job. When she wondered aloud how the staff were managing without her, he had laughingly told her they were probably all doing much better on their own. Helen had threatened to ring school to get all the passwords so she could log on and start running things from Australia. He had responded by forbidding her to touch the phone, although he knew that she would do what she wanted. He also knew that this precious slice of time was temporary, a brief respite during which they had agreed to put major decisions aside. David dreaded the possibility that as Helen improved and regained some confidence, he could start to lose his grip on things and they would end up being back where they started.

As much as he loved this renewed closeness with his wife, he couldn't stop his thoughts returning to Karen. He had picked up his phone on a few occasions and started to compose a text message, but the words escaped him. He wondered how she was and he hoped she had been telling the truth when she said she didn't expect anything from him, because he knew he had nothing for her now. He wondered how some men managed to keep a mistress for years and years, loving two women in different ways, each woman having needs and expectations.

But in David's thoughts, it wasn't living with the two relationships that posed the problem, it was living with the guilt. Each time he eased himself into this new feeling of contentment, his conscience jabbed at him. When Helen kissed him or took his hand, when they lay close, his arm across her waist, he wondered if he would ever be able to do all these things without feeling sad that he had deceived her. Perhaps that would only come if he was honest and confessed everything. He sometimes framed words and sentences in his head; *Helen, I need to tell you something..., it meant nothing..., I feel so ashamed.* But it never sounded right, and how could he ever be completely honest? If he was, he would have to explain why he had enjoyed being close with another woman, and how could he possibly do that?

That evening, after another scorching day followed by drinks and a barbecue, Helen took herself and Lottie off to bed. Chris disappeared, so it was left to David and Jenny to clear glasses and crockery and put uneaten food in the fridge.

'Leave the grill,' she said as David started to wipe it down. 'Chris can do it tomorrow, he always takes off when it's clearing up time.'

'Where's he gone?'

He carried a pile of plates through to the kitchen and Jenny indicated the settee in the open-plan lounge. A pair of long legs and bare feet rested on the arm and Chris's peaceful snores drifted across. David ignored Jenny's order to leave things and resumed cleaning the barbecue.

She came out to the patio with the remains of a bottle of wine and two glasses.

'I told you to leave that,' she said.

David didn't answer, admiring his work as he polished the stainless steel to make it shine.

'I want one of these,' he said. 'I love it.'

'I love it too,' Jenny said, emptying the bottle into the glasses. 'I love it because it's a man cooker. A pity *he* conveniently forgets that it needs cleaning.'

David sat opposite Jenny and swirled the wine around the glass. She rubbed her finger at a stain on the table, then sat back in the chair.

'You and Helen look so much better than you did,' she said. 'I couldn't believe how ill Helen seemed when we met you at the airport. Lottie looked better than she did, in spite of her accident.'

'We're not there yet,' David said. 'Lottie's making great progress, but with Helen it's hard to say. Some days she seems to be fine, then she'll go quiet and withdrawn again.'

'What about work?'

'She hasn't mentioned it very much.'

'She got away without eating properly, tonight,' Jenny said.

'You noticed?'

'I try not to, but I notice it every time we eat together. You've had a lot to deal with, haven't you? Lottie's accident was a shock, but I think Helen's been worrying you for a long time.'

David felt the weight of good food in his stomach and the effects of Chris's excellent wine on his mood. He looked at Jenny, who seemed to be waiting for him to speak. They had been friends since infant school and she was like the sibling he never had. He watched her ruffle, then smooth her fine, silver blonde hair.

'Can I talk to you about Helen?' he said.

'I think,' she said looking at him, 'that it's time you talked to someone. You've put all your energies into your wife and daughter since you got here, and I know you wouldn't have it any other way, but there's more to this, isn't there? Chris thinks I'm reading too much into it, but he's always very black and white.'

'It's where to start,' David said, running his finger around the rim of the glass.

'Just start,' she replied. 'Anywhere.'

Once he began, David found he couldn't stop. Talking about it, finding the right words, explaining how he felt seemed to rearrange things in his head. He described his anxiety about Helen's eating, his fear before Christmas that the nights away and increasing distance between them was because she was having an affair, and his frustration at her unwillingness to retire. He told Jenny what had happened on the evening before they flew to Australia. Jenny listened. She asked questions but didn't comment until he finished.

'But where are you now?' she asked, reaching across the table and putting her hand on his arm.

'Better. We've talked some things through. We're much closer. I still can't seem to get her to commit to finishing work, but she has admitted that she needs to do it.'

'And you've no reason to believe she's had an affair?'

'None, only the nights away and her lack of interest in me.'

David took another mouthful of wine. It was beginning to taste rather bitter, but it was fuelling a desperate need to confess even more, to put some pressure on the sore spot of guilt and see how it felt when he did.

'You're a great guy,' Jenny said. 'I've always thought so, and after these last few weeks I still do, more than ever. You built up a good business, raised two lovely girls and you obviously love your wife so much that you'll do anything to help her through this bad patch. I wonder how I ended up with Chris when you were around, you're even better looking than he is.' Jenny added this last bit with a short laugh.

David hesitated, opened his mouth to speak, then stopped. He stared at his glass and he knew he was going to tell her about Karen, had to tell her. Suddenly he felt an astonishing rush of emotion and as he put his hands over his face it was to touch unfamiliar tears. He couldn't speak, and Jenny, realising something was wrong, turned to look at him.

'David,' she exclaimed. She shook his wrist. 'David, no, don't cry. What is it? Tell me.'

He reached in his pocket for a handkerchief, which wasn't there, so he got up and headed inside for a paper towel. He tried desperately to control the feelings welling up inside him. Where had they come from? Probably too much wine and the accumulated anguish that had been allowed to fester. He stumbled outside, annoyed with himself for becoming emotional.

The night air was hot and humid, but there was a cool, thin breeze, insignificant now, whispering change. The next day was set to be fresher with a plummet in temperatures, so typical of Melbourne.

I need some freshness, he thought. I need an icy blast that blows right through me, cleaning everything out, hurting, punishing, because I deserve it. I don't deserve to have this easiness here, this lovely time with Helen and Lottie and our friends.

He felt Jenny's hand in his and he looked at her.

'Tell me,' she said. 'It can't make it worse.'

David paused and searched for words. Then he took a deep breath.

'I'm really not as great as you think, Jenny,' he said

wiping his face, 'because there's something else.'

Jenny waited, but David didn't speak. He looked at her again and knew that telling her everything was exactly what he needed to do. Chris's snores from inside made them both smile. Jenny squeezed his hand.

'Go on,' she said.

'I said I thought Helen could have been having an affair, that may still be true, I don't know. What I do know is that it was me, not Helen who had the affair.'

He glanced at Jenny expecting to see shock or at least some surprise, but she was looking at him seriously, her eyebrows raised.

'Well I didn't expect that,' she said. 'So?'

'So, I want to tell you about it, but you need to promise this stays between us. I'd hate Chris to know and Helen – or anyone for that matter. I feel so ashamed, yet, at the same time...' His voice tailed off.

Jenny folded her arms.

'I won't judge,' she said, 'and I won't tell anyone, so come on, get it off your chest. If you can't tell me, I don't know who else you can tell, and I have to admit, I'm intrigued.'

David paused, then he began.

'She was called Karen – is called Karen. I met her through the walking group. She needed some jobs doing at her house so I went round a few times to put shelves together, that sort of thing and we got on really well. We climbed Loughrigg in February with another couple, to plan a walk. They went off to check out a different path, so we were on our own. By the time we got back to the car I'd kissed her. It took its own course from there.'

'You slept with her?'

The question was blunt and David hesitated. Of

course he had slept with her, it wouldn't have been an affair otherwise, but it was as if he couldn't put it into words.

Jenny sighed and said, 'Silly question, isn't it?'

'Once. I stayed at her house the night before we got the news about Lottie.'

'I'm presuming it's over?' Jenny said. 'I say that, because I've never seen a guy as devoted to his wife as you've been since you came here.'

'It's over. It should never have happened. I've betrayed Helen, who I should have supported while she was going through a hard time, but I've also hurt Karen, and she doesn't deserve it.'

'You haven't been in touch since you came out here?'

David shook his head. 'I went to see her briefly the night before we flew, to tell her about Lottie and to let her know that I'd be going to Australia. I think we both knew that it was over. She didn't hesitate, she told me to put my family first but I could feel her disappointment. And the worst guilt for me is that the few weeks we had together, I really enjoyed. When Helen was being so difficult and could hardly look at me, Karen was offering me everything. And I took it.'

'It's not an excuse,' Jenny said pointedly.

'I know that.'

'Does Helen have any idea?' she asked.

'No,' David said. 'She's met Karen once, and I've never hidden the fact I was visiting her to do jobs on the house, but that's all. It's funny, but after they met on New Year's Day Helen joked that Karen fancied me and I felt flattered. At the time, I brushed it off. I liked her, but I never thought we would start an affair. It sounds rather flippant to say that it just happened, but it did, and now I need to end it in the right way. I don't know whether ending it in the right way also means I have to tell Helen.'

There was a grunt and a thud from inside the house.

'He's fallen off the sofa,' Jenny said, 'and not for the first time.' She got up and went through to tell Chris to go to bed. David heard the impatient, rather exasperated tone she often used with her husband, then he could hear Chris's bare feet flopping heavily down the hall. She came back with more wine and topped up the glasses as they sat in silence for a moment.

'I can't believe you went to bed with another woman,' Jenny said at last. 'Of all the guys in our group, you would be last I would have thought might have an affair.' She smiled slyly at him. 'Come on, tell me who made the first move.'

'It wasn't like that,' David protested.

'Come off it, David. I bet it was you. It's always the man, isn't it?'

'Actually, no. She made the first move. She suggested I stayed the night, said it wouldn't mean anything, it was the two of us needing each other at that moment. And in the end, she was kind of scared and that made it even more appealing.'

Jenny snorted. 'Huh, and you believed all that rubbish, did you? You're so naive. No woman says that sort of stuff and means it. Believe me, this Karen wanted you.'

David started picking up his glass and the bottle. 'Right, that's it,' he said. 'I've told you quite enough, and if you're not going to believe me, there's no point telling you any more.'

'Hey,' Jenny said. 'Don't take it like that.

Remember how well I know you, and I think you've been taken in.'

David looked at her. 'You don't know me as well as you think,' he said sitting down again. 'I'm not sure I know myself any more, and I daren't even contemplate what Helen or the girls would think of me.'

'I can't think of one good reason to tell Helen,' Jenny said abruptly. 'Have you thought about how she would react?'

'Of course I have. But if I don't tell her, I live with the guilt of knowing I've deceived her and honesty has always been important to me, regardless of the consequences.'

'It got you into trouble once or twice as I recall,' she said. 'Remember the milk bottles we dropped at the old lady's house across the road? If you'd told your mum the lie we prepared, we'd have got away with it, but you had to tell the truth, didn't you?'

'Come on, Jenny, I was only five, and you always were a bad influence.' David glanced across, trying to gauge her thoughts. 'I don't know what you must think of me now.'

'I think,' she said, 'that I like knowing you're not the perfect husband after all.'

'You're not shocked, disappointed in me, even a little bit?'

'Surprised,' Jenny said, as if she was searching for words. 'But I think that coming to terms with this is more about making a good end, like you said, finishing it in the right way. That means telling Karen it's over, but definitely never telling Helen. And if you have to live with your guilt, alone, then that's the price you pay, because there's always a price for this sort of thing, isn't there?'

David thought about this.

Jenny suddenly interrupted with a laugh that surprised him.

'Now what?' he said, curious that she could find something to laugh at in the middle of his confession.

'How would you feel,' Jenny asked, 'if you found out that Helen had slept with someone on one of her nights away?'

'I'd hate to think of her with someone else. The thought of another man touching her in a sexual way makes me feel so angry, and that sounds hypocritical, but it's the truth.'

'I was thinking that it would even things up,' Jenny said mischievously. 'Cancel out each other's infidelities so to speak. If she confessed to something, then you wouldn't feel so bad telling her about Karen.'

'And if she had nothing to confess?'

'Keep it to yourself. If you love Helen and know you wouldn't be tempted again, lock it away and deal with it.'

'It won't happen again. Ever.'

David looked at the wine left in his glass and decided against finishing it. Very slowly, all the uncertainty about what to do next began to settle in his head in a neat and now, rather obvious way.

'Is Karen anything like Helen?' Jenny asked.

'Not really, in fact not at all. She's gentle, lacks some confidence in herself. She's never had a career, just worked part time and brought up her boys.'

'So, walking apart, what could you possibly have had in common?'

Everything, he thought, glancing away.

'Nothing,' he said.

'So why...? How...?' She left the questions hanging

and shrugged her shoulders.

'It was the walking, I suppose, and I felt some sympathy for her. She was married for twenty-five years, but it seems to have been a rather stale relationship. She wants a man in her life, someone who could love her and she could love back. She isn't feisty and argumentative and always trying to be in control. She was appreciative of me and I have to admit, I liked that.'

'No doubt she thought you were wonderful?' Jenny said with a sarcastic undertone.

David opened his mouth to speak but was interrupted.

'She did,' Jenny said. 'She sounds desperate.'

'Thanks,' he said huffily. 'Thought you were my friend.'

'I am, and I know how easily led you are.'

'That was years ago, I'm all grown up now. But seriously, Karen has no need to be desperate. She's an attractive lady with a lovely personality. She'll find someone.'

Jenny leant back in the chair and yawned, stretching her arms above her head. David thought how well Australia had treated the family. They all looked tanned and in good shape.

'Bedtime,' she said, with a cheeky grin. 'I need to sleep on this shock revelation.'

'You're not taking me seriously.' David protested.

'I am, honestly, but I don't think it's such a big deal. It's over and you shouldn't spoil the rest of your future with Helen by dwelling on it.'

Then Jenny said suddenly, 'Ring Karen, do it now.' She looked at her watch. 'It's 3.30 in the afternoon over there, ring now. Use our phone.'

She got up purposefully, but David felt himself hesitating.

'I'm tired, and I've had too much wine. It'll sound like a drunken, late-night call. I need to think about this.'

'No,' she said. 'You've decided what has to be done, so you don't need to do any more thinking. Come on, do it, get it over with. You'll wake up tomorrow and feel different, so do it now.'

'The number's in my mobile,' he protested.

'Go and get it then.'

David didn't move. He really wanted to think about this with a clear head.

'I'm going to bed,' Jenny said. 'I'll leave it with you, but there's no time like the present, is there?'

He looked at her and he wished she hadn't suggested this, but at the same time, she was right, it needed to be done.

'Good night.'

David waited for a moment, listening to the sound of her footsteps, then he crept upstairs and pushed the bedroom door open quietly. Helen was asleep, the sheet tossed aside, the pillows scattered. He watched her turn over, a slender arm stretched across his side of the bed. At that moment, he felt so much love for her that it seemed to spread out inside him. He reached for his mobile – part of him willing it to be out of battery – but as he pressed the keys it came to life.

Downstairs, the house had settled into quiet. David sat on the sofa and looked at the phone for a moment before tapping in Karen's number. He listened to the familiar English dialling tone. It rang for a while, then the call was picked up at the other end.

Chapter 22

Karen's hands were uncomfortably hot inside the plastic gloves, one hand was holding a brush loaded with paint stripper, the other a metal scraper. Early April sunshine was warm on her hair, and the strong smell strangely pleasant. She swore under her breath when the phone rang. Her first thought was to leave it unanswered, but it could be her mother or one of the boys, and not knowing who had rung would trouble her. Once she had decided to interrupt the task, it was a race to stow the brush and the scraper on the rim of the tin, peel off a glove and get through the kitchen to the telephone.

'Hello,' she said, the handset between her shoulder and her ear as she pulled at the second glove. Then, for a brief, suspended moment, the voice speaking her name halted the action. She gave a final tug before dropping the glove in the sink and resting an unsteady hand on the unit.

'It's David.'

'Hello David.' Her words sounded distant and unreal. There was a pause then she said, 'Where are you?'

'I'm still in Australia. It's midnight here.'

Karen spoke in an automatic, unthinking way, surprised she could utter the very ordinary sounding words, 'Are you OK?'

'Fine. We're all fine.'

'How's Lottie?'

As David answered, she took a few calming breaths and made her way outside to sit in the garden. She put a finger to her neck and felt the pulse, strong and fast, and she listened to David describe Lottie's recovery.

It had been a miserable, lonely month, wondering if he would get in touch, sure that his family crisis would mean the end of things, allowing herself a faint hope that there could be more. She relived their night together, and his unexpected return when her heart had leapt at the sight of him. Minutes later, she had closed the door, the warm, emotional high vanishing. Karen had sunk to the floor in the hall and cried, ashamed that her tears were not for the girl lying injured in an Australian hospital, but for herself.

She realised he had stopped speaking. 'You sound so near,' was all she could think of saying.

'Hard to believe, isn't it?' He paused. 'I'm sorry I haven't been in touch before. Are you all right?'

'Yes, I'm fine. I was in the middle of stripping the paint from that little table you thought was oak. Dan's coming round later, he said he'll sand the rest for me. It's coming off very well.'

'Have you been out walking?' he asked.

'Once. It was a local walk. Bob hasn't been too well, he's had a problem with his knee, but he met us at the pub afterwards. I think he's going into hospital for a replacement joint soon. People were asking about you, but no one knew anything.'

There was another awkward pause. Karen waited. He had rung her, so he needed to say whatever it was he wanted to say. She had lived through various stages of anguish over the past few weeks, she wasn't going to make it easy. At times, missing him, realising what she already knew about the future, had turned to anger. She felt furious with herself for getting involved in the first place, but also angry with him for letting it happen and then not contacting her. Not a single call, not even a text.

Across the vast distance, she sensed some emotion, a break in his words, a hesitation. She tried to picture his face.

'Does anyone know you're ringing?' Karen asked softly.

'They're all in bed asleep.'

'Have you told Helen about us?'

'No, but I've had time to think things through while we've been here.'

'And?' Karen said, holding her breath, knowing exactly what was coming next.

'I'm sorry,' she heard him say, 'but when I get home, I can't see you again.'

Karen released a long, drawn-out sigh. It was a relief to hear the words, yet a bitter draught to swallow.

'There's so much I want to say to you,' he said. 'I was wrong to lead you on.'

'Lead me on? That sounds as if I didn't know what I was doing, and believe me, David, I did know.'

She let this hang in the air and waited.

'I feel bad,' he said at last, 'that I have to end things like this. I shouldn't have started something that really, we both knew had no future.'

Karen felt stronger than him. He was thousands of miles away, but she could feel his emotion as if he was there beside her.

'I wish you'd rung me before,' she said. 'It's not been easy waiting. I could have sent you a text, but I didn't want to do anything to take your mind away from your family.'

'I'm sorry for that, too. There's no excuse.'

'There's a lot I would like to say to you one day, and maybe we'll get the chance, maybe we won't. But I've no regrets, David, none, and I don't want you to have any.'

She heard a strange sound, almost a sob, but he didn't speak. She wanted to reach out and touch him, and when it came to her that she would never touch him again, she stopped trying to be strong.

'Put the phone down,' she managed to say. 'That's enough for now.'

There was still no sound from the other end, then she heard his voice, strangled and choked, 'I loved it, being with you.'

She closed her eyes.

'And I loved it too,' she said. Then she pressed the red button with her thumb, put the phone on the bench beside her and covered her face with her hands.

Karen had spent many years restraining her emotions, keeping the joys calm and dignified, never allowing the lows to overcome her. When Guy left, a wave of conflicting feelings had engulfed her and the sensation of drowning without the buoyancy of the usual coping strategies to cling to had been frightening. But when the emotional wave finally lost momentum and dumped her on the sand, she realised that giving in to her feelings was more liberating than finding the energy and will to contain them. She learnt to cry, to yell, to throw things. When she bought the cottage, and started to put her life back together, she allowed herself to laugh loudly, to dance in the kitchen to the radio, and to fall in love with David.

Would she rather it hadn't happened? She knew

the answer long before framing the question.

There was a small noise and she was aware of someone nearby. She wiped her eyes on the sleeve of the overalls and turned to see Dan smiling over the fence. His smile dissolved into concern, and in a second he had vaulted over and was sitting beside her, a hand on her arm.

'Don't tell me paint stripping is that upsetting,' he said. 'I look across and you're working away and when I come back to see how it's going, you're in bits.'

She tried a smile. 'It's the fumes,' she said.

Dan put his arm across her shoulders, the gesture releasing even more tears and she sobbed into his chest, unable to stop. Eventually, he pulled out a hanky and she was able to dry her face. He had the sense to let her finish before asking what was wrong. Karen took a few deep breaths and tried to think through how much she could tell him, because whatever she said would probably be shared with Tina. Eventually she pulled away and sat up.

'Is it your mum?' he asked.

'Nothing like that. Mum and the boys, they're all fine.'

'Tina thinks you haven't been yourself for a while now.'

'She's right,' Karen said. 'I haven't.'

Dan said, 'Do you want to tell me, or Tina?'

'Not really.'

'Can we help?' he asked.

'No, no one can help. I'll be ok.'

Karen was beginning to pull herself together, although every now and then a huge sob would come from nowhere.

'Thanks, Dan,' she said eventually. 'I appreciate

your concern, but I can't tell you. It was a man I was seeing and now it's finished and I'm sad, that's all. I'll get over it.'

'Bastard,' Dan said.

She smiled. 'No, he wasn't. If he had been a bastard, this bit would be far easier.'

Dan hugged her again, but Karen was determined to take control, so she stood up.

'What do you think?' she said, indicating the little table.

He picked up the scraper and started on some of the paint that was left. 'Still a bit more to do, but you're getting there. I can stay and finish it off if you like?'

'No thanks,' Karen said. 'It's the sort of job I need to do myself.'

She started to apply more remover with the brush, then took the scraper from him and attacked the remaining paint with vigour.

'Hey, steady on,' he said. 'You don't want deep scratches on the finish. It's some stupid guy, not the table that's dumped you.'

Karen eased off, giving Dan the best grin she could manage.

'Come back with the sander in half an hour,' she said. 'I'll be feeling a bit better by then.'

'You sure I can leave you? You won't start sniffing the paint stripper or anything stupid like that?'

'Don't be daft,' she replied. 'Leave me to it.'

As he climbed over the fence she added, 'And don't tell Tina,' but Dan had gone.

I could have told him, she thought. I could have confessed everything, and what would people think of us then? She suddenly realised that the knowledge she had about herself and David was powerful and the consequences of that knowledge could be catastrophic.

And if I did tell someone, and it became public, and his marriage blew apart, who would people blame? Would they see me as the one who led him astray, because he's a good family man, pillar of the community, or would he be put in the role of seducer? And what would Helen think? How would she react? Karen was sure Helen was not the sort of woman to be made a fool of.

She stopped scraping the table top and picked up a smaller tool to remove the remaining flecks of paint from the curves in the legs. As she worked, her imagination ran snatches of conversation in her head, where she and David were discussed and people made what they could out of whispered information, filling the gaps with detail that was based on speculation. In her mind, she saw a furious Helen, then imagined his girls and she knew that she would never tell anyone.

But I loved it, she thought fiercely. I couldn't bear it to be shared, to be picked over and enjoyed as a piece of nasty gossip, made more of or even made less than it was. Our families deserve better, we deserve better. If I tell just one person, it will diminish what we had. She scratched at a thick blob of white paint that was lodged in an awkward corner of the table leg.

'I'm angry with you,' she said aloud. 'How could you wait so long before you rang me? You could have contacted me weeks ago.'

Then she thought about the evening David had called to see her before he went to Australia. He could simply have picked up the phone and rung her but he came in person. Perhaps waiting almost a month to get in touch was because the decision to end things was such a difficult one.

Before long, Dan was back with two electric sanders and an extension lead in a wooden box.

'Show me how to use them,' she said as he took the larger one out.

He unravelled the lead and connected the tool to the power.

'It isn't difficult, but I told you I'd do it for you.'

'I know, but I'd like to have a go.'

Dan got the sander working and demonstrated how to hold it.

'This big one for the table top,' he said, 'then the little one with the pointed end for the nooks and crannies.'

Karen took the larger sander, squeezed the trigger and applied pressure as she moved it up and down. Dan reached for a soft brush from the box and swept away the dust. The surface looked raw, but the grain of the wood was beautiful.

'You need one of these as well,' he said handing her a face mask. 'The dust can get up your nose.'

Karen took the mask. 'Thanks,' she said. 'I'll be fine now.'

'Sure?'

'I'll shout over if I need you.'

'Come and eat with us later,' he said.

Karen started to shake her head, but Dan was persistent.

'Please come,' he persuaded. 'We won't ask you anything, and if you want, when you've had enough of us, you can scoot home early.'

'Thanks,' she said. 'I'd love to come.'

'Tina knew something was up,' Dan said. 'When we were away in York, she was convinced you were seeing someone, you seemed so happy and a bit secretive. But when we came back, you were quiet and sad. I hope he was good to you.'

'He was very good to me,' Karen said.

'Well, nothing like a bit of DIY to get things back on track,' Dan exclaimed. 'By the time you've got rid of all that old paint, you'll have got rid of him, too. He'll be out of your mind. Think about that as you're sanding it down, getting in all the corners.'

Karen laughed. 'I'll have to remind myself to stop sanding. If I get too carried away with erasing him there'll be no table left.'

Dan climbed back to his own garden, muttering about needing a gate, and Karen picked up the sander.

It was a noisy, messy, yet absorbing job, that left her headspace to think, albeit not too deeply. Within an hour she was wiping the wood down, enjoying the sight of pale brown oak.

Why would anyone want to cover this up with white paint, she thought? She tipped the table up and noticed a smear where the top was joined to one of the leg supports. It was tempting to leave it, as it wouldn't be seen once finished and she had thrown the last piece of sandpaper in the bin. She reached in to retrieve the crumpled sheet, spreading it out to find a section still rough. Then she started on the remaining paint by hand. It was slow to move, and far more tiring than using the electric sander. Karen sat back on her heels, pushed her hair back and let the sun warm her face.

It had been such a brief affair, positioned delicately between their lives, yet strongly, deeply experienced. I'm in the right place now, she thought, and despite all this hurting, he made me feel desired and wanted. What we shared was so special to me, every moment precious.

She looked at the table and the small scratch of white still left and recalled what Dan had said earlier about sanding away the man who had hurt her. She considered the paint, touched it with her finger.

In the end, she decided to leave it there, screwing the sandpaper into a ball and tossing it in the bin.

Chapter 23

The night air engulfed him as he stepped out of the house. He put his mobile phone on the table, then walked across the patio to lean against the glass panels around the pool. The sky seemed too close, heavy with cloud, blurring the lamplight at the rear of the house. There was no moon.

Last night they had all lounged out here and looked at the stars. David stretched out on the grass, hands behind his head, as Chris pointed to the Southern Cross and Orion the Hunter. The Warrior seemed to lie to one side rather than stand upright as he did when viewed from the Northern Hemisphere. Helen had sat beside him and taken his hand. He felt happy just to be there, slightly drunk with wine, but mostly with the joy of being alive and the prospect of more life like the one they were living in Australia.

He left the pool and sat on the edge of a garden bench trying to clear his thoughts. Jenny was right about him needing to make the phone call. What he hadn't known, and how could he, was how desperate he would feel after it was done and how ashamed of himself for not taking control of the situation sooner. What had Karen said, "Why didn't you ring earlier? Why have you left it so long?"

He thought about her words. Yes, he had loved their brief affair too, and that pleasure was eating away at his sense of what was right and honourable.

Complete lack of control, he thought. I kissed her,

I arranged our meetings to be with her, I wanted to take her to bed. I enjoyed it. It didn't have to be like that, we could have remained friends, but I was flattered by her attention, I was weak, it's as simple as that. And not to contact her for so long when I knew it had to end. I don't deserve to get away with this.

David heard a soft click behind him and he turned, expecting to see Jenny. But it wasn't Jenny, it was Helen, her white cotton wrap pulled in around her waist. A strange combination of guilt and relief made him light-headed; if he stood up his legs would surely give way.

Helen slipped through the door, her bare feet making no sound on the tiles. She looked up.

'What are you doing out here? I woke up and didn't know where you were.'

David reached out a hand. She was still anxious when he wasn't there. He tried to smile, but it didn't work.

'Hey, what's up?' she said. He shook his head slightly, but the words seemed stuck. His mouth couldn't utter a sentence without sounding emotional.

Helen sat beside him and rested a hand on his knee. He put both arms around her and pulled her close. Thinking about anything outside the moment seemed impossible.

'Tell me,' she said.

For a while, neither of them spoke, then David released her and said, 'I'm feeling a bit weary. I've had a long conversation with Jenny and it's brought everything to the surface.'

'Everything? What do you mean?'

'All the stuff we've been through lately.'

'But we're doing fine, now,' Helen said. 'Lottie's

going back to her apartment tomorrow, she's great, I'm feeling so much better, Lizzie and Pete are good. We spoke to your Mum and Dad last night and they're all right. Things are returning to normal.'

David nodded, but didn't trust himself to speak without all the bottled-up emotion pouring out. He had a moment when he desperately wanted to tell her everything, as if sharing this anguish with the person he had shared most of his life with was the most natural thing to do.

The moment passed.

Helen commented on the heat and the stuffiness of the air. He managed to say how tired he was, how too much wine and the relief that things were turning out well for all of them had, rather strangely, made him feel choked up and sad. For a while they sat together saying nothing and David sensed that there was a possibility of everything dropping gently back into place. His guilt would be part of this. It would find its own corner in his mind and he would live with it.

'You said things were getting back to normal,' he said eventually. 'being here like this feels normal, now. Our home, your job – they all seem so distant. I hope that going home doesn't mean life going on the same as it was before we left.' He looked at Helen, reached out to smooth her hair, still ruffled by sleep, then said, 'I want to take some of Australia with us and have part of it, or even all of it, in the UK.'

Helen gave a short laugh at his choice of words. 'OK then,' she said, 'which bits do you particularly want to take back as souvenirs?'

David thought for a moment.

'You, as you are now, not as you were. That's the only bit that matters. The you I brought out weeks ago can stay here.'

'I'm not sure that the way I am now would work for the life we have back home,' she said.

David turned to face her.

'Well in that case, the life back home has to change.'

'We've discussed this. I don't want to talk about it now.'

'Will there ever be a good time?'

'Yes.'

'When?'

'When I know for certain.' She met his gaze and her expression softened. 'You can let go of me, I won't run off.'

'Yes, you will,' he replied, gripping her hands. 'You'll run off before I have an answer. I love you so much, and yet there have been times when I thought I was losing you.'

'Really?' Helen frowned, but it was a look of concern, not irritation. 'I can't believe you felt like that. When? What did I do?'

He thought for a moment.

'Well, it was about the time we had that row about you finishing work, and you were away overnight a lot, and late home after spending evenings with Simon.'

Helen shifted the cushions on the bench. She leant back against the arm and lifted her legs to rest them across his knees.

'Simon?' she said. 'Surely you're not implying I'd be attracted to Simon? He's young enough to be my son.'

'No, although I did resent him and his school. He seemed to have something that grabbed your attention at the drop of a hat. No, it was all the nights away, I wondered if...' David hesitated again. 'You're very attractive, especially when you're in professional mode. I've seen other men look at you and I've enjoyed that. It never bothered me, because I knew we were close and I trusted you. Then a few months ago, things seemed to change.'

'It was work, my job,' she protested. 'It wasn't you, although there were times when you didn't seem to understand.'

'And all those overnights with other headteachers and advisers, you were never tempted, none of them ever made a move on you?'

'No,' Helen paused and seemed to think, 'and yes.'

'Do you want to tell me?'

'Nothing to tell, absolutely nothing.'

David wanted to ask her more, but something told him to stop digging, to leave this alone. He presumed that her "no" referred to never being tempted. If she wanted to keep the "and yes" thing to herself, then why not? He tried to see this as balancing things up a little, especially if she was choosing to keep something from him. But it wasn't a balance. His guilt still weighed heavily on his side of the scales. He ran a hand over her knees, down her shins to her feet and he started to rub each foot gently. Suddenly he remembered that it was something he used to do for Karen and he stopped.

He waited, wondered if Helen would question if he had ever been tempted. But she didn't and he was relieved. He knew that if she asked, he would have to answer with a lie. He swiftly brought the conversation back to her job.

'Why are you frightened of finishing work?' he said. 'I did it, and for me it was my business I was letting go, not just a job.'

'Just a job,' she repeated.

'I'm sorry,' he said. 'Helen I'm really sorry, I didn't mean to say that.'

'That's what I mean about not understanding.'

David didn't trust himself to speak again. He glanced at his watch and felt a desperate need to be in bed with his eyes closed and his own thoughts in his head. Starting this conversation was a stupid thing to do in his fragile state. He was about to get up when she spoke.

'I'm frightened,' she said, her voice hesitant, 'of losing... no, not losing, letting go of something that makes me the person I am. I'm in control at school, I'm important, people look up to me, ask for solutions, think I'm marvellous when I supply them. I'm frightened of not feeling essential and needed and in a place where I can make a difference to people's lives.'

'I understand all that,' David said, 'but you can't carry on forever, this decision will have to be made sometime soon, so why not now?'

Helen didn't answer.

'And *I* need you,' he said. 'I think you're important and necessary and you've always made a massive difference to my life. Isn't that enough? Am I not enough?'

Still Helen said nothing. He wished he hadn't asked the question. It was unfair.

'Of course you're enough,' she whispered. 'More than enough.'

She swung her legs to the floor and stood up, loosening then re-fastening the belt of her wrap. She looked out at the night, then back to him, her eyes glancing over the low table.

'Why have you got the phone out here?' she asked, reaching out for David's mobile. Her fingers touched it, but he scooped up the phone and put it in his shirt pocket. Immediately he knew it was the wrong thing to do. He watched as Helen withdrew her hand and looked at him, her body taut.

The atmosphere between them changed.

'Have you rung someone?'

David almost replied, then hesitated. Should he lie, tell a half truth, tell her who he had been speaking to? Before he could decide, Helen said, 'Why would you phone someone at this time?'

'It's the afternoon at home,' he said, this question an easy one to answer.

'Is that why you're upset? You've spoken to someone and it's upset you? It isn't Lizzie, is it?'

He shook his head, took a breath, started a word, but it never became more than a slight sound.

Helen waited.

'Tell me,' she said. 'Who did you ring?'

'No one, it isn't important.' He stood up and took her hand. 'Come on, let's go up, I'm exhausted.'

Helen shook off his hand and stood upright, facing him, her expression determined.

'Why won't you tell me, David? What are you hiding?'

He took her hand again and led her to the door and again she shrugged it off, this time quite deliberately.

'Are you coming inside or not?' he said shortly, 'because you'll have to lock this door yourself if you don't come now and it's tricky to close.'

'I might want to stay out here. I might want to make a secret phone call to someone,' she said.

'Now that's being childish...'

'No worse than you hiding something that's

obviously important enough to upset you.'

'Come in and let me do the door,' he said. She paused for a moment then stepped inside and stood watching him.

Fiddling with the door gave him a few moments to think. A lie, such as saying it was Bob from the walking group, he'd sent a text that needed answering, would be the easiest option. But David knew that this should have been his immediate response. His reluctance to explain had made a casual lie impossible now. With elaborate care, he pulled the sliding door across, taking two attempts to find the right groove. Then he pushed the handle up and locked it. The key dropped from his shaking fingers, and he found himself on his knees under the table feeling about in the half-light. Once retrieved, he slipped the key under a table mat. I don't want to say anything, tonight, he thought. She can stand there glaring at me for as long as she likes. If I tell her a little bit about Karen, she'll keep asking more and I'll end up telling her everything.

He turned to face her. 'Yes, I've spoken to someone in England tonight. It's upset me and I don't want to talk about it. For God's sake, accept it and come to bed.'

'So, you may tell me what this is about tomorrow?'

'Maybe.'

'Or maybe not?'

David's irritation, fuelled by overwhelming tiredness, turned to anger. He slammed a fist on the dining table next to him.

'Bloody hell, can't you leave it alone?'

She looked shocked, then hurt, then her eyes hardened. She set off for the stairs.

'Helen, please.'

She turned. 'So, you might tell me, you might not. I suppose that's up to you, isn't it? I won't ask you again, but in the meantime, I'll speculate and wonder and worry, but never really know. Is that what you want?'

David shrugged helplessly.

'You obviously think that's better than the truth,' Helen said. She stood in the doorway waiting, giving him a final opportunity to tell her.

David didn't speak. He wanted to rest his face on a cool pillow, his mind drifting into sleep and the triviality of dreams.

He looked up, ready to ask her again to forget it, but she had gone.

Chapter 24

Helen opened her eyes to dawn light piercing the gap between the curtains. Immediately, she knew life had changed. Her muscles tensed. David reached out, as he did every morning, and pulled her to him, but she stiffened at his touch, tolerating the embrace. What did he expect, that everything could carry on as normal? The truth would have been better than this. Part of her regretted saying that she would never ask him again, but Helen intended to keep her word. What she would do, however, was make it quite clear that she was thinking about what had passed between them last night and that she was angry with him.

He tried to placate her, made breakfast, offered to start the packing before their departure the next day. Her replies were deliberately curt and she spent the morning going through e-mails in her school inbox and reading the applications for the deputy head's job. When he asked if she wanted to come out for a walk or a bike ride, she refused, saying she had far too much to do. She also refused lunch, knowing that this was another way she could punish him. It was stupid, but her appetite had disappeared and it wasn't her fault, it was his.

In the end, David seemed to give up and went off on his own.

Without warning, he had spoilt everything. The end of the holiday should have been pleasurable. Yesterday she thought about their return home with some regret. Now she couldn't wait to get back, to throw herself into work again, to feel that she was pulling all the strings and watching things happen the way she wanted them to. Yet they had to keep the tension between them away from Lottie and from Chris and Jenny, which made being annoyed with him even harder. Then there was the prospect of a twenty-four hour plane journey, where she imagined them sitting beside each other, barely talking. Helen's anger deepened, twisting a knot in her stomach.

Standing on the sun terrace, Helen felt the change of air that Jenny had said would be on the way by early afternoon. There was a coolness in the breeze, barely perceptible unless you were looking for it. She hoped it would herald an easier sleep without the hum of the air-conditioning unit or the whirr of the ceiling fan.

Last night she had lain awake for hours, her mind revisiting David's words about the phone call. When his breathing changed and she knew he was asleep, she had slid out of bed and tried to find his mobile phone in the dark. It wasn't where he had put it in his shirt pocket, or anywhere obvious. It was a half-hearted search and part of her felt relief that she couldn't find it, because if she had, she wasn't sure what she would have done.

She couldn't remember him keeping anything from her before, except Christmas and birthday presents, and even then, he never lied. He would admit that he was keeping a secret but refuse to tell. Helen's thoughts had exhausted many options and always brought her back to the same thing; this was something which had upset him and he didn't intend to share it with her. Once her mind had entered the realm of what this could possibly be, she couldn't get Karen out of her head.

She remembered their visit on New Year's Day,

Dan persuading her to go in for a drink, feeling ill after the flu, noticing how attractive Karen looked in a red cashmere jumper, while she was wearing old jeans and a sweatshirt. She also recalled teasing David on the way home about how Karen obviously fancied him. And although the idea that something could be going on between them had crossed her mind, she always dismissed it as rather amusing.

I never took any of it seriously, she thought, and I'm still struggling to imagine that he would be involved with someone else, not David, surely? But what alternative could there be? Anything other than this and he would have said who he had telephoned and why. And if it was an affair, how far had it gone? More importantly, was it over?

Helen shook herself. This is mere speculation, she thought, and I need to get a grip. I'll go for a walk, then I'll e-mail school with my feedback on the applications. Harry's coming over later, so that'll relieve the atmosphere and we'll both have to try to be normal. She replayed their conversation about normal from the previous night and wondered, if her assumptions were true, how things could ever return to that again.

The seafront was quiet, although it was a beautiful afternoon. By five o'clock the kitesurfers, joggers and family groups would arrive to make the most of the evening. She hesitated about which direction to turn. David had said he would probably cycle towards the city, well in that case, she would walk the other way. She didn't intend to stroll. It would be a fast-paced, power walk, the intention to return with tired feet and aching legs.

As she walked, Helen gave her thoughts free rein, and by the end of her first kilometre, she knew that the only way she could get through this was to find out the truth. By the time she reached the cliffs above the harbour she had framed the conversation and prepared her reaction to whatever he was likely to tell her. She sat on a bench overlooking the ocean, which was flecked with white, whipped up by the changing wind. She had walked out some of the anger, and her determination to make him suffer was no longer so strong. Her stomach growled and a hollowness opened up inside her.

On the way back she stopped at the row of bathing boxes that lined Brighton Beach. She chose her favourite, painted a crisp blue with white stripes, and sat on the warm wooden platform to unfasten trainers, remove socks and rub her bare feet in the soft sand. It was warm out of the breeze and tempting to close her eyes and doze, enjoying the sound of the sea and the voices around her.

We've been so close these last few weeks, she thought. It's almost as if we've rediscovered each other, and suddenly it all seems ruined, pointless. But he has to be honest with me, because I don't think I could live with anything less. Whatever he's keeping from me can't be so terrible. She ran her hand over the sun-bleached wood, feeling its dry surface, every knot and split worn to a rounded smoothness by the sand.

She opened her eyes as she thought she heard her name called, distant at first, then nearer, then Jenny was powering across the sand waving madly, shouting back to someone further down the beach.

'I thought you'd be on the beach,' she puffed. 'We wondered where you'd got to.'

'I went for a walk,' Helen said, a little surprised that Jenny had thought it necessary to come to find her.

'It's nearly half-past six,' she said. 'Lottie and Harry

have arrived. David was getting worried.'

Helen exclaimed at the time.

'I'm sorry, I didn't put my watch on. I'd no idea it was so late. Half-past six, surely not?'

She looked up to see David taking long strides towards them.

'I'll get back,' Jenny said. 'Don't be too long.'

David didn't smile as he approached.

'You're doing this on purpose,' he said angrily. 'We didn't know where you were, your phone was on the bed, you didn't even leave a note. It's one thing to be pissed off with me, Helen, but to take it out on everyone else by disappearing isn't fair. Was this to get me into a state? Because it's worked, and it's inconvenienced all of us. Or didn't you even think about that?'

Helen gasped at his onslaught.

'I'm sorry,' she said. 'Honestly, I had no idea it was so late. How can you think I'd do this on purpose? That's hardly fair.'

'What did you expect me to think?'

'Sit down for a minute,' she said.

'We haven't time…'

'Yes we have, sit down. You're angry and you don't need to be. I've had a long walk, I lost track of time and yes, I should have taken my phone or left a note.'

David remained standing.

'Please yourself,' she said, 'but I'm having another few minutes here in the sun before I go back.'

She shook the sand off her feet, rubbed it out from between each toe and began putting her socks and trainers on. He sat beside her.

'We have to sort this out,' she said.

'Disappearing doesn't help.'

'I've told you, I went for a long walk and forgot the time. It wasn't deliberate. I needed the space to think.'

David rested his elbows on his knees. He glanced at her, then looked away. Helen laced up her trainers, stretched out her legs and put a hand on his arm.

'I said I wouldn't ask you about the phone call,' she said, 'well I am going to ask you. Whether you answer with a lie or tell the truth is up to you.'

She paused, tried to see his expression. He seemed to be following the movements of a particularly reckless kitesurfer who was racing out to sea with the waves, then choosing just the right moment to flip over, controlling the kite and the wind so expertly.

'Were you ringing Karen?' she asked.

He turned to look at her and she knew. 'Something has been going on between you, hasn't it?'

He hesitated, then said, 'Yes, but it meant nothing and it's over and I rang her to tell her that.'

Helen let the information seep in. He was feeling sad last night because he had ended it. She had thought about this possibility all afternoon, but knowing she had come to the right conclusion didn't make it easier to accept. They both sat without talking. She waited for him to elaborate, but he was obviously struggling.

'It's over?' she asked. 'To be over, there must have been something, then.'

'Yes, but as I said, it really wasn't important.'

'Have you been seeing her?'

'You might call it that, but it's finished. It has been for a while.'

Helen took a breath before asking, 'Did you kiss her, hold her hand?'

'That's all it ever was. I swear...'

'Did you enjoy it,' Helen interrupted, 'being with

her?'

David looked at his wife again, hesitated, then said, 'At the time, but afterwards I felt dreadful.'

'Because?'

'Because of you, and because of her. It was wrong. I'm making no excuse.'

Helen found herself battling a spread of anxiety that sapped her ability to rationalise. She forced herself to breathe slowly, shorter breaths in, longer, calming breaths out. The one question she desperately wanted to ask seemed impossible to put into words. Surely not, she thought. He wouldn't. He said it was nothing.

They both sat for a moment looking into the sun. Suddenly, the kitesurfer made a spectacular turning leap, then crashed into the water making them both gasp. David said, 'Thank goodness for that,' when the figure resurfaced and took control of the kite and the board.

'Why last night?' Helen asked. 'Why did you ring her last night?'

'I should have rung her weeks ago,' he said. 'I needed to ring her before we went home to say that I couldn't meet her again. I've known it was over since we came here and I'm annoyed with myself for not contacting her sooner to tell her.'

'Surely,' Helen said sitting upright, 'she didn't think there would ever be any future in it, surely you didn't?'

'Of course not. Never.'

'Then why... how did it happen?'

'This,' he said, 'is exactly why I didn't want to tell you. You know a little bit, then you want more and I can't explain it now. Lottie and Harry are waiting for us. After today we won't see them until September and I want to have a lovely evening with them, and we said we'd call Lizzie at seven o'clock. I don't want to talk about this. It meant nothing. I feel dreadful about it. You're my wife, Helen and I love you.'

'At least try to tell me why you did it.'

David didn't speak. He raised his shoulders, took a few deep breaths, scratched his head. He put an arm around her and she almost shrugged him off, but instead let her body rest lightly against his. She waited.

'I'm finding it very hard to say exactly why,' he said eventually. 'She's a lovely person, I enjoyed her company, and I was lonely, I suppose.'

'Lonely? How could you be lonely? You had me. You had the family, and lots of friends around you.'

'Please, Helen, can we do this another time, *please?*'

He stood up abruptly, put out his hand to help her up. Instinctively, Helen took it, then let go as soon as she was on her feet.

'You probably hate me,' he said, 'and I deserve that, but I love you and I only ever want to be with you. I'll do whatever it takes to make you feel better about this, I promise. I don't want you to ask me any more questions, now, because I honestly do not want to talk about it.'

They walked back to the house and she let him take her hand, but said nothing. She had pondered for most of the day about Karen, never managing to frame a picture of the two of them in her mind. Now the image was there.

What was wrong with him? Why would he need to look at another woman? Then it all flipped over and landed in a different way and she thought, what was wrong with me?

Chapter 25

Lizzie stood in the kitchen at her parents' house looking
through the pile of post that Debbie collected when she
came in each day to feed Floss. It had been tossed
haphazardly on the kitchen worktop, and Lizzie felt the
need to sort it out. She separated the junk mail and the
free newspapers from the letters and arranged neat
piles. Pete looked on with a smirk.

'What,' she said, 'is amusing you?'

'You,' he said. 'Little Miss Organised. Don't ever
change, I love it.'

Lizzie pulled a face at him. 'Make yourself useful.
There's a bulb out in one of the ceiling spotlights. New
ones are in the bottom drawer.'

Pete spent the next few minutes in precarious
positions between a chair and the worktop unscrewing
the light fitting and replacing the old bulb with a new
one.

Lizzie watched him, enjoying his antics, grateful for
the contented feeling that had gradually replaced the
worry about her sister and deep concern for her
mother. For weeks she had felt as if she was carrying
the anxiety around with her like a package she couldn't
put down. They had shared a Face Time call that
morning, which was completely dominated by Lottie,
who had so much to talk about. Her parents had
claimed the screen halfway through, looking windswept
after a walk on the beach.

Although it was her sister who had been through

the most serious and obvious injuries, it was Mum who had given Lizzie more to worry about. With Lottie it was simple; she'd had an accident, she was getting better, she would make a full recovery with time. Yet the change she had seen in her mum the night before her parents had flown out to Australia, had been a shock. Lizzie couldn't get her mother's distress out of her head and found herself returning to it on several occasions. Is this what stress does to you she wondered? If it can affect Mum, who's strong, then surely we're all vulnerable. She had spoken to Lottie, who seemed to think there was nothing to worry about, Mum had been working too hard. She needed to slow down a bit, eat more, let Dad look after her and start enjoying herself. Lizzie wasn't sure it was a simple as this.

They had called on Debbie and Ross before checking the post and later that afternoon, Lizzie was looking forward to visiting her grandparents.

'You're missing Dad, aren't you?' Lizzie said as she picked up Floss and stroked the ginger fur. 'Only a few days now and they'll be back.'

'Your mum's going to murder that cat when they do get back,' Pete said. He pointed to where Floss had scratched the wood of the back door frame. Lizzie looked.

'Heck, she's never done that before. She'll be banished to the shed.'

Lizzie put Floss down and looked round. She contemplated getting out a duster.

'You can tell they've been away, can't you?' she said. 'The house seems stale and unlived in.'

'And bloody freezing. They'll feel the cold when they get back. Is Debbie putting the heating on next week?'

'I expect so.'

Lizzie looked out of the kitchen window. Early rain had cleared and the sun was drying the wet pavements and lawns.

'Do you fancy a walk?'

'Short walk, long lunch in the pub,' Pete suggested.

Floss was treated to some extra attention, although Lizzie told her firmly not to scratch. The cat meowed as they locked up. Lizzie glanced back to see her take up a favourite spot on the sunny windowsill.

Pete took her hand as they walked through the village towards the pub, passing the school and then the church. She exclaimed at the number of banners tied around the railings of the playground. They read each one. There must have been a good dozen, all colourful, sometimes with children's drawings between the letters or small hand prints and beaming cartoon faces.

'So, what's all this about?' Pete asked.

Lizzie grinned. 'It's a cheeky two fingers to the Ofsted report. Mum said it started with one, then it snowballed.'

She stopped by the last banner and said, 'Look, the gate's open. Come on Pete, let's go in, I'll show you my old school. We can peep in the windows.'

Pete hesitated. 'Are you sure we won't be trespassing?'

'Even if we are, it's not that serious. If anyone says anything we apologise and leave. And anyway, I am an ex-pupil and Auntie Debbie is the deputy head, and Mum has helped to run this place.'

Lizzie didn't wait for an answer. She took Pete's hand and pulled him through the open gate.

It was Easter Monday so the staff car park was

empty. They sat on a bench by the playground while she recalled the events of a netball final from years ago. Pete listened with an amused look pretending to hang on to her every word.

Lizzie mimed the moves, then raced to the semi-circle, her dark hair flying, to demonstrate the end of the match.

'Then, Emma missed the goal, but I snatched the ball and...'

'Scored! Goaaaaal!' Pete ran around the court waving his arms in mock triumph. Suddenly he stopped, let his arms drop and walked back towards Lizzie looking more than a little sheepish.

'There's a man by that window watching us,' he said.

'Lizzie turned. He was right. A fair-haired guy was standing inside by the window, holding a small child. He was smiling at them.'

'Ooops,' Lizzie said. 'How embarrassing. Should we leg it?'

'Too late,' Pete said. 'Looks like he's coming over.'

The man came out of a side door. Lizzie walked towards him and started to apologise.

'I'm an ex-pupil,' she explained. 'I was showing my boyfriend the school. Sorry.'

He put the child down and smiled at her.

'No problem,' he said. 'I'm Simon York, the head, but I won't remember you, I'm fairly new.'

She shook Simon's hand and said, 'I think you know my mum, Helen Richards.'

Simon looked surprised, then he beamed at her. 'Yes I do, and now I look at you, you're obviously her daughter. Is she back from Australia yet? Your sister had an accident, didn't she? Your mum and I exchanged one or two e-mails before the Easter break but I've tried not to bother her.'

Lizzie updated Simon on her parents' news. She tried to recall what her mum had said about him and his family. Pete played a chasing game with Billy as they talked.

'Come in,' Simon said. 'I'll show you around.'

'I don't want to stop you working.'

Simon laughed. 'Working – with Billy to entertain? My wife dropped me off half-an-hour ago to take Jim to the clinic. I'm picking up some files and checking e-mails. She'll be back soon. Please come in. I'd love to show you the place.'

Lizzie had never met Simon before, but she felt as if she knew him. He showed great enthusiasm for his school and she thoroughly enjoyed the tour, recognising some things from her days as a pupil, noting many changes.

'You've had a difficult time with Ofsted recently, haven't you?' she said as they stood in the hall admiring a display of artwork.

Simon shrugged his shoulders. 'It doesn't matter any more,' he said. 'Your mum helped me realise that Ofsted reports are merely a snapshot. The real work happens every day.'

'She tells me that,' Lizzie said. 'But everyone makes such a fuss. I'm a teacher, secondary maths, and we were criticised. They said the kids weren't getting involved enough in the lessons, but they only dropped in on three. The head of maths was devastated. None of us could tell her not to take it so seriously because it's Ofsted, and what they say goes public and becomes the reality, even if it isn't true. You start to believe it yourself if you're not careful.'

'I felt like that,' Simon said. 'Then your mum and I unpicked the report and it was full of errors and judgements based on very little evidence.'

'I love the banners,' Lizzie said.

Simon laughed. 'Do you know it's made the local press? The Parents' Group started it, then there was a new one every week. There isn't much space left. There were thirteen when I last counted.'

Billy ran in and launched himself at Simon, who lifted him into the air and tickled him.

'How is your mum?' he asked. 'I've missed her. She's an amazing woman; very well respected for speaking her mind and knowing what needs to be done, rather than doing whatever the current trend is. Time flies on her courses and you feel you're leaving with something useful. Do you know,' Simon added, 'my friend Philip is in love with her.'

Lizzie laughed. 'Well you'd better warn him she's happily married and my dad is very possessive.'

'I think it's more a sort of admiration from afar.'

'She's fine,' Lizzie said. 'They're back in the next few days. Lottie, my sister, was going to come with them, but she's doing so well she's staying in Melbourne until September. She's got plenty of friends to call on.'

'That's good. Tell your mum I was asking about her and everything's going well here.' Simon glanced round. 'What happened to your boyfriend?'

Lizzie frowned. 'I've no idea,' she said. She called Pete's name, then turned back to check some of the classrooms. She found him settled on a beanbag in a corner of the infant library, smiling to himself. He was engrossed in an early reading book.

'The Magic Key,' he said when he looked up and saw Lizzie. 'I loved these books.'

'He seems nice,' Pete commented as they walked on to the pub.

'Mum has a lot of time for Simon,' Lizzie said. 'I'm glad I've met him. Hope he wasn't watching the replay of the famous netball match.'

'I think he was,' Pete suggested. 'Couldn't take his eyes off you.'

Lizzie gave him a playful shove and grabbed his arm. 'Most men can't,' she said. 'I've learnt to live with the admiration.'

The pub was busy, taken over by a group in walking gear who seemed to be holding some sort of meeting. Lizzie picked her way through mounds of rucksacks and walking poles and discarded anoraks to squeeze behind a small table where she pulled up a chair for Pete, who was at the bar. She listened to them discussing events, and noticed an attractive, dark-haired woman, taking notes. Lizzie's attention wandered to the black and white photographs on the wall. They were scenes of the village from 100 years ago and she wondered why she had never noticed them before. Then she heard someone in the walking group mention her dad's name. She glanced across.

'David Richards?' a woman asked.

'Tall guy, led that walk along the canal when we all froze to death.'

'No news, Bob?'

The older man, who seemed to be leading the meeting, shook his head.

'Not since the e-mail I had about four weeks ago. It said his daughter was improving, and he and his wife would be in Melbourne for the near future.

Lizzie hesitated, then stood up and approached the

group.

'Hello,' she said. 'I'm sorry to interrupt, but I overheard you talking about my family. I'm David Richards' daughter, Elizabeth.'

At first Bob looked slightly confused, then he beamed at Lizzie.

'Ah,' he said. 'You must be David's elder daughter?'

'Yes. It was my sister who had the accident in Melbourne.'

She suddenly found herself bombarded with questions. When she paused to take a breath, she thought how much this group seemed to think of her dad. Their concern was sincere, their pleasure that everything was improving for her family, genuine and warm. When Pete returned with drinks, she was sitting on the arm of Bob's chair telling them about her parents' time in Australia. As Lizzie got up to leave the group, the woman taking notes asked, 'How's your mum?'

Lizzie, who had hardly mentioned her mother, was a little surprised at the question. Perhaps this person knew her mum.

'She's fine,' she said. Something told her not to elaborate.

'I'll leave you to your meeting,' Lizzie said. 'We need to order our food before they stop serving.'

'Give our best wishes to your parents,' Bob said. 'We look forward to seeing them on a walk very soon.'

'I'll do that.'

Lizzie said goodbye and made her way back to where Pete was sitting with the drinks.

'There's a better table free over there,' he said. 'We're a bit squashed in this corner. Who on earth are that lot?'

'Dad's walking group,' Lizzie explained as they carried the drinks across to a larger table. They passed the group and she heard Bob say, 'What was that date, Karen?'

The dark-haired woman looked up from her notebook.

'The date for the June walk?' he asked again.

Lizzie stared, remembering something. The woman glanced at her then looked away.

As they settled at the new table, Lizzie whispered, 'That must be Karen. Do you remember? Granny made that comment about her carrying on with Dad.'

Pete looked completely blank. 'Who?'

'When we came to visit before Christmas? I was driving and I had to stop the car on the way home because I got upset.'

'You thought your Dad was having a bit of a fling or something, yes, I remember now.'

'I never really thought that, but Granny suggested it in fun. When I came over at February half term, Mum made a snide comment about Karen. Dad defended her and I went home convinced their marriage was on the rocks.'

Pete leaned over to catch a better glimpse of Karen. 'So that's her?' He continued to look. 'She's quite attractive for an older woman,' he said.

'That,' said Lizzie fiercely, 'is not what I want to hear thank you very much.'

'But,' Pete said quickly, 'if I was your dad, married to your mum, I'd never contemplate an affair.'

'That's more like it,' Lizzie said, glancing as casually as she could in Karen's direction. She noticed how her face lit up when she smiled, and the animated way she used her hands when she spoke. Suddenly Karen met her gaze. Instinctively Lizzie looked away, then she glanced back to see that Karen was smiling. She returned the smile, sat back and put her hand on Pete's arm.

Lizzie thought about her parents. They had looked fine. She wondered how she could ever have worried about them. Pete seemed to read her thoughts.

'Your parents are OK, now,' he said. 'It was a bad patch, nothing to worry about.'

Lizzie agreed. 'Food,' she said. 'Better order, it's almost half-past. I'll have a prawn sandwich please.'

Pete got up and went over to the bar. He gave in the order, then came back with cutlery and serviettes.

'I hope Mum's less stressed when she goes back to school,' Lizzie said, as she watched him arrange the table. 'She can be such hard work when she's got a lot on.'

'We men like a bit of hard work,' Pete said. 'Makes life interesting.'

'Really?'

'Why do you think I'm with you, babe?'

Lizzie shook her head in exasperation, but sought his hand and linked her fingers through his.

'I love this village,' he said looking around the pub. 'Don't you ever get sick of the city?'

'Sometimes,' she replied. 'Not sick of it, more as if I'm gasping for different air and open spaces.'

'Perhaps it's time to consider a change. I'd like to live in a small community again.'

Lizzie was too preoccupied with her own thoughts and didn't answer.

They enjoyed lunch, ordered more drinks and watched the walking group disperse. Then they left for the short drive to see the grandparents. Pete took the wheel and whistled along to the radio as Lizzie looked out of the window and mulled over the possibility of moving away from the centre of Manchester. It was time she changed schools, possibly looked for a promotion. Pete did much of his graphic design work from home, so they could move anywhere. It would be good to be near her family. Suddenly she was aware of him pulling off the main road well before the turning to Granny and Grandad's house.

'What's the matter?' Lizzie asked.

He stopped the car and switched off the engine.

'I've thought of something,' Pete said, 'something I want to do. I haven't planned it and it won't be done properly, but I want to do it now and it can't wait, it can't wait another minute.'

Lizzie turned towards him. Pete released his seat belt, then he released hers. He took her hands.

'I would like to ask you to spend the rest of your life with me,' he said, 'to marry me.'

Lizzie's eyes widened. She put a hand up to her face.

'You said I was hard work,' she whispered, teasingly.

'I also said I like hard work.'

'Well as long as you understand what you're taking on.' She deliberately paused, as if she was giving his proposal some long and serious thought. 'As long as you understand that, I think I can say… ' she leant over to kiss him, 'Yes!'

Pete put his arms around her and in spite of the gear lever and handbrake between them, he held her close and buried his face in her hair, both of them laughing, Lizzie close to tears. She thought about her parents and their thirty-year marriage and hoped that she and Pete would be together for as long.

When Pete let her go she brushed her face with her hands and said, 'We need to calm down before we get to Granny's. She's very quick to notice something's up.'

'I don't care who notices how happy I am.'

'Yes you do, we can't tell anyone yet.'

She pulled the sun visor down and looked at herself in the mirror. 'Why now?' she asked.

Pete sat back in his seat.

'Surely it's not completely unexpected? We've discussed the future and things we want to do together haven't we? But today, visiting Fellburn, looking at your old school, meeting Simon and Billy, it's as if I've had the chance to look around the corner, see what might happen next, and I like it.'

'You like it?'

'Yes, I like what could be in the future for us. It's made me feel excited and happy and the moment felt right.' He suddenly looked concerned. 'You're not disappointed are you, that I proposed in the car at the side of the road? It isn't very romantic.'

Lizzie kissed him. 'Not disappointed at all.'

Pete started the car and pulled out. He looked at her briefly. As they continued the drive, she felt as if she was being hugged from the inside. She placed a hand on his knee.

'Happy?' he asked.

Lizzie thought about this. 'I think I need a word that doesn't exist,' she said, 'and that's fine, it doesn't need a name. Happy sounds like something that's on the surface, something good but it isn't enough for what I feel at this moment, so don't ask me to give it a name, because I can't.'

She stretched her legs, and looked at Pete, then out of the window, overwhelmed by a desire to see her parents and her sister safely back from the other side of the world.

Chapter 26

They left Melbourne in the afternoon. Chris and Jenny drove them to the airport and it was a short, but emotional parting. After hugs and thanks and final goodbyes, Helen found herself struggling to get a grip as they waited at the check-in queue. David took her arm, squeezed her hand, tried to lighten her mood, but she found it hard to keep her emotions in check.

'We'll come back,' he said, 'and they'll be over in Lancashire in the summer. Lottie will be home in September – it's not long to wait.'

Helen nodded, but said nothing, irritated that he thought it was so simple. There was no point trying to talk to him or even to try to reason with herself about why she was so distressed.

Once the plane took off, they abandoned themselves to the ordeal of a long flight in the limited space that economy class afforded. It was a twilight world, crossing time zones, the hours crawling by yet moving inexplicably in reverse as they flew west. It could have been a chance to talk, to focus on themselves and their marriage and what the future held. But it was enough to get through the journey, to eat when the trays arrived, doze fitfully, try to let the entertainment relieve at least some of the boredom.

The change at Singapore was uneventful. They sat at the boarding gate and Helen turned to David with a faint smile as they listened to snatches of northern English accents in this foreign airport.

'Almost home,' he said. 'Only fifteen more hours of sitting still, being waited on hand and foot and watching every film I never wanted to see.' He wrapped his fingers around her wrist as if measuring it, then he took her hand. It was one of many affectionate gestures he had kept up as she sat beside him, sometimes a touch, an arm across her shoulders, a kiss on her cheek. Twice he had told her he loved her and she had responded with an automatic, "I love you too", but it meant nothing.

A few hours into the second flight they both stood at the rear of the plane, stretching cramped limbs, and watching the cabin crew at work. Helen noticed David follow the movements of a particularly pretty girl as she swished past in the immaculate airline uniform. When he glanced back to her, he seemed embarrassed, and stared through the window awkwardly. Normally she would have nudged him, teased him, made a comment about his wandering eye, but she also looked away and felt miserable.

This was how it would be from now on. It dawned on her that it was trust that had been lost, the absolute certainty that however difficult she was, however distant or short with him at the end of a long day in school, he would always be there, solely for her. This is what she had thought and she had been wrong.

He said he had kissed Karen. It sounded trivial, like teenagers on a first date, but the more she repeated the words to herself, the more offensive it became. It wasn't the action, it was the intention, and he said he enjoyed it.

Quite helplessly, she created images that went far beyond small affectionate gestures. Then, inevitably, she wondered if they had slept together.

No, surely not, she thought. But what if they had? And not only sex, but sharing a bed, overnight. They would have had several opportunities when she was away.

She pushed on the tender spot even harder. Our bed? No, he wouldn't do that, would he?

She pictured confronting him, asking the question, receiving the answer.

Did you...?

Yes, we spent some nights together.

She tried to imagine her reaction to the response, to feel how it might flood through her like a cold panic attack, but she stopped herself.

No, not David, she thought, glancing at him. Some hand-holding, kissing, but that's all. Yet I have to know, and if I ask and he says yes, can I cope with the answer? Yet if I don't ask and never know, would that be worse? I can't talk about this yet. I need to be in control of all the stuff in my head first.

David's voice interrupted her thoughts.

'Do you want to sit down again?' He slipped an arm around her and pulled her towards him, and Helen wondered why she was still accepting this closeness when she felt angry and hurt.

'Do you think they'd make me a cup of tea?' she asked, pushing him away.

'Of course they would. You go and sit down, I'll sort it out.'

Helen apologised for disturbing the man in the aisle seat and slipped into her space by the window.

She peered out at the lights of some vast, unknown city below. Will the balance between us change now, she mused? He'll be forever trying to make up for hurting me, always feeling guilty, overdoing his side of things. I don't want that, either. I want things back the way they were a few days ago when we were relaxed and happy. Everything seems to be muddled and uncertain, and I can't sort out what we need to do next.

She recalled how David had cared for her when they first arrived in Australia. She couldn't have asked for more from a husband. He had been the certainty, the calm presence when she had found herself drowning in the fear of failing at the simplest of tasks.

As he settled into his seat beside her, he handed her a feeble looking plastic cup, half-full of weak, milky liquid.

'Sorry,' he said. 'They don't have cups and saucers. It's the first thing I'll do when we get home – make you a real cup of tea.'

She accepted it gratefully.

'Thanks,' she said, rubbing her hand along his arm. It was the first sign of affection she had shown and he looked at her for a moment.

'It will be ok,' he said.

'Will it?'

'If we both want it to be.'

Helen sipped her tea, the unfamiliar scented aroma surprising, but not unpleasant.

'But you are thinking about it,' he said gently, 'aren't you?'

'What do you expect? I can't help it. I'm trying to get hold of what you said about you and Karen.'

David leant back in his seat, but turned his head to look at her.

'All you need to know is how much I love you,' he said. 'Don't worry about anything else, because it doesn't matter.'

'It's easy to say that.'

'I mean it.'

Helen wanted the conversation to end there so she said, 'I just need to be home.'

The only time she slept was a brief hour after some passengers disembarked in Munich and David moved so that she had the row of three seats to herself. But it was almost worse than not sleeping at all and it took all her efforts to wake up as the plane came into Manchester. Her legs felt unsteady – it was like stepping off a rolling ship, but she felt relief at having landed safely with the hours and hours of flying behind her.

As they walked out into the arrivals hall, Lizzie and Pete were at the front of the sea of faces holding a handmade sign that said, *Taxi for Mr and Mrs D Richards.*

Helen smiled, then she hugged her daughter.

'We must look dreadful,' she said. 'I don't know what time it is, I'm not even sure what day it is.'

'It's a quarter to eight in the morning,' Lizzie said, 'and yes, you do both look dreadful, but I am so pleased you're back.'

A biting wind made them shiver and they were demanding heat as soon as they got in the car. Pete drove, with David in the front. Helen and Lizzie sat in the back and talked all the way to Fellburn.

'I wish Lottie had come home with you,' Lizzie said as she opened the front door to the house and held it back for the two men to carry in the luggage.

'So do I,' Helen said, 'but she insisted she wanted to see the year out, although she won't be able to do her stint on the farm. Harry's lovely, you'll like him. I'm sure he'll take care of her.'

David looked aghast as the cases were spread across the hall and Helen started to rummage for the gifts they had brought back.

'Can't it wait until the weekend when we're a bit more sorted out?' he protested. But she ignored him and soon the house looked as if someone had scattered their belongings around during a burglary. Debbie turned up with a casserole, and a bottle of wine for supper and Floss leapt through the cat flap, meowing at everyone, refusing to be picked up and cuddled, even by David. It was a noisy, lively hour and Helen was surprised to have found a renewed energy.

'I think we need to keep going,' she said. 'If we go to bed early this evening, exhausted, we may sleep and wake up tomorrow in a normal routine.'

Debbie left them to it, but Lizzie and Pete seemed reluctant to leave. Helen had noticed something different about her elder daughter – something excitable. When they all sat down for a second cup of tea and there was a gap in the conversation, she saw Lizzie and Pete exchanging glances.

'What are you up to?' she asked.

'Nothing,' Lizzie said. 'But we would like to ask you out for a meal, perhaps Friday or Saturday night. It'll be somewhere in Manchester. Pete's parents are coming over too.'

'That's fine,' David replied. 'We're free both evenings.'

'Great, we'll let you know.'

'It'll be good to see your parents again,' Helen said to Pete. 'Are they both well?'

'They're great,' Pete said. 'Mum's finally going to retire at Christmas.'

'Is she?' David remarked, looking at Helen, but his wife wasn't going to be drawn into this.

'Right,' she said to Lizzie, 'you're very welcome to stay, but we must get some of these cases upstairs. If I stay in this chair much longer I'll fall asleep and that isn't the plan.'

Pete jumped up. 'Come on, I've got work to do. We don't all get teachers' holidays you know.'

Lizzie rolled her eyes at him then she turned to her mum.

'Are you back in school on Monday?' she asked as she gathered up their presents from Australia.

'I'll go in before then,' Helen said. 'There'll be so much to do.'

She hugged them both but let David see them to the door, then she stood amongst the half-empty cases and bags and felt desperately tired. She carried the smallest case upstairs and looked at their familiar bed longingly. Suddenly, an image of David sharing it with Karen came into her head. She dumped the case on the floor and descended the stairs. David was loading up the washing machine, Floss rubbing around his ankles and making as much noise as she could. Helen paced across, picked the cat up and tossed her gently outside, closing the back door and clipping the cat flap shut.

'Why did you do that?' David said.

'She's getting on my nerves, and I want to talk to you, now.'

'Helen…'

'No, I think we need to talk now. We can't keep putting it off because we're tired or other people are here or there are things to do. It could go on forever like that, and we have to get this thing sorted out.'

'All right, but I don't see what else we need to say.'

Helen shot him a look, irritated at his attempt to brush aside something so important, then she went back into the lounge. When he sat next to her and tried to put his arm round her she pushed him away.

'No,' she said firmly. 'I want to see you when we talk. I may allow a cuddle when we've finished. The touch of humour softened the action and he slid across to the other end of the sofa, arranging the cushions to make a mock barrier between them.

'I need to tell you all the things that have been going round in my head,' she said, 'about you and Karen. And then you need to be honest and tell me what went on between you.'

She noticed an intake of breath, but he said nothing, so she carried on.

'I knew about Karen, of course, that you were going over there to do some jobs at her house, but I never once imagined that there was anything else. I thought we had everything in our marriage. We're different in lots of ways, we have bad patches, but I absolutely trusted you. It never crossed my mind that you would need or even want another woman. And did you ever stop to think of the girls, us as a family? How do you think they would feel if they knew?'

David contemplated the floor. 'I didn't think,' he said quietly, glancing up at her, 'I am so sorry.'

'I know you say it's over, and I want to believe you, but I feel hurt and betrayed. You've gone behind my back, shared a closeness with someone else; that's devastating for me. And if you can't imagine it, think how you would feel if it was the other way around.'

David hesitated, then said, 'I have thought of that, and I would be jealous, angry, and I would want to punch the other guy, but maybe that's a man thing. You might not understand.'

'Oh I do,' Helen said, sitting upright, facing him. 'Perhaps not the punching bit, but I do feel jealous and angry and I wonder what she was able to give you that I couldn't?'

She waited for a reply.

'I don't know how to answer that,' he said eventually. 'But, if you had another man in your life, after I'd punched him, I would want to be better than him, in fact I'd be absolutely determined to be so much better than him, you would only want me.'

Helen thought about this and found that it was mirroring her own thoughts. The *why* had been troubling her, and she had kept returning to the disturbing idea that she was partly responsible. Her distance, her lack of time for him, her obsession with her job had been unacceptable; there were faults on both sides. She grappled with the right words, then said, 'In that respect, I feel the same. I want to be better than her.'

'You are better,' David said immediately. 'It was me, my fault entirely. I've been carrying this guilt around with me and it's heavy, but it's deserved, I know that.'

'It isn't only your guilt,' she said carefully. 'I feel it too. If I'd been a bit more considerate of your feelings, you wouldn't have needed to start this thing with Karen.'

She pulled her legs up and packed a cushion behind her aching spine. The jet lag and lack of sleep had drained almost everything, but she had started this and she couldn't stop.

'What I want, now, is for you to be honest with me, tell me about you and Karen, where you met, what you did,' she took a short breath and looked directly at him, 'how far things went. I need to know.'

When he spoke she was surprised at the tone in his voice, the definite way he said, 'You don't need to know, love.'

'I do,' she said indignantly. 'How can I carry on imagining things? I need to know the truth.'

'What you need to know,' he said firmly, 'is that it's over, and I love you.'

'It isn't enough, David.'

'It'll have to be enough.'

Helen knelt upright, arching her spine, pushing her hands into the muscles of her back until it hurt.

'Whatever I say,' he insisted, 'won't help. It won't be what you want to hear. If I say it was all wonderful, you'll hate me, if I say she was unattractive and boring, you'll want to know why I bothered with her. It's far better for both of us if I say that it's over and, although I'm repeating myself again, I love you.'

'And what exactly does that mean?' Helen asked, surprised at the sarcasm in her voice. *'I love you.* It's easy to say, isn't it, and you've said it enough times since you told me about her, but how do I know you mean it?'

David stood up and paced towards the window. He sat on the low sill and she noticed his hands shaking, his face red. She recognised the signs, pleased that she was making him angry. Did he really think that all he needed to do was tell her he loved her and say it was over with Karen?

He looked up. 'Why do you always have to be so difficult?' he said.

'I'm being difficult? How can you say that?' Helen slammed her hand on the arm of the sofa. 'You're the one being difficult because you won't tell me what I'm entitled to know.'

David raised his hands in a gesture of hopelessness and let out a short breath. He glanced at her, then turned away. Helen pushed him again.

'So, you're not going to tell me anything?'

'No.'

'Did you sleep with her?'

David put his head back and gazed at the ceiling in exasperation, then said, 'I'm not even going to say *no* to that question.'

'Well, I'll ask her then. I'll go round and knock on her door and ask her.'

'You wouldn't do that.'

'Oh yes I would,' Helen said, anger in her voice. 'And I don't know how you can stop me.'

Now, I'm in control, she thought. He can't sit there and refuse to tell me how far his little affair went. She looked at him and wondered what he would do next.

'You will do as you please,' he said, eventually. 'As usual. But before you do anything, please Helen, just listen. You don't need to know about Karen and me because there's nothing more *to* know. Whatever I tell you won't be enough, you'll ask more and more and want endless details and dates and times and stuff, and it really doesn't matter. Why do you have to know everything? For once, stop trying to be in charge. Accept what I'm saying and let's move on.'

'This is nothing to do with taking charge,' she said furiously. 'I'm entitled to know what you've been up to with her – I'm your wife. Do you want our marriage to survive this? Because it won't unless you're completely honest with me.'

She uncurled her legs and sat on the edge of the sofa. For a moment, she contemplated life without him. It was a brief, yet terrifying thought, and if she stood her ground, it might become a possibility. And if she left him, would he seek Karen out?

'I desperately want our marriage to survive,' he

said. 'Haven't you listened to a word I've been saying? Whatever happened with Karen is over, and I think the best way forward is if we put it behind us rather than holding up all the details for some sort of pointless discussion. And going round to confront Karen – what sort of a stupid idea is that?'

Helen stood up suddenly and glanced around for the car keys. They were on the table by the door. She took three steps then reached out to snatch them away, seconds before he got there. David grabbed her arm, and she felt his grip below her elbow and the sharpness of the keys cutting into her clenched hand. She waited for him to prise them from her fingers.

'Do what you want,' he said, 'I can't stop you.'

He released her arm. For a moment, Helen imagined herself leaving the house, driving to Karen's, knocking on the door, but she never got as far as seeing Karen open it. The keys dropped to the floor. The room retreated, falling from reach, taking her anger with it and leaving David's voice, muffled and unreal. It was as if she was listening intently, but couldn't understand what he was saying.

She felt the sofa beneath her, the footrest pushed under her legs, his hand grasping hers and she heard her name, spoken repeatedly. Her hands and feet started to tingle, but this helped to bring things back into focus. She was aware of his arm around her and at first she tried to push him off. This wasn't the right time to be touching each other, although she couldn't seem to remember why.

As the room settled and her body relaxed, she knew that she would never have confronted Karen. Threatening to do so had been a bluff, a way of getting him to tell her what she wanted to know, and it hadn't worked.

'Are you OK?' he asked.

Helen shook her head. 'That didn't feel too good,' she said putting a hand to her forehead. Then, rather carefully she reached out and laid the hand on his knee, knowing that the gesture was enough to tell him that she was feeling calmer. He kissed her cheek.

'We need some sleep,' he said, 'a few hours. This wasn't the right time...'

'Can I ask you one thing?' Helen interrupted.

David didn't speak. She waited for a moment then said, 'All of this – it isn't going to happen again, is it?'

He hesitated, then said sharply, 'What isn't going to happen again? Me and Karen, or you being so involved in your job that you're impossible to live with?'

'Ah,' Helen said. 'I meant you and another woman. You're changing the subject. This isn't about me.'

'It will never happen again. Never, ever, I promise you.'

He continued to hold her, seemed to be waiting for a response, but she wasn't sure what to say.

'I don't know if I can do as well as that. But I promise you, I'll try not to revert back to the person I was.'

'There's one way of making sure you don't,' David said.

Helen didn't reply. It was enough to sit beside him and try to accept what he had said. She was realising that he was probably right. The truth of his affair, or whatever it was with Karen, needed to stay with him, at least for the moment.

David was quiet, his breathing soft and regular, then she heard a gentle snore and felt his hands loosen. Helen sighed.

'Bloody hell,' she whispered. 'This is one of the most crucial moments of our married life and you fall asleep on me.'

She shook him gently, then pulled herself upright, lifting his arms aside.

'Come on, we need to sleep,' she said. 'Let's go up to bed.'

They picked their way through the cases and the contents that had spilled out across the hall and the lounge.

In the bedroom, they shed shoes and clothes and slipped beneath the duvet. Helen felt her whole body sink gratefully into the mattress, the duvet soft, infused with the familiar scent that belonged only to them. David pulled her to his side and pushed his knees to fit the shape of hers.

Can I live without knowing she wondered? I'll have to, I don't have a choice. It's him I need to concentrate on now – our marriage – not her and what went on between them.

In her head, she began to frame the first few sentences of a letter.

Chapter 27

'It's as if Australia never happened,' Helen remarked the following Sunday morning.

David looked up from the newspaper.

'Really?'

'Yes. You reading the paper, me looking through e-mails and stuff. In a minute you'll check the time and ask if I want a coffee.'

She placed her iPad on the low table and reached over for one of the Sunday supplements. David watched as she rearranged cushions on the sofa and started to flick through the magazine.

He was grateful and relieved that they had managed to get through the rest of this week. At times they seemed to resume some of the closeness they shared in Australia, but an underlying, careful tension, remained. He couldn't work out what she was thinking, and was reluctant to ask, as it could so easily upset the delicate balance he was trying to maintain. Helen hadn't returned to the subject of Karen since confronting him, and he wouldn't raise the issue again. In fact, he was desperate to let it lie.

Helen spent two days in school, brought a pile of work home and withdrew from him as she ploughed through it methodically. The sight of her sitting at the table surrounded by folders depressed David's spirits and, with their relationship less certain, made it feel as if there was a formidable mountain to climb.

Nevertheless, he made a point of touching her

affectionately and telling her he loved her. Once, she stared at him when he said it, as if she wanted to make sure he knew she was questioning the words, but he just said it again and kissed her before she could speak.

On Friday evening, things had changed. She sat down beside him and put a sheet of paper in his hand.

'What's this?' he asked.

'A letter, well, a rough draft of a letter,' she replied, her expression giving little away. 'Read it and you'll see.'

David scanned the first few lines before realising that it was her letter of resignation. It was the last thing he expected, convinced that this was the one subject he wouldn't be able to touch on in the near future.

'You're certain about this?' he asked, incredulously.

'Yes,' she said, 'quite certain.'

David hugged her with such enthusiasm she had to tell him to let go.

'I'm not sure I believe it,' he said. 'You won't regret it, I have so many plans.'

Helen said pointedly, 'I might have a few of my own.'

'What's brought this on?' he asked. 'Why now? I thought it was out of the question with your deputy leaving.'

Helen seemed to think about this. 'Us.' she said. 'Our family. They're more important than my job.'

She smiled at him, but didn't offer anything further. Then she went back to her laptop and another pile of papers.

David had wondered if her decision had been influenced by his relationship with Karen. I have an affair with another woman, he thought, then, when the dust starts to settle, my wife does the very thing I wanted her to do in the first place. Yet if she'd agreed to finish work when the shop sold, none of this would have happened.

It was easy to look at things in this way, to convince himself that Helen was partly to blame, but what David knew he would find if he looked deeper was a reluctance to let go of what he had shared with Karen and that was the force behind his continuing guilt. He hadn't loved Karen – of course he hadn't, but he had needed her, especially at a time when he didn't seem needed by his wife. He would probably never tell Helen that they had spent the night together, that he had lied to her and made out it was little more than a few illicit meetings. And he would never fully understand why, on the evening Karen invited him to stay, he had found it so easy to say yes.

David folded the paper carefully, and put it down on the pile next to his chair.

'We could do this every morning when you finish work,' he suggested with a grin.

Helen shook her head. 'We'll be too busy to laze around, there's a wedding to plan.'

'It was great to see them both so happy last night,' he said. 'I was touched by the way Pete took me to one side when we arrived and asked if he could marry Lizzie. I didn't think young people did that any more.'

'I don't think it's usual, but Pete obviously wanted to do the right thing.'

'Do you fancy going out for coffee this morning?' David asked.

'Like we used to in Melbourne? Yes, let's do that, although it won't be the same as sitting outside looking over the beach and the sea.'

'Nuts and Bolts cafe will be open,' David said. 'I noticed their new Sunday opening hours on my way back with the papers.'

'Well, I suppose we'd better support them. I'll find some shoes. I hope Rosemary still makes that delicious apple cake.' She threw her magazine on the pile and went to get her coat.

'Come on,' she called from the hall as she zipped up her boots, 'or we'll end up buying lunch as well.'

It was drizzling softly as they made their way through the village, although spring-like temperatures had encouraged a flourish of daisies and dandelions in the grass verges. The trees, mostly bare, seemed to be holding their breath before a sunny day persuaded them to burst into leaf. David thought he might need to get the lawn mower out before the end of the week.

They paused outside the school gates to read the banners, just as Lizzie and Pete had done. Helen wondered aloud who had been the motivation behind so many.

'Rosemary and Mike may know more,' David said. 'We'll ask them.'

When they reached the hardware shop, Helen stood back for a moment.

'I'm remembering when it was ours. When I look back I feel so old, so much time has passed. I can't believe we once lived here.'

'Look forward,' David said. 'There's so much to come, I can't wait.'

He opened the door enjoying the familiar clang of the old-fashioned shop bell, one thing that hadn't changed since Mike and Rosemary took over. They moved through to the cafe area, which was busy and had that damp, wet-day atmosphere, with steamy windows and umbrellas drying by the door. The mismatched wooden chairs and tables seemed such a contrast to some of the smart places they had frequented near Chris and Jenny's, and the menu for hot drinks was far less comprehensive.

'Thank goodness for that,' Helen said reading it. 'Coffee with hot milk, please, easy choice.'

Rosemary, who seemed rounder and more pink-faced than ever, was bustling between the tables and a new girl was busy behind the counter. Rosemary stopped and came over when she saw them settling into one of the sofas.

'I heard you were back,' she said, her face beaming. 'How's your daughter? Did you like Australia?'

'Loved it,' David replied. 'And Lottie's doing fine now.'

'Good to hear that. What a shock for you, especially with her being at the other side of the world. It's a long way, isn't it?'

'Not too far,' David said, 'but we're glad to be back.'

Rosemary wiped her hands on her apron. 'Your mum and dad were in last week,' she said to David. 'Looking well, aren't they?'

'They're fine, yes. We're going to call on them this afternoon.'

'Are we?' Helen asked, surprised, but David was already giving Rosemary their order.

'Mike will be pleased to see you,' she said to David as she finished scribbling. 'I can't tell you how busy we are. He really needs some help – that's if you're available?' She glanced at Helen with a short laugh as if David needed his wife's permission.

'I'm available,' he said. 'I'll pop over and have a

word before we go.'

Rosemary threaded her way between the tables and pushed their order across the counter where it was pinned up with half a dozen others. David looked around, glad that this couple were making such a success of their business. He looked forward to helping Mike out again, especially as Helen would still be working until Christmas at least.

'You never mentioned we were going over to Whalley,' she said. 'You were only there on Thursday.'

'Didn't I? They were asking about you, and if we don't go today, it'll be next weekend before we see them. We don't have to stay long.'

'You could have run it past me first,' she protested, mildly. 'I might have school stuff to do.'

David took her hand and, weighing up her relaxed mood, decided to take a risk. 'Not on Sundays.'

'Since when?'

'Since today. And there's no need to sound so defensive. Sundays are going to be special. I promise not to help Mike on a Sunday and you are not to do any school work. That isn't a suggestion, it's going to happen.'

Helen looked at him, but he could tell she was amused.

'Is this the new you?' she asked. 'The bossy, I'm in charge, you?'

'It isn't new,' he insisted. 'It's the old me resurfacing. Things will be much better, you'll see.'

Helen laughed. 'Well you'll have a fight on your hands,' she said, 'I hope you're prepared.'

David squeezed her fingers together until she pulled her hand away. He whispered in her ear, 'I'm looking forward to it.'

It was Mike who brought their drinks over. He shook hands with David and kissed Helen on the cheek. Helen exclaimed at the size of the cakes and Mike tapped his nose secretively.

'They're specials,' he said. 'Don't tell everyone.'

As Mike and David discussed business, Helen started to cut her cake into smaller pieces. She asked Mike about the school and the number of new banners.

He shouted something to Rosemary, who unhooked a frame from the wall and came over. She handed it to Helen. It was an enlarged copy of the newspaper report, with a photograph of the banners and a rather bemused looking Simon. As Helen read the brief report, she noticed quotes from Mike and a few other parents.

'That Ofsted woman was in our school for a day,' Rosemary said. 'What could she know in a day? Well the kids are in there every day, and they decided they wanted to tell everyone how great their school is. It's been good to see Mr York smiling again.'

She took the frame from Helen and hung it back on the hook, taking a moment to straighten it before hurrying to another table.

Helen turned to Mike. 'Great stuff,' she said. 'Your support will make a real difference. It's about time someone stood up to Ofsted.'

'Better get on. See you Tuesday,' Mike said to David, who nodded, his mouth full.

Helen sipped the mug of coffee and continued to attack the slab of cake.

'I could ask Rosemary to wrap up some of this for later,' she suggested.

'No, eat it all now,' David replied. 'If you get through three quarters I might help you when I've

---

345

finished mine.'

Helen tapped his stomach, but he wouldn't be drawn into the implication that he had put weight on in Australia.

Hoods up against the drizzle, David took his wife's arm during the short walk home.

'You don't mind us calling on Mum and Dad?' he asked.

'No, but let's not stay too long, and don't say anything about me finishing work. If we tell your mother the Chair of Governors will get to know before I even give her the letter.'

'Hardly fair,' David said, pretending to be offended. 'So, I can't tell anyone?'

'We'll tell the girls, but that's all,' Helen said. 'These things have to be done in the correct order. I've e-mailed Chris Harrison.'

'Chris who?'

'School adviser. You met him at that Christmas do in Chorley.'

'Blousy wife, if I remember.'

Helen laughed. 'Blousy? You can't say that.'

'You know exactly what I mean,' he said.

'She left him last year. I thought I told you. He was devastated at the time.'

'Can't think why, she was so loud.'

Helen put her feet up when they got back and he was concerned when she refused lunch.

'I'm full of cake,' she insisted. 'And I still feel weird. I don't think my body clock has reset itself yet.'

David wondered if this was to get out of visiting his parents, but when he came in from splitting and chopping logs, he was pleased to see the remnants of some cheese and biscuits on a plate beside her.

'I'll drive,' Helen said. 'Let's take the Audi, it needs an outing after so long in the garage.'

David smiled as the car started easily and seemed no worse for its months of idleness.

'Do you remember that red Escort? Never started until at least the third or fourth try.'

'Yet you loved that car,' she remarked, reversing off the drive and pulling away. 'I always preferred the Mini.'

They sifted through memories of their previous cars and David was happy to have found an easy, safe subject, one that reminded them both that they had been happily married for almost thirty years, but didn't venture into more difficult territory.

When they arrived, Marjorie was opening the door before they got out.

Helen whispered, 'She looks pleased to see me for once.'

'I think,' David whispered back, 'that Lizzie must have rung with her news.'

He was right. His mother was full of Lizzie and Pete's engagement and the prospect of a wedding.

'How are you?' she said, kissing Helen. 'You still look a bit thin, didn't they feed you in Australia? I'll bet you're glad to be home.'

David took a sharp breath, but Helen seemed to accept his mother's comments, and he relaxed as they sat in the lounge. Helen talked to John as David listened to his mother, who was excited about Lizzie's wedding.

'I've told Lizzie we'll help out,' Marjorie told them, 'but I don't know if the bride's family pay for it all nowadays.'

'Lizzie said they're prepared to foot the whole bill if they have to,' David said. 'But we can't expect everything to be traditional, Mum. I think they want something informal.'

'Surely they'll get married in the parish church?' Marjorie protested.

'It's up to them,' Helen pointed out. 'It's their wedding.'

Marjorie ignored this comment and tried to impress on David the importance of persuading Lizzie and Pete to get married in church.

An hour passed, then Helen began stifling yawns and David remembered that she was at school the next morning.

'We'll have to get off,' he said, 'work tomorrow.'

'If you finished work, you could both take things a bit easier.' Marjorie directed her comment towards Helen.

'Yes, but she loves her job, don't you?' John said, coming to Helen's defence.

'I do, and it's going to be a busy week after I've been away for so long,' Helen replied. 'David's right, we'd better get going. It's been lovely to see you.'

On the way home, David apologised for some of his mother's comments, but Helen shrugged them off.

'I'm not bothered any more. Your mum loves the girls and that's what matters.'

'She once said you were a very good mother.'

'You never told me.'

'Didn't I? I can't remember.'

David looked over at his wife. He enjoyed watching her drive. She seemed surprisingly calm and he recalled many occasions when he had spent this journey listening to her indignation at something his mother had said.

'You keep looking at me,' Helen said.

'Are you going to get your hair cut?' David asked, 'because I like it as it is now.'

'What, long and tatty?'

'It isn't tatty, it's more natural, more like you used to have it when you were younger.'

'You mean when we couldn't afford a hairdresser and I had to cut it myself.'

'It's up to you,' he said, 'but I prefer the colour, too, it isn't quite so blonde.'

'I'll do whatever you want when I finish work,' she said, smoothing her hair with one hand. 'But for now, I haven't time to fuss with it.'

'Whatever I want,' he repeated teasingly. 'That sounds promising.'

'When I've *finished* work,' she replied, then, stealing a quick sideways glance at him, added, 'And possibly on Sundays.'

Chapter 28

Perched on a rock by the car, Helen threaded new laces through the holes and hooks in her walking boots, tugging at them impatiently.

'Don't pull so hard,' David said. 'They'll break.'

'We should have done this last night.'

'We?' he said, amusement in his voice. 'They're your boots.'

'Thanks for that,' she replied. 'Very helpful.'

David took the other boot and started threading. She looked up to scrutinise how he was doing it.

'I haven't done it like that,' she said. 'Look, I've crossed the laces, like yours.'

David took both boots from her.

'Do I have to do everything?' he said in a tone of mock exasperation. 'I make your sandwiches, prepare the flasks, pack the rucksack, and I still managed to bring you a cup of tea in bed – as usual.'

She looked at him smugly. 'It's only what I deserve. And anyway, you're so much better at lacing boots than I am.'

'Go and look out for Lizzie and Pete,' he told her. 'Make yourself useful while I finish this.'

Helen rolled her eyes at him, tutting loudly at his bossy tone, then she got up and crossed the car park. She leant against a tree to watch for Lizzie's car and turned her face to the sun considering how glorious this September was proving to be. At the end of August, they had celebrated their 30th wedding anniversary with a party in the garden and had been blessed with a sunny afternoon followed by a long, warm evening. Since then, the sun had shone every day.

They were both more content. She was giving less time to her job and more to David, and it seemed to be working. When she handed in her letter of resignation to the Governors, she expected to feel apprehensive about the future of her school, anxious about what life would be like without it. Instead, she was filled with a sense of excitement and anticipation. David was delighted, but he still didn't know her plan to continue with some part-time advisory work.

The only time Karen had been mentioned was when David returned from the pub a few months ago where he had met Dan and Tina. He told Helen that she had resigned as secretary for the group and was too busy to join the walks.

'Tina thinks she's seeing someone in Kendal,' David said.

Helen didn't comment. The frayed ends of the Karen saga were still waiting to be tied up neatly and put away, but for the moment, living with the sense of a matter unfinished seemed the right thing to do.

At the beginning of September, Bob rang to ask David if he would be available to lead a hike over one of their favourite Lakeland fells. Helen listened as David was non-committal in his reply.

'E-mail the stuff,' she heard him say, 'and I'll let you know.'

When Bob's mail came through, she had looked over David's shoulder at the list of people who had signed up. The name she was looking for wasn't there.

She felt the bark of the huge oak tree with her fingers as she watched the road for Lizzie's car to appear. A sleek, red cabriolet caught her eye. It pulled into the car park, shiny paintwork catching the autumn sunshine. Helen watched with admiration.

We should have brought the Audi, she said to herself. It's a perfect day for an open-top car.

She walked back to find David sitting on the tailgate of their old hatchback, consulting the map. Her boots had been placed neatly by the rock, the laces tucked inside.

'Are they with us?' she asked.

'Don't think so,' he said giving a quick glance in the direction of the sports car, which had pulled neatly into a space between two trees.

A tall man in walking gear got out and she saw Dan stride across to shake his hand.

'They are with us,' she said. 'Dan seems to know them.'

David straightened. 'It's so long since I've walked with everyone, it must be some new people I haven't met, but I thought I recognised all the names on Bob's list.'

Helen was staring intently. 'I'm sure I know him,' she said.

David looked again. 'Do you?'

'I do, in fact I know exactly who it is, it's Paul Eagland. Do you remember that course I went on when I'd been headteacher for a few years, the one where we stayed in Elterwater and you were really jealous?'

'Sort of.'

'You must remember,' she insisted. 'I had a room overlooking the beck, king-sized bed, jacuzzi bath, wonderful food.'

'So?'

'He was on the same course. I got on well with

Paul and we kept in touch for a while. He was head of a school in Kendal. Unfortunately, his wife was always ill – I think she was an alcoholic.'

David had a vague recollection of what Helen was talking about, but she had been on so many courses and met so many people.

'I'll have to talk to him,' she said. 'I wonder if that's his wife in the passenger seat. Perhaps she's better.'

Helen walked across. She was instantly recognised by the man, who hugged her with delight.

'Helen!' he exclaimed. 'Great to see you. Are you with this walking group lot?'

'Yes,' she replied. 'My husband's leading the walk today.'

A woman with dark hair was getting out of the car on the other side. Helen watched as she put both feet carefully on the floor as if she had been practising alighting from the low vehicle as neatly as possible.

It was Karen.

Helen was suddenly aware of David behind her, his hand on her elbow, an arm around her waist. As she introduced Paul and glanced across to where Karen stood, she felt panic in her stomach and thumping in her chest.

'I thought she wasn't coming,' she whispered to David.

Karen approached them with a half-smile and David, still holding his wife's arm with one hand, reached out and greeted her with a kiss on the cheek. Helen said a small hello.

'We must finish getting ready,' David said brightly. 'And we're waiting for our daughter and her fiancée to arrive, so we'll catch up with you both later. Helen felt his arm around her shoulders, turning her back towards the car, and for a few paces she let him propel her away from Karen and Paul, then she stopped and shrugged him off.

'I'm going back to talk to her,' she said.

David took her arm. 'What's there to say?' he said urgently. 'Come on, Helen, leave it. Neither of us knew she would be here, it would be stupid to do something without thinking about it first.'

Helen hesitated.

'And we need to look out for Lizzie, they should have arrived by now. I don't want them to miss the car park.'

Helen glanced over again and noticed Karen standing to one side as Paul talked to Dan. The two men went round to the front of the car and Paul opened the bonnet.

A feeling of being carried along by something she had to do was taking Helen towards an inevitable confrontation with this woman. She was suddenly outside the normality of lacing boots and deciding which jumper to take. It was as if this moment was the only one and would slip away if she didn't act. There was no time to plan or to think. She pulled away from David, ignored his urgent voice speaking her name, and strode back across the car park until she was standing close to Karen who was brushing her hair. Karen turned.

'I know what went on between you and David,' Helen said in a low voice.

Karen didn't respond immediately. Helen expected to see shock, nervousness, but Karen carried on putting her hair in a ponytail then she threw the hairbrush on the seat and said clearly, so the others could hear, 'I need to get my stuff out of the boot,' and she moved away from the guys who had their heads bent under the bonnet. Helen followed.

The two women stood by the rear passenger side and Karen placed a hand gently on the red paintwork, then rubbed her finger across a smear of wax. Helen folded her arms.

'I had no idea you would be here today,' she said. 'But I've thought, many times, about what I would like to say to you if we did meet.'

'Helen, I really don't...'

'You don't what? You don't think this is the right time? You don't want to hear it?' The rise of anger was strong in Helen's voice.

Karen didn't speak. She opened the boot and started getting things out.

'I want to tell you,' Helen said, moving closer, 'how deeply hurt I feel, how let down. I've told David that and you need to hear it too. As you probably know, we've been married for thirty years and when the trust you've built up over the years is betrayed, it takes a long time to get it back again.'

'I'm sorry.' Karen said looked up, then away, as if meeting Helen's stare was causing her physical pain. 'I don't know what David's told you, but I was in a mess. I lost all my confidence when my husband left. David was only being kind to me when I really needed it.'

'Only being kind?' Helen spluttered. 'You took advantage of that kindness.'

Karen seemed to think for a moment, then she met Helen's angry gaze.

'It takes two,' she said.

Helen was incensed. 'You're saying he wanted you?'

'We wanted each other, we needed each other. It wasn't right and I am so sorry we hurt you. If David's told you anything about me you'll know I'm not someone who relishes hurting others.'

'Have you any idea how I felt and what effect it had on me, on both of us?' Helen said, her words coming out in a furious, almost uncontrollable manner. She was suddenly aware of someone approaching and when she looked up she saw Paul coming towards them, smiling. David stood a few paces away. Not surprisingly, his face bore a look of anguish. Helen met his eye briefly, but ignored his gesture to come away.

Karen took a step towards Paul and touched his arm.

'Give us a minute,' she said, 'if you don't mind. Ask David about the route for the walk or something. We really need to finish this conversation, it's important.'

'I didn't realise you two knew each other,' he said. 'You both look very serious.'

'Well, we do know each other,' Karen answered. 'Now go on, please, we won't be long.'

She turned back to Helen, who was standing by the open boot.

'No,' Karen said, her voice low and emotional. 'Of course I don't know how you feel, how can I? How can I know about being married for years to someone who loves you more than anything else, who admires you, who will do anything to make you happy? In my marriage, I never had what you've had with David, what you will carry on having. He's kind, generous, intelligent, but most of all he loves you, Helen, and if I were you, I would do anything in my power to make him happy.'

She took a breath, made an impatient gesture with her hands before continuing. 'Do you ever stop to think how lucky you are?'

Helen started to speak, but the words seemed to stick in her throat. She shook her head a little and let Karen carry on.

'Well, do you?' Karen asked again, but didn't wait for an answer. 'You have years and years of closeness, a good marriage and everything to look forward to together. I'll never have that and if David chose to pay me some attention for a brief while, believe me, it meant nothing to him, nothing, and I know that because of what he said to me about you.'

Helen took a step back as if Karen's words had struck her. When she had pulled away from David a few moments ago and walked across the car park, it was with no expectation about what she would say and how Karen would react. She had been completely overcome by an urge to face the source of her anxiety, and give vent to the anger she felt towards this woman. Karen's words had taken away her animosity as if a strong wind, blowing in noisy, hurtful gusts, had suddenly dropped. She didn't know how to respond.

'I can only say I'm sorry,' Karen said. 'I can't change what happened, it was wrong, and I am so sorry if it's affected you, both of you, in any way.'

Helen put a hand on her chest. She glanced at Karen and noticed her dark eyes, her smooth skin, some strands of hair escaping the blue elastic tie. There was a strength about her, a dignity. I'm the one who's nearly lost it, Helen thought. I could make a fool of myself here, I need to get a grip.

'Are you OK?' Karen asked when Helen didn't speak. Helen let out a slow breath and said, 'Yes, I'm fine. I accept what you've said, and I think I can accept that you're genuinely sorry but it doesn't make it right.'

'Paul and I, we'll leave,' Karen said. 'I thought Bob

was leading this walk, your names weren't on the list. I'd no idea you would be here and the last thing I want to do is spoil your day. I'll tell Paul I'm not well or something, we'll make some excuse and go.'

'No, you don't need to do that,' Helen said, 'really, you don't. It won't spoil my day.'

Karen turned to where the three men were standing. Paul had his back to them, relaxed and unaware, Dan was describing something with huge hand movements, David was looking nervously in their direction.

'Perhaps he's waiting for us to thump each other,' Karen suggested, the lighter tone of her voice diffusing the remaining tension.

Helen couldn't help smiling a little. 'Well, he'll be disappointed,' she said. 'I'd better go and put him out of his misery.'

As Helen started to move away, Karen spoke.

'You're sure you don't want us to leave?'

'Only if you're happier doing that,' Helen said. 'I've said what I wanted to say and I appreciate what you've said to me. To be honest, I'm glad we got this chance to meet. I think it helps to bring things to a close.'

Karen hesitated and seemed to think about this.

'I wasn't sure what you knew,' she said.

'Oh I know everything, David's told me everything.' Helen watched to see what Karen's response would be to this, but she said nothing and went to gather her things.

Helen walked over to where David stood with Paul and Dan. He looked at her with a face like thunder. She slipped an arm around his waist, but he pulled away.

'It's fine,' she said, surprised at how angry he seemed to be.

'It isn't fine,' he said, his voice low and furious. 'It isn't fine at all.'

Chapter 29

When Helen marched over to confront Karen, David stood alone. Around him, people were enjoying the sunny morning, getting ready for a walk he was expected to lead. He felt foolish, uncertain, helpless to stop Helen speaking with Karen. It was typical of her to jump in without any real thought, and to ignore his wishes. He should be the one in control of this, talking to Karen himself, perhaps later on when he'd had time to think. Helen had no business taking things into her own hands leaving him completely wrong-footed.

He took a few steps towards his car, then changed his mind and turned back, hesitant about going any nearer, desperate to stay close. He scanned the parking, expecting to see someone looking at him, but they all seemed engrossed in their own preparations. The anger was now becoming fear about what could happen next. Karen was a calmer, more gentle character than Helen, but she wouldn't be confronted unfairly, and in the heat of a moment she might reveal the one thing he desperately didn't want Helen to know.

He watched the two women as they faced each other. Helen was standing tall, and she had her arms folded. Karen clasped her hands in front of her.

Realising he couldn't remain in the middle of the car park forever, he went to look at the sports car with Dan and Paul, closer to the two women, but not near enough to hear what they were saying.

'Don't know what they're talking about,' Paul said

as he approached. 'I've been warned off.'

'Women,' Dan said with a short laugh.

David faked a smile, then he tried to show an interest in Paul's description of the engine, which Dan seemed to find fascinating. Every few moments he looked over to where Helen and Karen stood, noticing changes in their movements and the expression on Helen's face. He held his breath when he saw Karen move nearer to his wife. His heart thumped, but the noise was in his head rather than his chest.

Then, they both seemed to be looking at him. Karen said something and he was surprised to see his wife smile. The women parted and Helen came over, slipped an arm round him and whispered that everything was fine.

The pulse in his head refused to slow down. He pushed her arm away, told her it wasn't fine at all. Then he took her hand and led her over to the car, not trusting himself to speak.

'David,' she said. 'It's all right. There's no need to be angry. We said what we had to say and it's finished.'

She sat on the tailgate, took off her trainers, and started putting on the newly laced boots. Standing with his back to the other cars he put his face close to hers.

'You think I'm angry?' he said. 'I'm bloody furious. Why did you have to do that? I had no idea what you were going to say, or do, for that matter.'

'Neither did I,' Helen said. 'I had to speak to her, what did you expect?' She rammed a foot into her boot and pulled the laces tightly round the metal clips.

'I asked you not to speak to her and, as usual, you didn't listen, but went off to do exactly what you wanted. Just imagine if the two of you had started a row or something, in the midst of all these people.'

'Well, we didn't,' Helen said fiercely. She tried to stand up but he was in the way and didn't move. When she looked at him he said, 'I haven't finished yet.'

'Finished what?'

David felt things inside him begin to settle down. He stood aside as Helen reached for her other boot.

'How do you think I was feeling, watching you two talking together,' he said, his voice levelling out. 'Honestly, Helen, I didn't know whether things were going to explode into something neither of us could control. It could have been so embarrassing.'

'Is that what you're worried about, being embarrassed?' she hissed. 'Do I need to remind you that you started this – what shall I call it, *affair* – in the first place?'

David shrugged and opened his mouth to speak, but Helen continued.

'So as far as I'm concerned, you've no right to be angry with me, because this embarrassment as you put it is completely your fault.'

'I didn't think she would be here,' he said defensively.

'Well she is. I've dealt with it my way and I've no problem with her being here. You, on the other hand, obviously have.'

David paused to think about this implication. He definitely had a problem with Karen turning up so unexpectedly and with another man. But it was Helen who had become his immediate worry, and, as he realised what could develop and what could be revealed, anxiety took over, then anger. His thoughts were a mess, and the urge to be alone, somewhere he could regain control of this turmoil of emotions, was overpowering. He had to get a grip. His daughter would be arriving soon and he had the responsibility of leading the walk.

'I was concerned about you,' he said. 'And yes, I know this is my fault, all of it, I know that.'

Helen stood up and grabbed her jumper, which she tied around her waist. She looked into his face and gave a short sigh, then she reached up and touched his cheek.

'I'm sorry I dived in,' she said. 'But for me it's resolved. I said what I wanted to say to her, she told me how she felt, we ended it fairly pleasantly, and that's it.'

'Are you going to tell me what you said?' he asked. 'What Karen said?'

Helen seemed to hesitate, then gave a tight smile. 'No need. I think we'll keep that between us, Karen and me.'

They both looked up as Lizzie's car pulled in with Pete at the wheel and their daughter waving madly. Helen leapt up to indicate the space beside them. The next few minutes were taken up with hugs and handshakes and chat. David reminded himself why he was there and started to gather the group together to check everyone had arrived. He noticed Paul help Karen with her rucksack, loosening the straps until it sat comfortably, planting an affectionate kiss on her nose. He experienced a sharp stab of jealousy that surfaced quite unexpectedly, then disappeared before he had time to understand where it had come from.

When everyone was ready, David went through the brief safety talk before describing the walk.

'We ascend the path by the waterfall to Tarn Hows,' he said. 'It's steep in places, but we'll take it slowly. Then we walk alongside the tarn before we leave the crowds behind and branch off towards Black Crag.

It's a steady climb, with a short pull to the top. The view will be worth it, especially today.'

Most of the walkers had visited Tarn Hows before, but David enjoyed watching their faces as they emerged from the shady wooded path to blue sky and sunshine. A breeze moved through the trees and across the bracken, rippling the tarn, shaking out the last warm pockets of summer. Another week and the browns and oranges of autumn would colour this landscape.

'Do you remember watching the skaters?' he said to Helen. 'New Year's Day a few years ago. It looked effortless. It reminded me of that Wordsworth poem we all had to do at school.'

She took his hand and walked beside him.

'You all right now?' she whispered.

'I think so.'

'You've calmed down?'

'I'm getting there.' David squeezed her hand gently. 'I just want to enjoy the walk,' he said. 'I wish she hadn't come.'

'How do you feel, seeing her?' Helen asked suddenly.

He thought for a moment, unsure of himself and his feelings. 'Surprised, shocked.'

'I don't mean that.'

'I don't feel anything.' he said. 'Nothing like you're implying.'

They walked in silence for a few minutes, then she said, 'Have you spoken to Karen since that phone call in Australia?'

'No, I haven't,' he replied. 'I would have told you if I had.'

'Well I think you should,' Helen said.

David looked at his wife in surprise, but her

expression was serious. He had meant to ring Karen when he got back to the UK, to see how she was, but he could never bring himself to pick up the phone and do it. Then time had passed and it had seemed inappropriate to get in touch.

'She offered to go home, not come on the walk,' Helen said.

'Did she?'

'Yes. She said it would spoil our day, so she'd make an excuse to Paul and they would leave.'

'That was considerate of her,' David said.

'I thought so too. I told her it wouldn't spoil the day, and it won't, unless you let it.'

'Are you sure you're OK her being here?' he asked tentatively, trying to gauge Helen's mood.

'I am now,' she said. 'I've said what I wanted to say. It's sorted out in my head, it's finished. But you need to finish it properly, for you, for her, and for me. Today's an ideal chance – you won't get another.'

They walked in silence for a while. David wondered what on earth he might say to Karen and knew that he would rather not say anything; let it lie as it had been doing quite easily for the last few months. What could he say other than, *Are you all right? How long have you been seeing Paul?* It all seemed very trivial.

Lizzie came to chat with Helen about her wedding plans and Lottie's return to England next week. Pete wanted to talk through a problem with the car. David listened, then he heard Karen's laughter as she conversed with Irene and Jane, who were striding out with their walking poles. He remembered Karen referring to them as the "not lesbians" after the freezing walk along the canal. Everyone quietened down a little as they began the ascent up the rocky track and the group spread out, slower walkers taking things more steadily.

At the top of the first climb, he leant on the gate and looked back at the straggle of trees that had once been an evergreen forest, cleared to allow native species to grow. As she reached the gate, Helen placed her hands on top of the wood and turned her face to his. David kissed her on the mouth, then again, then a third time before she wriggled through.

'Speak to her,' she said in his ear.

David wrapped an arm around her shoulders and pulled her to him in a brief hug, then he opened the five-barred gate to let the rest of the group pass.

She gripped his arm, then let go.

'And remember,' she said, 'I love you.'

Chapter 30

'Pete and I can lead the next bit,' Lizzie announced as she passed him.

'You'll get us all lost,' David joked, but Lizzie would have none of it.

'Sandwiches on top?' she asked.

'Of course. But don't rush off, some of them won't be able to keep up with you young things.'

With everyone through, David pushed the gate. The catch was refusing to click in, so he lifted it a little to compensate for the dropped hinges, although it took a few moments for the bar to finally latch. Helen had left him to talk to Paul and he could hear her voice, although they were almost out of sight round a corner of rock. He set his rucksack down and took a welcome swig from a bottle of water. The sun warmed his shoulders, the heat releasing all the earthy scents of autumn from the damp, bracken-covered earth. He took a moment to enjoy the familiar view of the Langdale Pikes across the valley before surveying the upward path. Between him and the last of the group, Karen stood alone, her bag resting on the floor as she shrugged off her jacket.

'Hello,' she said as he approached.

'Hi.'

Karen shook the jacket and folded it over her arm, then reached for her rucksack.

'How are you?' she asked.

'We're fine,' David said. 'What about you?'

'I'm good, too.'

David felt awkward. On previous walks, they would have chatted easily. He would have taken her hand as they crossed a stream or scrambled over rocks. Now he was afraid to touch her. The distance between the two of them and the group widened so they were out of earshot, but he didn't know what to say.

They started walking and he quickened his pace. She reached out to put a hand on his arm.

'David, don't rush off,' she said. 'I've things I need to say to you and we might not get another chance.'

He slackened his pace. Why was this so hard? He had wept over this woman, covered himself in guilt because of her, been as close as you could possibly be to anyone, but now he couldn't even talk to her.

'Don't be scared of me, David,' she said. 'I want to be able to talk with you as friends would talk. Don't feel that what we did was wrong. It happened. I was sad when it was over, but I'm not sad any more.'

The tension inside him eased. He had no right to be offhand, she deserved some honesty.

'I'm sorry about Helen confronting you earlier,' he said.

'It was bit of a shock. I didn't think you would have told her about us.'

'I didn't want to. She found out when we were in Australia. I didn't want her to speak to you, but she ignored me and barged straight in.'

'She needed to tell me how hurt she felt,' Karen said, 'and I needed to tell her that I was sorry.'

David started to speak, then he hesitated. Finally he admitted, 'She doesn't know everything. She thinks that we met a few times, that's all.'

'Good,' Karen said. 'It's better like that. You don't

need to tell her, or anyone for that matter.'

David stopped walking briefly and looked at the crooked line of hikers spread out across the fell. He could see Lizzie at the front, dark hair against a pink shirt. Helen and Paul were still together and he could just catch the sound of his wife's laughter.

She's changed, he thought. I still can't believe she's managing this so calmly. And she was the one who suggested I talk to Karen, finish things off. It suddenly dawned on David how much Helen trusted him, not only to have this conversation, but also to handle things with integrity. He wouldn't let her down.

'This feels strange,' he said, turning to Karen. 'Thank you for keeping it to yourself. You could have told Tina or any of your friends. You could have come round and told Helen the truth and really made things difficult for me.'

She sounded surprised. 'Did you think for one minute that I would do that, make things hard for you, caused you any trouble?'

'No. No, I knew you wouldn't do that.'

They walked on a little without speaking. David wondered whether to ask her about Paul and was turning words over in his head when she said, 'I've been seeing Paul for a few months now, and we're both in it for the long haul. He's a nice guy, a bit like you in some ways. But if you and I hadn't met and if you...' she hesitated, 'if you hadn't shown me what things could be like, I wouldn't have believed that another man could ever be interested in me.'

There was a pause as David tried to understand this.

'I feel so guilty,' he said, 'not only because of Helen, but because of you.'

'Feel guilty for Helen if you must,' Karen said, 'but not for me. If I thought for one moment that I'd spoiled anything in your marriage, I *would* feel guilty and then what we did would have been wrong. But we haven't spoiled anything, have we? And you've made things better for me.'

David wanted to hug her, to take her hand, to embrace her as a friend because her words made so much sense.

'I know it's a cliché,' she said, 'but I'm going to say it anyway. What we had was special. I loved it and I'm going to make sure it stays special by keeping it all to myself.'

'It was special to me too,' he said.

'So, don't be embarrassed with me, or avoid me. I'd hate that, although if I spend more time in Kendal with Paul, I might not be walking with the group as much.'

She stopped to take in the view and asked David to put her jacket in her rucksack. Standing behind her as he fastened the drawstring, he took in a faint scent of her perfume and a small part of him ached to place a kiss on her smooth skin where a few wispy strands of hair had escaped the pony tail band.

Karen carried on telling him about Paul.

'He's a lovely man, a walker, and he's also into cycling. You won't believe it but we climbed Great Gable on our third date.'

'Really? And you made it – all the way to the top?'

Karen pretended to be hurt. 'Of course I made it. Good job I'd had some practice hikes with you, though. He keeps hinting about buying me a bike, but I'm not so sure about that one.'

David smiled. 'Go for it,' he said.

'Has your daughter fully recovered?' she asked.

'Almost,' David replied. 'She's coming home next week and she's got a job that starts in October.'

'And what about you and Helen?' Karen said tentatively. 'Did Australia give you time to work things through?'

'Sort of. Helen almost had a breakdown because of the stress at work and then the shock of Lottie's accident. But it gave her some space to look at things in a different way. She's leaving her school at Christmas, retiring. It was a hard decision, but now that she's made it, she seems very optimistic and there's so much we plan to do next year.'

'I'm pleased for you both.' Karen said. 'She's very lucky, I hope she realises it.'

'Thanks for the compliment,' he said with a grin and a shake of his head, 'but believe me, I'm the lucky one.'

The path narrowed and they walked without speaking as the climb became steeper, catching up with Jane and Irene who were taking each step carefully.

'Admiring the view,' Irene said as they passed. 'Don't wait for us.'

'You're both managing?' David asked.

Jane laughed. 'I wouldn't say no to a piggyback.'

'You go on,' he said to Karen. 'I'll keep an eye on my two favourite walkers, make sure they get to the top and don't slope off to the pub.'

Karen touched his arm before striding ahead, the wind lifting her hair. Suddenly she turned back to flash him a wry, almost mischievous, smile.

The ascent of Black Crag took less than an hour and as they gained height, the view opened up, with higher fells to the north and lakes to the south and west.

Windermere glinted in the sunshine, smooth except for the curve of a power boat grooving its surface. At the summit, David listened as Lizzie showed off her ability to name every lake and fell, something she had learned from him when she was a child and they took turns to pose for photographs by the trig point.

Everyone spread out on the rocks and the grassy patches to get out sandwiches and flasks. David did a quick head count, then he heaved his pack to the ground and dropped beside Helen who was lying on the grass, her face to the sun. She sat up wrapping her hands round her knees.

'You were right,' he said, 'about talking to her.'

Helen said nothing, and he was grateful she didn't question him.

He watched Karen and Paul, noticed him take her hand, look into her face with affection. It was exactly what David wanted. He allowed himself a brief memory of his arm across her body, his fingers resting over hers, but deliberately allowed the image to pass, the feeling dissolving easily. He wondered if he would ever tell Helen the truth, but felt a huge relief that for the moment he wouldn't need to. David knew that regardless of the guilt he would carry for a long time, he would do whatever was in the best interests of his wife.

The conversation with Karen ran round in his head and he was moved, so much so that for a while he didn't speak.

'You're quiet,' Helen remarked.

David paused.

'I was thinking,' he pondered, 'that next year we can climb every one of these fells, and we'll be free to do it during the week. We can decide the night before if the weather looks good or if we just fancy a day's walking – it'll be up to us.'

'I feel like I've been climbing a mountain for the last twelve months,' she said. 'I might want a rest.'

'I would have climbed the mountain with you,' David insisted, 'if you'd let me; carried the rucksack, read the map, pointed you along the right path. But you wouldn't let me, you had to go it alone, rushing on ahead, never pausing to admire the view.'

Helen gave a short laugh.

'Really? You'd have come with me? Or were you on a different walk?'

David looked at her, then he realised the tone was teasing, flippant.

He reached over and took out the picnic boxes, searching for the right response, then he glanced sideways at his wife. She held his gaze for a moment before turning away.

David reflected that for rather too long, the two of them had been walking apart, and for some of that time, he'd even been walking with someone else. Deep inside, his inner-self was telling him that his parallel walk had been but a brief interlude – he and Helen were, once again, on the same path.

There's nothing else to say about my different walk, he thought. At least, not today.

About the Author

During her thirty years in teaching, Catherine Finch wrote lovely stories, plays and musicals for children and tedious documents for school inspectors. Although reluctant to leave the village school where she was headteacher for eleven years, she is delighted to have found space in her life for some real writing.

She has been shortlisted and placed in a number of competitions, including the Bath Short Story Award 2017, Flash 500 and TSS. She has completed two novels so far.

Catherine is married with two grown-up children. She divides her time between the green and pleasant hills of east Lancashire and the warm sunny fields of south west France.

Acknowledgements

Heartfelt thanks to:

Gary, Anita, Mandy and Jean for expressing their honest opinions as the story and the characters unfolded,

Chris, Joanna, Ian and Steve for critical feedback and encouraging responses to the first drafts,

Sheila for thorough, detailed editing,

Jane Dixon-Smith for bringing the cover design to life.

Finally, a special mention for the authors who make up the unique and inspirational Parisot Writing Group in the south west of France. They provide endless and abundant support, cheerful encouragement and, most of all, sincere friendship.

Catherine Finch
January 2018

catherinesfinch7@gmail.com
Twitter: @chatffinch
Instagram: catherinesfinch

Printed in Poland
by Amazon Fulfillment
Poland Sp. z o.o., Wrocław